All of the charact
and any resembla
or dead, is purely coincidental.

MARUTA
(Log of Wood)

by
Jack Roberts

Acknowledgement

'UNIT 731'
by Peter Williams and David Wallace

Hodder and Stoughton

Castle of Dreams Books

published by
Castle of Dreams Books
8 Pease St
DARLINGTON
DL1 4EU
UK

ISBN 1 86185 122 7

MARUTA
(Log of Wood)

Jack Roberts

for Marjorie

Chapter 1

The Russian soldier suppressed a yawn as he stood and gazed without interest at the passing fields of stunted wheat. The open window of the carriage door rattled loosely in its grooves, and a sudden drift of thick smoke briefly obscured his view as the decrepit engine laboured up the gentle gradient.

He shifted his feet and changed his grip on the barrel of the rifle upon which he was leaning. Then his expression abruptly changed as the belching smoke was caught and momentarily cleared by a flurry of wind. The heavy creases beneath the youth's eyes crinkled in a smirk of amusement as he raised the rifle and pointed it through the gap above the window.

There were two sharp cracks. The two stooping figures in the rock-strewn field suddenly straightened and bounded rabbit-like in the opposite direction to the train. The soldier shouting with laughter cupped his mouth with his hand to hurl insults at the disappearing targets. Still grinning, he straightened himself, and hooking a pack of cigarettes from his breast pocket, he turned to stare down the narrow aisle of the crowded railway carriage.

"Nipponski!" he shouted engagingly.

The rough-looking passengers seemed scarcely perturbed. A few heads had turned with curiosity to seek the cause of the shooting, but mostly they continued with their talking and card playing, or simply snored with open mouths and lolling heads.

The young soldier shrugged uneasily and dragged heavily on his cigarette, whilst holding the rifle loosely by its rough webbing strap. These men, they puzzled him. Crop-skulled and gaunt featured, with jackets discarded or loosely buttoned, they lounged in unsoldierly attitudes on the slatted wooden seats.

One of them wearily flung down his remaining cards.

"OK fellas! That's me finished I guess." He yawned and rubbed a hand over his bristly face. "Jeez! My arse is getting blisters, sitting on this bloody seat." He turned slightly and looked over his shoulder at the man with the rifle.

"Hey Ivan! why did you shoot at those bleedin' peasants?"

The Russian grinned and made an extravagant gesture with

5

his free hand.

"Nipponski." he said. "I shoot all Nipponski."

The other man rose slowly to his feet, and paused to massage his bony buttocks.

"Niet, niet!" he answered. "Niet Nipponski." He stepped carefully into the aisle and moved towards the insanitary toilet near where the armed man was standing. His voice had a strong Australian accent.

"Those jokers weren't bloody Japs. They were just poor bleedin' Chinkos, trying to scratch a living." He was almost face to face now with the young guard. He leaned against a partition to support himself as the clanking train gathered speed on the downward slope.

"Look!" he went on, raising his voice above the racket of the wheels, "The bloody war's over man! We've won! You Russki, me Australian!" He waved his arm towards the others. "Americanski! Ingliski! We've all bleedin' won! Now be a good lad and stop the bleedin' shooting!" He shrugged and reached for the toilet door, ignoring the young guard's angry stare.

"Oh what the hell! Why do I bleedin' bother? The flimsy door slammed as he disappeared inside. "What worries me," he muttered to himself, "is that some bastard might shoot back!"

Stefan Gregorovitch flicked the remainder of his cigarette through the window and moodily resumed his stance. The Manchurian landscape through which the train was doggedly pounding reminded him of his home in Kazakhstan.

He was sixteen years old and had been a soldier of the Red Army for more than a year. Those shots he had fired had been a symptom of his rage and frustration. Since he was eleven years old his country had been at war. He had seen his father, two uncles and an older brother marching to defend the motherland. His father had died at Kiev. His uncles had been missing for many months after the fighting before Moscow. Then one had returned with a half-healed stump in place of one arm. The other had been ground into the rain-sodden earth beneath the tracks of a German tank. His own brother had been with General Zhukov's Western Army, which had stormed into the ruins of Berlin. But he, Stefan Gregorovitch, had remained in the house of his mother until he was fourteen.

He had gone to school, then helped grudgingly on the collective farm, filled with shame at having to work with the women and girls. His young Cossack blood had surged with pride and excitement when he had heard day by day on the radio of the filthy Fascist invaders being halted and then rolled back across the border by the heroism of his people.

But when his turn had come, he had found himself posted to an isolated garrison, near the town of Khabarovsk, set deeply in Eastern Siberia and close to the northern border of Japanese-occupied Manchuria.

His disconsolate reflections were broken by the crash of the lavatory door as it was flung back and its muttering occupant re-appeared.

The skinny Australian, still struggling with the belt of his baggy denims, staggered as the carriage jumped across a gap in the badly laid track. He stabbed out with a free arm to regain his balance, missed the door post, and cannoned into the brimming chemical toilet. The rickety contraption promptly fell over, discharging its contents onto the floor where they both stood. The Russian's jaw sagged with disbelief as the horrid mess sloshed around his feet.

Still clutching his trousers, the cursing Australian did a quick hop, attempting to escape from a second more turgid and increasingly evil wave. He failed. With his trousers now around his ankles, and the train almost falling apart on the unnerving downward stretch, he was launched past the swearing Russian, into the carriage. A nauseating stench preceded the hideous stream as it followed him down the aisle.

A bald-headed British corporal was sitting near the door, with folded arms, his bearded chin sagging on his chest. His closed eyes opened wide with shock, as the frog-hopping figure tottered past, one free hand grabbing desperately for the nearest seat back. He missed, then tripped over a carelessly stowed kit bag. The corporal leaned forward to peer open-mouthed at the floundering Aussie. Then his gaze dropped to the carriage floor, and he covered his twitching nostrils with a large hairy hand. He gave an outraged bellow as he saw the disgusting mess lapping its way past him.

"Lockie – you clumsy, bloody yard-bird! What the hell's going on?"

"Steady on, Corp. The bleedin can just fell over!"

Other loud voices now took up the protest as the foul smell mingled with the blue tobacco smoke, which already filled the stuffy carriage. Missiles flew. The man on the floor ducked as a corned

7

beef can whistled past his stubbled scalp.

"Jeez you fellas, what's all the bleeding fuss about?" He clutched at his shirt tails and attempted to thrust them into his pants whilst still on his knees.

"That's right! Cover your arse before we bloody puke," a voice shouted.

"It's handsomer than your bleeding face, any day mate!" returned Lockie.

The unabashed Aussie was struggling to fasten his belt, whilst scrambling to his feet. He hurriedly clutched at the back of a seat as the train swayed round a bend. He dodged another volley of flying objects, and genially ignored the insults as he aimed a broken-toothed grin at a straight-backed young American.

"Which would you choose Rosie? His face or my arse?"

Private First Class Ross flushed, and half rose to his feet, one bunched fist held threateningly towards the leering Lockie.

"Cut that out, you sonofabitch. I don't take that kind of crap from nobody. If you weren't covered in shit, I'd come over there and beat your godammed head in!"

Shrieks of encouragement came from around the crowded carriage, as the bored passengers temporarily forgot the appalling stench, and selected their champions.

"I'll lay six to four on Rossi." A big-boned Top Sergeant, with a Tennessee drawl, pulled a wad of Japanese yen from his pocket, and licked a calloused thumb.

"Any takers?" he shouted

"Yeah - you're on," came a voice.

"Like hell! I'm offering three to one on Lockie." A pug-nosed Australian with an Apaché hair-cut loudly took up his countryman's cause.

"Aw knock it off Bongo! Can't you see I've sprained my bleeding wrist?" Lockie, middle-aged, ex pig-farmer, ex-sergeant, ex-corporal, and hoping soon to be ex-private, held up a dangling hand at the end of a knobbly fore-arm.

"That's a load of crap," the top sergeant jeered. "Look, you're fastening your god-dammed buttons."

Lockie flipped his braces, then delicately raised each foot in turn from the repulsive puddle surrounding them.

"OK then, Tiny. Come over here. I'll wrestle you, or anybody else for that matter." He sniffed and made to wipe his nose on the back of his hand. Then, thinking better of it, looked around at the bad-tempered faces of his suddenly silent comrades.

"No takers, eh? Right then, what do I do now. Any bleedin' suggestions?"

Pandemonium broke out once more, as Lockie kicked aside some soggy biscuit packets and squelched towards his empty seat.

The unhappy fellow-countryman with whom he shared it, opened his mouth to protest, but a knotted, smelly fist thrust under his nose, promptly changed his mind. Instead of speaking, he gulped and flung open the window between them. His action had been repeated along the length of the carriage, and the occupants were coughing and cursing as they breathed in the smoke and soot flung in from the belching engine.

Stefan Gregoravitch peered through the open door and surveyed the chaos with wide-open eyes. The stink from the can which rolled around the floor was overpowering. He gasped with relief as the increased draught from the opened windows cleared the air a little.

"What should he do?" After all, had not he, and the comrades of his platoon, been given strict orders to escort these crazy scarecrow-men and to ensure their safe delivery to the port of Dairen. A sudden thought brought a look of horror to his face! He tried in vain to blink away the dreadful image. Quickly, he thrust his forage cap back high on his brow to wipe away the erupting beads of ice-cold perspiration.

"Great God! What if his sergeant saw this?"

Too late! A flat-handed shove between the shoulder-blades sent him reeling. A loud voice was bawling curses in his ears as he ducked to avoid a shower of blows aimed at his luckless head. His feet slithered in the hideous slime. He checked the slide, floundered as he regained his balance, and spun round to stand at attention. He slammed the butt of his rifle smartly on the floor - and sagged with despair as he noted the shower of filth which was sprayed over the thick lisle stockings of his platoon sergeant.

A plaintive shriek came from the ancient locomotive as it reached the end of its downhill run, emerging from a shallow valley, between distant copper-hued hills. Streamers of steam and fine ash were added to the funereal plume of black smoke which enveloped the train and its impatient passengers as they bumbled on their way across the stark dun-coloured plain.

"Look at it!" someone observed morosely, "Miles of sweet Fanny Adams!"

"Hey there's a bird!" yelled a cockney voice, his finger pointed through the haze of dust and smoke. The singular absence of life in this cheerless stretch of country caused every ones' eyes to follow the pointed direction, where a large black carrion crow fluttered frantically in the up-draught from the fume laden air.

Taffy, a red-haired Welshman, was staring intently.

"Can you see that?" he muttered with Celtic gloom. "That bloody shite-hawk is going to fly right past us. If we can't do better that this, it'll reach the bloodyboat before we do."

Indeed the train was slowing down again, as it approached another gradient. The ragged winged bird, released from the slip stream, wheeled away with splendid disdain, to soar into a yellow-tinged sky.

The foul smell from the floor became stronger as the incoming draught was reduced, and heads, which had returned to card games and clattering dice were again turned towards Lockie with huge indignation.

"Hey, come on there! Why don't you clean up this goddammed mess?"

Tiny, the Tennessee top-sergeant, was glowering at the slumped Australian. Lockie was unperturbed. He replied from behind half-closed eyes.

"Up yours mate! What the bleedin' hell can I do, with no water, no mops, no nothing?"

His arms were folded. His filth encrusted boots planted comfortably on the slats of the opposite seat. He slowly opened one eye to look slyly at the complaining American.

"Why don't you do it yourself?" he remarked. "Your mouth's big enough. You wouldn't even need a shovel. And you're full of crap anyway!"

Tiny, giving an enraged shout, leaped across the aisle to grab the seated man by the front of his shirt. The skinny Australian was sinking his teeth into Tiny's ear, when they were frozen by a loud female voice. They both dropped their arms and looked towards the

10

communicating door. Sergeant Tatiana Chokovska of the 1st Eastern Siberian Battle Group, Russian Red Army was standing there.

One hand was clutching the arm of a downcast Stefan Gregoravitch, and the other supported a rifle which hung by the webbing strap from her shoulder.

"What is happening?" she shouted. "What is this, that is happening?" She glared at the abruptly silenced men, then shook the arm of her young compatriot. Scummy water slopped out of the bucket he was carrying. He retained his balance only by using the long-handled straw broom which he held in his other hand. She pushed the red-faced youth into the carriage and pointed to the rapidly drying filth on the floor.

"Now you," she ordered, "You Ukranian runt of a mis-begotten donkey, you will sweep. Make this clean".

The young Russian staggered as she thrust him forward, then sulkily dumping the bucket, he plunged the sparsely-tufted broom into the water, and angrily scraped the ordure around the floor. There were groans from some of the seated men as the murky tide began to spread beneath their feet again. But their protests were drowned by the voice of the Russian N.C.O.

"You must be clean," she called out. The rifle she carried scraped noisily against the wooden seats as she turned to confront the watching faces.

"We soldiers of the Russian Red Army have made you free from the pig-shit Japanese." She grimly tightened her lips and closed her eyes, with frustration, as a chorus of derision and sarcastic laughter momentarily silenced her.

"Like hell, you did!" came an American voice. "It was them Yankee Paras who got there first!"

"It took your lot a bloody week to find us!"

An angry British voice had joined in the clamour, but the bearded corporal reached across swiftly, to push the owner back into his seat.

"Knock it off, Jim," he warned "We've a long way to go yet. We don't want to get the Russkis' backs up." His companion, a black-browed, hard featured man, subsided unwillingly, as Tatiana Chokovska abruptly opened her eyes and silenced the rowdy objections with an upraised arm and clenched fist salute. Her plump-cheeked face was humourless, as her snapping black eyes took in the

11

squalid carriage and its occupants.

"Remember," she barked, "You must do as we tell you, then you will go home."

The clamour broke out afresh.

"Bullshit!" someone yelled.

"You try bloody stopping us!" The irate Jim was on his feet again.

"Come on mates, fair goes! The shiela's doing her best."

Lockie was struggling to squeeze past the generous buttocks of the strapping Russian lady. As he did so, she gave an involuntary shriek, then swung a fist in a mighty blow at the grinning Australian's head. He ducked in time to avoid it, then dodged behind the sentry, with an apologetic smile smeared across his ugly face.

"Sorry, miss! My hand just sort of slipped. No offence meant. Look! I'll do this bloody cleaning up myself!" He snatched the broom from the young Russian and started to wield it with exaggerated vigour, causing the sloppy mess to surge forward to threaten her blunt-toed shoes.

Pete Brodie, the corporal, had joined in the mirth at Lockie's unexpected act. He was relieved to note the change of mood. Even Jim, whose thick eyebrows had met across the top of his prominent nose, relaxed with a reluctant smile, and sat back in his seat with folded arms.

Whilst watching the formidable lady twist her lips into a curl of disgust, Pete became mildly aware of an increased draught through the open window and a spume of fine dust made him blink. He continued to watch closely, however, as she glared wordlessly at the innocent-looking Lockie. Without removing her eyes from him, she unhitched the sentry's rifle from her shoulder, and flung it back to its owner. Then she leaned slightly forward so that her face was even closer to the scruffy Australian's. Her fingers clenched and unclenched as she lowered them to her side.

Lockie now stood with his fish-like mouth agape, until her eyes were only inches away from his. Then she released her breath to scream an awesome sounding Russian oath. There was a sudden respectful hush in the carriage as she straightened and tugged savagely at the hem of her high-necked tunic. Even Lockie, a Queensland-bred Australian, was impressed, and watched admiringly as she spun on her heel and thumped out of the compartment.

"Jesus, Lockie! I reckon she must have fallen for you."

'Bongo' Wilkins, pointing a finger towards his mate, spluttered as the smoke from the cigarette he was smoking caught in his throat.

Then suddenly everyone was coughing. Laughter turned to shouts of dismay as clouds of yellow dust, driven by savage blasts of wind, whipped through the carriage.

The train had slowed down even more - almost to a standstill, and the engine's thick smoke now added pungency to the smothering particles as they clogged the nostrils and stung the eyes of the yelling, scrambling men. The banging of hastily slammed windows ceased when the last one was closed, and the howling assault of the dust-devil became an angry screech as the agate-like grit scoured the outside of the glass.

The breathless men choked and swore as they hawked the dust from their throats and tried to protect their eyes and faces from purposeful streams which forced their way through cracks and open louvres.

Then, with eerie suddenness, the noise diminished, and the foggy air outside became less thick as the miniature whirlwind slid away in a grey, swaying cloud across the dust-laden plain.

"Bloody hell!" Pete gasped. He turned to wipe his lips with the back of his hand, but filled his mouth with fresh grit which spilled from his bearded cheeks.

Jim was already on his feet, shaking his body and causing runnels of yellow powder to stream from his blouse. He looked along the carriage, peering down its noisy length through the murky air, which thickened in bad-tempered bursts as irate men slapped the gritty deposits from their clothes.

The train had ground to a halt when the way ahead had been blotted out. Now, as the dusty air began to clear, and the afternoon sun showed weakly through a trembling yellow haze, the engine snorted and took up the strain again.

Men, who were standing, grabbed wherever they could for support as they were shaken by the jolting of the carriage, and steam squirted noisily from leaking cylinders as the wheels spun protestingly in an effort to grip the sand-blasted rails.

Pete and Jim flopped back on their seats and looked at each other. Disgustedly, Pete tried to lick his lips, but dislodged still

13

more grit from his face. He leaned forward to shake his head and to rake his fingers through the bushy growth. Jim now stood up, swaying slightly as he watched the turmoil. He easily shrugged off his camouflaged blouse and shook it briskly outside the re-opened window.

He was unsympathetic with Pete's predicament.

"You should have got rid of that beard weeks ago, corp!" he snapped. "No excuse now. Plenty of razor blades."

Pete shook his head again, rather wearily, as he felt fresh dust trickle down his shirt front.

"Jim was always so dammed certain that he was right." Pete thought. His restlessness and energy were a constant reminder to Pete of the burden of his own thirty-six years.

Someone brushed past his out-thrust elbow, causing him to look up as a new voice was added to the clamour.

"Holy saints! Come on you guys. What the hell's going on here?"

Pete recognised the voice as that of Lt. Schroeder. He had to lean sideways in his seat as the American officer edged further into the carriage, his baggy denim jacket and webbing belt scraping roughly past Pete's cheek. Close behind him was a lanky British sergeant who was looking at Pete with an ill-concealed grin. Pete struggled to his feet against the lurching of the ancient coach, and shouted to make himself heard.

"Sorry sir!" he yelled. Then feeling foolish he lowered his voice a little as he realised that most of the racket had died away. "It's the sand-storm, sir."

The lieutenant was staring speechlessly along the dust smothered carriage and at its harrassed looking yellow occupants. Then he turned and cocked his head sharply in Pete's direction, his jaw half-clenched to suppress his mirth.

"OK corporal. I get the picture, but why were the goddammed windows wide open? - Oh never mind!" He turned and made to push his way further along the carriage.

"Look out, sir!" But Pete's shout was too late. The officer's feet had slithered in the congealed slime. He had to snatch at the overhead rack to save himself. His gaunt, heavily-lined face screwed up with disgust as the smothered smell rose up afresh. He looked down at his be-spattered boots.

"Jesus H. Christ!" he breathed heavily. "Who's been shitting on the goddammed floor?"

The flustered Pete tried to collect himself.

"It wasn't that, sir." he stammered. He looked appealingly at the sergeant, who was staring at the ceiling. "It was an accident."

Lt. Schroeder's gaze was disbelieving as he looked around. His shoulders sagged momentarily.

"Yeah, yeah! I guess so." he growled after a pause. He made to take a deep breath, then changed his mind.

"Listen to me you guys," he went on. "This goddammed rust-bucket is set to arrive at Dairen around 05.00 hours tomorrow morning. It may be daylight then, it might not. I don't know. But sit tight, you'll be told what to do." He paused again and looked carefully at the staring faces. "In the meantime, we'll be stopping to take on water in about thirty minutes. I suggest, I strongly suggest, that you'll do something about cleaning up this goddammed mess."

He swung round to thrust his way along the cluttered, noisy aisle to continue his inspection of the train, still trailed by the silent British sergeant, who, before disappearing through the door, turned his head to smile encouragingly at the glowering corporal.

Pete sank furiously back into his seat.

"Why did he always have to open his big mouth!" And even worse, "Why could he never think of the right thing to say? Officers always made him feel nervous. After 15 years in the army he had no great opinion of officers of any kind.

"What's on your mind, Corp?"

Pete silenced Jim with a murderous look, and resumed his train of thought.

"Mebbe that Yankee lieutenant was something special, though."

He had been one of the small group of paratroops who had stepped from a B29 U.S.A.A.F. bomber high over Manchuria. They had been dropped to secure the isolated prison camp. The breath-taking cheek, and the courage of the operation made Pete shake his head at the recollection. Unexpectedly, the Jap camp garrison had surrendered quietly after having heard their Emperor's message on the radio.

"That bloody sergeant, however, he was something else!

15

Supposed to be a mate! Known each other since the far-off days in Singapore. Off-duty, it was always 'Pete' and 'Johno'. Helped each other in and out of all kinds of scrapes."

He folded his hairy arms and relaxed a little as he mused. He remembered the time when Johno's Bren carrier had lost a track at the edge of a pineapple plantation. Pete cocked an eye at his nodding partner. Jim, the driver, had been struggling to move it under cover on its remaining track. But it had spun itself further into the spongy soil, and those bloody Jap mortars were thumping away, filling the noise-wracked air with flying spiky fruit.

Pete suddenly grinned, when he thought of the unhandy little vehicle rotating like a top, and Jim's furious expression as he struggled with the controls.

So, OK, he and Taffy had got them out, but that was the way things were. They all stuck together. Then, somehow, there'd been a mix-up when they were boarding the train at Mukden and they were separated.

"Just a few hours, to Dairen," someone had said.

Pete gave a contemptous snort!

He rose clumsily to his feet to follow Jim's example and shake his jacket outside the window, ignoring his partner's protests when most of the grit blew back into his face.

A short time later the train stopped again. The flabby hose from a rickety tank was slopping water into the engine's boiler. A grimy, horse-toothed driver, with ingrained soot in the seams of his face, hauled cheerfully on the long, rusting chain, whilst his equally wrinkled fireman, with a skimpy beard, directed the flow from the roof of the cab.

"Is that the goddammed crew?" came an amazed American voice. "No wonder this trip's lasting forever!"

"Quit the griping," someone drawled. "They were both just kids when they started!"

Most of the passengers had jumped down from the train. A short distance further along, the line ran beside a raised wooden platform, with wind scuffed timbers supporting a corrugated iron canopy. Behind it were scattered a few wooden dwellings, grey as the surrounding earth, slotted deeply into the ground beneath shallow-pitched roofs of mud and straw, which leaned away, as though cowering from the winds of the far-reaching wilderness.

"Gee, sarge! This sure is a Nowhere place." PFC. Ross, who had been the butt of Lockie's earthy humour, squatted down to speak to Tiny, the huge sergeant from Tennessee.

Tiny was sitting on a pile of old, wooden sleepers, scooping food from his mess-tin: a mixture of beans, sliced peaches and macaroni pudding. He held the container close to his mouth as he rested both elbows on his great bony knees.

Rossi drew some wavy lines in the dust with four outspread fingers.

"What's going to happen, Tiny?" he queried. "We sure do seem a long way from Stateside."

Tiny shoveled another spoonful of food into his mouth.

"How in the goddammed hell should I know?" he demanded.

"Hey kid, come over here!" He called to a small boy clutching a hard boiled egg in each hand, who stood and looked appealingly at the scattered men. "Here gimme them." He tossed a couple of notes to the boy, whose button eyes disappeared in a grin of delight, as he turned and ran towards the station, where among a group of puzzled villagers, a woman was holding a full basket.

Tiny looked disgustedly at the two small objects.

"The hens must have small asses in these parts," he grumbled. He broke off the shells and pushed an egg into his mouth.

"Well, I was just thinking," Rossi continued patiently. "You've been out east a long time. I mean before all this". He watched fascinated as the other egg disappeared between the big sergeant's chomping teeth.

Tiny swallowed the egg and before plunging his spoon into his food, paused to wave it under the young soldier's nose.

"Yeah! you're dammed right," he said. "One of the Battling Bastards I was. 'The Battling Bastards of Bataan', all regular army soldiers we was, and don't you forget it"

"Regular bastards, that's right! How could we forget it?"

Lockie flung the remark over his shoulder as he slouched past them, carrying an aluminium mug filled with water.

"No offence, mate! Just joking," he added hastily as the big man's expression changed. Tiny's face in repose, had the squashed nose and pushed in features of a battered chimpanzee. His ring-worm scarred scalp resembled a threadbare carpet. When he looked

17

threatening he was a hideous sight. Lockie's nerve failed him.

"How about a nice cup of tea, mate?" he asked.

He was standing close to the enormous wheels of the panting locomotive. He reached out gingerly to turn a small tap, which spat a powerful jet of steam into his mug. The water boiled immediately, and the Australian, quickly turning off the tap, popped in a "K" ration tea-bag. He swirled it round a few times on the end of its string, then held it invitingly towards the big American.

Ross got to his feet, stuck his thumbs inside his belt and looked decidedly unfriendly as Lockie ambled over to them, holding his can of pale-yellow liquid.

Tiny, however, had resumed his eating, slurping appreciatively as he gulped down the revolting mixture. The spoon rattled noisily as he scraped away at the last remnants. He gave an enormous belch before looking suspiciously at Lockie's peace offering.

"Hey! What's that supposed to be?" he demanded.

Lockie looked offended.

"That," he replied indignantly, "is a nice cup of tea, and I'm offering it to you, you big ape! Take it or bleedin' leave it."

The Australian's voice rose as his patience started to fray.

Tiny followed suit.

"Shove-off!" he shouted. "You can just...His voice broke and his shoulders heaved as a ravaging cough shook his giant frame. He leant forward to rest his forearms on his knees, as the bout continued. He lowered his head to spit out the green phlegm which dribbled from his cracked lips.

Lockie watched silently, as the big sergeant, slowly recovering, raised his eyes to look at him.

"I said beat it," he gasped. "I wouldn't drink that hoss-piss if I was dying. Us Americans, we only drink coffee, eh Rossi?" He nudged the young man by his side, and panting to recover his breath, he wiped his mouth with the back of his hand.

The Australian took a swig of the tea, and looked thoughtfully at the wasted giant. When Tiny had leaned forward, his open shirt front had shown the great bony racks of his protruding ribs. The rope-like tendons crawling beneath the scaly skin were all that remained of the once massive shoulder muscles.

"Feeling better now, mate?" Lockie asked.

18

"Are you going to be OK?" he went on cautiously. "You know you could have been flown home with them other sick guys."

Tiny shook his head and glared at Lockie.

"What made you think I was sick?" he growled. "It's just that goddammed dust. All I need is a lotta chow - and then you watch me!" He pointed a threatening finger at Lockie. "First thing I'm gonna do, is screw your head right off your goddam shoulders!"

Lockie shrugged and ambled off still carrying his mug of tea.

"Good luck, mate!" he called back.

Tiny's face relaxed into what might have been a grin.

"Yeah, thanks!" he muttered under his breath. "Thanks, you interfering little bastard. I guess you might just mean that."

Pete and Jim had been joined by Johno, the defecting sergeant, outside an open carriage door.

"Why couldn't you have said something?" Pete had grumbled. "Properly up the creek I was! Why did the Yank officer have to pick on me?"

"Because you just happened to be the nearest to him." Johno had soothed. "Just like he picked on me, because I'm British. Said he couldn't understand the Limey lingo half the time, so I'd better be around to translate."

Jim looked indignant. "Limey lingo." he repeated. "He means English, doesn't he? That's the bloody language they're supposed to speak. Maybe nobody told him." He looked accusingly at the sergeant.

"He speaks good Russian anyway." Johno was addressing Jim, but he was watching two approaching figures. Lt. Schroeder and Sergeant Tatiana Chokovska had been standing together some distance away from the eddying clusters of men. Now they had turned and were striding back towards the train. As they drew closer, the trio could see that their faces were serious.

The pair passed very close to where the little group was standing. Just beyond them, the Russian N.C.O. reached up to grasp the door handle and climb into the coach. As she did so, she turned and said something to the American in a deep, tight voice. Pete could have sworn that he saw the glint of moisture on her cheek. Lt. Schroeder stepped back wordlessly and snapped a

19

courteous salute.

"That looks to me like a very touching farewell."

The three of them turned to stare at Lockie who had sauntered up and was pouring the dregs of his tea onto the ground.

Lieutenant Schroeder, who had started to move away from the slammed carriage door, jerked suddenly to a halt, then spun round to face the innocent looking man.

"I heard that remark soldier." he said in a quiet voice.

"Sorry, sir. No offence meant." Lockie shuffled his feet and stared at the ground.

"As it happens, you were right. It was a touching farewell. Just take a look over there." Lt. Schroeder pointed to where, about two hundred yards away, almost invisible against the dusty earth, three upright wooden posts were planted in the ground. "They are the graves of three Russian soldiers who were killed in the fighting around these parts." He turned away from the silent men and suddenly clapped his hands. "Come on you guys," he shouted. "Everyone aboard. Slap it about now. The train's leaving in five minutes.

As the four men remained standing, he looked around and glared at them.

"Well come on, get moving. Or is there something on your minds?"

The lieutenant's sarcasm was clear. He had had a long day.

The stringy sergeant cleared his throat.

"Was she all right, sir? I mean the Russian non-com. We thought she sounded angry. I-that is-we hope it wasn't us."

Lieutenant Schroeder looked thoughtful.

"No nothing to do with you guys. But she might have been kinda angry - with herself I guess. She just said to me, 'But someone must weep for those who are gone'!"

He moved off, waving his arm, canteen and accoutrements jangling on his dusty uniform.

"Come on now!" Move it along there! Everybody aboard.

Johno, the lanky sergeant, was fighting for breath. He was nailed tightly into a rough wooden box. He could hear around him the shrieks of the others who had died. But some disembodied particle of his being had escaped from the coffin and watched with horror as lumps of cold hard earth were hurled into the open pits.

The shrieking became louder. His lungs were pumping painfully. Watching from the outside, he tried to move, to tear open the lid. But which one? There were hundreds of them. They stretched away endlessly side by side, placed in shallow, raw trenches, which scored the surface of the frozen ground.

His legs refused to move. He felt the coffin suddenly lurch as a massive boulder crashed down upon the lid. The shrieking became louder. He attempted to scream himself, but the sound refused to leave his throat. Then his manic struggles were abruptly stopped by a violent blow on the head.

The pain awoke him from his nightmare. He opened his eyes, and there above him, only inches from his nose, was the underside of the seat which he had been occupying.

But the shrieking and the bumping continued. He raised a hand to dash the sweat from his eyes and rubbed his forehead where it had struck the wooden boards as he fought to escape.

It was dark outside, and the carriage lights were dim. He hastily dragged himself forward to release his head and shoulders from their suffocating confinement. Then, half-sitting, he withdrew his long legs from under the opposite seat, where he had tucked himself in the hope of finding sleep.

Men around him were standing shakily or clinging grimly to their places as the screeching of the brakes subsided, and the derailed train bounced and scraped to a painful halt. Some of the coaches were tilted at an alarming angle. There was a smell of hot steel. Steam spurted noisily from ruptured brake lines.

Someone grabbed for the nearest door-handle and others followed suit. There was the usual volley of oaths, shouted questions and contradictory orders.

"Everyone must stay where you are." A familiar voice could be heard almost along the whole length of the train. It was Sergeant Tatiana Chokovska.

"Everyone must stay where you are," she kept repeating, as she forged her way through the confusion in the coaches, closely followed by two of her youthful brood.

Lt. Schroeder was moving from the opposite end to meet her.

"So what goes on, Sergeant?" he drawled. "Seems like we've had a little accident!" He had removed his tunic and his face looked pale in the sickly half-light.

Thick tobacco smoke swirled heavily in the air again, as men nervously lighted their cigarettes.

She looked disapprovingly at the American's stubbled cheeks and red-rimmed eyes. Then she seemed to relax and briefly spoke to him in Russian. Beckoning her escort to follow, she moved off quickly in the direction of the engine.

The lieutenant's hand scraped thoughtfully at his bristly chin, as he stood aside for them to pass.

"OK you men!" he shouted. "Just do as you're told and stay where you are for now. Don't move around or you might rock the goddammed coaches. Our Russian friends are checking things out."

He reached up to the rack to pull down his tunic and harness. He remained on his feet, whilst he donned them, keeping a careful eye on the nervous, grumbling men.

A little later, in the thickest part of a dank, cold night they gingerly climbed down from the few end coaches which had remained on the rails.

Pete followed Jim, cautiously stepping over the parallel metal tracks and slithering down the side of a low embankment. Their boots crunched on the loose stone ballast as they regained their balance and paused to wait for the other scrambling men.

Tatiana Chokovska had mustered her small troop of escorts and deployed them in a straggling line to keep the stumbling passengers from straying too far away.

The word went down the line that Lt. Schroeder wanted to speak to the senior N.C.Os. They gathered around him, whilst the Russian sergeant stood by his side.

Along the length of the disabled train men moved around with anxious faces. Light clouds partly obscured the stars and a thin grey mist was weaving its tendrils amongst the scattered groups.

Pete sniffed the damp air.

"We can't be too far from the sea," he muttered to Jim.

Taffy overheard him.

"Not too far to walk I hope," he observed gloomily. "This bloody train wont be going any further."

Cigarettes glowed and hands were thrust deeply into baggy pockets. Some men gathered together their scattered kit. Others chatted, huddled in small groups, uneasily shuffling their feet.

"Nothing ever bloody changes," Taffy grumbled. "All the officers, they flew them out. Why couldn't they have done that with us, instead of putting us on this shitty train?"

"Oh shut up!" Jim snapped. "The old tin can got us this far. Anyway, what about Schroeder? He's an officer. If we have to walk, we'll bloody walk. All the bloody way back to Blighty if we have to," he added fiercely.

"OK you lucky lads! Get your stuff together. We're going to take a little stroll.!"

Johno's feet slid noisily on the loose gravel as he left the N.C.O's briefing session and made his way towards them.

Metal fastenings clicked and snapped as belts and packs were buckled onto skinny shoulders. The fittest helped the weakest and the young Russian soldiers did what they could. Then, led by Sergeant Chokovska and the American lieutenant, the grumbling unkempt band of frustrated travellers wound slowly on its way through the darkness.

About ninety minutes later, the twin tracks of the iron rails began to divide and sub-divide. A goods train had lumbered past them, heading north, into the hinterland from which they had come. To their left, a faint crack of light was appearing on the eastern horizon.

"Hey look there! straight ahead!"

Bongo Jordan, Lockie's mate, pushed back his cap and pointed a finger.

Lockie grunted and screwed up his eyes.

"Why the excitement?" he asked.

Bongo jerked to a halt and pointed again, one of his elbows digging painfully into Lockie's ribs.

"Can't you see, you bloody drongo?" There's a kind of glow in the sky."

"It's just the dawn." Lockie muttered doubtfully.

But ahead of them and behind them, the straggling column was slowing to a halt, and other fingers were pointing. A charge of spontaneous chatter flowed down the line.

Bongo dragging off his cap to reveal his Indian hair style, wiped a sleeve across his brow.

A grin spread over Lockie's face.

"Yes you're right, mate! There's lights over there all right! We must be near the bloody port!"

He eased the chafing strap over his bony shoulder.

"Oh you bloody beaut! Come on let's get going then!"

Lt. Schroeder stood waiting patiently whilst Sgt. Chokovska harangued a surly Russian officer at the entrance to the dockyard. The heavy iron gates were firmly closed. The exasperated men were grumbling and making belligerent noises in the direction of the Russian guard room.

Schroeder turned and shouted down the lines.

"Let's just be quiet now, you guys. There's some documentation to be taken care of."

A rebellious murmur came from the impatient men.

"What a load of goddammed crap!" Tiny exploded.

In the harsh glare of the surrounding lights, his face had a greenish tinge. Beside him, Rossi looked worried as Tiny's protest ended with a bout of harsh coughing.

The ex-prisoners' unlikely guardian angel had produced a wad of papers from a capacious pocket distended by her generous bosom. She shook the papers under the officer's nose.

There was more argument, but finally he snatched them from her, his irritation obvious in every movement. Some shouted orders brought several more soldiers from the guard room. They lined up smartly to follow their captain. He paused to exchange a few sentences with the American lieutenant, whose quiet manner seemed to reassure him. Then, followed by the dock guards and a fire-breathing Tatania Chokovska, the pair of them moved off towards the waiting men.

The counting of heads and the checking of national origins was going to be a tedious business. Schroeder was glad that he and his own men had taken care in doing the paper-work before the trip had started. He hitched up his canvas belt to ease an aching back, the legacy from a poor landing.

Prior to his leap above the unfriendly soil of central Manchuria, his experience had been limited to one practice jump. His orders

24

from a two-star general in the Philippines had been brief but specific.

"Find this tinhorn town called Mukden and get to those guys out there before the Nips pull any tricks."

He had later met Major "Hank" Mullholland, who was to command the operation, and who had filled in some important extra details.

"There's a buzz going around that General Wainwright and that Britisher from Singapore General Percival, are prisoners somewhere near the Mukden P.O.W. camp."

Schroeder had hunched forward to look as the other man spread a map of the S.W. Pacific on the rough deal table. They were alone in a tin hut at a temporary camp located near Manila. Outside the open door, the red earth was awash with water from a tropical downpour. The major had to raise his voice to make it heard above the roaring of the rain on the low metal roof.

"We've had reports," he continued, "that American and British top brass were moved north to Manchuria after we had re-taken the Philippines."

The lieutenant nodded thoughtfully, peering more closely at the map.

I'm beginning to get the picture," he said slowly. "Seems like we were getting too close to Taiwan."

The major sat down, tugging at a damp shirt to ease it from his sweating shoulders.

"You're dam right." he agreed. "We know they'd been kept in Taiwan, and now that we are getting nearer, our little friend General Tojo decided to pull them out and move them north"

He struck a match at the fourth attempt and lit a thin black cigar. The younger officer recognised the brand. A local Phillipino product, allegedly cured with rum, but the smoke smelled like fish oil. He dug out a Camel and lit up himself, exhaling hard to dilute the cigar fumes.

The sky outside was dark with rolling clouds. Morose-looking men sloshed around dismally with water streaming from their rubber ponchos. He dragged again on his cigarette whilst he leaned closer to study the map.

Major Mulholland sat down and explored the crevices in his teeth with a sharp thumbnail whilst he waited. Soon Schroeder raised his eyes and turned to gaze at the seated man with a wary calculating look.

"OK Sir!   Seems like a hell of a long way.   So what's the plan?"

Schroeder had had a hard war." Guam", "Saipan," "Iwo-Jima".
Infamous names that reeked of blood and carnage.   He had hoped
the worst was over.   The Major's reply confirmed that it was not.

The thickset, slightly balding   man shot him a hard bright
smile.

"Have you ever made a parachute jump?" he had asked.

It had taken only three weeks to get together a specialised
group of volunteers.   Schroeder had been chosen for his Russian
speaking prowess, as well as his experience in battle. He had
majored in modern languages at Yale.   He had thought, at the time,
that learning Russian was a good idea.   Now with hindsight, it
seemed that maybe he had been wrong.   For, according to the
vagaries of war, he had found himself fighting the Japanese, and
killing had become his business.   A business at which he had learnt
to excel.

Kino Naguchi, a top sergeant, and a second generation
American Jap, was volunteered as interpreter. He didn't really have
a lot of choice.   Most of his relatives were in American internment
camps.   He, too, had learned how to kill – and did it with a fearsome
efficiency.

Major Bernie (Hank) Mulholland was a Wall St. broker who
had made a fortune by taking risks in the money markets.   His
piratical instincts had led him to join   the U.S. Army Special
Operations Section, with a token pay-cheque of one dollar a year.

"Just for the hell of it!" he would say.

"Most of his pleasure," he admitted, was derived from "kicking
asses," preferably Japs or Krauts, but he didn't care much if anyone
else fell between.   He usually got what he wanted.

The others in the final squad of twenty-four were chosen
fighting men of various skills, mostly concerned with the arts of
destruction.   Schroeder never asked how it had been accomplished,
but had no doubt that there were many sore butts along the way.

Now, in the diminishing glare of the floodlights outside the dock-yard gates Schroeder followed watchfully behind the Russians, answering the odd question, whilst they carried out the scrupulous head-count. He stared with mixed feelings at the massive steel gates. Once these men were through there and aboard the waiting ship his job with them was done. There were others who would take over.

"'But what was a guy supposed to think? How should he be feeling? It was not just the end of a journey, but the end of the war - the end of the killing. He thought he should thank some kind of God for his deliverance – but he felt only emptiness. There was nothing there.'"

He looked along the line of haggard, tired faces, with eyes that were cold and bleak. The Jap bastards should be made to pay for this. He hoped Mulholland would make sure they did.

"So we aim to take care of the generals," he had agreed with Mulholland at the conference. "But what about the rest of the P.O.Ws."

Mulholland had leaned forward to take a closer look at the map, his mind already busy with plans and logistics. He turned his head a fraction and cocked a sharp eye through the cloud of fish oil smoke.

"Yep! them too!" he said.

Schroeder had pressed his question further.

"How many?" he asked.

But the other man's attention had seemingly wandered again. He was gazing intently at a second ringed circle about two hundred miles north of Mukden.

"How many prisoners will there be, sir?" Schroeder had repeated.

There was a pause before the major replied.

"About fifteen hundred." he said. Then he had turned in his chair to look him squarely in the eyes,

"Could be a lot less if we don't get there soon enough."

But they had finally made it, just in time. These men, unlovely as they were, they were on their way home. Remembering this, might, someday, make Schroeder's war seem worthwhile.

He drew back his shoulders and rejected his musings with a dismissive shrug. Mulholland would have no such notions. He was single-minded. He was ruthless. Everything he did, he did with a

27

purpose.

He had got them all to Mukden, a bunch of battle-wise, hard nosed men, with sufficient fire power to blast their way through those twelve foot high brick walls if necessary – and with enough extra weapons to equip a private army.

It was Mulholland who had confronted the threatening Jap guards, and convinced the stony-faced Commandant that they should lay down their arms. Which the Japs had done, without a shot being fired. After seeing the prisoners, Schroeder half-wished that they had resisted.

They had found the generals, hungry and ill-kempt along with many other high-ranking officers, American, British and Dutch. They had been in a separate camp only a short distance from the main one. Dakotas had been flown in to the nearby airstrip to ferry them away, quickly and discreetly.

Then as the air-link with the captured island of Okinawa became established, the twin engined planes arrived in greater numbers. The strip could not take the larger aircraft, but gradually, in small batches, the worst of the sick prisoners had been flown out. After them went the remaining junior officers. The rest of the men were here, being counted.

It was almost daylight, but the mist remained, patchy and chilling. The men were rubbing their hands and shuffling their feet, anxiously watching, waiting for the next order.

The Russian was finally satisfied and with an unexpected smile and nod to the American officer, he waved an arm at the two sentries by the dock yard entrance. One of them slung his rifle and marched into the guard room to pull a switch. All eyes were turned towards the gates as they rumbled back and the space between them widened.

"Praise be to the Lord," a pious voice breathed. Schroeder broke the spell.

"OK you guys," he shouted. "Grab your things. Form up in threes and let's get your asses over there."

He stood back quickly as Tatiana Chokovska bustled past him, followed by four of her men. She halted by the open gates and busily ushered two of her troop inside to lead the way as the ex-prisoners shuffled forward.

"You will follow my men," she called out importantly.

28

Schroeder shrugged and allowed himself a wry smile as he picked up his own gear to follow behind as the end of the column straggled through.

Staring around and talking in restrained voices, they tramped along a narrow strip of cement, which ran at the foot of the mildewed walls of an endless line of windowless concrete sheds.

The dawn had been grey and flat. The sea-washed sun still struggled to disperse a chilling mist. It clung soft-edged and insubstantial to everything around them. The path was wet and slimy. Moisture dampened the iron roofs of the buildings and a film of droplets dulled the steel of the railway line which ran alongside.

"Must be close now." Jim craned his neck to peer ahead as he spoke to the trudging Pete and Taffy.

Johno, walking behind, them felt a quickening of his pulse and a breathlessness which threatened to choke him. He almost collided as the head of the column slowed to a halt. It was concealed by a curve in the line of the buildings. He heard the cheers, then found himself stumbling as those behind surged forward.

The movement rapidly gathered force. The loose formation fragmented then coalesced. There was an uncontrollable rush of men to join the others already on the wharf. They were cheering wildly. Some started to cry. Tears streamed from eyes whose well-springs had been dry for many years. Others prayed. Without exception, their gaze was focused on the tall steel sides of the ship which was moored at the jetty and on the flag which waved at her stern. A gangway had been dropped from the boarding hatch on to the quay. On it was the name "Harriet L. Lane."

There was a sudden loud click and a voice boomed from a Tannoy, drowning the riotous noise below.

"Men from Mukden, the Captain and crew of the Harriet L Lane welcome you aboard. We are here to take you home."

The short address was followed by another click. A blast of music from the speakers on the ship mingled with the delirium below.

"Hear what they're playing?" someone sobbed.

His gum-chewing listener did not know.

"It's 'Sentimental Journey'," the weeping man shouted. "The goddammed Andrew Sisters." His friend still shook his head.

"Goddam it! Don't you know anything?" the other man raged.

29

"We heard it before we left."

He almost broke down.

"Jesus Christ, so help me! I think I'm gonna die if I don't get on that ship right now."

Schroeder stood at the foot of the gangway and watched them file aboard. With him was a Russian guard and a ship's officer. He wished he were sailing with them, but he had to return to the Mukden camp. Mulholland was busy making deals with the Russians about the take-over of the camp. The former camp guards were wanted by the Americans to be tried as war criminals. The Soviets produced reasons for trying them in Russia. Their claims had startled Schroeder. They were insisting that Russian and Chinese prisoners had been used in germ warfare experiments. They had vividly described a vast research complex which their forces had overrun in northern Manchuria. The Japs had demolished it before fleeing, but human remains showed evidence of their gruesome work.

Mulholland had listened politely, but had shown only scepticism as they argued. Schroeder, however, had seen them showing him a map.

The finger of the excited Russian had been stubbing at the very place north of Mukden, which had so preoccupied Mulholland at the time of their first meeting in Manila. Schroeder had been left with an uneasy feeling that there could be a link between the location of the Mukden P.O.W. camp and the proximity of the Japanese germ-warfare unit. If there were, had Mulholland known about it? And if he had, why was he denying it now?

Chapter 2

Johno chose a bunk above Pete's. It was of tubular steel and strictly functional, but the sheets and pillows were fresh and clean, with the blankets neatly tucked-in.

He remembered a spattering of nurses' white uniforms among the crewmen's dungarees as they had received the dazed but delighted men aboard. His brain still reeled from the stunning effect of the reception as they had stumbled up the gangway: the music, the shouted greetings, handclasps, the shoulder-slapping; then the sudden warmth and comfort of the sleeping quarters. These were tiers of metal bunks in a vast soulless space, with bright overhead lights, whining fans, and the smell of fresh paint.

Face splitting grins expressed disbelief as cracked, grimy hands fingered the laundered sheets. Johno sniffed and brushed a dirt-stained hand across his running nose. The supporting chains rattled as he dumped his meagre belongings on the upper bunk and turned to speak to Pete before climbing up.

Pete's head and shoulders had been concealed as he bent to stack his things on the narrow shelf. Now, as they emerged, Johno opened his mouth to make a comment, but abruptly changed his mind. Stepping carefully on the lower bunk, he pulled himself up to the one above. He rolled over, flat on his stomach, and buried his face in his arms. His shoulders shook, and soon, like Pete's, his face was wet with tears.

Most of them slept the clock round, leaving their bunks briefly, but only for the most urgent reasons. They lingeringly adjusted to the sensual pleasures of clean and comfortable beds, yielding, only slowly, even to the clatter of plates in the adjoining galley, and to the heady aroma of bubbling coffee. However, with the smell of eggs and bacon, the strongest resistance crumbled.

"Hey! C'mon' you fella," Lockie shouted. "Breakfast's ready! Can't you smell it?"

His hook-nosed face was screwed up with impatience as he shook the bunk of his snoring friend. He reached up and tugged at Bongo's sheets. But Bongo slept on.

"C'mon and get outa your fart-sack. Or have you stopped being bleeding hungry?"

Bongo swiped out with a protesting hand and half opened his

eyes.

"Sod off and get lost," he muttered drowsily.

Lockie shrugged. Planting a foot on the lower bunk, he bent to lace up his boots.

"Suit yourself, mate!" he snapped peevishly. "I'll see you later."

But Bongo had changed his mind. He dropped down from the upper bunk and blundered into Lockie as he hopped around to drag on his ill-fitting trousers. His round good-natured face looked ecstatic as he sniffed the air like a pug-nosed chow.

"Why didn't you tell me breakfast was on?" he complained to the stormy Lockie.

Wearing only trousers and a vest he set off towards the mess-deck.

"Come on then," he shouted. "What the heck are you waiting for?"

The ship's chief cook was a sad looking man. He was stooped and shrunken, with a tragic expression as though always re-living a life-time of taunts. But even he looked happy as he watched the way the food was attacked.

"Hell's bells!" Pete mumbled. His tomb-stone teeth were part-way through a buttered bread roll, and crumbs sprayed around as he tried to speak. "The Yanks know how to feed the troops!"

Jim looked doubtfully at the flap-jack on the end of his fork.

"Don't know about that," he said. "Pancakes for breakfast don't seem right to me."

"I suppose you'd prefer dried egg and tinned tomatoes." Taffy sounded sarcastic as he belched and dug into his eggs and bacon. "Or maybe even that cornmeal mush the Japs gave us." His voice had risen as he dwelt further on Jim's ingratitude.

Jim was chewing steadily, but rested his knife and fork momentarily on the table to shoot a swift glance at the freckle-faced Welshman.

"You want to watch it, Taff," he warned. "We've all had trouble with our guts - you especially."

Pete waved the remains of a T-bone steak in Taffy's direction.

"And don't forget," he hiccuped earnestly, "we could be at sea in a few hours time."

Taffy's short red fringe showed like a smudge on his damp forehead as he mopped up the plate with his bread.

"Balls!" he scoffed as he sat back looking satisfied. "I reckon we'll be stuck here for ages yet."

He tried to ignore Pete's smug expression as the deck beneath their feet began to tremble. The confused rumble from deep inside the ship settled down to a steady beat.

The Tannoy clicked noisily and a casual American voice announced, "Now hear this! Now hear this! In one hour's time the ship will be leaving the port of Dairen. Our destination is Okinawa."

"Oki bloody where?" came a puzzled voice from the crowd. "Is that on the way to Australia?"

Shipboard sounds became louder as the preparations for sailing were made. Excited men pushed their way between the closely packed bunks. Billowing steam hung like a fog in the shower room. Moisture streamed down opaque mirrors as razors scraped on roughened cheeks.

"Come on then you blokes. How about getting up topside?" Johno had rejoined his trio of friends, who were busy making up their bunks.

"Hey mates, did you hear that? This bloody Pom sergeant thinks he's a sailor already! Topside eh! Do you mean upstairs sarge? Why don't you bloody say so?" Lockie, further along the alleyway had overheard Johno's remark.

"Hey watch it there mate!" He backed away and squeezed himself hurriedly against his bunk as Jim's determined hand was planted firmly against his chest, while the four men pushed their way past him. Pete, at the end, called back, "Come on then, Lockie. Don't you want to say goodbye? We're leaving this bloody dump." The companion ladders leading to the main deck were steep and crowded. They had to join a line of men and wait their turn.

The air was refreshing when they emerged into the daylight and squinted at the brightness of the sky. Pete felt his spirits soar as he breathed deeply and looked around. There was a knife-like sharpness in the morning air, and a tang of salt, and tar, and rotting fish. The ship's gang-ways had been drawn in. The quay side was deserted apart from a few Russian guards. Standing by the iron bollards some dockyard workers were waiting to cast off the mooring ropes.

33

Johno grasped the ship's rails and felt an unexpected lurch in his stomach. He thought he was going to be sick. Pete's sunken eyes were dark with unspoken thoughts. Although the ship's sides were thickly lined with the waiting men there was little sound.

"As though everyone held his breath," thought Pete. It seemed funny, not wanting to wave. All those troop-ships he had sailed in, from good places and bad. There had always been something, sometimes even "someone", to stir his emotions. This place felt stale and dead. From the corner of his eye he could see Jim's brooding expression. Almost unnoticed, the last rope splashed into the water. Crewmen heaved to pull it inboard. A clanging of telegraphs sounding from the bridge could be heard by the silent men. A grimy, smoking tug took the strain on its thick hawser. The ships siren droned its farewell, but there was little sound from the rows of ex-prisoners. A few minutes later the tow was released. Unattended, the Harriet L. Lane slipped easily through the water towards the out-jutting mole on the south side of the harbour. At intervals along its length, lonely anglers could be seen, precariously perched upon the massive boulders which formed the breakwater.

"Hey look! There's somebody waving, right at the end there!"

Lockie screwed up his eyes to follow Bongo's pointing finger. Where the mole ended at the mouth of the harbour, he could see a giant steel tripod which supported a beacon. Near its base were three small figures. They were waving at the approaching ship. Other eyes had seen them now. As the ship drew closer someone suddenly shouted,

"Its the Russian broad and Lieutenant Schroeder."

"And one of them school-kid guards." another voice yelled.

The homely sight of the waving figures released a charge of emotion which exploded in a burst of wild cheering. Schroeder's trousers flapped untidily around his ankles. The stiff sea breeze flattened the woman's uniform against her Brunhilde shape. Stefan Gregoravitch had removed his cap to wave it in circles around his head.

"I notice he's holding on to his rifle," Lockie muttered darkly. "Let's get the hell out of here."

A single blast on the siren as the ship slid past, and the waving trio was left behind. But the confused, uneasy mood which had subdued the spirits of the departing men had changed completely.

"Never knew you had so many friends, Tiny. I counted three of them to see you off."

Lockie cowered in simulated terror as the big man turned from the rail to raise a threatening fist.

"Get lost, you Aussie asshole!" he growled. But there was a big grin on his seamed face.

The sound of the engines took on a deeper note as the ship left the protection of the harbour. Her blunt bow rose to meet the ocean's swell. The mast-head gyrated slowly against the background of the sky as the ship's head swung lazily south, into the muddy waters of the East China Sea.

Chapter 3

Schroeder and his two companions remained where they were, long after the ship and its cheering passengers had swept past them. They shielded their eyes and watched until the vessel rounded an out-jutting headland and disappeared completely from sight. An occasional breaker flung up needles of salt spray from where the waves surged beneath them against the base of the mole.

Tatiana Chokovska's cheeks were fresh and ruddy as she stood to face the buffeting breeze. She glanced at the American, who, with folded arms, was gazing thoughtfully at the empty ocean

"You are wishing you were with them - yes?" she said. She tilted her head sideways and clasped her hands behind her back as she looked up at his serious face. The wrinkles at the corners of his eyes creased momentarily on seeing her earnest expression.

"Yeah! You bet your life I am. But in fact it's something else I have on my mind right now."

With a dismissive shrug. she turned abruptly to face the sea again.

"Bah!" she said drily. "You men are always too much the same. You will find women and drink in Dairen!"

His amused smile quickly faded as he reached out to grasp her arm.

"Not quite what I was thinking about," he said.

She looked at him suspiciously, but, yielding to the firm pressure on her elbow, accompanied the grim-faced man as he walked slowly back along the mole.

He released his hold as they walked together in silence for a few moments, followed by Stefan Gregorovitch, who looked around with watchful suspicious eyes. Schroeder appeared to be carefully studying the circling, squawking sea-birds.

"Are you going back to Mukden?" he asked, with a sidelong glance.

"Yes, I must go back, but my men, they stay here. Except for him." She pointed a thumb over her shoulder. "You understand," she continued, "There must always be two people. There is still danger."

Schroeder permitted himself a change of expression. "Gee!

Thanks for telling me. That leaves me the odd one out I guess. Mebbe we should travel back together?" He was half-smiling now as he spoke to her in Russian. He noted her appreciative nod.

She paused for a moment before replying. "You have the permit - yes?" she enquired.

"Sure," he replied. "That's all taken care of." He produced a hand written document from his pocket, but looked at it doubtfully. He paused in his stride and turned to her as though with a sudden thought. "Who knows, though. Maybe those guys of yours can't read."

They had left the mole and were back on the quayside, among the brooding warehouses, with their network of roads and railway sidings. Chattering Chinese stevedores busily unloaded goods to feed the buildings' cavernous interiors. Heavy cranes clanked noisily, filling the holds of two single-funnelled ships berthed further along the concrete jetty. Schroeder gestured towards the unsmiling Russian soldiers guarding the various exit roads.

"I'd appreciate it," he went on, "if you'd at least help me get out of here, and through the main gate." He was regretting his jibe about the guards' illiteracy, because whilst he was speaking, she had stalked off, with her armed escort hurrying behind. Schroeder was becoming impatient. He swore and followed after them.

"Hey! godammit! Why can't you answer my questions?" he called. In his exasperation, he had lapsed into American again. She had heard him, though. She turned her head to look at him.

"Very well," she answered tersely. "Follow me."

He was grateful for her help when they had to be checked out by a different officer and a new set of guards. Once away from the claustrophobic atmosphere of the dockyards, her mood seemed to improve.

"Now," she said, with a thoughtful stare, "We must find you a place to stay until tomorrow."

She led the way, through half deserted streets, to a requisitioned hotel, with a crumbling facade. Russian banners fluttered importantly from many of the windows. She introduced him to a suspicious uniformed clerk, who finally gave him a lengthy form to complete, together with the key to a room.

She was half-way out of the lobby door before he realised.

"Hey!" he called after her. "What about you?"

She replied, with an almost imperceptible shrug of her

37

shoulders and a wry smile.

"You," she said, " Are an officer comrade. I must stay in a different place."

He looked bemused as the door swung closed behind her.

"Jumping Jehosaphat!" he grunted. "So what's so different about the Reds?"

The following morning when he appeared, looking downcast and ill-tempered, she was waiting in the lobby. Tatiana Chokovska was shining and fresh. She conveyed, with tightly pursed lips, her disapproval of Schroeder's bloodshot eyes and pale, sunken cheeks.

"You have been drinking vodka – yes?" she affirmed with a heavy sigh.

Schroeder nodded and winced. The movement had pushed his eyeballs back onto the sharp steel spikes inside his head.

The Russians had been in convivial mood the previous night. They were mostly junior officers who had advanced with the Red Army from the Siberian border. They were at the hotel awaiting movement orders for their return to the U.S.S.R. After some confusion about his identity, and long explanations to a sharp-eyed civilian commissar, they had proved to be hospitable and high-spirited. They had been delighted with his knowledge of their language, and had insisted on his being their guest.

"Nostrovia!" they had shouted as they had drained their glasses, and had flung them against the bar room wall, there to be crunched beneath the waiters' feet. "Nostrovia!" they had shouted, and loudly clapped their hands as he had climbed a human pyramid to autograph the ceiling.

"Tovarich, Americanski." they had hiccuped as they staggered with him to the door of his room, and departed with roistering embraces.

There were other wan faces around the desk this morning, but the Russian N.C.O. ignored them and pointedly addressed the American.

"There will be a train in two hours," she said with a sadistic smirk.

"Another bloody train!" he groaned to himself.

On the third morning of the voyage the Harriet L. Lane was pushing her way into waves which heaved with a sullen ochre sheen. There was no wind and the thick air had become oppressively warm. Below decks the men wore little more than their underwear, yet their bodies were permanently damp with sweat. A small team of American doctors and nurses had sorted out the ones most in need of attention and installed them in a make-shift sick bay.

"Looks like they should have taken Taffy," Pete observed morosely. He wiped his glistening forehead with the back of a hairy hand.

Johno nodded his agreement. The red-haired Welshman had taken to his bunk at the first uneasy movement of the ship, and flatly refused to leave it.

Jim twisted his lips in disgust.

"The lazy sod should be told to get up. He stuffed himself too much at the beginning."

Pete and Johno exchanged glances.

"If I was a sergeant, or even a bloody corporal, I'd make him turn out," Jim grumbled on. He looked with huge significance at the two N.C.Os. perched on the opposite bunk.

"Well you're bloody not!" came Taffy's voice from above where Jim was sitting. "So shut your bloody gob and let me get some kip."

Pete grabbed hurriedly at the edge of the bunk. His expression changed to sudden alarm as the tilting deck beneath their feet sank dizzily for several seconds.

"I'm going to take a look outside," said Johno shakily. He gulped and moved unsteadily towards the ladder, followed by Jim and a reluctant Pete.

They leaned on the ship's rail and watched the yellow heaving waves slide flatly beneath the keel. Other men were standing there, seeking relief from the stuffy humidity below decks.

"We're heading for a storm," observed Lockie, with a knowledgeable twist of his lips.

"Since when were you a godammed expert? Tiny sneered.

"I'm telling you mate. I've seen this kind of sky before. In Queensland."

Tiny's pitted jaw was moving steadily on a wad of chewing tobacco. Spitting a dollop of juice over the side, he looked doubtfully at the bilious coppery hue which coated the sky and the sea.

"You mark my words," Lockie's voice had an ominous ring. "When it looks like this, we tie the bleedin' houses down and hide in the bleedin' cellars."

The expression on Tiny's face remained unchanged, but the crevices became more deeply hatched, as black-edged clouds pushed angrily through the sulphurous orange haze. He clung to a metal stanchion whilst the ship's bows lifted heavenwards again.

"Sonofabitch!" he exploded as his ungainly body was thrown against the metalwork. Rossi's face had turned pea-green. He was throwing up over the side. Tiny bit off another chew of his tobacco.

"Guess it's as well we'll be in port pretty soon," he muttered uneasily.

"Yeah! sure. I only hope we make it." Lockie turned away to hurry back below. "I'm goin' to get me bleedin' lifebelt," he shouted over his shoulder.

"Sonofabitch!" repeated Tiny savagely. He spat again into the sea. A thread of wind was now stirring the turgid air and white-caps were flickering and dying in the confused waves. Tiny swore again as the spittle spattered back to stain his shirt

An hour later the men below looked anxious. The wind had been strengthening. Those who were standing, staggered and flung out their arms to grab something as the first great wave crashed with a jolting shock against the side of the ship. The cumbersome vessel heeled violently as though caught unawares. Pale faced men hung on again as she rolled ponderously back and sank into another deep trough.

A pallid Johno sat opposite Jim and watched him tuck into a meal as though nothing was happening.

"Do you really fancy that tinned salmon?" Johno asked.

Jim looked surprised. "Yes – why not?" he said. "We used to have it every Sunday tea-time.

"And the chips?" Johno's voice was getting fainter.

Jim shrugged. "Well those Yankee cooks insisted."

"What about the sliced peaches?"

"They should have been separate," grumbled Jim, "but the ship rolled when he was dishing them out."

The struggling vessel dropped into a sudden hole that was fifty feet deep and everything rattled and groaned. Johno's lunchtime beans and bacon rushed up to his throat. He swallowed them back and his face turned green. Several coca-colas foamed in his stomach and forced the contents up again. He bounded to his feet and fled from the galley.

Jim grabbed at his tray, which had shot across the table and resumed his eating, his heavy brows creased in deep thought.

"What's got into him?" he wondered. A ruminative gleam came into Jim's eyes as he munched steadily at his food. He'd worked in a boat yard before the war. "Why not start a small place of his own?"

A few hours later the ship was at anchor in Okinawa harbour. The sky was a uniform leaden-grey, heavy with impending night and the threat of still worsening weather. Beyond the harbour walls, the wind continued to blow. Spindrift from the breakers mixed with squally showers which sheeted across the open decks. The anchor cable creaked as the ship strained against her moorings. The shoreline was scarcely visible in the driving rain, but occasional twinkling lights appeared invitingly at its edge. The jubilant men below were preparing to disembark.

"Stands to reason," Taffy said smugly. "They'll want to put us ashore tonight, before it gets too rough." He had risen from his bunk and was standing in his underpants, fresh from the shower.

Jim spat on the rough suede of his boots, trying to remove the dust and salt-rime with an inadequate piece of rag.

"American army issue," he grumbled. "These boots always look bloody scruffy."

"Knock it off, Jim." Johno said. He was stuffing a few of his things into a haversack. When he had finished he sat with Pete on the edge of the lower bunk. He was looking unusually worried. "Wish they'd tell us what's going on," he said.

"We're getting off this bloody ship! That's what's going on," Taffy answered emphatically. He had dragged on his slacks, and pushing in his shirt tails, he glanced anxiously at the others who were already dressed and waiting.

"Don't bust yer bleeding braces, mate," came a glum Australian voice. "We won't be goin' anywhere tonight." Bongo brushed past them, his jacket dark with moisture. Water still dripped from the peak of his cap. Johno followed him to his bunk, where the pale-

41

faced Australian unbuttoned his jacket. He flung his wet cap on Lockie's blankets and lit a cigarette. His expression was serious

"What's the problem?" Johno asked.

Bongo drew on his cigarette.

"I'm telling you sport, it's getting real bad out there!"

"So what?" Johno said. "We're in harbour. We should be OK"

The young Australian shook his head wonderingly. "Stone a bloody crow! You Poms don't know a bloody thing, do you? If that's a typhoon blowing up we're not safe anywhere."

"What's got into him?" Pete asked Johno, a few moments later. "It's not like Bongo to blow his top like that."

Johno hesitated. "Hell, he's just getting impatient like the rest of us, I guess."

He patted his shirt pockets unavailingly.

"Do you happen to have a fag handy Pete?"

Pete handed one over and lit up himself. They sat on Pete's bunk and puffed in silence, ignoring Jim's dark looks as the smoke drifted around his head.

"D'you know, Pete," Johno said. "I'm beginning to have a funny feeling about this trip."

"How come, sarge?" Pete delicately tapped the ash off his cigarette and the fans blew it over Jim's clean boots.

"Too many things have gone bloody wrong since we started." The sergeant drew again on his cigarette.

Pete showed his big teeth in a grin.

"Hell's bells sarge! Don't say you're getting superstitious. It's like being on a bloody holiday as far as I'm concerned!"

Johno smiled mirthlessly, giving a sceptical glance at the ebullient Pete, who continued, "Remember we're still in the bloody army!" Pete was on his hobby horse now. "A day at a time, that's what I say. Take what's coming and bugger the rest!" With which profound remark, Pete sat back with a satisfied smirk and airily raised his cigarette to take another puff.

Johno, watching him carefully, asked the next question.

"Ever been in a typhoon, Pete?

Pete nodded slowly. He looked very thoughtful.

"Yes, once. When I was in Shanghai. We just caught the edge of it, but I thought my number was up. Buildings came down like bloody cardboard."

The sergeant got to his feet and scratched his chest.

"Right then. We'll see what happens." he said.

Pete suddenly sat up.

"Hey! hold on a minute. Why the interest in typhoons?"

Johno shrugged carelessly. "It's just that Bongo reckons there's one blowing up."

Pete's thick eyebrows shot up into his forehead.

"Bloody hell!" he said.

Tiny turned away from the steaming coffee urn and helped himself to a handful of sugar cubes. The cardboard beaker looked very small in his large hand as he stirred the hot liquid into a thick black syrup.

"Say! What the hell goes on?" He paused, with tilted head, to listen to a new sound. He swore loudly as the scalding coffee sloshed over his fingers.

Overriding the busy humming of the fans and the clatter of crocks and cutlery beyond the stainless steel counter, he heard the familiar thumping of the ship's engine. Beneath his feet the deck-plates had begun to quiver again. Rossi, looking at him, made off towards the door.

"I'll find out," he said.

From the deck above came the sounds of loud voices and hurrying feet as crewmen prepared the ship for sailing. There was the whine of powerful winches, and the rumble of heavy gear being shifted. He could hear the thud of hammers as wedges were doubly secured around the hatch-covers.

Rossi gasped as he forced open the door at the top of the ladder and felt the strength of the wind and rain in his face. He dashed the water from his eyes and beneath the powerful lights could see the glistening oilskins of men as they rigged safety lines along the main deck. Turning his head away from the force of the wind, he saw the dark shape of the wallowing tug as it prepared to push its blunt nose against the stern of the ship. A waving dripping figure shouted at him.

"Get below there! Nobody's allowed topside from now on!"

43

As he returned below decks, the Tannoy was repeating a message about the ship leaving harbour, "Because of an impending storm."

"Bloody unsafe here?" yelled Taffy, his normally pale face red with anger. "What's happening out there then?" He jerked a quivering thumb roughly in the direction the ship was heading.

Chapter 4

Schroeder groaned and looked hopelessly at the crowded station platform. There were several hundred armed and equipped Russian soldiers jammed closely together. They were mostly laughing, eager young men, looking forward to their journey back to the Motherland.

"Hope it's quicker than the last one," thought Schroeder sourly. He belched, and the taste of vodka-flavoured goats milk cheese rumbled up from his stomach. He sucked a hollow tooth and dug out a sliver of raw fish.

"What a godammed awful breakfast," he thought with a shudder.

He had been coerced into the dining room by some of his friends from the night before. The coffee had been ersatz, but his breakfast companion, with a nod and a huge wink had topped up his half empty cup with vodka from a hip flask. Schroeder had nibbled at a token quantity of the cheese with some crumbs of rye bread. He had eschewed completely the dishes of raw fish. His protesting stomach had reacted audibly at the sight of the flaccid pink flesh, but his helpful neighbour had wagged an admonishing finger. With the discerning eye of a connoisseur he had rummaged around with his fork and placed several choice morsels on Schroeder's plate.

Schroeder had looked miserably at the black skin and warty scales, then closing his eyes, had chewed a small piece valiantly until the other man had turned away. Shortly after, when he had met Tatiana, the remaining bits of fish had been safely in his pocket. The taste in his mouth now, made him remember they were still there. She used her arms and shoulders to good effect, as she pushed through the throng, beating aside any protests, and waving some papers in a clenched fist.

"I have your tickets," she shouted

They sat in comradely silence on opposite facing seats as the train pounded noisily on its long haul to the northern border. She looked relaxed now, with closed eyes, tunic unfastened and hands clasped across her middle. Schroder wondered about her. She was tough and resourceful. She lived a hard life in a world of men.

He remembered her expression of disbelief at the Mukden camp, when Flying Fortresses had thundered over, low enough to shake the flimsy buildings.

"Godammed idiots!" Schroeder thought.

The zealous bomber crews had almost leaned out to shake the hands of the men below. He remembered fleeing for illusory shelter as heavy containers plummetted from the planes' open bellies. They were often too low for the parachutes to open. After a week of this, everyone had become very jumpy. Most of the roofs had holes in them and craters dotted the ground.

They had talked about the wealth of food and supplies before she had fallen asleep.

"We'll be moving out soon," Schroeder had said. "We sure as hell won't be taking it back with us. Mebbe the Chinese'll get it," he had added, with his tongue stuck firmly in his cheek.

She had sat bolt upright, with narrowed eyes and burning cheeks.

"No!" she had said. "I do not think so."

Schroeder had suppressed a smile as she settled back, still looking angry.

Tatiana and her men had been outside the walls, fighting off hordes of the local Manchurians who had appeared like gophers in the desert. She had been in the thick of it, with flailing arms and bunched fists, as they fought in hand to hand combat. It was a battle she had lost however. Sorely outnumbered, her small band of men could not restrain the peasants without using weapons. The victors had made off with the wayward containers as they had fallen on and around their sometimes scarred, but welcoming heads.

She had flicked open one eye before nodding off.

"The piano," she had said, "the piano we will keep."

This had been her greatest victory. The giant crate had floated down, way off-target, but surprisingly, almost intact. It had been too heavy for the peasants to lift, and her panting, red-faced men had clawed it back from the indignant hands of the local entrepreneurs.

Schroeder grinned. "Sure, why not? And the records, and the P.A. system. If it's music you want, you'll have it!"

He shuffled uncomfortably on the hard wooden seat. His buttocks were numb. The bare slats behind him dug into his back. He sniffed and remembered the raw fish was still in his pocket. His bladder was feeling uncomfortable too, so he decided to dispose of the

46

fish in the lavatory. No elaborate chemical toilet here, just a very draughty hole in the floor.

The train was crowded with the boisterous soldiers - a generous sprinkling of women amongst them he noticed. He waited with a group of the men outside the lavatory door, answering curious questions and sharing in their bonhomie. It was accepted that two people could use the lavatory at the same time, if another one held open the door. On one occasion a desperate third party tried to get in, but staggered out backwards with a bleeding nose.

The American waited his turn then darted for the door. He was thankfully directing a stream through the draughty noisome hole, when the door banged open again. Someone greeted him noisily in a voice which was vaguely familiar. He raised his eyes and recognised his companion from the breakfast table.

The Russian officer was capless. The neck of his tunic was unbuttoned. His eyebrows rose towards his sparse, sandy hair in a smile of happy recognition. He took a comradely stance alongside Schroeder. After a few moments he breathed a sigh of deep relief and looked at the trapped American.

"My friend," he said. "How good it is to meet again."

"Hi there!" Schroeder replied. "Sure it's great. Mebbe the place could have been better."

As the Russian roared with laughter, Schroeder could smell the vodka on his breath. He, himself, had recovered from his hangover and now felt he could use a snort of something. When this new friend took him by the arm, he immediately followed.

There were others he remembered from last night's wild party, cheerfully sprawled in several seats at one end of a crowded coach. Schroeder's new acquaintance found a place for him and introduced himself.

"Sergei Petrokov." he said.

He squeezed himself into the narrow seat alongside the American. The leg-room was not too generous. Schroeder apologised when his knees brushed against those of the man sitting opposite. The man's eyes were closed, but they flicked tiredly open at the sound of Schroeder's voice. He eased himself from the corner where he had been slumped and stretched himself painfully, rubbing the back of his neck whilst Petrokov introduced him.

"This," said Petrokov, "is Nicolai Yukovlev."

47

He leaned forward as he spoke to reach beneath the seat. Schroeder heard the encouraging clink of bottles as a large canvas valise was pulled out.

The Russian's broad smile displayed a gold tooth as he introduced his friend. He delved into the valise and produced a large bottle with a familiar label. He held a cigarette between his lips whilst using both hands to unscrew the stopper. The smoke made him cough as he thrust the bottle into Schroeder's hands.

"Thanks!" said Schroeder. "Your very good health gentlemen."

He raised the bottle briefly and nodded in the direction of the beaming Russian and his friend, before taking a good long pull. The liquid went to work. He hiccuped loudly. Tears came into his eyes. He gasped and shook his head as he handed the bottle back to its owner.

The Russian looked offended.

"No! No!" he said. "That is for you."

The gold tooth gleamed again as he produced another bottle and waved it in Schroeder's face.

"See," he said, "there is more of this – and we have a long distance to travel."

The stopper was off, and the bottle raised to his lips.

"Na starovya! my friend."

"Na starovya!" Schroeder replied and promptly followed suit.

As the warmth spread from his stomach, he could feel his tensed muscles relaxing. The ache in his back had gone almost completely. He sat back with a contented sigh and smiled with approval when Sergei Petrokov produced a greasy paper parcel. He unwrapped it with great care to reveal the crispy golden carcase of a roasted chicken.

"Beats raw fish," thought Schroeder. "This trip is getting better."

The man sitting opposite had not moved from his corner seat. His features were dark and angular. Schroeder held out the bottle invitingly. The man seemed not to notice for a moment. His deeply-set eyes were flat and unfocussed. Both his hands were dug deeply into the pockets of his tunic. He removed one suddenly to reach for the bottle. Schroeder noticed the tremor. The vodka gurgled in the bottle as the man took two greedy gulps. He returned the bottle to

Schroeder wordlessly, then sank back into the corner, a tightly clenched fist once more in his pocket.

Sergei Petrokov sighed and shook his head. He handed a chicken leg to Schroeder.

"My friend Nicolai Yukovlev, you must excuse him please. He is not very well."

Schroeder grinned and nodded understandingly.

"Yeah! sure! You mean he's had a little too much to drink. He must've started early!"

The Russian suddenly looked serious.

"Yes he has been drinking," he said slowly. "But we have been friends for many years, and always before when he drinks, the vodka makes him happy."

Schroeder looked at the silent, withdrawn man, who was gazing unseeingly out of the window.

"He sure isn't happy now," he whispered. "What made him change?"

Sergei Petrokov ignored the question and sank his teeth into his piece of chicken.

"Come," he said. " Let us eat. Then there will be time to talk."

He fumbled in the bag again and brought out some rye bread, a slab of butter and several hard boiled eggs.

A short time and several drinks later, Schoeder burped and rested against the hard seat back. He allowed his head to move from side to side, in time with the unhurried clanking of the train. He shared a glow with his fellow passengers. Further along the carriage two of them were singing a mournful duet. One had a high falsetto voice, the other a booming baritone. As the song went on, the Slavic emotions took over, until they dissolved in an alcoholic burst of tears, collapsing in a drunken stupor on each others shoulders.

The man sitting opposite gave a sudden grunt. Schroeder opened his eyes and saw that he was bending over with his arms clutched tightly across his midriff. His face had turned grey. He rocked back and forth several times, before getting to his feet and lurching into the corridor. Schroeder drew back his legs and shot out a hand as the other man tripped and almost fell. He started to his feet and was about to follow, when he was restrained by his companion. Sergei Petrokov shook his head.

"It is not what you think, comrade. It is a feeling deep inside his soul, which is hurting him. Sometimes it tries to break out, and he has to be alone, to weep."

Schroeder felt bewildered. These consuming Russian emotions were alien to his cynical New World temperament.

"But can't something be done?" he asked wonderingly. "The guy should see a doctor."

The Russian looked at him sympathetically.

"My friend," he said very slowly, "I have to tell you. Nicolai Yukovlev, he is a doctor."

A few moments later, with the opposite seat still vacant, Petrokov was explaining to Schroeder.

"It was just before the Japanese surrendered," he said in a sad quiet voice. "In Manchuria they did not always fight very hard." His lips curled with disgust and he almost spat. "Our soldiers defeated them everywhere. The Japanese knew they had lost the war. Just sometimes", he went on, "In special places they would stand and fight."

Schroeder nodded. "Yeah! I know what you mean," he said. "Did you lose many men?"

The Russian spread his hands and shrugged. "Yes. sometimes. Sometimes many, sometimes not so many. But we are soldiers," he continued, "we expect to die."

Schroeder was feeling drowsy by now. The alcohol still swirled inside his brain. He could feel his eyes closing as the deep pleasant voice droned on.

"It was at one of these places," he heard it saying, "that my friend Nikolai Yukovlev lost his reason. Since then he has been very strange."

Schroeder's interest was faintly revived.

"What place was that?" he asked, stifling a yawn.

"It was a factory," the Russian answered. "A very large. a very modern factory. They were blowing it up when we arrived."

"Oh yeah" Schroeder queried. "So what were they making that was so important?"

The Russian lowered his voice still further. The train rattled so much Schroeder could barely hear him. Words were filtering into his befogged mind. Some of them he held on to. They stuck, sank in,

50

and slowly crystalised.

"Germs, chemicals, disease, gas, explosives," were some of the words he was listening to. But there was something else.

His senses were suddenly alerted. He could feel his heart beginning to quicken. What he was hearing about, in the Russian's solemn voice, was of a vast germ and chemical warfare establishment. Unknown, and on a scale undreamed of by the U.S. Government. The cigarette smoke in the carriage had thickened the mucous in his nostrils. His eyes felt sore and raw-edged. He snorted loudly to clear his head and rubbed his eyes with the balls of his fingers. Turning slightly sideways, he blinked painfully at the grave-faced Russian. Now Schroeder's voice became urgent.

"Can you repeat that?"

Petrokov looked puzzled

"I mean what you were just saying. About the other things – the dead people you found in the ruins"

Petrokov hesitated, as though unwilling to talk further about what they had discovered. "Yes", he said slowly. "It is true. We found the remains of Russian prisoners who had been killed by the Japanese. They had tried to burn the bodies outside in the yard."

A niggling thought in Schroeder's mind was expanding at a frightening rate. The Russian sounded weary. His voice was becoming slurred. He was unscrewing the cap from his bottle again. Schroeder stopped him.

"Was this when your friend, the doctor, started acting strangely?"

The Russian nodded sleepily, then changed his mind and shook his head.

"No! it was later. Below the ground. In the cells. He found more dead people. He turned me away. To me – it was of no matter. We were leaving."

Brushing away Schroeder's hand, he took a long drink.

Schroeder felt helpless as the other man's head began to loll. He shook Petrokov's arm roughly, then had to grab the bottle as it almost slipped from its owner's grasp. The movement roused the Russian slightly. He opened his eyes again.

The train wheels screeched protestingly as they took a bend on a downhill stretch. The lurch threw the Russian forward. Schroeder caught him by the shoulders.

"Listen!" the American hissed. "Please, you've gotta tell me. What was it that turned your comrade's mind?

The niggling thought had become a profound suspicion. It was clamouring insistingly in his brain. There was something he had to know.

A familiar voice from slightly behind made him turn his head sharply.

"Here is the one who can answer."

It was Tatiana Chokovska. She was half-supporting the angular bowed figure of the doctor.

With Schroeder's help she guided Yukovlev into his corner, where he settled with a heavy grunt. She sat down beside him and looked disgustedly at the red-eyed American and his snoring companion.

"I was searching for you," she said. "And found him alone out there." She indicated the door with her thumb.

Schroeder, feeling embarrassed at having left her, began to explain, but she stopped him with an emphatic gesture.

"He was standing in the corridor and talking to himself. He looked very strange. I heard him saying, 'The American should be told.' so I brought him with me." She settled back with folded arms, and looked at Schroeder suspiciously. "I thought it was the vodka, but now I am not so sure. I think he might be sick." She rose to her feet and tugged at her tunic. "Now I will leave you."

Schroeder pushed out a restraining hand.

"No, please don't go. I'm sorry I left you like that, but I met these guys..." He shrugged helplessly. "Well, you know how it is, I guess."

Still looking hostile, she wrenched her arm free.

"Say, why don't you have a drink with us?" Schroeder picked up the bottle, but it was empty. He flung it back onto the seat.

Her tight lips relaxed into what might have been a smile, as she looked at his bristly hair and tired, confused expression. She dropped her eyes to avoid his gaze. The train lurched as she turned to move away. She staggered. He clung to her shoulders to prevent her falling backwards. He held on, pushing her firmly downwards, until she shook him off and sat down with a defiant tilt of her head.

52

"Listen!" he began earnestly. He seated himself and leaned forward, searching in his fuddled mind for the words to explain. His insides were feeling queasy. Blue tobacco smoke made the air beteween them thick and heavy. He discovered that his hands were sweaty as he rubbed his palms together.

"Listen!" he said again. "The Japs have been up to some pretty nasty little games,"

She did not look impressed.

He cleared his throat and continued. "There were things that no one knew about. Neither your government, nor mine." He could see that she was getting impatient. "Your soldiers discovered this place. These two men were there."

She gave a harsh laugh and looked contemptuously at the comatose Petrokov and the huddled Yukovlev. "Tell me what they discovered." Her sarcasm was crushingly heavy.

He exploded and she jumped slightly.

"Goddammit! That's what I aim to find out! It was a kinda factory place. The Nips were manufacturing bugs–"

He broke of when he saw her look of puzzlement.

"Bugs?"

"Yeah, bugs! That's what we call 'em – germs, bacteria, poison-gas, chemicals for killing people. That kinda thing." His voice became more urgent as she nodded, showing interest at last.

He pointed to the silent man in the corner. "Look at that guy there. He's a doctor. He saw something in what was left of the place. And it was enough to send him half out of his mind."

"What could I do?" she asked doubtfully.

But Schroeder felt suddenly better. The old brisk authority was back in her voice. Her back was straight. The alert gleam had returned to her eyes. He swallowed to relieve his parched throat. He lowered his head to stare at the floor whilst he tried to think. After a while he raised his eyes to look at her with a rueful stare.

"Well, now that you ask me, I'm not so sure!" He looked at the motionless figure in the corner. "Unless we can persuade him to tell us what he saw."

The doctor's head was laid back in the corner between his seat and the window. His black hair spread in a lank fringe across his forehead. Between his eyes there was a deep furrow. His lips were tightly closed, his balled-up fists compressed between his drawn-up knees.

Reaching over slowly, the Russian woman carefully released his hands. Holding them between her own, she slowly massaged the knotted fingers, all the time speaking quietly like a mother, in a crooning sing-song voice.

"Babushka, babushka." Schroeder heard him say.

As the younger man watched, the Russian's fingers relaxed. He released his pent up-breath with a shuddering sigh. After a while Tatiana, with unbelievable care and tenderness, drew his head towards her, to rest it on her shoulders. She put her lips to his ear and spoke to him in the same caressing tones. Schroeder could see the man's adam's-apple moving as he answered her in a scarcely audible voice. When the American attempted to ask a question, she shook her head warningly. He had to contain his impatience. The doctor's breathing became regular. His staring eyes gradually closed. The sergeant eased the sleeping man back into his corner, the creases in his forehead smoothed away.

Schroeder watched open-mouthed. "Well. I'll be a son-of-bitch!" he said. "If that don't beat everything I've ever seen. Do you know the guy or something?"

She snorted contemptuously as she dusted her palms and straightened her tunic. "No never! He is a pig, just like all the other Russian men."

Schroeder swallowed hard, then nodded reluctantly.

"OK" he said. " But from what I heard, he found something there, which came straight out of hell, and it kinda snarled him up."

"I think," she said slowly, "it made him ashamed of being a doctor."

He looked at her intently, his face serious.

"If all that was true," he said, speaking very slowly, "the hangman's going to have quite a time. There was a word he kept using..." Schroeder hesitated, wishing he didn't have to ask. "I didn't understand. It sounded like 'Maruta'. Do you know what it means?"

She nodded slowly. She looked suddenly very weary.

"Yes it was a word used by the Japanese, for some of their prisoners. It means 'log of wood'. To them such people are no longer human."

"Jesus Christ!" Schroeder breathed.

The pupils of her eyes were enlarged. Beneath them blue crescents showed through the pale skin. She groped in her pocket to produce a crumpled handkerchief. She blew her nose violently as she rose to her feet. Schroeder stood with her. She looked around, swaying slightly with the movement of the train.

"That place," he persisted. "Did the doctor tell you the name of it?

She stuffed the handkerchief back into her pocket and rebuttoned the flap, before moving sideways into the corridor. Schroeder had been unwittingly holding his breath. He released it to repeat the question, but she forestalled him.

"The name of the devil's workshop was Pingfan." she said in a quiet voice.

"Pingfan," thought Schroeder.

He'd remember the name. When he got the chance he'd check it out on a map. He was sure he'd know exactly where to find it. Since the time they had first met in Manilla, he could recall Mulholland's interest in that small red circle north of Mukden.

"Hey!" he called out suddenly. He had heard the crash of the corridor door as it slammed shut behind her. He remembered uneasily that he had not thanked her. He recalled her sniffle and blotchy cheeks as she had answered his last questions.

"What the hell goes on with these Russians?" he grunted to himself. "They're always goddam crying." He seemed to be out of cigarettes, and fumbled around in his pockets. His frustrated expression turned to one of disgust. His fingers had encountered the unwanted fish.

Chapter 5

Johno listened with increasing fear to the wind which had changed to a constant high-pitched shriek. The intermittent hammering of the waves had become a continuous, skull-cracking roar. He tried not to think of the mountainous seas being hurled with pile-driving force to thunder across the open deck.

He raised his head a little to take in the sights around the room. Someone with a broken arm was screaming with pain as a frantic doctor and orderly struggled to fix a temporary splint.

The pool of water at the foot of the ladder had by now become a miniature lake. It was kept in violent motion by the movement of the ship. It made a rushing, sucking sound of its own as it was tossed furiously around. It picked up loose clothing, bits of kit, containers filled with vomit and excreta. It became a frisky tidal wave which washed over Pete in his lower bunk.

He gasped and swore. He shot up from his dripping pillow, dashing the water from his face with one free hand. He looked across the alleyway for Jim. The atmosphere reeked of sour sweat and sewage. The ventilation intakes had been closed off to keep out the water, but with only limited success.

Tiny's chest heaved painfully as he coughed and choked to clear his lungs of mucus. He had a graze on one cheek which looked raw and sore. The semi-conscious Rossi below him had earlier been thrown onto the deck. Tiny, somehow, had clambered down and heaved him back. He had knotted Rossi's sheets to hold him in place. Now Rossi was struggling to free his arms as he was swamped by the erratic rush of cold, filthy water. It soaked his mattress and pillow before instantly receding as the bucking deck plates swung away in a new direction.

Johno became aware of a pair of hands grasping the frame of his bunk. They were followed by Pete's shining pate as he peered over the edge. Pete's arms were spread and his chest and shoulders pressed hard against the mattress as he struggled to hang on. The confusion of noise and movement was so great, that though Johno could see Pete's lips moving, his words could hardly be heard.

The sergeant felt bruised and exhausted. His scowl was unwelcoming as he glowered at his friend's worried face.

"What the hell is it?" he yelled.

Pete's cheeks were pale beneath his beard. His forehead and half-soaked body were glistening with the water from his wave lapped bunk. His shoulders sagged against the cold metal as he took a breath and waited hopefully for a lull.

Johno stretched our an arm to give him extra support. "Come on. What's happening?" he shouted.

"It's Jim." Pete answered. "He's disappeared." He turned his head slightly in the direction of Jim's bunk.

Johno looked. Jim's bed was empty, with the sheets neatly folded at one end.

"Bugger him!" said Johno emphatically. On the bunk above Jim's, he could see the back of Taffy's ginger head. His inert body was lying face downwards. Both arms locked securely around the steel framework.

"Something might have happened." Pete insisted. The two of them were almost head to head, bellowing into each other's ears.

"Too bloody bad." replied Johno. He clung to his bunk with one arm, looking with disgust at the slopping mess below still swilling with haphazard gusto in every direction. "You're not getting me into that bloody mess," he said with flat finality.

A few minutes later, the pair of them were painfully edging their way along the narrow gap between the rows of bunks.

"Bloody madness this is." Johno's grumbling voice was jerky as he was thrown from side to side.

"He can't have got far away from here," Pete panted. "The water-tight doors are all sealed off."

"Hey! Where do you two think you are goin'?" Lockie's suspicious eyes showed darkly from their sunken sockets.

"Lifeboat bloody stations!" the irate Johno shouted back. "We're going to be first in the soddin' boat."

"Hey no! You're kiddin'!" Lockie looked alarmed. He was clinging, fully dressed, to his sodden mattress. He half rose to go after the two stumbling figures, but was thrown back with a painful thump as the deck reared again to an impossible angle.

The two searching men glanced quickly round the toilets and the showers, but they were empty. A hideous smell came from the disrupted plumbing. They gagged and held their noses as they splashed through the stained scummy water.

"Where the hell can he be?" Pete sounded out of breath. He had paused to rub a shoulder, bruised when he'd been flung hard against the steel counter of the coffee-bar.

Johno didn't hear him. He was holding on to the metal handle of a door at the end of the bar. "Would you bloody look at this?" he bawled. He was staring through a small glass panel at the top of the door.

Sliding along the counter to join him, Pete exploded,

"The jammy bloody bastard!"

On the other side of the door in a small snug kitchen they could see Jim. He was engrossed in a game of cards with a black American cook. They were both sitting on the floor of a small alcove. Jim's feet and shoulders were firmly wedged between the walls. His forehead was furrowed as he stared at the cards in his hand.

Johno beat furiously on the glass with his fists for what seemed a long, long time.

It was the cook who finally heard him. Jim, obviously startled, turned to stare as the crewman reached above his head to grab a rail and haul himself to his feet. The cook lurched to the door and quickly threw it open.

Johno was hurled through the space by a vicious movement of the deck, rasping his ankles painfully on the raised coaming. Pete followed with the speed of a projectile. They crashed together against the opposite wall, finishing on the deck, in a breathless, swearing heap.

Jim was annoyed by the interruption. "I was just having a good run," he protested. "I hope you busting in hasn't changed my luck." He broke off when he saw the sergeant's furious expression.

"You bloody stupid sod!" Johno blazed. "We were thinking you'd gone over the side."

"Who me?" Jim scoffed. "As if I'd do a bloody silly thing like that."

Johno shook an outraged fist under Jim's nose.

"Come on, come on, fellas. Knock it off, and let's all be friendly now." The cook's voice was deep and jovial.

Falling back on all fours, the sergeant shook his head and took a few deep breaths, whilst Pete watched with wide expectant eyes. The cook took the cards and shuffled them with expert hands. He

58

licked a thumb and stared to deal.

"Come on now you guys. My name's Luke. If you've never played Black Jack on a roller coaster, now's your chance to learn." His wide smile welcomed the overwrought men.

Johno scrambled to his feet and immediately lost his balance again, to be flung against the wall. Pete crawled over to squat alongside him.

Jim grinning smugly, eased himself more comfortably into his corner. "Right then," he said to the dealer, "I'll take two."

The tiny galley was less noisy than the bunk room. They were able to continue the game without straining their voices too much. Luke's wide smile and apparent unconcern encouraged the others. Even he, however, occasionally paused and cocked an eye at the groaning steel walls and the deckhead as the ship clawed its way through the demented seas.

There came a moment two hours later, when Johno felt the muscles of his back had unknotted very slightly. He was wedged tightly against the angle of a girder in the bulkhead. He looked quickly at the others. Pete had paused before making a call. Luke's expressive eyes were momentarily closed.

"I think she's riding better," he ventured. But even as he spoke the wind must have shifted. It caught the struggling vessel on her beam. She heeled over to a terrible angle and remained there helpless, engulfed between ramparts of solid wind and the pulverising seas.

"Jesus Christ! She's broaching." There was a breathless, awed expectancy in Luke's voice. The others clung on in frozen-faced terror.

The remorseless pressure of the wind suddenly eased. The hideous shrieking subsided to a malevolent drone. The battered ship was slow to respond. Its welded seams creaked as the propellers bit deeply again. With a ponderous, wallowing roll the bow climbed upwards and swung to take up its new heading.

Pete tried to swallow as he pulled himself back into his cramped position, but his mouth felt parched. He licked his lips. They were dry and tasted salty. The pressure of his legs against the wall of the alcove had caused a cramping pain.

Johno groaned as he rubbed a sore back which had been pummelled against a hard-edged stanchion for the past two hours.

He stopped rubbing and attempted to pick up their scattered cards with one hand. His other arm was locked around the metal base of a garbage grinder.

With the falling wind, the ship's ungainly motion had become slightly less erratic but the crazy, spiraling pitch and roll continued undiminished. Sheer weariness was taking its toll on the men.

Jim rubbed his red-rimmed eyes and suppressed a huge yawn. The air in the galley was stifling. On the opposite side of the hard-tiled floor, Luke had fallen asleep. His eyes were closed. His chin was jerking around on his chest in time with the movement of the ship. He had pulled his tall chef's hat far down over his ears to keep it on. The high crown now sagged limply over his shining forehead.

"Mebbe we should be getting back to the others." Johno's voice sounded tired as he looked at them.

Pete reluctantly nodded an exhausted assent. "My arse is sticking to these bloody tiles." he said with a pain-filled grunt.

Jim shrugged non-committally. "If you say so," he answered.

"Right! Come on then!" Johno wedged the pack of cards behind a pipe.

Luke opened his eyes, rudely roused by the noise of their grunting and stomping as they stretched cramped limbs and found their feet.

They tried to thank Luke, exchanging friendly slaps on shoulders already bruised. A playful parting punch from Jim skidded off Luke's chest to become a right hook to his jaw leaving him slightly cross-eyed.

Johno took a deep breath.

"Come on!" he shouted. "Let's go."

The trio scrambled towards the galley door. It swung violently open as Johno released the heavy latch. He thrust the other two ahead of him. They shot out as though flung by a catapult. He chose the best moment to stumble over the treacherous coaming, and skated after them down the steeply tilted alleyway. Some of the water on the floor had drained away, but a sludgy residue remained. It slopped and swirled against the steel walls of the suffocating bunk room.

The wild-eyed men hauled themselves along between the rows of bunks, alternately pausing, then running with teetering footsteps as the ship rose and fell. They grabbed at any object with their outflung hands as each steep climb became an impossible slope down which they skidded and slid. Hard objects were thrown after them as they startled their recumbent comrades.

They arrived together by their bunks in a shaken, sweaty tangle of flailing arms and legs. Breathless, Pete flung himself face downwards on the clammy sheets and wrapped both arms around the frame of his bunk.

"Who said the bloody wind was dropping?".

Jim was hopping around in his underpants, stoically trying to fold his shirt.

"Hey you. you idle sod, have you bloody died?"

He reached up to rattle Taffy's bunk before scrambling into his own.

Johno, hanging on with both arms, waited for the ship to roll, then heaved a leg over and dragged himself up. He pulled off a sweat soaked vest and thankfully flopped backwards onto the mattress.

Pete groaned when the wet bed squelched beneath him. He raised his body slightly to fumble behind the pillow. He produced a semi-dry towel which he stuffed between his chest and the bedding.

"I'm too bloody old for this lark," he decided.

He listened with renewed alarm to the howling of the wind, which had taken on a mournful cadence. Its persistent rise and fall made him think of werewolves and haunted houses. He pulled the wet sheet over his head and shoe-horned himself more tightly into the confined space of his bunk.

The sorely tried vessel shook and rumbled as she clung with a slithering hold to the racing vertical walls of solid water. Their jagged, overhanging crests were torn and shredded by the ferocity of the cleaving wind, to smash across her bows and push them down and under.

Johno flinched with each gut-wrenching lurch as the ship haltingly lifted in jerky sporadic stages. Then he waited, the muscles of his belly rigid with fear, for the roll and tilt and the sickening swoop as the contemptuous breakers rushed under the keel to push the stern skywards yet again. He struggled over to lie on his side, watching the trickles of condensation as they ran down the steel posts of his bunk. The sight of the wriggling droplets made him shiver. Goose pimples prickled in the small of his back.

He clenched his teeth to prevent them chattering and took a fresh grip on the cold bunk rails

Chapter 6

"Jesus Christ Schroeder! What the hell are you talking about?"

Major Mullholland was angry. Now he glared challengingly at Schroeder and demanded an explanation. The chair behind him rocked as he got to his feet. With his fingers splayed he leaned on the desk, glowering at the disheveled young officer.

Schroeder was all-in. His head thumped with the level of alcohol still in his liver. He'd had one night's dubious sleep over the past four days. He'd been in motion for most of that time. His skin was itching, he needed a bath. He was also very hungry. He struggled to keep his voice level

"I'm sorry, sir," he said, "But I have evidence that that place exists."

"So what?" Mullholland growled more quietly. "The godammed Nips are capable of anything."

He jerked the cigar butt from his lips and ground it into a tar-stained porcelain dish on the desk.

"What if this bug-joint does exist? I'm telling you it's none of your godamm business."

He sank back in his chair and changed the conversation.

"Anyway, those boys of ours, at least they're on their way home."

He showed his teeth in a grin of satisfaction, and lit another cigar.

"You've done a good job, Schroeder. Why don't you get some chow and take a bath. We'll talk again tomorrow." His voice hardened.

"That bug-factory, Schroeder. Forget about it. There's nothing we can do".

"If you say so sir."

The grim-face Schroeder saluted and turned towards the door of the white-walled room. He paused before leaving.

"By the way, sir. I've brought along a few friends who got off the train with me. Is it OK for them to stay the night here?"

Mullholland's gaze was flinty. "Friends! In this asshole of a country?"

Schroeder nodded. "I came up on the train with them. They're Russian army, sir. On their way north."

"O.K! Why not?" He gave a nonchalant shrug and raised his eyebrows slightly "Make them comfortable. I'll see you all tomorrow."

He wrinkled his nose suddenly and stared around the room.

"Say! Can you smell something funny, like dead fish or something?"

"Mebbe its your cigar, sir."

Schroeder slapped on his cap and stalked out slamming the door behind him.

After he had left, Mulholland sat and gazed at the closed door for several seconds. There was a quizzical expression in his half closed eyes. He opened his desk drawer and took out another cigar. He sniffed it suspiciously, then picked up a portable phone.

"Naguchi," he snapped, "come over here. I want to talk to you."

The young American sergeant who appeared a few minutes later was tall for a Japanese. His nose, also, was straighter than usual, with a finely boned bridge. He saluted when he entered and stood at attention whilst the major lounged back in a cloud of smoke and stared at a spot on the blotchy ceiling.

Mullholland dropped his gaze suddenly to stare at the interpreter.

"At ease," he said.

Naguchi relaxed and took of his cap. Mullholland nodded towards a chair.

"Take a seat."

He leaned forward, both arms on the desk, the black cigar gripped firmly between his teeth.

"Any news yet from Pingfan?" he asked.

The interpreter shook his head. "Nothing positive, sir," he answered. "The two contacts we have up there are having a bad time. The Russians are as mad as hell about the treatment of their prisoners. They suspect everybody."

His accent was pure mid-American. Mullholland nodded

agreement.

"You don't have to tell me that," he said. "I've done my dammdest to get their permission to send a party of my own. I've even told them I won't believe it's as bad as they say, unless I can see it."

Naguchi shook his head slowly.

"It's as bad all right, sir.   There's no doubt about that. Prisoners of war were used as guinea pigs."

His sharply angled eyes narrowed as he spoke, until only the polished blackness of the pupils could be seen.

Mullholland waved at the empty air with his cigar, leaving tendrils of thick blue smoke. He jerked open a desk drawer, then slammed it shut again with a bang.

"Godammit!" he exploded. "Hundreds of the yellow sonso'bitches were employed there. We can't find a solitary one!"

If Naguchi were affronted he didn't show it.

The major continued to grapple with his train of thought.

"The godammed place was nearly as big as the Pentagon.   I don't believe that everyone of those motherlovin' bastards has disappeared without trace.   We've got to make contact, somehow, with some of those people.   As things are with the Russkis, that's our only chance of getting information about the work done there. It could be important to Uncle Sam.

Naguchi's voice was clipped, but his eyes continued to burn as he answered.

"Trouble is, sir, the Russians think we are already doing just that.   They say the top Jap scientists have slipped through their fingers too.   They could be mixing with civilian refugees or remnants of the Kwantung army.   They suspect that we might be harbouring some of them."

Mullholland tapped some ash into the bowl and toyed thoughtfully with a ruler.

"Kinda checkmate isn't it?" he mused. "They know that we'd like to get our hands on the sonsobitches, and we are convinced they're doing their dammdest to stop us. They've got that place closed up tighter than a duck's ass." He flung down the ruler and leaned forward, peering ferociously through a cloud of smoke. "In the meantime, the cunning yellow bastards are probably getting clean away."

Patches of paler skin suddenly emphasised the outline of Naguchi's cheek bones as his features tightened.

"Sir," he said, "those two men we dropped into Pingfan. They're posing as Jap P.O.Ws, helping to clear the wreckage from the demolished site. They say it looks like a bombed-out iron foundry. But the Reds are very nervous. They think there could be some lethal bugs still around. The place is in total quarantine. It's become very dangerous, sir."

The officer cut him short. "Look, relax," he said. "I know those two guys are buddies of yours. You trained together in the States. With any luck we'll get them outa there. Mebbe even with a fat Jap scientist or two!" His heavy brows puckered. "Fact is we've only got three days. That's when the last American plane leaves here and we hand over this junk yard to the Russkis."

Naguchi saluted. "Yes, sir. But with your permission, sir, I'd better stand by the radio. They're due to report in ten minutes."

Mullholland nodded and massaged a bulky shoulder.

"OK dismiss. But there's one other thing," he added, as the N.C.O turned to leave, "Not a word about this to Schroeder, yet. He sure as hell suspects something's going on, but if he gets too inquisitive and makes the Reds suspicious, the shit could really hit the fan. Yes, siree!"

His teeth gleamed white as he slowly shook his head, at the same time stubbing out his cigar in the overflowing bowl.

Half-an-hour later, he snatched impatiently at the phone to still the shrill burst of sound.

"Yeah what is it?" he listened intently, looking suddenly wary. His eyes flickered towards the door and windows. "OK!" he snapped, "I'll be right over." He held onto the receiver and urgently rattled the hook until a tinny voice replied.

"Tell my driver to come round with the jeep." he said.

He buckled on his pistol belt with a hard expectant smile.

Schroeder had shared a communal bath with his two Russian friends. It was in the former quarters of the Japanese guards. The bath was a fairly basic object. A small rectangular tank made of smoothly rendered cement, sunk into the ground and fed with steam

66

from a coal-fired boiler.

Sergei Petrokov had welcomed Schroeder's invitation for them to break their journey and visit the camp. The dark-visaged doctor had also assented with an indifferent shrug and a shake of the empty bottle in his hand.

Tatiana had scowled, as, with her one man escort, she had joined the trio alighting from the train.

They had ridden to the camp together, in the back of a requisitioned Chinese lorry. It was fuelled by a wood-burning contraption, set in a corner behind the driver's cab. A skinny gap-toothed Manchou chose a couple of small logs from the stack alongside, tossing them into the fire-box as the grubby travellers climbed aboard. They squatted on the gritty wooden floor and waited whilst the stoker vigorously turned a handle. A gush of acrid smoke and red-hot sparks shot skywards from the long tin funnel as his knobbly arms became blurred by the speed of their rotation. A triumphant gasp, a bang with his hand on the roof of the driver's cab and the truck started with a jerk. The man slumped gasping to the floor.

Schroeder had watched with open-mouthed wonder.

"Jesus Christ," he said. "Is that what makes this thing go?"

Sergei Petrokov, alongside him, raised both hands in a tolerant gesture.

"It is something to do with the hot gases which drive the engine. The Chinese, they can be very clever." He placed a knowing finger to the side of his nose.

They were talking later, in the makeshift Mess, after a meal of cold ham, turkey, slabs of sliced beef, jacket potatoes, asparagus, sweet corn, ice-cream. coal black coffee and brandy. Petrokov was expansive and full of praise as he sat back and puffed at a cigar.

"You Americans," he said, "you are so fortunate. You have so much. Why did you fight in this war?" He blinked through the smoke at Schroeder's gaunt features and noted the harsh lines which scored his cheeks.

Schroeder stared silently into his drink as the Russian continued.

"The Japanese. Yes I understand. They attacked you and sank your ships. But the Germans! It was my country they tried to

67

destroy, and the Empire of Great Britain."

Schroeder carefully placed his empty glass on the small round table. He slumped back in the chair, with hands clasped comfortably across his chest.

"Who the hell knows?" he growled. "Why does anyone fight a godammed war?" He beckoned to the mess-waiter for another drink. He leaned forward and shrugged, looking slightly embarrassed. "You guys, sure you had to fight. It was your own soil, your own country. Us! Aw, what the hell! Mebbe we just thought that other people had their rights."

Nicolai Yukovlev stirred in his chair. his straight black hair hung loosely across his forehead. His voice was surprisingly deep for such a slight frame.

"Those that are dead," he murmured, they have no rights."

His mistrustful gaze moved slowly round the bare walls of the sparsely furnished room. It took in the scattering of young American officers, chatting and laughing over their drinks. They were mostly air-crew from the nearby field, staying overnight.

He looked again at Schroeder.

"This war," he said, "Has been much too long."

Schroeder looked at the hollow eyes and sunken cheeks, and pitied this husk of a man. He stretched across to take the Russian's empty glass and called to a waiter.

"Fill 'em up again," he said.

He looked deliberately at Yukovlev and spoke in a quiet voice.

"What was it that you wanted to tell me?" he asked. "Why are you so afraid?"

Schroeder watched carefully as the doctor's eyes appeared to dilate. The man's mind appeared to be perilously unstable. Then the Russian took the re-filled glass and grasped it between both hands. He slowly dropped his eyes to gaze unseeingly at the floor between his feet.

"I arrived at Pingfan before the ruins were guarded," he began. His voice now, though clear enough, was little more than a whisper.

"Tell me about it." Schroeder urged.

"We had a little knowledge of what the place had been. But the size of it astonished us. There were many large buildings. Some had been laboratories, some had been workshops. There were the

68

remains of underground rooms with sealed doors to shut them off from the world."

Yukovlev's wax-like skin shone with sudden perspiration. He raised the glass half-way to his lips. Before he drank he turned his head to look oddly at Schroeder.

The American nodded. "Yes, go on." he said, speaking slowly.

There was something in the Russian's expression. A warning? A question? Something unresolved perhaps in Yukovlev's own mind? He finished the drink with two large gulps and replaced the glass carefully on the table. When he spoke again, his voice was calmer.

"One thing I did not understand," he continued, "Was where were all the Japanese scientists and doctors who did this work, The place was very large, many hundreds of people must have worked there."

"How about maintenance staff?" Schroeder asked. "They must have had engineers and power-plant workers, cleaners, that kinda thing. They might have been local people?"

Yukovlev shrugged. "A few of them were captured, but no one of importance. It was a place only for the dead."

Sergei Petrokov interrupted.

"Yes. I remember," he said gravely. "The smell of death, it was in the ground. The remains of the prisoners they had tried to burn were left in the embers of the fires, outside in the yard."

His good-natured face had turned ugly. Both fists were clenched on his knees.

Schroeder listened carefully, as Yukovlev resumed his story.

"A few years ago," he said, "in 1942, we had outbreaks of anthrax in villages near the Russian border with Manchuria. We captured some Japanese soldiers. They confessed that they had infected the streams. Hundreds of our people died. In China, even before the war with America started, the Japanese Air-Force sprayed fields of wheat with cholera germs."

Schroeder's expression was serious.

"Holy cow!" he breathed. "Germ warfare, and the bastards were getting away with it!"

The swarthy Russian nodded, his thin lips were twisted with revulsion.

"They were small experiments, my friend. Pingfan was a factory for producing these diseases on a very large scale."

"What happened to all the stuff they were working on?" Schroeder's knowledge of biology was sketchy. He felt confused, but what he was hearing curdled his blood.

"Could it still be around, is there any danger?" he asked. His voice was urgent.

The Russian shrugged his shoulders, looking drained and tired.

The American caught the waiter's eye and nodded towards the glasses.

"Keep 'em comin'", he said grimly. "What about the explosions and fires?" he persisted. "When the Japs blew it up, would the germs be destroyed?"

Yukovlev shook his head doubtfully.

"Perhaps!" he said, "but perhaps it is too early to know. There were so many things. At a meeting of Army doctors in Moscow, two years ago, we were informed by the Soviet Intelligence, about outbreaks of strange diseases in various parts of China."

Sergei Petrokov looked perplexed. "But there is always disease in China."

Schroeder nodded. "Sure! he said. "We used to hear about their epidemics in the States."

The Russian doctor made a dismissive gesture with one hand.

"Epidemics," he said, "take place in particular areas, and follow logical patterns. These were in unexpected places. They did not spread as quickly, but the effects were more deadly."

The American took a deep breath. Much of this was over his head, he admitted. But even the most limited imagination could picture the horror of what he was hearing.

"What kind of - uh! - things are we talking about?" he asked.

For the first time, the doctor turned his eyes directly towards Schroeder.

"Bubonic plague." he said deliberately, "And epidemic-haemorrhagic fever are two we know of."

Schroeder was looking very thoughtful. Petrokov puffed vigorously on his cigar as his dark-visaged friend continued.

"There may also have been others, but these two diseases have

70

one thing in common."

"Yeah, what's that?" asked Schroeder, as the Russian paused for breath.

"They are spread by fleas from infected rats and mice." The doctor's voice was dull again.

"Well, sure." said Schroeder. "We all learned that at school."

"In that factory," Yukovlev persisted, "in underground rooms, there were thousands of cages containing rats and mice."

Schroeder whistled silently.

"Go on," he breathed. "Were they dead?"

Yukovlev nodded. "The ones we found, yes." he said slowly. "I hope the carcasses were burned very carefully by those who came after."

"What about the ones that got away?" Schroeder murmured quietly.

The Russian shrugged. "Nobody knows." he said. He continued quickly. "There were also other rooms, many, many rooms, which had in them glass containers with millions of dead fleas, and strange, unrecognisable insects. Most of the containers had been broken by the explosions."

He looked helplessly at Schroeder.

"Do you not see what this means?"

Schroeder felt a sudden itch in the middle of his back and had a sudden desire to scratch it. Petrokov's face was getting redder. One hand was inside his tunic exploring an armpit. A curious sound came from Yukovlev's lips. It might have been the ghost of a chuckle.

"It could be worse than you think comrades. It is my belief that biological changes have been created in both the insects and the rats, to produce much stronger strains of these infections."

"What the hell makes you think that?" Schroeder knew now that his hunch about the place had been more than justified.

"How much of this had Mulholland known?" he wondered.

But the Russian was answering his earlier question.

"Remember the prisoners. We must not forget they used them for their experiments. Over the years they had taken many Russians and Chinese in skirmishes near the borders. I saw photographs which were hideous beyond belief. Even to me, a doctor. They were

71

pictures of men who were still alive, but unrecognisable as human beings because of the swellings and peeling of the skin. When they had died parts of their bodies were so monstrous that they had been preserved in glass jars. The remains were still scattered around."

Yukovlev shook his head.

"I tell you, my friends, what I saw in Pingfan - it remains with me as a picture of hell. Now I am afraid to die, or even to sleep."

The three of them remained silent, whilst the waiter re-filled their glasses. Schroeder was scowling. Perhaps he should ignore the whole thing.

"No damn business of mine," he told himself. "A few more days and I'll be on my way back home."

He toyed with his glass and glanced uneasily at the two silent Russians. Petrokov, clearing his throat noisily, tugged at the collar of his tunic.

"Perhaps we should find our sleeping quarters," he suggested.

Schroeder nodded. "Sure, I'll get someone to show you." He nodded towards the slumped figure of the doctor.

"Your friend. Is he going to be OK?"

The Russian waved a hand in front of his face to clear away the smoke.

"I think so." he answered doubtfully. "But for Nicolai Yukovlev, this has been a long war. He was there at the very beginning. He has seen too many things perhaps."

"Yeah, perhaps!"

Schroeder helped Petrokov to rouse the doctor. As he looked around for a mess-waiter to help them, a sudden thought struck him.

He gave Yukovlev's arm a gentle shake.

"There was something special you said I ought to know." He had dropped his easy-going drawl. His voice sounded strained.

"You told Sergeant Chokovska on the train. What did you have on your mind?"

The Russian doctor was on his feet. As he deliberately disengaged his arm from Schroeder's grip, he raised his head to stare at the American.

"I wanted you to know about Pingfan," he said in a suddenly sober voice. "Those scientists who were doing this devil's work. Did

72

they ever visit your countrymen and their allies, here in Mukden."

"Sure, some guys did come to do some tests," Schroeder replied uneasily "That came out in the de-briefings."

A shadow from an over-head light passed across the doctor's face, as he turned away.

"Remember this very carefully," he said. "We believe they had discovered a way of delaying the action of these deadly diseases."

Schroeder's breath caught in his throat.

"For how long?" he stammered, "Those guys of ours, could they be taking these things back home with them?"

The Russian's voice was very sorrowful.

"That my friend is a possibility. It is my duty to warn you."

"Is there something I can do, sir?" The waiter was at his elbow.

"Yes please. Show these officers to the visitors' quarters."

After they had gone, the American dropped heavily back into his chair. "Sonofabitch! Those poor bastards on their way back home. They could be human time-bombs. They were from different States, different countries. Each one, a possible carrier of hideous death for himself and countless others."

The following morning, before breakfast he rapped on the door of Mulholland's quarters. Mulholland's servant answered it.

"Sorry sir! The major isn't dressed yet."

"Let me in godammit!" Schroeder pushed the man aside and swung open an inner door. Mulholland was sitting at a table, tucking into a plateful of eggs and bacon.

"What the hell's all this about, lieutenant?" The Major's voice was sharp, his hard eyes enquiring.

Schroeder pulled off his cap and stood at attention.

"Sir." he said breathlessly, "I have some serious news. I thought you should hear it as soon as possible."

Mulholland nodded slowly.

"Sure, OK Come on in. Relax. Sit down. How about some breakfast?"

Schroeder seated himself, but shook his head.

73

"No breakfast, just coffee, sir."

The major, dressed only in olive-green singlet and slacks called to the orderly. He resumed his eating, looking steadily at the younger officer, from under heavy brows.

"Well come on then, Schroeder. What's on your mind"? He picked up a dripping bacon rasher with his fork and stuffed it into his mouth.

Schroeder made a small gesture with his crumpled cap, then subsided under the major's stony stare. He took a deep breath.

"It's the guys we've just sent home, sir."

Though Mulholland continued to eat, his gaze was unwavering.

The orderly appeared and placed a cup of coffee on the table. Schroeder picked it up and took a sip. His eyes returned Mulholland's gaze uncertainly

"I thought I had something to tell you, sir, but mebbe you already know. It's about that place they call Pingfan".

Mulholland picked up the napkin and wiped his lips, before reaching for a toothpick.

He gulped the remains of the coffee and leaned back in his chair, both hands placed palm downwards on the clean white cloth.

"Sure," he said slowly. "I can tell you now that I do. They've known at the Pentagon for quite a while about Pingfan. They were worried as hell about the allied P,O,W. camp being so close."

"Even before the generals were sent there?"

Mulholland ignored Schroeder's jibe.

"Part of my brief for this mission," the major went on, "was to find out what the Japs had been up to."

Schroeder interrupted him. His tense expression made the major pause. "We know from the prisoners' statements that they were given injections by scientists from Pingfan."

Mulholland's eyes narrowed. "Sure, so what? The Japs said they were vaccinations."

Schroeder leaned forward. "My Russian friend is a doctor. He visited Pingfan. He claims the shots contained a new kind of plague which would stay dormant 'til the guys got back home."

For once Mulholland looked startled. His eyes opened wider as

74

he stared at the younger officer.

"Jesus Christ!" he breathed softly. "So that's the godammed plan!".

It was Schroeder's turn to gape as Mulholland rose noisily from the table. There was a rustling of starched material as he pushed his arms into the sleeves of a freshly laundered shirt. He snatched up a pack of cigars. His cap was hanging on a hook by the door. He grabbed it on the way out.

"Come on!" he flung back to the astounded lieutenant. We've got a date with some Japanese eggheads."

"They turned up last night", he explained as they were being driven to the nearby camp vacated by the P.O.W. generals. The jeep rattled as it bounced on the ruts of the temporary road.

"The sonsobitches have used an escape route through the Russian road blocks. They wanted to surrender to us, rather than to the Reds."

"That figures." Schroeder growled. "Its just as well the generals' camp is empty," he added. "You wouldn't want word of these Japs to get around."

He held on with one hand to the side of the jeep and shot a swift glance at the major.

Mulholland bit on his cigar.

"You're damn right, I wouldn't." he snarled.

"How many of them?" Schroeder asked.

"Eight of the bastards – so far."

The jeep jolted to a halt by a guard-house manned by a burly M.P. Saluting Mulholland, he swiftly opened the gates.

The small vehicle ground its way across an exercise yard towards a cluster of wooden huts.

"Naguchi should be here." The jeep doors clanged as Mulholland alighted. "He's been here most of the night. I left him two hours ago."

Schroeder was white-faced with excitement. "Have they done any talking?"

"That's what we're here to find out."

Another M.P. opened the door of one of the huts. Mulholland

and Schroeder brushed past him.

"Where's Naguchi?"

The guard pointed towards an inner door.

"In there, sir."

The interpreter was sitting alone at a desk, busily making notes in a book. He jumped to his feet when Mulholland entered.

"Any more news?"

Mulholland flopped down in a chair and motioned for the other two to follow suit. He leaned an folded arms, to stare at the bleary-eyed Naguchi.

Naguchi nodded. "Some sir. But they're wanting guarantees from us before they'll tell us any more."

"We don't want the godammed history of Japan. We don't have the time. Those boys of ours.... What exactly did those bastards do to 'em? We have to know - and pretty dammed quick!"

The interpreter looked worried.

"They're not saying much. There's one of those guys, he seems to be the spokesman, but he's pretty cagey. What he's really talking about, is doing a deal."

Mulholland's face turned brick-red. He shot to his feet.

"Deal my ass! Bring the bastard in here."

Naguchi held out a placating hand. His voice was serious.

"Hold it, sir. There is something. I've talked to each of them separately and they all agree that one of their teams had visited the Mukden camp to do some kind of tests on our guys."

He looked at the grim-faced officers, and paused as though reluctant to continue.

"Yep, go on then." Mulholland's voice was suddenly cold.

"Well, sir." Naguchi shrugged. "The prisoners were given a course of injections, over a period of, about two years."

"What are the chances of some coffee?" Mulholland sat back slowly. "I guess we might have a problem on our hands."

When Naguchi had left, the major got to his feet and walked towards the grimy window. He jingled some keys in his pocket, then spoke from behind a cloud of smoke.

"One thing's for sure," he said. "Those poor bastards can't be

76

allowed to return to their godammed homes."

"I'll radio H.Q. in Tokyo.   But I think the Pentagon may have to decide."

"Decide what for Chrissake?" The young officer's face was pale.

The major sounded very thoughtful.

"Just what the hell to do with 'em," he replied.

Chapter 7

The sound of people moving around woke Johno from his uneasy sleep. His bunk was see-sawing lumpily, but he realised he was no longer holding on to the rails. He sat up slowly.

"Damn!"

He had to grab the rail again, as a lunging wave slammed into the side of the ship. He hung on as it heeled painfully over. A shudder ran through its thrumming steel plates. He looked cautiously about him, taking in the signs of activity.

"Hey, Pete!"

There was no response from the bottom bunk. Johno clambered down. He shook the shoulder of the snoring corporal. The deck beneath Johno's feet was pitching and rolling uneasily, but the violence had gone.

"What the hell do you want?"

Pete was dreaming of Nellie's bar in pre-war Singapore. He reluctantly opened his eyes.

"Come on you lazy old sod. Time to show a leg." Johno grinned smugly at Pete's look of alarm.

"What's going on?" Pete demanded.

He raised himself to rest on his elbows and squinted along the narrow aisle. Some damp looking men were dragging at wet sheets and mattresses. Soggy garments were being sorted out. A few hardy souls were stumbling towards the ablutions carrying towels.

Pete swung his legs over the side and groped among his things on the tiny shelf, to produce a curling cigarette pack. He yawned and rubbed his hairy chest, whilst Johno hunted for matches in the upper bunk.

"Jim's buggered off again," Pete observed, looking at the empty space opposite.

The sergeant swore when another heavy wave rolled him backwards as he searched for the matches.

"Big bloody deal," he snapped.

They sat smoking together in relative peace, listening to men around them describing in loud voices their own particular sufferings. Fans were whining again, but the foul smells persisted.

The smoke from their cigarettes was sucked upwards to join the clouds already swirling in the foetid air. They moodily watched some Filipino crew-men, who were making a brave attempt to clear the floor with mops and a trickling hose.

"Hey! What's this?"

Johno stood upright to peer between the alleyways as a door at the far end of the bunk room swung open with a sudden clatter.

"We've got visitors," he said to Pete.

A burly ship's officer, with several days growth of beard stepped through the hatch. His eyes looked sore and tired. He picked his way along one of the aisles to the sound of a few weak cheers, which rose in volume as he progressed. His dripping oil skins were streaked with salt. A saturated towel was wrapped around his neck.

Pete showed his large teeth in an admiring grin.

"How the hell did they survive up there?" he asked Johno.

The officer's voice was husky with fatigue.

"OK you guys? OK? We're going to be OK now. Hope you're OK"

Behind him came a crumpled-looking figure with a ghostly-white face.

"Probably a doctor," said Johno sarcastically.

There was a fresh burst of cheering when a nurse stumbled through to join them.

"Sick bay's open fellas. Sorry you've had a bad time." Her voice sounded young and reviving.

"Report for treatment if you need it."

"I need it!" shouted Lockie. He grinned lasciviously, nudging Bongo in the ribs.

"What do you think, mate? She's the first bleeding sheila we've seen for years."

"You're forgetting your friend," Bongo guffawed.

"Who the bleedin' hell's that?" asked Lockie suspiciously.

"Why, the bleedin' Russian sergeant-major." Bongo ducked as Lockie aimed a blow at his head.

The nurse was a bulky, bundled-up figure in her baggy trousers and army issue gear, but appreciative eyes followed her every move.

The trio paused from time to time, to check on individuals. The nurse made notes in a book whilst balancing on the swaying deck. Before they disappeared the officer called out,

"There'll soon be chow in the galley, you guys. Why don't you go and get it?"

Taffy had been unmoved by the new excitement. He remained immobile beneath his sheets. Johno looked at the strangely still shape. He gave Pete an enquiring glance. Pete winked and nodded his head. They reached up to drag off the tightly wound sheet, but failed to remove it.

Taffy raised his voice in protest.

"Bloody hell!" he complained. "Leave me alone can't you. I want to bloody stay here till the bloody ship stops moving!"

He raised himself on one elbow. His pallid face showed huge indignation.

"Grab him Pete!" shouted Johno.

Pete was only too willing. They each took one end and they both heaved.

"Jesus!" said Pete. "What a bloody pong."

The struggling Taffy almost fell on top of them. They had to fight to stay on their feet.

The reactivated showers were much in demand. They had to share a single spray. Pete snorted noisily and grinned at the grumbling Welshman.

"Cheer up, Taff. You're not dead yet old son."

Taffy cocked a sceptical eyebrow.

"Up yours mate! We've a bloody long way to go yet!"

A little later, they haltingly made their way to the mess-deck, where they held out their metal food trays to a line of heavy-eyed servers.

"Is this all there bleeding is?" Lockie looked with mock dismay at the scrambled eggs and bacon rashers, which were slapped haphazardly onto his tray.

"Shut up, you stupid bastard! They might think you bleedin' mean it!"

Bongo grabbed an extra bread roll. He followed his fellow-countryman to the nearest table. The tables had brightly coloured shiny surfaces, and like the benches on either side, were firmly bolted to the deck-plates.

Lockie was rapidly recovering from his dread of the storm. His hair was damp and tangled from the shower, but his cheeks remained black and unshaven. He ducked as Tiny's tray narrowly missed the top of his head. The big man eased his way round the table, to sit at the opposite side. He was closely followed by the unsmiling Rossi, who slammed his tray down and gave Lockie a hostile glare.

"What are you grinning at, you ugly sonofabitch?" he demanded.

Lockie's jaws were working overtime, as he chewed on a piece of bacon.

"I was just admiring Tiny's black eye," the Australian mumbled, pushing back some food into his mouth.

"Have you two been fighting or something?"

Tiny fingered the raw-looking bruise on his cheek-bone.

"Mind your own godammed business, you little Aussie asshole," he grunted.

He pulled his tray towards him and plunged a fork into the scrambled egg, then paused to stare intently at the munching Lockie.

"Say, what's the matter with your face?" he enquired. He leaned across to look more closely.

The indignant Lockie shifted back to avoid a closer scrutiny.

"Mind your own bloody business," he spluttered.

The prickly-eyed Rossi was following Tiny's stare.

"I know what it is," he sneered. "He ain't got no godammed teeth."

A startled look came into Lockie's eyes. His nut-cracker jaws stopped moving for a moment. Then his lips parted in a puckered grin.

"Yeah, that's right!" he said. "I took 'em out, when I was being sick. Must have forgot to put them back in!"

He rummaged around in a pocket until he produced some dirty yellow objects. He swilled them around in his coffee, before stuffing them into his mouth. He displayed them with a sickly leer.

"That's better." Tiny nodded approvingly and stolidly resumed

81

his eating.

It was then that the ship hit the floating mine. The explosion ripped through the bows. It lifted the vessel clear of the sea as though pushed by a giant hand. The impact of its descent tore open the damaged steel plates. As she settled there came the hollow boom of inrushing water. The beat of the engine died away.

The shock wave sucked the air out of Johno's lungs. He was flung into an abyss where there was only complete silence. A crushing blackness bore down on his half-stunned senses. He fought to regain his breath, but his mouth and nostrils were filled with a salty liquid. He turned to shout, but the shout was only a gurgle. The thought of drowning made him panic. Instinctively he struck out with his hands, but something heavy was pressing on his face and the upper part of his body. He struggled to push the stifling object away, but it didn't move. His chest felt as though it would explode with the effort to breathe. The terror of his recurring nightmare flared afresh in his mind. He thrashed with arms and elbows to escape from the suffocating pressure, managing to free his head and shoulders. He sucked the foul air into his lungs. It smelled of hot metal and scorched paint. It was thick with dust and the hovering fumes of cordite. A final desperate shove and he was able to drag himself free. He found himself retching as he tried to clear his throat and nostrils. He realised he had the taste of blood in his mouth.

The lights had gone out, but reflections came from somewhere beyond the open door. As Johno sat up, his arm brushed against a bulky shape, which was lying face downwards. A sudden intake of breath made him cough again as he scrambled to his knees. The motionless figure by his side was Pete. It was his body which had been so difficult to move. There was a sticky feel of blood beneath Johno's fingers as he struggled to turn the inert figure over, praying that it would still be alive.

He found himself swearing incoherently as he was thrown off-balance by the jerky pitching of the deck beneath his knees. In the elusive patches of dim light, between the shifting shadows, he could see the blood on Pete's face. It came from a deep wound on his forehead. A ragged flap of skin had been peeled back, partly covering the right eye. Its white edges contrasted sharply with the crimson flesh. In the centre of Pete's chest, Johno noticed another circle of blood. It was slowly increasing in size. He tore at the buttons of his friend's shirt, then discovered that the spreading stain was caused by the large drops which were falling from his own nose.

He was puzzled by the utter silence. He could see things happening. People were moving about, but he could hear nothing. He shook his head stupidly, then realised that he was deaf. Something was also blocking his nostrils. He drew the sleeve of his shirt across his mouth, trying not to vomit. He noted thankfully that Pete was breathing, but his head was moving limply with the movement of the ship. Johno pulled off his shirt to make a pillow for the unconscious man. He strained his eyes to see through the semi darkness looking for help. He tried to call out, but congealed blood clogged his throat, bringing on a violent bout of coughing. The coughing threw up a large clot, which hung stickily from his lips, until he dislodged it with the back of his hand, where it left a bloody smear.

The rush of air as it entered his straining lungs made him gasp. More blood spattered from his dripping nose as he shook his head when the coughing re-started. He swallowed several times to clear his throat again. There was a startling 'ping' in his ears. At first, very quietly, then with a sudden roar, the capsule of silence was shattered.

There were men's voices, shouting, calling, whimpering. They were blanketed by the remorseless thudding of heavy seas, still battering the plates of the wallowing ship. The dying wind had the muted snarl of a thwarted wolf, still waiting for its prey.

When Johno bent closer to listen, he could hear the rasp of Pete's breathing. It was laboured but regular. The wound on his head was still oozing fresh blood. Johno heard the sound of hysterical sobbing. He glimpsed a weeping man being led away, half-supported by a nurse, whose face in the grey half-light, looked shocked and pale.

He noticed that a beefy American bo'sun was trying to create some kind of order. He was using his harsh voice to speed the scrambling survivors though a single open door.

Johno looked around for help. A few more nurses and orderlies had appeared and were stumbling about, giving what aid they could to victims unable to move. A line of those with minor injuries was being passed through another alleyway in the direction of the sick bay.

"Over here!" he tried to yell, but his voice was choked off by another fit of coughing. He was worried by Pete's open wound, and the blood which continued to trickle. He looked around hopelessly for something to staunch the bleeding.

With a resigned sigh, he dragged off his thin singlet, shivering slightly from the draughty air. As carefully as he could, he rolled back the gruesome flap of skin, and pressed the grubby garment gently over the wound.

"Hope this doesn't give you gangrene, you old bastard," he thought anxiously.

"Is that you sarge?" A familiar voice came from the gloom.

Johno recognised Taffy coming slowly towards him, stepping carefully to keep his balance, and to avoid the debris on the deck. His pale-blue eyes were staring. There was a vagueness in the way they searched around the rapidly emptying mess-deck.

Crackling sounds were coming from the Tannoy. They added to Johno's worries and confusion. The ship was still afloat, but the rolling had become more sluggish.

He covered his fear by shouting at Taffy.

"Of course it's bloody me!" he replied.

Taffy jumped slightly. and his expression became less vacant. He beckoned towards the crouching sergeant.

"Come on you silly bugger," he called. "The bloody ship's sinking."

"Bollocks!" Johno answered loudly. "Can't you see I've got Pete here."

Taffy came closer. He looked shocked when he saw the injured Pete. His pallid face turned even whiter.

"Bloody hell!" he gasped. "Is he dead?"

Johno snorted impatiently, then winced as he felt the pain inside his head.

"No. Pete isn't dead!" he answered thickly. Johno stopped himself. "Look," he went on in a quieter voice. "We can't leave Pete like this. Besides, they haven't even sounded 'Life-Boat Stations' as far as I know."

Taffy moved closer very slowly. He suddenly dropped to his knees to look at Pete more carefully

"Stuff me! He looks pretty bad doesn't he sarge?" He switched his gaze to Johno. Then the Welshman's lips began to twitch, his face became contorted as if in pain.

Johno became even more alarmed. Now Taffy was cracking up.

"Come on you silly sod!" he snapped. "Have you gone mad?"

In reply, the Welshman's shoulders heaved. His voice became a cackle as he pointed a derisive finger.

"No sarge, it's you, your nose! It looks like a bloody great tomato, and you're getting a black eye. It's going to be a real beauty!"

He broke off with a cry of alarm as Johno's arm shot out to grab him by the front of his shirt.

"If you don't shut your trap," the sergeant threatened, "yours is going to be a bloody sight worse."

Taffy wrenched himself free to stare with ghoulish fascination at the blood soaked cotton garment held in place by Johno's hand.

"Hope that doesn't give him blood-poisoning," he muttered darkly.

Johno's rage was increasing. "Why don't you do something useful?" He was trying to yell, but the effort was too painful.

He sat back on his heels to look desperately around. With a gasp of relief, he saw a white-coated orderly, a few tables away. He was doing something to the limp arm of a groaning casualty.

"Look! Over there." Johno gave Taffy a shove. "See if you can get him."

He switched his gaze to the deck-head as the lights blinked on. Just as suddenly they went out. Another second, another blink, then they stayed on.

Words started to stream from the Tannoy, but so loudly that Johno was almost deafened again. Abruptly, the sound became more normal. He was able to pick up a few sentences.

"Explosion for'ard. Suspected mine. Awaiting reports from damage control. Passengers return to quarters. Await further orders."

Taffy's voice rose an octave with his indignation. "A bloody mine! The soddin' war's supposed to be over! What about getting home then?"

Johno wasn't listening. His frantic wavings had caught the attention of the orderly. The young man was lurching across the few

85

yards of floor, in their direction. He dropped on his knees beside Pete. Carefully, he raised the sodden dressing. Through the welling blood, Johno caught a glimpse of something white. The orderly felt Pete's pulse, then raised his eyelids to examine the pupils.

"Can you do something?" It was Taffy, his voice surprisingly anxious.

"Yeah, I guess, but not here. Sick bay for him. We're going to need a litter."

"I'll get one." Taffy clambered to his feet. He scuttled away, half-hopping as the deck angled away from under him.

The kneeling orderly tossed aside Johno's sticky singlet and replaced it with a pad of clean gauze from his bag. For a few moments he held it there, resting his other hand on the front of his white trousers, where it left bloody finger marks. He looked across at Johno from under raised eyebrows.

"Been pretty bad for you guys hasn't it?" he said. "What a helluva way to be going home!" The note of sympathy in his voice was unexpected.

Johno sniffed, then wiped his nose again with the back of his hand. He tried to clear his throat.

"What about him?" He gestured towards Pete's still shape. "Is it bad?"

"Bad enough," the orderly answered. "But don't worry. I think your buddy's goin' to be OK His eye reflexes seem good, and there's no bleeding from his ears. I guess his skull's pretty thick," he added with a grin.

Johno knew that most of this had to be guess-work, but there was something reassuring about the casual American accent. He felt a surge of relief. He brushed the blood from his nose again.

"Here, take this." The medic handed him some gauze swabs. He looked around for Taffy. "Where the hell is that guy with the litter?"

Johno suddenly shivered. His eyes wandered to the blood-soaked garment on the floor of the shattered mess-deck. He heard himself talking to take his mind off the shivering.

"It's a pity about the singlet," he said.

The medic, who was checking Pete's pulse again, looked up, startled.

"The singlet?"

Johno pointed to the bloody object on the rubbish strewn deck. "Almost brand new. Special delivery. Fell out of the sky!" His teeth were starting to chatter. He had to clench his jaws.

The orderly looked thoughtful. "I guess Uncle Sam owes you that one," he said quietly.

"Here it is, Sarge. I've found a stretcher." Taffy was stumbling towards them, hampered by the unwieldy burden on his shoulders. His face was pink with exertion.

"Good man!" gasped Johno. "Come on let's lift him onto it."

They unfastened the leather straps to place it alongside the unconscious man. Johno's hands had started to shake. He found himself being clumsily shoved aside by Taffy, who, with the orderly, gently lifted Pete. Between them they raised the stretcher. Johno tried to help, but Taffy pushed him away again.

"No, sarge. I'll manage this."

They moved slowly off, shoulders sagging with the weight, struggling to keep the stretcher level. Taffy shouted over his shoulder, "Bugger off and find youself a shirt, sarge. You're going to get bloody pneumonia."

Johno got to his feet, still shivering. The air was becoming colder. He looked around the almost deserted mess deck, searching for the best way out.

"Hey you! This way!" The bo'sun had reappeared. He was waving an arm in the direction of the bunk-room.

"You OK?" he asked, as Johno tripped over some debris.

"Oh sure. Yes, I'm OK"

"We want all you fit guys together." He held out a friendly hand to help Johno over the coaming.

"Fit guys?" The sergeant allowed himself a hollow laugh. He hauled himself along the short alleyway, past the door of Luke's tiny galley, where the atmosphere was decidedly warmer.

"Stay near your bunk," the bo'sun shouted.

Johno nodded. He started to hurry. For the first time since the explosion, he was feeling real alarm about the fate of the ship.

"Bugger all I can do," he told himself uneasily.

"Hey, sarge!"

Johno halted abruptly. That voice. It was Jim's. He glanced sideways through the open door of Luke's galley. Jim was there. His face looked red and aggrieved.

"I've been looking for you, everywhere," he shouted.

Johno's drooping spirits sank even further. He was relieved to see his friend again, but something in Jim's voice spelled out more trouble. Jim had been about to leave the galley through a hatch on the opposite side. One leg was already half-way through.

"This way, sarge. We need some help here!" He beckoned urgently.

Johno noted with further misgiving the excited gleam in Jim's eyes. "What the hell are you up to?" Johno's voice was a snarl as he ducked through the open hatch to follow in Jim's wake.

The amplified shriek of a klaxon came over the Tannoy. It was followed by a message:

"Passengers assemble immediately at life-boat station. Please carry lifebelts."

Chapter 8

Mullholland told Schroeder to return to the main camp.

"Naguchi and I will be talking to these creepy bastards." He jerked a savage thumb towards the adjacent hut. "You'd better take care of your Russian buddies." he grunted.

The young lieutenant agreed reluctantly.

"Sure! They'll be wanting to be on their way home, I reckon"

Mulholland shook his head.

"Try and keep them here for a while. I guess there won't be a train 'til tomorrow, so it shouldn't be too difficult."

Schroeder looked puzzled. "Keep 'em sir? Any special reason?"

Mulholland shrugged. "Just let's say a guy can't have too many friends, lieutenant. But for Chrissaake, don't tell 'em about these prisoners here," he warned.

Back in the main camp a little later, Schroeder located his visitors. They were in the mess-hall having a late breakfast. The Russian doctor looked lethargic. His manner was taciturn again. Schroeder wondered if he was taking drugs. "Perhaps he came alive only at night?"

Tatiana Chokovska had joined them. Schroeder thought her eyes looked a little puffy. He greeted her with a guarded smile.

"Hi there! Did you have a good night?"

On the previous evening, which he had spent with the two Russian officers, he had introduced her to a few of the American non-comms. They had snapped up the chance of some female company. The firm-jawed Tatiana, suspicious at first, had succumbed to their hospitable advances. When Schroeder had left they had shown signs of preparing for a convivial evening.

In answer to his question, she looked at him from under lowered eyebrows, whilst sipping her coffee. She carefully nodded her head. Schroeder shot her an unsympathetic grin when he recognised the symptoms.

"I guess you must have enjoyed yourself." he said.

The look she gave him discouraged further comment.

He wandered over to the counter to pick up a cup of coffee. One of Tatiana's G.I. friends from the night before was also helping himself. His gravelly voice was tinged with awe as he stared in admiration at the Russian woman

"Some dame you got there, lootenant. She must have been the only one left on her feet last night."

Schroeder nodded and grinned.

"But before that, she took us to the cleaners. At shooting the craps," the man explained. "We ain't got a dime left between us." He moved off, still muttering to himself, – but he'd given Schroeder an idea. He remembered Mulholland's instructions to keep the Russians from leaving.

"Say wait a minute," he whispered. "How would you like to get your money back?"

The man looked interested, but his voice was sceptical.

"Are you kidding, sir? Like I told you, we ain't got no dough!"

Schroeder noticed that Tatiana was saying something to Sergei Petrokov, who turned to look with faint curiosity in their direction. Schroeder walked towards the outside door.

"Follow me." he whispered to the man beside him. The gaping N.C.O. ducked through the door as the officer held it open. Once outside the lieutenant pulled a wad of money from the pocket of his blouse.

"Here! Take this!" he said.

The sergeant's eyes bulged. "But sir...?"

"Cut out the thanks," Schroeder snapped. "It's local wartime currency. Not worth a shit. But those guys won't know the difference. Listen!" he went on. "I want you back in here, in one hour's time. I want you to bring a couple of your buddies."

The man was listening now. He stuffed the money into a pocket. "Yes sir!" he said.

"Then," the officer continued, "I want you to invite these friends of mine to a game of poker."

The sergeant's eyes brightened, then he looked disappointed.

"Does it have to be poker, sir? That ain't my best game".

"Well blackjack, then, shooting the craps. What's the difference, goddammit? Get 'em drunk, feed the bastards. Do anything you godammed like, but keep them busy".

The sergeant stared at him in disbelief.

"Is that an order,sir?"

"You bet your sweet ass it's an order!" Schroeder's voice was low and fierce. "Just one more thing," he went on, "Don't let 'em out of your sight 'til I get back. Is that clear soldier?"

The delighted man grinned and saluted.

"Sure, sir. I've got it. We'll be there in one hour's time, sir."

"Remember what I said," Schroeder repeated. "Don't let them out of your sight! If you should need me, I'll be with Major Mulholland. Oh! by the way. When you arrive, don't make it seem like you've been invited to Uncle Henry's party. Make it seem kinda accidental. Mebbe you shouldn't all turn up together."

The man nodded eagerly. "Sure, sir. Leave everything to me and my buddies sir. See you in an hour's time, sir."

Schroeder nodded. "OK Dismiss sergeant." He watched with some misgiving as the man marched jauntily away. Looking quickly at his watch, he went back inside to rejoin the others. An hour should be long enough to check again on Yukovlev's information. Then, if his plan worked out, he'd be free to join Mulholland for the rest of the afternoon.

Yukovlev's intense emotion of the previous evening was no longer evident. When the American cautiously questioned him again, however, he quickly dowsed whatever hope had remained in Schroeder's mind.

"If your prisoners were visited by the men from Pingfan", he asserted, "they will die."

"But how can you be so sure?" Schroeder persisted.

The Russian gave him a scornful glance. "Because that was their work – to kill. Just as it is a soldier's duty – to destroy the enemy."

"But they could have killed them in so many other ways." Schroeder was hanging on to his last shred of hope.

A momentary glitter showed in the Russian's eyes. "The difference is, my friend, that when they die, it will be in their own countries. In their own towns and cities. Many, many others will die with them. Perhaps, even so long ago, the Japanese thought they might lose the war. This would be an act of revenge."

91

"It's lunacy," Schroeder breathed. "Sheer godammed lunacy."

The Russian doctor nodded as he sipped his coffee. "I agree with you," he said in a quiet voice.

Schroeder's lips were tightly compressed as he drove back to Camp B. Despite Yukovlev's change of mood, there was no doubt that he believed the Japs had discovered a means of delaying the onset of plague-like diseases for whatever length of time they chose. He looked straight ahead. The small vehicle bounced as he pushed his foot down harder. "Where are the ex-prisoners now?" he wondered.

For the remainder of that morning, and part of the afternoon, he sat with Mulholland whilst the Japanese captives were led before them, one at a time. Naguchi was there to translate. His eyes looked heavy-lidded. Once or twice he seemed confused by the prisoner's evasive replies. Schroeder remembered that the interpreter had been up since very early morning.

Mulholland, from time to time, referred to the notes before him, which Naguchi had prepared from the scientist's earlier interrogations.

Schroeder found it difficult to conceal his loathing as each of them faced Mulholland's hostile gaze. Several times he had to restrain himself from interrupting as they produced their glib replies to the major's biting questions. The most senior of the party was particularly unhelpful. He was small and rotund. An arrogant smirk was ill-concealed beneath his obsequious manner. He insisted that neither he nor his colleagues had been involved in any way with the Allied P.O.Ws. He pulled back his shoulders and looked angry when Mulholland said,

"Bullshit! Listen to me, you little jerk," the major continued. "Almost without exception, those other guys admitted that they knew something was going on down here. Trouble is, they don't know exactly what. What makes you so different? Why do you deny it? What are you trying to hide? Why the hell are you godammed lying?" The major's voice was a threatening growl.

The prisoner looked less confident as Naguchi translated in his flat unemotional style.

Schroeder was watching closely. The man's moon face was damp with perspiration. but his glasses flashed as he stubbornly shook his head. He spoke rapidly in Japanese.

"He still says he knew nothing about it." Naguchi repeated to

Mulholland. "What's more, sir, he claims they have come here seeking asylum. He says there are others still in hiding, who could tell us more, but they are demanding a guarantee of safe conduct to Tokyo, sir."

Mulholland's face darkened with anger. He placed both his fore-arms on the desk and leaned forward menacingly, towards the prisoner.

"Listen to me, you little shit-head," he rasped. "I've got sixty of your fellow-countrymen, who were guards in this goddammed place. They're over there in their quarters." He indicated, with a jerk of his thumb, the direction of the main camp.

"Tell the bastard," he said to Naguchi, "that our Russian allies handed them over to me to do with as I pleased. They suggested that I should cut their throats. Why should he be different?" He sat back with a cruel smile as Naguchi translated.

The Jap looked visibly shaken. His eyes flicked shiftily towards the impassive interpreter.

"Now you tell me," Mulholland barked, "just why you and those other mother lovin' scum from Pingfan should get special treatment?"

The man's clenched fists were trembling as he replied in a hoarse uncertain voice. "It is my duty to die if there is no other way of serving my country with honour."

"Duty!" sneered Mulholland. "Killing innocent civilians in China. Spreading your filthy diseases. Torturing helpless prisoners."

There was a sharp rap on the door. Mulholland broke off.

"Yeah. what the hell is it?" he shouted.

"Your coffee, sir." came the reply.

"O.K! Bring it in."

The three Americans sat back as the orderly brought in a jug and several cups. Naguchi did the pouring.

"Help yourself." Mulholland invited the stone-faced M.P. who stood close to the prisoner. The Jap stood watching them as they drank and chatted. He said something in a guttural voice to Naguchi.

When Mulholland raised a questioning eyebrow, the interpreter replied "He's asking for a chair, sir."

"Not on your godammed life. Let the bastard stand," the major

93

answered.

The three men at the table were smoking. The atmosphere in the small room was stuffy and thick with tobacco fumes.

The prisoner coughed. He spoke again to Naguchi.

"What is it this time?" Mulholland drawled in a lazy voice.

"He says can he have a drink of water?"

Mulholland seemed about to refuse permission, then shrugged and said reluctantly, "OK. Why not?"

He nodded to the M.P. who moved quietly towards the door.

Schroeder had a sudden thought. "Tell one of your guys to piss in it," he snapped.

The M.P. halted. He looked enquiringly at the major. Mulholland had a sudden fit of coughing. He checked it and dusted the spilled ash from the front of his blouse.

"I didn't hear a dam thing corporal. Do as the lieutenant said."

When the unsmiling man returned a few minutes later he held a brimming tumbler stiffly in one hand. He placed it carefully on the table, in front of the prisoner. It contained a pale amber coloured liquid.

Cocking one eye in the direction of the tubby man, Mulholland said, "Go ahead! Have a drink."

The Jap looked at it suspiciously. He shook his head and turned to look at Naguchi.

"Go ahead, pick it up." Mulholland's voice was sharper.

The man stretched out an unwilling arm to pick up the glass. Holding it cautiously to his nose he sniffed it. His podgy face turned darker. He placed the glass back on to the desk, with a hand that trembled with rage. Turning to Naguchi, he pointed to the offending liquid and spat out a torrent of Japanese.

Mulholland leapt to his feet to move swiftly round the desk. The protesting man's teeth rattled from a back-handed swipe.

Schroeder rose, involuntarily, from his chair.

"Sir." he said in a warning voice.

"Shut up!" Mulholland hissed, without taking his eyes off the prisoner. "Now you, you crappy-assed bastard, you said you wanted a drink."

94

He picked up the glass to thrust it under the man's nose.

"Go on! Drink it!"

The cringing man, his teeth clenched, his eyes tightly closed, continued to shake his head.

Mulholland stepped back. He replaced the tumbler on the table. He spoke to the M.P. guard, in a voice which had the rasp of a freshly ground blade.

"Corporal," he said. "When I give you the order I want you to shoot this man."

"Yes sir." The guard unbuttoned the flap of his white-blancoed holster. He withdrew the pistol and pushed the muzzle hard against the prisoner's temple.

Schroeder was on his feet now. His eyes opened wide with horror. The M.P. was having to support the man's shaking body with his free arm.

Mulholland turned to Naguchi. "Sergeant," he said. His voice retained its cold impersonal ring. "I want you tell the prisoner exactly what I am saying. He is not a prisoner of war. He is a civilian wearing military uniform. I have the right to have him shot as a spy."

Naguchi translated the major's words in a few sharp sentences.

"I shall give him exactly five seconds to tell us what he knows about the treatment of the allied prisoners in Mukden. If he refuses he will be shot."

Nuguchi translated again. The man shook his head and started to moan.

"Get ready." Mulholland looked at the M.P., who nodded. The hammer of the pistol clicked as he cocked it.

Schroeder averted his eyes.

"You do the counting." Mulholland stood back. He placed both hands on his hips as he spoke to the interpreter.

Naguchi looked tense. "Now, sir?"

"When I give the order. Count in Japanese so that we'll know he understands."

The major's eyes were unwavering as he stared at the half-fainting man. "Now!" he said.

"Ichi, Ni," Naguchi sounded short of breath. "San, Shi…"

There was a thud as the prisoner's body slipped from the M.P's grasp.

Naguchi stopped counting.

"Sorry, sir." gasped the red-faced guard. "I couldn't hold him. He must've fainted. Should have had him on a chair, sir."

Mulholland's teeth showed in a vicious grin. "Forget it," he said. "Let's try and bring the slimy bastard round."

Holstering his pistol, the M.P. bent to shake the fallen body.

"Here, try this." Mulholland picked up the tumbler. He threw the contents over the Jap's mottled face. The man spluttered, and opened his eyes. He rolled onto his stomach, groaning and coughing.

Mulholland crouched over him. He had lit a fresh cigar. It was between his teeth, as he grasped the man's tunic to pull him over. He removed the cigar with his other hand.

"Wakey, Wakey!" he sneered. "Now isn't that just too bad. We'll have to try again won't we?" He got to his feet. "This time Corporal, we'll take your advice. We'll put him in a chair."

Schroeder came round to stand by the side of the grim-faced major. "You can't do it, sir." The words came out in a breathless rush. He stared at his senior officer with wide-open eyes.

"You keep outa this, and mind your own dam business." Mulholland's voice was harsh.

The frail chair creaked, as between them, he and the guard lifted the prisoner and dropped him on to it. The man was sobbing desperately. He covered his face with his hands whilst rocking backwards and forwards.

"Right, then! Are you ready corporal?" Mulholland looked at the guard, who was panting slightly. The man nodded. He unholstered his pistol again. There was an agitated tic beneath his right eye as he pulled back the hammer. He got no further. The Jap gave a despairing wail. He slid from the chair to fling himself at Mulholland's feet.

Mulholland's face was flushed. He shot a triumphant glance in Schroeder's direction.

"He says he'll tell you as much as he knows, sir." Naguchi sounded relieved as he spoke to Mulholland.

96

"It had better be godammed plenty," Mulholland growled.

He released his breath in a quick impatient cough as he sank back into his chair. He tossed the mangled cigar butt into a tray. Schroeder thought he looked suddenly older.

The guard helped the collapsed prisoner back onto his feet. He pushed the chair behind his knees, so that when he sat he faced the major across the desk. Mulholland nodded approvingly.

"You'd better get yourself some coffee," he said to the taut-faced man. "I guess you must be needing it."

The M.P. looked grateful. He saluted. "Yes sir. Thank you, sir." He turned to leave. "What about the prisoner sir? Shall I send someone else in?"

Mulholland looked at the shattered man opposite. He gave a thin-lipped smile. "Don't worry about him. He's got nowhere else to go. Have some coffee sent in for us, and something to eat." He settled himself, placing one arm comfortably on the back of his chair. "We may be here for sometime."

His eyes seemed to skewer the abject scientist with a mean hard stare. The tired look had disappeared.

"Now you, you bastard. Start answering some questions?"

Naguchi moved closer to the desk with the notebook on his knee.

Some two hours later, he leafed trough the papers as he referred to the notes he had taken.

The prisoner had been locked up again in his isolated room.

Mulholland got up from his chair. He eased his shoulders, then scratched his ribs furiously as he stomped around the room.

"Fleas," he was muttering. "Some kinda stuff from godamm fleas. What a way to make war!" He shook his head wonderingly. He stopped his pacing to fling himself back into the chair. Running his fingers through his bristly hair, he gazed thoughtfully at Schroeder.

"Sure takes some believing," Schroeder said. He licked his lips which were suddenly dry. "And they even used women and kids."

He switched his gaze to the grubby windows, where a large blue fly buzzed monotonously, caught in the dust-grey skeins of a spider's web.

Mulholland seemed not to have heard Schroeder's comment. He

97

was chewing at a dead cigar, whilst reaching across the desk. He snatched up Naguchi's notebook to flick rapidly through the pages whilst breathing thickly through his nostrils. He sniffed as he looked at the two other men.

"If it's true what that piss-ant told us, we at least know that not all our guys were given this slow acting plague shit." He sat back with a thump, to stare at the younger officers.

"Trouble is, he doesn't know the names of those they chose. They all of 'em had shots of some kind, so how do we find out which of 'em had the dangerous ones?"

Naguchi interrupted. "He did say there were records, sir. Kept in vaults at Pingfan with all their other stuff."

Mulholland nodded. "Sure, yeah. That's just what I was thinking about." A calculating gleam came suddenly into his eyes. He spoke quickly to Naguchi.

"How long have we got before you hear from our guys in Pingfan?"

The sergeant glanced at his watch. "A little over an hour sir."

"Right, then," Mulholland snapped. "Tell them to prepare to move out. In the meantime, have another word with that fat-assed creep and get him to give you some sort of a plan of the layout."

"Yes sir." Naguchi rose to leave. "What if...?"

"What if nothing!" the major stormed. "Just tell him the M.P.'s gun is still loaded" His face turned ugly. "And boy would I like to use it!"

"One more thing, sir."

Mulholland was still angry. He raised an eyebrow.

"Yeah, what is it now, sergeant?"

"How do we get those men back here sir? There's only two more days before we leave."

The major's face relaxed in a sardonic smile. "Yeah," he said. "I've got something figured out. Tell them to choose a place and be there from midday tomorrow. I want to see the pair of them back here." His voice had a curiously threatening growl.

"Right, sir. I'll see to it." The interpreter hurriedly left.

Schroeder had been listening carefully. He became aware of a warning tingle somewhere in the back of his mind. He dismissed it by recalling the details of the scientist's reluctant admissions.

"It sounded like the Nips did a pretty thorough demolition job," he said, "detonating trucks filled with explosive around the main buildings. All that wreckage on top of the cellars will make the search for those records difficult, especially with so little time."

Mulholland nodded heavily. "They did it that way because they were in a hurry. Mebbe they were not as thorough as they'd hoped. It's our only godammed chance to help those poor bastards who think they are going home."

He picked up Naguchi's notebook again. It was still open at the page he had been checking earlier. "Unless that Nip crap-head was lying, and I sure as hell hope he wasn't." The major's voice dropped ominously as he thumbed back another page.

"There can't be more than a handful who are going to cause problems."

He turned quickly to look at Schroeder, pointing with his finger to the page he had found.

As the younger man read the scribbled transcript he began to breathe more easily.

"That's right," he said. "See there. It looks like twenty Americans, five Limeys and five Aussies."

"Don't forget," Mulholland warned. "The sonofabitch could have been lying."

"Sure he could," Schroeder agreed. "But he also told us that at the time, they had only small amounts of the stuff to use for the injections."

Mulholland slammed down the notebook. Leaning back in his chair he stretched his arms above his head. He relaxed with a grunt. "One thing's for sure," he rasped. "We've gotta try to find the names of those guys, then the rest of 'em will be in the clear."

Schroeder unbuttoned his jacket. The room was becoming much warmer. "I guess a lot depends on those agents of ours in Pingfan, doesn't it?"

Mulholland looked thoughtful. He shot Schroeder a sideways glance.

Schroeder suddenly knew what it was that had nagged in his brain when this conversation had first started.

"How are you proposing to get them out?" he asked.

The buzzing of the trapped fly stopped with startling suddenness, only to restart in a higher, desperate key.

The major turned his head to stare directly at the junior officer. His voice became harder. "I guess I'll be counting on you to help 'em."

There was a silence between them for a few moments. Mulholland was unconsciously scratching again whilst he paused to collect his thoughts.

"With any kinda luck," he continued, "it'll be a straight-forward two-way trip. Those guys should be waiting. Just pick 'em up and bring them back here."

Schroeder was starled. "How the hell do I get there?" he gasped

"We've got less than forty-eight hours," Mulholland went on. "So it'll have to be by air." He was speaking more quickly now. "When you get back, I'll be waiting with the egg-heads. We can haul-ass out of here."

Schroeder's brain was racing. Unpleasant images were forming in his mind. He heard Mulholland's voice again, but this time it was slow and deliberate. "But before you leave Pingfan, I thought maybe you might take a look around for those records," he was saying.

Before Schroeder could respond, the major continued. "Those two guys on their own don't stand a chance. They think their cover's been blown. They're already in hiding."

Schroeder's expression was incredulous.

"Take a look around you say. Just how the hell would I do that?"

Mulholland's confident grin was back again.

"Just go along there with your Russian buddies," he said. The wrinkles at the corners of his eyes showed briefly as he watched the younger man's start of surprise.

The major continued. "That's what I had in mind when I told you to keep them here. Listen, Schroeder. That Russian doctor may be a screwball, but he sounds like a regular guy. He might be prepared to help you."

His words gave Schroeder another jolt.

"How the hell do you know about him?" he asked. "You haven't met the guy."

Mulholland made an impatient gesture. "How, for Chrisake, do you think this army operates, Schroeder? I know every dam thing that goes on around here." His grin returned. "That dame you brought. She seems to be a real tough cookie. You could make quite a team."

Schroeder gave a disgusted snort. "Come on, sir," he retorted. "Do you really think they'll go along with this? They're on the other side, remember?"

"No they're godammed not!" the major snapped. "They're still officially our allies, but as they are in control of this country we have to let 'em call the shots. Put it to them, at least," he urged. "That doctor sounds like a guy with a conscience. What the hell!" Mulholland airily waved his foul smelling cigar. "Doctors are supposed not to take sides anyway."

"Mebbe you're right." Schroeder sounded very doubtful. He gave a resigned shrug. "Oh what the hell! OK I'll get back and try talking to them. Yukovlev, though, most of the time he's stoned out of his mind." He buttoned his jacket, then bent wearily to pick up his cap. "When's the deadline for starting, sir?"

"I'd say not later than sun-up tomorrow," Mulholland replied. "Naguchi is fixing the pick-up for our agents sometime after midday. Remember, Pingfan's 300 kilometres from here. You won't have much time."

"What if the Russians refuse to cooperate?" Schroeder was turning away, about to leave.

"In that event," the major replied softly, "the bastards won't get away from this camp 'til after we've left, or maybe we'll take them with us"

As he spoke there was an urgent rap on the door. Mulholland turned to look.

"Yeah. What is it?"

The messenger handed him a note. "They say it's urgent, sir".

Mulholland was rising from his chair as he unfolded the slip of paper. His eyes became bleak as he slowly took in the contents. He whipped round to look at Schroeder with a disbelieving stare.

"What is it, sir?" Schroeder knew that something was terribly wrong.

101

"Jesus Christ!" the major answered. "That ship you put 'em on. It's hit a mine. This message from Okinawa says she's sinking."

Chapter 9

Johno could hear the sound of sudden movement from the bunk-room. A clattering of feet, loud voices seeking directions. He almost turned back, expecting at any moment to feel a sudden lurch as the ship began its final plunge.

"This way sarge, down here!"

All Johno could see of Jim was his head. It was disappearing through a tiny hatch in the deck as its owner climbed down a short steel ladder. The rungs of the ladder were slippery as Johno followed him down. His feet hit the deck below with a sudden thud.

"This way sarge." He followed the voice again. There was a turn to the right, another short corridor, then a main passageway with handrails. Still following hard on Jim's heels, he was gathering speed along the canting deck. A sudden left turn brought him up sharply before an open steel door. Jim was waiting there. Johno was panting. By now his damaged nose was making breathing difficult.

"What's the bloody idea?" he stormed. "They were sounding life-boat stations. What the hell are we doing down here?"

Another voice broke in, deep and unruffled.

"Come on there now. All we need is a little help here." It was Luke's voice. He was on the other side of the door struggling to lift something heavy from the floor. Johno stared in astonishment at the object. It was a bulky, wooden beam. It looked about the size of a telegraph pole, but was square at the ends. It seemed to stretch endlessly behind Luke as he straddled it.

"What's the idea?" Johno gasped. "Are we building a bloody raft?"

Luke shook his head impatiently as he heaved on the end he was grasping. to rest it on the raised coaming of the doorway. He managed to grin, but his face was glistening with sweat.

"The pair of you take the other end," he gasped. "I'll handle this." The muscles bulged under his shirt as he heaved again. Johno noticed that Luke's finger's were bleeding as he and Jim scrambled past him to take their places at the opposite end – two pallid, skinny figures compared with Luke's heavy frame.

103

"Come on, sarge. Heave!"

They both grunted, as together they took up the weight. With Luke pulling, they lifted and pushed until the unwieldy length of timber slid reluctantly through the door, where it dropped with a thud on the other side of the high threshold.

"What the hell's going on?" demanded Johno, as they struggled to pick it up again.

"It's needed down below," Jim panted. "There's some trouble with a bulkhead. It needs shoring up."

Johno's knowledge of ships was limited, but when he thought of a bulging metal wall between him and Davy Jones' locker, it had an astonishing effect.

He stooped with Jim to raise the beam sufficiently to get their hands beneath it. Then, lifting together, with Luke's encouraging voice ahead of them, they tottered a few more yards along a passageway, which dipped and rolled as the ship wallowed drunkenly in seas which remained high as an aftermath of the storm.

"How the hell does it happen to be us?" Johno's question came in breathless bursts, as they tugged and swore at the inanimate object.

Jim explained that he had been with Luke when a call was made for volunteers from the crew. "Trouble was," he panted, "the timbers were stored aft. No question of opening the hatches. They had to be man-handled through the ship."

"And you decided to help?"

"Yes." Jim replied.

"Why just you two and one bloody piece of wood? Fat lot of bloody good this'll do."

"We took a short cut. Luke made a mistake. We've lost the others."

"Now it looks like he's bloody made another-"

Johno broke off to swear loudly as a rough corner ground into his shin. Luke had suddenly stopped. He was faced with a blank wall of steel.

"Holy cow!" he gasped. "The godammed safety shutters!" He released his grip on the beam, allowing it to fall with a heavy thud on the corticene covered deck. His chest was heaving with his efforts. He turned to face the other two men, spreading his arms in a

104

helpless gesture.

"Sorry you guys," he panted. "Looks like we'll have to goback."

On the deck above them, Taffy had remained with Pete in the sick-bay.

"Get movin'!" the orderly told him as the klaxon screeched its warning. "We'll take care of the guy on the litter."

The Welshman looked apprehensive when he heard the sound of hurrying feet outside in the passageways. Around him in the crowded room there was hardly room enough to move. With some difficulty the two of them had found a place at the foot of Pete's stretcher.

"Go on, get the hell out of here!" the orderly had urged.

Taffy clamped his teeth obstinately. Pushing Pete's stretcher closer to a corner, he crouched down beside it looking anxiously at the roughly taped dressing on his friend's head.

The orderly had been called away to something more urgent. Taffy squatted on his heels, drawing himself as close to the wall as he could. The klaxon continued with its intermittent shrieking. He shuffled round slightly so that his body gave the stretcher some protection from the stumbling feet passing by. Someone cannoned into him, swearing savagely as he almost tripped. Taffy lurched forward, frighteningly aware of the ship's uneasy rolling. As his hand hit the stretcher he felt Pete's body move. He knelt to get his face closer.

"Pete!" he said fiercely, "Come on. you bloody old lead-swinger. Wake up!" Taffy's voice was edged with approaching panic. He had a firmly implanted dread of the sea. This climax to the previous days of torment was deeply offensive to his confused religious concept of fair play.

"What the hell's all this about?" he moaned to the non-conformist God of his early youth. "I'll join the bloody chapel choir again, if you get me out of this lot."

Knowing the limitations of Taffy's voice, Pete would have been the first to point out that from God's point of view, Taffy's deal was a bit one-sided. Its familiar, grumbling sound, however, helped Pete's submerged senses to surface a little.

"Jesus Christ!" he groaned. "What's going on?"

105

The many other noises in the over-crowded room obliterated the croaking sounds which came from his dry throat. He licked his lips, wincing with pain as he tried to turn his head.

Taffy leaned over him eagerly. "Come on you stupid old bugger. Wake up!"

Pete's eyes were closing again. He screwed them up tightly as the noise of the klaxon screamed out once more. He could feel his brain swelling. It threatened to burst out of his skull.

"Bloody hell! What happened?" Pete's voice was hoarse, but Taffy now had his ear close to his friend's face.

Taffy sniffed disgustedly. "Got your bloody head in the way of a table, that's what happened."

Pete was struggling to unscramble his thoughts. He dimly remembered the eerie feeling as the table rose up to hit him.

An orderly came hurrying by, holding a small syringe. As he stood over Pete, he turned to push Taffy out of the way and grabbed hold of Pete's arm. The cuff of Pete's blouse was buttoned.

"Sonofabitch!" the orderly growled. He had to hold the syringe between his teeth as he used both hands to unfasten the sleeve.

"Hey, what's that stuff you're giving him?" Taffy's voice was querulous with suspicion.

"Come on, move away, slackass!" This orderly was not the one they had seen before. He sounded impatient.

Pete was protesting weakly. He tried to pull his arm away.

Taffy was looking stubborn. "What's it for?" he demanded.

"Just a shot to keep him quiet." The white coated man was getting angry. "All the litter cases have to have one," he explained. "Just in case."

Taffy's face turned a shade paler, as the man made a significant downward-pointing movement with his thumb. He moved closer to Taffy to hiss confidentially.

"This stuff'll knock 'em out for a while. Makes it easier to handle the litters if we have to abandon ship."

Pete was reviving rapidly as he watched with mounting alarm the pantomime between the other two men.

"He wont be needing it," Taffy was saying. "Look he's coming round."

The orderly shook his head sadly as he expelled some bubbles from the syringe. "That's just what we don't want to happen," he warned. "If he comes round he'll be in a lot of pain."

Pete heard a disembodied voice, which turned out to be his own. "Bugger off." it was saying.

It was weak, but perfectly clear. The man with the syringe must have heard it. He hesitated before getting to his feet. He turned to look carefully at Taffy.

"Do you think you'll be able to handle your buddy?" he asked. "You know! if..." Again he made that gesture with his thumb.

Taffy swallowed hard before nodding reluctantly. "Yes, you can leave him to me," he answered.

The orderly shrugged as he moved away. "O.K! O.K! Your asses not mine," he said.

Ignoring the buffetting from passers-by, Taffy crouched once more by the stretcher. He looked doubtfully at his friend's pale face. Pete's eyes were closed again, but they opened when Taffy shook his arm.

"What the hell are we going to do now?" Since his encounter with the orderly, Taffy's imagination was sending a depressing stream of pictures to his brain. He could see the ship sinking lower by the minute. "We ought to get up to the bloody lifeboats. Can you manage to walk do you think? Come on try! I'll give you a hand."

Enough of Taffy's agitation seeped through Pete's barrier of pain to make him grip the poles of the stretcher. Pushing with all his available strength, he managed to raise himself slightly from the canvas. Taffy slipped an arm beneath his shoulders.

"Come on mate," he urged. "Let's try to get upstairs with the others. Then we can all keep an eye on you."

He glanced desperately from side to side as he struggled with Pete's bulk to raise him a little further. Pete grunted with the effort. He cursed with a pithy descriptive fluency. He cursed in Urdu, Arabic, and Cantonese. He cursed with the dedicated professionalism of the long-serving soldier, until finally, he was sitting upright, still supported by Taffy's arm.

"Do you think you'll be able to walk?" Taffy's anxiety was increasing by the second. Around them, the work of treating the injured continued at a brisk pace. Pete was feeling sick again. It was not only caused by the movement of the ship. The air was heavy with the pungent smell of anaesthetic and disinfectant.

He noticed other stretchers with their helpless occupants being carried through a door in the opposite wall. A doctor busy at an operating table, kept looking curiously in their direction.

"Come on mate. Can you walk?" Taffy repeated.

Pete couldn't reply. He was aware only of the white-hot, piercing spicules which flickered between his throbbing temples. He was no longer swearing. He had stopped to regain his breath. He was afraid to shake his head. His comrade's question remained unanswered.

Taffy jumped at the sound of an angry voice which came from the direction of the adjoining mess deck.

"Do as I godamm tell you. Get up there to your boat station with the others," it was shouting. He remembered the voice as that of the bo'sun. He cocked his head to listen with mixed feelings when he heard someone else replying.

"All right! Keep your flippin' hair on," the other man was saying. "I'm just lookin' for me bleeding teeth. I'd just put 'em in, right here, I tell you. Where I was sittin'"

"I don't give a monkey's fart about your sonofabitchin' teeth," the bo'sun bellowed. "Are you gettin' outa here? Or do I have to kick your ass?"

Taffy's sudden hope turned to caution.

"It would have to be bloody Lockie," he thought.

His sense of grievance became almost unbearable. Throughout his years as a prisoner, he'd dreamed of the ship that would take him home. During his brief, but eventful war in Malaya, his declared intention had been "to finish off the bloody Japs and bugger off back to Wales".

He'd imagined being picked up by a majestic liner, to cruise home blissfully through tropical seas. Nobody had been more astonished that Taffy, to find himself on the losing side. His lustful plans for lotus-eating holidays in Llandudno had had to be postponed.

Now here he was with an injured mate, waiting for the bloody ship to sink. His pale-blue eyes darted wildly from side to side. There seemed to be fewer people around. The doctor was busy stitching something with a large curved needle.

"Just hang on mate!" Taffy made sure that Pete could remain sitting upright, whilst he dashed across the passageway.

"Lockie!" he bawled.

The protesting Australian, closely followed by the bo'sun was heading for the nearest companion ladder. He looked back over his shoulder when he heard his name being called.

Taffy, standing by the open door, waved his arms.

"Over here!" he yelled.

Lockie stopped walking to turn and stare. He looked for a moment in Taffy's direction, squinting short-sightedly from under lowered brows.

"What's the trouble, mate?" he called. "Have you lost your way or somethin? Come on. I've got a personal bleedin' body-guard here."

Taffy shook his head desperately. "No!" he shouted. "I need some help here. It's Pete. He's been hurt." He waited anxiously whilst Lockie, with outspread arms appeared to be arguing with the bo'sun.

"Look, mate," he was saying. "I can't leave a friend of mine in the shit, can I?" Whilst the bo'sun hesitated, Lockie sidled away, to head in Taffy's direction.

The Welshman grabbed his arm. "In here," he said quickly, dragging Lockie with him.

By now the bo'sun was close behind. "Ya can't go in there," he ordered. "That's the sick-bay."

"'Course its the bleeding sick-bay," jeered Lockie. "We're just goin' to visit a friend." He stopped when he saw the blood-stained Pete sitting up on a stretcher. "Jesus Christ, mate! What hit you?"

"They want to knock him out with something, put him somewhere else, chuck him overboard for all I bloody know." Taffy's voice was rising hysterically.

"Take it easy, mate. We'll soon sort things out." The Australian shot a sideways glance at the bo'sun, who was looking critically at Pete.

"You'd be crazy to try to move him," the big man pronounced. "The medics'll take care of him."

Taffy shook his head determindly. "Balls!" he said. "We're going to keep him with his mates."

109

Lockie grinned showing his toothless gums. "That's telling him, old son. But we can't get that stretcher up the bleeding stairs, can we?"

The two considered Lockie's unhelpful comment.

The bo'sun wrenched his unfriendly glare away from the scruffy speaker. He let forth an explosive curse.

"OK Then for Chrissake, let's lash him on to the litter."

The doctor had finished his stitching. He came over to investigate, swaying unsteadily on the rolling deck as he removed his gloves and apron.

"What the hell's going on here?" he demanded. "Why isn't this guy with the others.?"

He broke off at a gasp from Pete, who fell partly sideways, held back only by Taffy's grasp. He lowered Pete carefully to a prone position, where he started to moan and shiver.

The doctor looked angry. "Get a godammed blanket," he told them. "I'm going to give him a shot."

He looked around the almost deserted room. His assistants were removing the patient from the operating table. The doctor moved clumsily away, to fumble in a surgical pack for a loaded syrette.

As the doctor searched, Taffy watched, sullen and resentful. Suddenly he stooped to take hold of the handles of the stretcher. Lockie, at the other end, looked at him in bewilderment.

"Come on, grab hold!" Taffy urged. "Let's bugger off away from here."

The skinny Australian grunted as he took up the weight.

"Hey you can't do that!" The bo'sun's eyes popped with disbelief as the pair disappeared through the door.

"Stop them!" the doctor yelled.

"Yes sir, right sir! The bo'sun lumbered after them.

"Just a minute" the doctor called. "Oh what the hell! You'd better take this," he said in a resigned voice, as the confused bo'sun halted. Picking up the blanket the doctor tossed it towards him. "Take this as well." The bo'sun caught the small syrette. "Tell 'em to take damn good care of him," the doctor growled. "Mebbe I'll catch up with 'em later."

As the bo'sun disappeared, the doctor pulled off his surgical gown. He sat down with a sigh on a nearby stool, a thoughtful expression on his tired face.

"What is it about those guys" he wondered, "that makes them so suspicious of doctors?"

Carrying the bouncing stretcher between them, Taffy and Lockie headed for the exit leading from the deserted mess-deck.

Pete, jolted into increasing consciousness, made no pretence of suffering silently.

"You clumsy bastards," he shrieked. "For Christ's sake, take it easy." He almost blacked out again as the effort of shouting brought on another wave of pain.

The breathless Taffy, from his position looking down on Pete, tried to be reassuring.

"Try not to bloody fall off," he panted. "We're getting you to a boat before the bloody ship sinks."

Pete had heard enough. "Put me down," he called weakly. "I'm going to walk."

The furious bo'sun caught up with them. "You stupid bastards," he shouted. "Just what the hell do you think you're godammed doing?"

The stretcher tilted precariously as the two bent hurriedly to dump it on the deck. Taffy stood irresolute as the American produced the blanket he had been given.

"Come on for Chrissake." The seething man hurriedly unfolded the blanket. "Can't you see he's shaking with cold?"

When it dawned on Taffy that the bo'sun was trying to help, he hurriedly grabbed one end of the blanket. Between them they covered the half-senseless patient. Lockie, shifting his feet impatiently looked with trepidation at the steep companion ladder.

"Don't fancy our chances of getting him up there," he sniffed.

The bo'sun gave the hapless pair a withering glance.

"It's as well for your buddy we don't godamm have to," he grated. "If it's the Limey's boat-station you were heading for, there happens to be another way."

Lockie's face brightened. "Come on then, mate. Let's get going.

111

What are we bleeding waitin' for?" He bent unexpectedly to lift his end of the stretcher. Its unfortunate occupant gave a hollow moan.

The bo'sun's face turned bright red. "Sweet Jesus," he ground out. "Are you trying to kill the poor bastard?" Breathing heavily, he glanced down at the toothless Australian, before switching his gaze to Taffy's staring, washed-out eyes.

"Are you guys sure it wasn't a nut-house you got out of?"

Taffy's white face turned a little pinker under the other man's critical scrutiny.

"Oh what the hell!" the bo'sun continued with a sudden change of mood. "Come on, we've gotta hurry. Let's get him outa here."

Whilst he was speaking, he had knelt by the stretcher. He took from his pocket the morphine syrette. Biting off the protective cap, he sank the needle into Pete's arm, before firmly squeezing the tube.

"Guess that'll take care of him for a while," he said.

Lockie was becoming more fidgety. "Come on!" he pleaded, "let's get up to those bleeding boats."

From somewhere far beneath their feet, a sound like the rumbling of thunder could be heard with each sluggish roll of the helpless vessel. The bo'sun's eye searched swiftly round the echoing space of the mess-deck as he got to his feet. He stooped to grasp the handles of the stretcher at one end.

"You two guys take care of your end," he ordered, "and follow me."

Taffy and Lockie tried to match the purposeful stride of the big man in front of them, but got hopelessly out of step.

"Bugger this for a game o' darts." Lockie grumbled shakily. If I hadn't lost me bleeding teeth, I'd 'ave been safe upstairs with me mates."

"Shut up and watch your bloody feet," Taffy warned as a large can of tinned fruit rolled backwards and forwards in their path.

Stumbling behind the stretcher, they jolted their way behind the bo'sun through some heavy swing doors leading into the ship's main galley.

"Right over here," their helper grunted, "There's a hand operated elevator from the food store. It's big enough to take the

112

litter. We'll get it in there and haul it to the deck above. It's used for crates an' trolleys an' such-like," he explained as he slid back the flimsy gates.

The stretcher fitted comfortably on the floor of the small elevator, with just sufficient space for one person to crouch beside it. The burly seaman turned to jab a large finger at Lockie.

"Now you get in there," he ordered, "and me and your partner here'll haul it up."

"What if the bleeding rope breaks?" Lockie objected.

The bo'sun gave him a push. "Stop godamm bleating," he snorted. "Don't know why I'm wasting my sonofabitchin' time with you guys," he rumbled, as he slammed the gates together. "Godammed ship could be sinkin'. Crew thinkin' I'm lost overboard, and here I am, stuck with a pair of screwballs." He grasped the rope savagely with both hands. "Stick around on the next deck," he shouted. "We'll see you there."

Taffy watched tight-faced, as the clumsy contraption jerked its way upwards with the protesting Australian and the blissfully unconscious Pete. A solid THUNK finally told Taffy it had locked into position on the deck above. He jumped as a telephone jangled on a nearby panel.

The bo'sun darted forward to grab it hurriedly. Taffy watched the man's expression change to one of respect as he heard an angry voice shouting from the other end.

"Sure, sir." he was answering. "Yeah, still here sir. Makin' sure the mess-deck and sick-bay are clear, sir. A coupla problems, sir." He squinted pointedly over one shoulder at Taffy, as he spoke. "All taken care of, now sir. Yes, sir!"

The man's face became more serious as the other voice continued. It was speaking more rapidly. The bo'sun was nodding his head in quick, affirmative movements.

"No 2 hold. Still making water. Bulkhead givin' trouble? Sure I heard the call earlier. Lotta guys hurt down here, sir. All hands? Right, sir. I'm on my way sir."

Slamming the phone back into its holder, he turned. Taking the startled Welshman roughly by the arm, he moved with him towards the doorway.

"Listen, soldier," he said. "You use that ladder to get up there and take care of your buddy. You'll find your lifeboat station pretty close."

Taffy stood for a moment, numb with disbelief; his imagination producing dreadful images. There were no further explanations.

The bo'sun moved quickly across the galley to where a steel staircase was set into the metal floor. He grasped the rails to slide easily down to the lower decks.

Two levels down, above the rumble of the moving water, he heard a sound of prolonged scraping, followed by a regular thump. He interrupted his downward flight to take a few steps along the passageway, tracing the source of the strange noise. Taking a swift left turn, he almost collided with three sweating men. One of them he recognised as Luke, who worked in the galley. The other two he didn't know. One of them was shortish, with an angry expression and fierce black eyebrows. The other was tall and skinny, with a swollen nose. The three of them were pushing and shoving at a huge baulk of timber.

"Where in Christ's name are you takin' that?" the bo'sun demanded.

"We're looking for No. 2 hold," the short angry man exploded. "But no bugger can tell us where it is."

"Why didn't you use the godamm 'tween decks passageway? It's a godamm straight route from No 3 hold?" The bo'sun directed his angry question to Luke.

Luke looked confused. "Well, bo'sun," he answered, "I kinda thought I knew a nearer way, but it sorta didn't work out."

"Why are these guys here?" The bo'sun pointed furiously at the two other men. "They should be at their godamm boat-stations with the others."

"We volunteered to help him," the stocky belligerent one interrupted.

The bo'sun's eyes swung from him to his lanky partner. He noticed that the tall one wasn't wearing a shirt. His arms and back were red from scuffing against the walls.

"Well, as of right now, your help is no longer required. This guy," he pointed at Luke. "is coming with me. I'm mustering all spare hands below where they're needed." He thrust a warning

114

finger at the others. "You two report to your boat-stations. There'll be a roll-call remember."

Luke gave them an apologetic shrug. "Sorry fellas." He grabbed each of them by the hand as he eased his way past them, to join the bo'sun. "This is as far as we go I guess!"

With a parting wave from Luke, the seamen moved away.

"Godamm Limeys," the bo'sun was muttering. "Are they all godamm nuts or something?"

With a sigh of relief, Johno flopped down on the end of the beam. "Well, that's that then!" he said.

Jim made no reply. He had his head round the corner to stare after the two Americans. Johno rose to join him. He rubbed his arms, suddenly chilled.

"Come on then," he said briskly. "We might as well get back to the others. We can't take this bloody thing any further."

Jim stared at him with a thoughtful expression. "Oh yes we can," he stated firmly. "All we need is some more help."

Chapter 10

"Chase it baby! Box cars for daddy." Corporal "Dead-Eye" Groger rattled the dice between his palms before flinging them along the table. As they rattled against the upraised backboard, he clapped his hand over his one good eye.

"Holy Cow!" he groaned, as he scooped them up. "This game sure ain't what it used to be. One more?" he pleaded.

A chorus of shouts came from others around the table.

"Make him run for it baby!"

"Why not just take his dough?"

The fair-haired woman looked fiercely around the room. She pushed back the damp fringe from her forehead, before snatching up the dice.

"OK," she said. "It is too much or nothing?" She showed her teeth in a challenging smile.

Dead-Eye didn't grasp her meaning. His expression was blank as he stared around the room.

"She means 'Double or Quits', you stupid bastard." someone yelled.

Dead-Eye's face cleared. "Oh! sure. Yeah!" he said with a delighted grin.

Tatiana Chokovska looked at him suspiciously. "Have you got the money?" she asked, suppressing a slight hiccup.

Amidst a renewal of hoots and jeers, he sidled closer to her. "Not here right now, lady," he told her in a gruff whisper. Then looking quickly round the room, he plucked out his glass eye from its socket, to plonk it with a flourish on the table.

"I'm offering this as collateral till pay-day tomorrow," he shouted, in a voice which rose in pitch to overcome the tumult from the surrounding men.

Tatiana Chokovska looked at the eye and its owner with equal distaste.

"Tell the sonofabitch where to shove it," someone yelled.

"Go ahead, shoot the dice." another voice sang out. A heavy palm thudded down on a table. Someone else took up the beat.

116

"Shoot the craps, shoot the craps!"

The woman shrugged and reached for the dice with a defiant smile, as the noisy chant rang round the room. She had taken off her tunic. The high neck of her belted blouse was unfastened. Her generous breasts shook as she vigorously rattled the ivory cubes.

A shout of approval created rifts in the thick pall of tobacco smoke as the dice hit the backboard and the upturned numbers were displayed. With enormous aplomb, Tatiana Chokovska picked up Groger's staring orb, to drop it delicately into her shirt pocket.

Dead-Eye looked bereft. "Take care of my sharp-shootin' friend," he sobbed dramatically, "Or I'll never knock-off another godammed Jap."

"You never did, anyway!" a sarcastic voice replied. "Come on, lady. Let's all have a drink."

There were further moans as Groger reached out to fondle his eye, now nestling in the woman's pocket. She swung a formidable fist, which caught him in the belly.

The hubbub suddenly subsided as the outside doors swung open. The chill of an autumn evening crept into the stuffy room as Major Mulholland stepped inside. With him were Lieutenant Schroeder and the two Russian officers. Following close behind was Grosberger, the sergeant whom Schroeder had detailed to keep watch on the Russians.

"I had to leave the dame with my buddy Dead-Eye," he'd explained. "These guys preferred Poker." He had shrugged dejectedly, as he remembered his losses. "She wanted to shoot the craps. Dead-Eye's great at shootin' craps. sir." But Grosberger was now looking worried when he saw his friend's empty eye socket. He closed the door behind him, as he moved with the small group further into the room. "He's godammed lost it again," he muttered.

There was complete silence now. The major's set expression and his unusual stillness made them realise something was wrong.

"Sorry to bust in on your recreation," he said in a quiet voice. "But I am here to pass on a message I received from Okinawa, a short time ago." He lowered his gaze to read from a slip of paper:

" 'From OIC Docks and Shipping Okinawa:

Troop transport vessel Harriet L. Lane reported struck a mine. Stop. Weather poor. Stop. No further news. Stop. Message ends.' "

The major looked around at his suddenly silenced audience.

"Our mission in coming to Mukden," he said, "was to help those guys. We did it as well as we could. It seemed like a good way for us to finish the war."

His searching gaze took in the startled expressions on the faces of the twenty or so men of his original party. He waved the scrap of paper he was holding.

"Mebbe this isn't as bad as it seems. Mebbe if the weather improves, the ship will still make it. I'll keep you informed." He held up a hand as a ripple of subdued sound came from the shocked men. "In the meantime, our orders remain unchanged. We'll be getting the hell outa here in less that 48 hours. Any questions? Yes, what is it Hanson?" He looked at a fair-haired giant, whose hand was in the air.

"What do we do with the Nips we've got locked up, sir?"

"You mean the ex-camp guards? That's easy. We turn them over to the Russians."

Shortly after dinner that evening, the four officers were relaxing in the mess. The heady aroma of good brandy mingled with the smoke from excellent cigars. Schroeder had prevailed upon Mulholland to forego his fish-oil variety for this one occasion.

"It's important we don't offend the Russians," he'd insisted at their earlier meeting.

Mulholland had shot him a suspicious glance. "You suggestin' my cigars are offensive, Schroeder?" He'd waved aside Schroeder's stumbling reply.

"Don't worry too much about those guys," he had said to Schroder. "Like I said before, if they refuse to cooperate, they dam well stay here, until we're on our way home. Just leave the talking to me."

There were many things, however, which had remained unclear in Schroeder's mind. As he sat back in the comfortable chair he reflected on Mulholland's response to the dramatic news of the stricken ship. He had stared unseeingly out of the window of the interrogation room until Schroeder ventured to speak.

"What happens now, sir?" he had quietly asked.

Mulholland swung round to face him. For a few further

moments he remained silent, meeting Schroeder's questioning eye with a thoughtful expression.

"Mebbe this news could change things." he said abruptly.

Schroeder watched carefully as the Major seemed to hesitate again

"Are you changing your mind about the mission to Pingfan, sir?"

Mulholland shrugged uncomfortably. "I guess we'll have to give it some thought," he grunted. "We can' afford to take unnecessary chances."

"I know that, sir, but it's my ass that's on the line. What else is there to lose? If we don't get the Mukden records, with the names of those thirty guys, the whole dam bunch will have to spend their lives in quarantine - or worse."

The major gave Schroeder a long, hard look, then he slowly shook his head.

"Lieutenant," he said. "I think I'd better explain my meaning. Your ass - sure it's important to you, but strictly non-essential to Uncle Sam - as you well know! But have you considered how the Russians would react if you were caught searching for those records? They'd guess immediately that you were acting on information from some place, and that place could only be here."

"Then why not do a trade-off?" Schroeder persisted. "Let them have those shit heads, in return for permission to search what's left of Pingfan."

Mulholland shook his head. "Not a chance." He twisted his lips in a snarl of disgust. "We've got to keep these bastards. They've been doing research which could never be copied in the States. We don't experiment on human beings."

"But we'd sure as hell like to know what they discovered," Schroeder butted in with heavy sarcasm.

"My orders," Mulholland continued doggedly, "are to get those sonsabitches back to Tokyo H.Q. at any price."

"At any godammed price?" Schroeder was trying to contain his anger. "Does that mean forgetting the guys who are on that ship?"

Mulholland's voice turned steely. He looked sharply at the younger man. "Best to cut out the sentiment," he ordered. "We don't even know if they're still afloat."

119

"So what's the difference?" retorted Schroeder hotly. "If there's no godammed place where they can go!"

Mulholland got up from his chair. He leaned over to open one of the desk drawers, taking from it a manilla envelope. With a sharp movement of his arm he offered it to Schroeder, who took it from him with a questioning stare.

"Take a look," the major ordered. "It's a sketch of Pingfan. Naguchi got one of those guys to co-operate."

Schroeder glanced at the rough ground-plan. It showed a network of underground corridors and rooms. Near the end of one of the corridors, a room had been outlined in red pencil.

He laughed shakily as he raised his eyes to where Mulholland was sitting.

"I guess you're telling me it's OK to go," he said in a subdued voice.

"Like you said, Schroeder, it's your ass," the major answered brusquely. His voice hardened. "Now here's what you've gotta do. You'll take-off at sun-up tomorrow. No fancy flight plans. We don't have time to fuck around. Remember, that so far we have our own air-controllers there. The Russians are supposed to supervise, but they're pretty easy-going. Some cigarettes and vodka to the right guys can work wonders."

Schroeder opened his mouth to interject, but Mulholland continued. "We'll have the flight logged as instrument testing. Or," he continued thoughtfully, "mebbe even sight-seeing, if we can persuade your Russian friends to go along for the ride."

Schroeder shook his head doubtfully.

"Well it's up to us to work on 'em." Mulholland continued with his plan. "You'll be flown to some place we'll decide about - as near Pingfan as possible. The plane will land, then return here immediately, to pick you up at a later time."

"So a place will have to be chosen where a Dakota can land and take off as secretly as possible?"

Mulholland nodded. "Shouldn't be too difficult. The country around there is pretty flat and thinly populated" He looked at his watch. "Jeez," he said, "Eight o'clock. I wonder if your friends have eaten?" He plucked his jacket from the hook. "Come on," he said. "Let's get back to the camp."

On the way out, he stopped as Schroeder held the door for him.

120

"I suggest you take along Naguchi, and also a couple of enlisted men to guard that precious ass of yours."

Schroeder slammed the door behind them with unnecessary force. The major appeared not to notice. His hands were thrust deep into his pockets, as his eyes picked out the path in the darkness. He looked sideways at Schroeder.

"There's somethin' else," he added. "Whether it's with or without your guests, when you go in there you'll be wearing Russian uniform."

Schroeder almost fell as his feet missed the uneven slabs.

"Jesus Christ!" he said. "You can't mean that, sir. What the hell, if I got caught? I'd be shot. I wouldn't have a chance."

Mulholland's voice was flat and final as they climbed into the jeep "It's the only way to do it Schroeder. That's the deal."

When Schroeder remained silent, he added, "I want to stop off at the mess-hall and speak to the men. I have to tell them what happened to the ship."

They were passing the bar where Schroeder had left his visitors earlier in the day. A sound of lugubrious singing was coming from inside. In spite of Mulholland's chilling instructions, Schroeder's grim features relaxed in a smile. The voices were unmistakably Russian. He slowed the jeep and looked enquiringly at Mulholland. The major pushing back his field cap from his forehead, nodded acquiescence.

"Better check it out," he said.

Schroeder shoved open the bar-room door. Several heads turned in his direction. He held it open whilst he looked around the smoky room. Several beer stained tables were occupied by men with grubby decks of cards. Others were lounging by the trestle table being used as a counter. Most of them wore resigned expressions as they tried to ignore the wretched duet. A pianist, with a long nose and slicked hair, had given up his struggle to accompany them on a lop-sided piano. He sat looking miserably at the keyboard whilst the two embracing Russians, their faces awash with tears, continued with the mournful song.

Grosberger, the sergeant whom Schroeder had detailed to watch them, was sitting at their table. His feet were resting on another chair, while from his open mouth came the sound of loud snoring. Schroeder made his way carefully to the table. A scraping of chair legs on the wooden floor told him that some of the men were attempting to stand as Mulholland appeared in the doorway.

Schroeder placed his hand on Grosberger's shoulder to give it a vigorous shake. The singers, whose eyes had been tightly closed, opened them with deeply hurt expressions, as the chair supporting Grosberger's feet fell over with a loud crash. For a moment Sergei Petrokov looked confused, until he recognised Schroeder. Then his glistening features reformed themselves into their normal joviality. Schroeder tried his hardest to look apologetic, whilst Mullholland took in the scene with cold unsmiling eyes.

"Sorry to bust in like this," Schroeder growled, "and - uh!- kinda spoil your song." he ended lamely.

"Not at all." The Russian looked around uncertainly, as though the walls were moving. "Come! Join us my friend. I will buy some more whisky. See, I have lots of American money." He pulled a thick wad of Schroeder's notes from his pocket.

Schroeder shot a sour glance at the dejected N.C.O. who had now got to his feet, before addressing the smiling Russian.

"That's very good of you," he said as brightly as he could. "But, first, I want you to meet Major Mulholland."

Sergei Petrokov reached down to shake the shoulder of his comrade Yukovlev, who, so far, had scarcely stirred in his chair. He had remained seated, with half-closed eyes; his body now slowly swaying, as though still listening to their interrupted song. Leaning heavily on Petrokov's arm, he rose to his feet as Schroeder performed the introductions. A perfunctory nod caused the black straight hair to fall again across his forehead as he and Mulholland exchanged handclasps.

Schroeder had been observing Yukolev with understandable misgivings, but as the two men faced each other, it seemed to him, for a brief incredible moment, that a spark of understanding had flashed between them. Had the intuitive Russian recognised a challenge in Mulholland's direct gaze? Schroeder could have sworn that something had flickered in the dark pits of Yukolev's eyes. A strange, still watchfulness, which had instantly disappeared.

"Tell 'em thanks for the offer of a drink." Mulholland instructed Schroeder. "But we are on our way to get some chow, and we'd be very privileged if they'd care to join us."

The ebullient Petrokov immediately agreed. His friend nodded silently, whilst clumsily pushing his arms into the sleeves of his tunic.

Mulholland was unusually silent as they followed the patches of dim light escaping from the steam dribbled windows. They were approaching the men's mess-hall, from which shouts and roars of laughter could be heard.

"You'd better tell the Ruskis," he said to Schroeder, "that I'll have to look-in here for a few moments." He lowered his voice to a whisper. "Make sure they know what I'm saying about the ship being mined," he said. "Lay it on as thick as you can. We want to get 'em feeling sorry again. It shouldn't be too difficult. Try singing it to 'em. Might make it easier!" He took the cigar from his mouth to give Schroeder a wicked grin, as he reached for the handle of the door and pushed it open with his shoulder.

"So I guess that just about sums up the position. I hope they understand that we only want to help our men who are on their way home." Mulholland picked up his glass whilst waiting for Schroeder to translate.

They had dined well. Now they were sitting at a table close to the bar. Mulholland had done most of the talking. Schroeder had struggled to rephrase some of his pithier comments.

The Russians had listened intently, Yukovlev in heavy-lidded silence. The more open-faced Sergei Petrokov occasionally betrayed his uneasiness as the American had tentatively sketched in the outline of his plan.

Tatiana Chokovska had also listened. But now her mind was drifting back to her game with Dead-Eye and the others which had ended shortly before the appearance of Mulholland and the group of officers. Her soldier's instinct had recognised the fatalistic response of the Americans.

"Shit!" someone was heard to say. "I sure hope they make it. There's a skinny Australian bastard who owes me fifty bucks."

Dead-Eye was more sympathetic. "Those poor sonsabitches oughta get home, he observed to his friend 'Dum-dum' Donovan. "They ought to be given a break sometime."

Dum-Dum nodded his shaven head. "Ain't that the truth?" he agreed. "It's time somebody else started calling the shots. Them guys have been the goddammed losers right down the line."

Tatiana Chokovska had been listening with some perplexity to this exchange. Her limited English was bogged down by the slang. Her flushed face still registered the dismay she had felt after realising the import of Mulholland's short statement. It seemed that her efforts in escorting them safely had been to no avail. She remembered the eventful train journey, with its confusion, its fights, its pointless arguments. She remembered the ones who were always in trouble. She remembered Schroeder's sympathy when she had wept at the grave of the Russian soldiers. Her eyes were burning now, as she turned to look at the grizzled Dead-Eye.

"Given a break?" she asked. "What is it, that it means?"

"Aw! it just sorta means a change in their luck. You know... they've kinda had a rough deal ever since Pearl..." He looked desperately at his friend for a bit of support.

"Pearl?" said Tatiana, looking blank.

Dum-Dum came to the rescue. "Yeah," he replied sagely. "Pearl Harbour and Singapore. They got their asses shot off there, when they'd nothin' to hit back with."

Dead Eye took up the theme in a doleful voice. "Since then it must seem like it's been all downhill."

"Sure thing!" Dum-Dum's ugly face turned solemn. "What they'll be needing right now is mebbe a little help from up there." He pointed a pious finger at the grubby ceiling.

She nodded with a fixed half-smile.

"Ah yes, help." she replied slowly. Her deep voice outdid Dum-Dum's solemn tones. She squared her shoulders as she spoke, and quickly looked away. She had scant knowledge of the possible machinations of Dum-Dum's deity. It was clear to her, however, that those strange men, whom she had got to know so well, were in serious trouble.

"Watch out, here comes the lootenant." Dead-Eye's hoarse voice sounded a warning as Schroeder approached.

"OK guys, take it easy!" He stopped in front of Tatiana, to tip her a courteous salute.

"Major Mulholland's compliments, Sergeant Chokovska, and please would you care to join us for dinner?" His smile was strained as he passed on the invitation very correctly in her own language. She realised she had rarely seen him really smile.

She drew herself to attention, and inclined her head slightly. "I shall be very pleased," she replied gravely.

Dead-Eye dug Dum-Dum in the ribs as they watched the pair move off when they'd excused themselves.

"Well how d'ya like that?" he grinned as he lit a cigarette. Then a look of alarm spread suddenly across his face. He clapped a hand to his empty eye socket.

"Sonofabitch! She's still got my godammed eye!"

These parting comments had passed unheard by Schroeder and the others as they had left the din behind them.

Now sitting in this quiet room after listening to Schroeder's halting translation of Mulholland's plan, Tatiana Chokovska thought of Dum-Dum and Dead-Eye and their gambler's superstition. Like the two men, she knew that a soldier's fate was as chancy as the roll of a dice. She understood that kind of philosophy. Survival was largely a matter of luck. Earlier in the war, she had played her part with fervent patriotism. They were mostly grown men who had first passed through her training depot. They had been hard and strong. Then, after the first years of the holocaust, the men had been replaced by hot-eyed, vengeful youths. Later still, they were mere schoolboys whose ranks had marched proudly off to battle. But she had secretly grieved over the deaths of her young boy soldiers. Now that the war had ended, those echoing barracks and wind-swept parade grounds where she had drilled and bullied them, would soon be empty – cheerless and soulless like the orphanages of her childhood.

Schroeder was watching her as they shared the uncertain silence about the small table. He was vaguely aware of distant sounds. There was laughter and casual conversation coming from the room next door, but here it seemed that the air they breathed had suddenly thickened and hung heavily around them.

Yukovlev was the first to stir. He reached out to take his brandy glass, holding it between cupped palms as he looked carefully at the contents. What would have been his response, Schroeder wondered, if he had known of that thin-coloured liquid offered by Mulholland to another of his guests earlier in the day?

Mulholland had been careful not to tell them about the captive Jap scientists. To expect the Russians to concur with their surrender to the Americans would surely have been asking too much. It had been Yukovlev, however, who had first convinced Schroeder that the Allied P.O.Ws had been used as guinea pigs by the Japanese from

Pingfan. Would Yukovlev now believe Mulholland's glib story, that he had confirmed the doctor's suspicions by the questioning of the prison camp officers and guards?

Mulholland, also, was watching the Russians, with a feigned expression of anxious suspense.

"The bastard," thought Schroeder, "he knows he's got them trapped." A moment later, he was not so certain.

Yukovlev, from beneath his darkly etched brows, was gazing thoughtfully at Mulholland, "How can you be sure that only a few of your men were infected?" The doctor's voice sounded casual. He almost murmured the question in a drawl which implied indifference.

Mulholland waved his arm in a nonchalant gesture.

"Well, I suppose the Pingfan medical team must have told the old buzzard." he said airily. He checked himself. "I mean, of course, the Jap Camp Commandant."

"He knew how many, but he did not know the names?"

"Yep. I guess that's just about right."

There was no need for Schroeder to translate the major's emphatic affirmative, but as Yukovlev sank back into the chair, still clasping his almost empty glass, Schroeder sensed again, the unacknowledged understanding that had flashed between the two men earlier.

He looked again at Mulholland, who was now smiling affably through the cloud of unaccustomedly rich-smelling smoke.

"Very well," Yukovlev was saying, "I will do what I can to help you." His cheek-bones showed up more starkly as he leaned his head against the back of the chair. "I think, Major, that you have understood very well that I have to go back to Pingfan."

"But, comrade, why return to suffer again?" Sergei Petrokov's fresh features showed bewilderment. "Especially on such a mission. We could be in great danger. When we were last there the N.K.V. were taking charge."

"Did you say 'we' ?" Schroeder interrupted, looking at the younger man.

Petrokev looked confused for a moment.

"Forget it, Schroeder," Mulholland broke in, "the doctor was explaining something. Perhaps the pair of you should listen."

"My good friend, Sergei Petrokov," the doctor said. "Major Mulholland has guessed correctly that I am very sick." He shook his head at Petrokov's shocked stare. "No, not because of Pingfan. It is one of man's much older enemies. It is destroying me from inside. I have known for many weeks," he added with a tight-lipped smile.

Schroeder felt suddenly embarrassed. He remembered his recent contempt for this man's need of drink and drugs.

"Then you should go to hospital and be taken care of." There was deep concern in the voice of Tatiana Chokovska.

Yukovlev shrugged. "I have accepted the sickness of my body," he muttered with a sudden in-drawn breath. "But since Pingfan, I have also felt a sickness in my soul." He managed a wry grin in the direction of Mulholland, whose lip was curling sardonically. "Oh yes, Major. Even a communist is allowed to have a soul."

Schroeder swirled the brandy in his glass. He nodded his understanding. "Yeah," he said slowly. "I remember you telling me something about your nightmares." He was discovering to his relief, that as the evening progressed his translation was being needed less and less. The Russians each had at least some basic English, the doctor more than average.

Yukovlev's voice sounded far away. "I should not have left Pingfan," he murmured very softly. His waxen features seemed to dissolve. They became almost formless with loathing and horror, as he stared directly ahead. "You see," he continued in the same low voice, "I cannot escape from the things I remember. I should have stayed there, to fight them. They were doctors, who created that place. It will need doctors to repair the harm they have done."

"But the war - it had lasted so long, you had done so much. You also knew that you were very sick." There was a hint of puzzlement in Tatiana's voice.

Schroeder was distracted by Mulholland's cynical sniff, which the major covered with a hasty cough.

"No need for you to feel guilty, doctor." Mulholland said. "Hell! we've all done things in this war, which perhaps one day we'll regret. We'll all have to live with our memories I guess. Mebbe we all feel guilty because we survived, when better guys than us didn't make it."

Yukovlev drank his brandy in short, greedy gulps before replying. "We are all familiar with death," he breathed, in a voice which was little more than a whisper. "Sometimes it is even

127

welcome as a friend. But Pingfan could give men a foretaste of hell. What comfort, then, would even death have to offer?" He was hunched, now, in his chair, ignoring the silent group, as though addressing the question to himself.

Schroeder cleared his throat self-consciously. "Well, at least if we can get hold of that list of names, we'll be helping those guys of ours - that's if they survive the shipwreck." he added lamely.

Tatiana Chokovska spoke up unexpectedly. "I think they should have the break," she said with startling finality. "We must save them from the pigshit Japanese."

Schroeder struggled to conceal a grin. "I guess Miss Chokovska has just about summed things up." he suggested.

"And what are your feelings lieutenant?" Mulholland put the question, in a brisk voice, to the ruddy-faced Sergei Petrokov. Sitting between the two other Russians, he gave a lop-sided smile. Looking from one to the other, he raised both his hands in an expressive gesture. "But of course I will go with my friends," he replied.

The major's expression remained relaxed, but there was a grudging note of quiet respect in his voice when he spoke.

"Thank you all for your decision," he said. "Your help will be appreciated by Lieutenant Schroeder here." He picked up a decanter from the table to refill their glasses. "I'd like to drink to the success of this mission. It could mean a lot to those guys on their way home."

The glasses clinked as they drank the toast.

"What the hell," thought Schroeder, who was feeling slightly drunk, "Mebbe it'll turn out all right." He wondered if he had spoken out aloud. He was aware of a sharp glance from Mulholland, who was preparing to leave.

"I take it we are all agreed about my plans," he was saying. "You, gentlemen," he addressed the two Russians, "And you, Miss Chokovska, will fly to Pingfan with Lt. Schroeder and a couple of my men. As Americans we aren't allowed to enter. I decided that in the short time available, the only way for Schroeder and his men to get inside, would be in Russian uniform."

A grim smile appeared on Yukovlev's saturnine features.

"They will also need to get out," he said.

Petrokov was vigorously nodding agreement. "Lieutenant Schroeder speaks very good Russian," he added. "That also will
128

help."

Tatiana Chokovska was sitting on the edge of her chair, leaning forward with an intent expression. Without her cap, she looked different, Schroeder had observed. Like the men, she had also removed her tunic. Her hair was surprisingly fair. It contrasted with the blackness of her eyes, which had a fierce excited gleam.

" 'A daughter of Tamerlaine', " he found himself reflecting, "'King of the Tartar Tribes'."

"Try not to take any chances." Mulholland's orders were seeping through into Schroeder's wandering mind. "Remember, the time you have there will be limited. Be ready to leave here soon after dawn tomorrow. I'll arrange for the Dakota to be standing by. Memorise the place where it lands. Be sure to be there when it returns to pick you up."

Mulholland stopped talking to look at the others. Two vertical creases appeared between his eyes as he frowned. "How you go about searching when you get there, I'm afraid will be up to you. Schroeder has a drawing, which should help."

"Ah yes, the drawing," Yukovlev repeated. Again he spoke as though musing to himself. "I had hoped that there would be at least a drawing. Your Japanese camp guards have been very helpful."

Mulholland picked up his jacket as he got to his feet. He ignored the doctor's comment. "Sorry, folks, but I've got things to do now. Unless you have any questions, I'll see you in the morning to wish you luck."

Schroeder was also standing as the major nodded briefly to each of the three Russians. "Goodnight everybody."

Petrokov and the woman rose partially from their chairs. Yukovlev remained seated. "Good-night, Major Mulholland," he said. There was a twisted smile on the doctor's face. There could have been a hint of mockery in his voice.

Again Schroeder had the uncanny feeling that these two men were playing a game, with rules he did not understand.

Crouching in the small elevator, at the foot of Pete's stretcher, Lockie screwed up his face, in anticipation of something going wrong. The sudden bang when the jerky movement stopped was a signal for him to open his eyes. He hastily scrabbled for the handle, to slide back the steel-latticed door. An unexpected yaw in the movement of

129

the ship almost threw him onto his face as he tripped on the stretcher in his effort to reach the opening. The passage-way in which he found himself was narrow and empty. He bent to seize the stretcher handles to tug it out of its box-like compartment. The end of the stretcher slid sideways. One tubular steel foot stuck firmly in the space between the elevator floor and the corridor.

Lockie could have ground his teeth in rage. This forced recollection of their loss increased his frustration. As he struggled to pull the stretcher free, he looked with mounting resentment at the contented smile on the sleeping Pete's face. "It's all right for you, you big lazy bastard," he mumbled with increasing desperation. "Why couldn't it have been me that was asleep?" He speculated briefly on a missed opportunity of stealing a syrette and injecting himself. He was sweating. There was no ventilation. The air around him was stale and humid. He heard a double clang as though someone had opened and closed a steel door. The sound was followed almost immediately by a welcome thread of fresh air. Lockie quickly came to a decision. There was someone else not very far away. He would have to risk leaving Pete to get some help.

"Hope somebody doesn't move the bleeding lift, with you half-way out," he sniffed. For a moment he wondered about dragging the patient from the jammed stretcher, but decided not to take the risk. "Just hang on a minute, mate."

With a quick backward look at the stretcher and its occupant, he made his way carefully along the corridor.

"Bleeding shut as usual!" He looked anxiously at the heavy steel door. "Still," he thought, "This must have been the one that some perisher had opened."

He struggled with the heavy handles which clamped the hatch to the bulkhead. As he pushed it open, a blast of wind forced the breath back down his throat. He gulped and almost fell as he slammed the heavy door behind him before reeling across a short stretch of open deck to reach the steel walls of a deck house. He gasped with relief when he realised he was on the boat deck. But his relief turned to horror when he saw that the life-boat davits were empty. "Oh God! they've bleedin' gone and left me."

His shocked eyes took in the surrounding devastation. A wilderness of twisted metal, splintered wood and shattered glass seemed to be all that remained of the boat-deck in the aftermath of the great storm. Loose pulley blocks swung forlornly from where the boats had hung on the heavy metal arms. A drenching spray from

130

waves still crashing across the decks below, swiftly soaked him to the skin. His body began to shake. He clung to some steel rungs which were welded to the walls of the battered deck-house. "Jesus Christ!" he moaned. "I'm goin' to be bleedin' drowned."

Slightly to his left and at shoulder level was a broken port-hole, which had been roughly boarded over on the inside. There was a sudden lull in the droning of the wind. He abruptly stopped his wailing, when he thought he heard the sound of voices coming from behind the boards. Turning his head from side to side, his eyes searched wildly for some sign of a door. The painted steel showed dribbles of rust and was thickly encrusted with salt, but it was otherwise blank.

Letting go his grip on the rung, he lurched round the sharp-edged corner of the superstructure. He pulled up short with a cry of alarm when he noticed the missing rail at the edge of the narrow strip of deck. Alongside him was a firmly closed door with its faint hope of sanctuary. He grabbed at the handle to shake it with all his might, whilst battering with his other fist at the unyielding steel. He almost screamed with relief, when he felt the handle shifting as it was levered free from its heavy clamps by someone on the inside. The door opened slowly, for a grudging few inches as though the person inside was afraid of a draught.

"Let me in!" screeched Lockie. "It's bleedin' me. I'm goin' to be bleeding drowned out here!"

"Holy Cow!" came a startled American voice. "See what we've got here you guys." All eyes were turned to the speaker, as the bedraggled Lockie staggered in.

"Throw it back!" someone shouted in mock terror. "It looks like it's been washed in by the godammed sea."

The dripping figure stood and glanced around at the thirty or so Americans who occupied the cheerless room. One of them came over to look at him curiously. "Say, where've you come from?" he asked. "Nobody's supposed to be allowed out there."

"I got bleedin' lost," Lockie shouted angrily. "What about a bleedin' towel or something? Can't you see I'm half-bleedin'-drowned?"

A gruff, familiar voice made him quickly turn his head.

"Here take this you Aussie asshole." It was Tiny, who was offering him a damp looking sheet. The giant shrugged his shoulders at Lockie's look of disgust. "It's the best we can do, I guess. There

131

ain't many comforts around here."

Lockie smeared it miserably over his face and hair, removing some of the wetness. His toothless mouth was clamped tightly, in an expression of disgust, as he looked around at the crowded, disorderly room. "Right bloody shit-house this is," he sniffed. "Where's all me bleedin' mates?"

Tiny shook his head unhelpfully. "All the Limey's are together somewhere, I guess. We was told to report right here. But it seems like the sonofabitching boats have been blowed away. We might've well stayed where we was," he grumbled.

Lockie's voice rose to a new level of indignant protest.

"That means we can't get off this bleedin' ship!" In a mood of bleak despair, he screwed up Tiny's sheet, to fling it onto the glistening, damp floor. "Oh bloody hell!" He'd suddenly remembered Pete. As he sank wearily to his haunches, his strangely fore-shortened face gave his mouth the contours of a scallop.

"Hey! What's eating you buddy? You goin' crazy or somethin'?" Tiny moved over to a nearby corner where he picked up an unused life-jacket. "Here, put this on. Mebbe it'll make you feel better." His knees creaked loudly as he squatted beside the Australian, to hand over the depressing object.

Lockie irritably pushed it away. He lost his balance attempting to get to his feet, and for a few moments was tangled with Tiny as the pair of them rolled on the sloping deck.

"Well! If that ain't just the dandiest godammed sight!"

From where he was lying, flat on his stomach, Lockie looked up at the grinning Rossi. The Aussie scrambled to his feet, at the same time stretching out a hand to pacify the swearing Tiny.

"You clumsy sonofabitch," the giant started to shout, but his voice broke off in a fit of coughing.

"What the hell's goin' on? There's always godamm trouble when you're around." Rossi wiped his hands on the seat of his pants after helping the pair of them to their feet.

The Australian grabbed Tiny's arm. "It's my mate, Pete," he gabbled. "I had to leave him."

"Leave him where, for Chrissake?" growled Rossi. "Can't the sonofabitch look after himself?"

There was now an evasive expression on Lockie's unshaven

face. "No he can't, as it happens. He was blown up in the bleedin' explosion, an' I had to leave 'im stuck in a bleeding lift."

Rossi's face gave an involuntary twitch, as the toothless Australian tried to explain. But he bit back the jeers when he saw the wild expression in Lockie's eyes.

"Sounds like his buddy's hurt and stuck in a godamm elevator," he drawled. "Sonofabitch! The poor bastard might be dyin'. Was he hurt bad?"

Lockie hesitated. "He was bleedin' unconscious," he answered. "If it hadn't been for me an' that ginger Pom, he'd have been dead already I reckon. But, of course, the Pom had to bleedin' run off didn't he?"

Tiny looked impressed by Lockie's account of his heroism. Even Rossi had turned serious. "Where is this godamm elevator?" he snapped.

"Yeah, come on. We've gotta find him." Tiny's gruff voice was determined.

Lockie immediately regretted his rash boasting, as they looked at him expectantly. He tilted his head towards the tightly closed door. "Out there." he said weakly.

A few moments later, Tiny was pulling open the door, whilst Rossi held the protesting Lockie securely by a fold in the back of his jacket. "Why can't you two bleedin' go and leave me here?" he was pleading.

"Not a chance!" answered Rossi grimly. "Where we go, you godamm go."

Someone on the inside stood by to slam and latch the door behind them, as they braced themselves on the narrow strip of deck with its missing rails. Oddly enough, Lockie felt comforted by Rossi's rough grip on his billowing jacket as the three of them stumbled through the stinging spray. Lockie continued to complain as he led them to the hatch, from which he had recently emerged. Once again it was Tiny who manipulated the heavy handles. He was breathless as he pushed it open. "Come on," he panted. "Let's keep movin'."

"It ain't bleedin' fair." Lockie's gnome-like features worked alarmingly as he spluttered with indignation. "Why couldn't you split-arsed Yankies get him yourselves? If I hadn't gone back to find me bleedin' teeth, I'd have been safe with me mates. It's all your bleedin' fault." He tried to accuse the lumbering Tiny, while all the time being held in his humiliating position by Rossi's unrelenting grasp. "It was you made me put me bleedin' teeth back in. If I hadn't they'd have been safe in me pocket, wouldn't they?"

Tiny pointed to a patch of deeper shadow on the wall of the narrow corridor. "That must be him," he grunted.

Rossi gave Lockie a shake to silence him. "Quit yappin'," he ordered. "Let's see if your buddy's OK"

Pete's stretcher was where Lockie had deserted it, with one of its feet still jammed immovably in the narrow gap. Rossi relinquished his hold on Lockie, to kneel beside the silent figure lying there. He turned to look up at the other two men, brushing a hand across his cropped hair, as though uncertain. "I guess he's OK" he said uneasily. "He's pretty damn quiet though."

"Course he's bleedin' quiet," the outraged Lockie broke in. "He's been given an injection, hasn't he. He'll probably still be asleep when the perishin' ship sinks. I wish I bleedin' was," he sniffed. He glared with something close to hatred at the bearded face of Pete, which still wore its expression of benign serenity.

Tiny was tugging in vain at the jammed leg of the stretcher. It was stuck in such a way that it was partly in and partly out of the lift. In spite of Tiny's efforts, the metal stump remained firmly stuck. He stopped his tugging to poke a large knuckled finger into the narrow space, hoping to push the leg free from underneath. The leg refused to move, and so, as well, did Tiny's finger. He was kneeling in such a way that his body took up the width of the corridor. "Holy shit!" he growled. He bent lower to put his eye to the gap, as though looking into it would somehow make it wider. He struggled again to pull his finger free, and looked increasingly worried when he failed.

Rossi gave Lockie a shove. "You get into the elevator and pull the godammed litter from that side. It might open up the space."

"Why me?" the smaller man protested. "Why don't you get in there yourself?"

"Because you're only the size of a turtle's turd. It's easier for you. That's godamm why!"

The disgruntled Australian stepped grudgingly over the stretcher into the confined space of the small lift, where he couldn't stand upright. When he worked his elbows to push, there was a grinding sound and a bellow of pain from Tiny.

"Jesus Christ!" he howled. "You mother-lovin' sonofabitch!"

Lockie was unusually dumb-struck as he witnessed the big man's rage. "Sorry, mate," he mumbled at last. "I hope there's nothing broke."

"It's as sure as hell, your godammed neck's gonna be broke when I get outa here," the trapped Tiny groaned.

"What the hell do you stupid sonsabitches think you are doing?" From further along the gloomy passage a loud voice was shouting, and purposeful footsteps were heading towards them.

Lockie knew who it was. He crouched down further, to make himself smaller. As the bo'sun stopped behind him, Tiny, still on his hands and knees, turned his head wrathfully. "Watch out who you're calling godammed names," he rumbled.

"Sorry I thought you were praying." The bo'sun sounded sarcastic as his eyes took in the predicament of the sorry looking group. He bent to look more closely at the shape of the figure on the stretcher.

"Holy Mother!" His voice expressed profound disbelief. "Ain't this the stiff I got rid of a while back?" He peered more closely into the dark recesses of the lift, where he saw the crouching Australian.

"Godammit to hell! Why are you still there?"

"Why don't you quit talking and do something to help?" Rossi's sullen voice caught the bo'sun's attention.

The burly seaman shook his head in patient acceptance.

"Like I said before, I think somebody musta made a mistake, an' we picked you guys up from a nut-house." With a deep sigh he pulled a heavy-handled knife from a sheath on his belt, ignoring Tiny's expression of sudden alarm. He pushed the handle into the crack to open it a little more.

Tiny's mouth opened wide with a gust of relief, as he pulled his finger free. "Jeez! That feels better." he breathed, as he stuck it into his large mouth to soothe the throbbing.

"When you've finished sucking your godammed finger, mebbe you could help out here."

Pete's stretcher hadn't moved.

Tiny and the bo'sun were now both on their haunches, glaring balefully eye to eye.

"What do you want me to do?" Tiny grated, holding back his
135

rising temper.

"Get in there, with that little sparrowfart, and give the godammed thing a shove when I say the word."

Tiny looked doubtfully at the constricted space. Bent almost double, he carefully stepped over Pete, to edge himself alongside Lockie, who almost disappeared behind Tiny's large frame.

"Right - now!" The bo'sun levered with the knife handle. The crack widened. The leg came out as he lifted. Tiny pushed from the inside. Pete's stretcher slid into the corridor. There was a clunk and a whining from invisible pulleys. The bo'sun stared aghast into empty space, as the rickety cage slid downwards, carrying Tiny and Lockie.

"Now look what you've bleedin' done." Lockie sounded incredulous as their unexpected descent came to a jarring halt at the lower deck level. "I'm back where I bleedin' started from."

Tiny, too was losing his temper. As they stumbled out of the shaky contraption, he turned, painfully aware of his throbbing finger, to shake his fist at Lockie.

"Why don't you quit complainin'?" he shouted. He pointed to a stout looking length of rope in a recess alongside the lift. "All we have to do is haul on this and pull the godammed thing up again." He demonstrated by giving it a hefty tug. But the rope moved loosely in his hand, apparently attached to nothing. "Sonofabitch!" he rumbled fiercely. "We'll have to find some godammed stairs."

"Just like I bleedin' said. We're bleedin' lost again."

Lockie's unhelpful comment was drowned by a burst of coughing from Tiny.

"You all right, mate?" Lockie asked with a note of anxiety as the big man slowly recovered.

Tiny reached into a pocket to withdraw a large chunk of black tobacco. Deliberately, he placed the end between his teeth, worrying at it until a sizeable piece was torn off. His jaws worked rhythmically as he fixed his rheumy eyes on his skinny partner.

"Yeah, I'm all right," he answered with terrible emphasis, "But if you don't quit squawkin', I'm gonna twist your head right off your sonofabitching neck." He made a threatening gesture with the remaining length of tobacco. "Now, are you coming with me or ain't you?"

Momentarily silenced, Lockie weakly nodded his head.

"OK then. Let's try going this way, godammit." Tiny lurched heavily off, with Lockie trailing dejectedly behind. Tiny had taken only a few strides when he suddenly stopped. Leaning with one hand on the wall of the passage to support himself, he thrust his head forward.

"Can you hear something funny?" he asked the brooding Lockie.

The Australian's scowl became even deeper. "Bloody hell". he replied. "I feel as if I've got me head in a perishin' bucket, with somebody bashing at it."

The unremitting rush and rumble of the wildly churning waves reminded Lockie of tropical storms in his Queensland home-town, where thunder shook the heavens and torrents of rain gushed from the clouds, battering his humble tin roof.

He suddenly flinched. "What's that?" he gasped. There was a jangling clash like a load of old iron being dropped down a deep shaft. It was followed by the crunching sound of torn metal plates grinding together with devouring zeal.

Tiny dismissed the noise with a shake of his head. "Aw, that's just somethin' fallin' off."

"Bleedin' fallen off? There's nothin' else left to bleedin' fall off, unless it's the bleedin' funnel! I'm gettin' out of here!"

But Tiny grabbed him by the arm. "I can hear somethin' else," he said. His seamed face was set in serious folds as he listened intently. "There it goes again!"

This time, in an unexpected lull, Lockie heard it too.

It was a shuffling scraping sound, accompanied by noisy wheezing and panting. Then there was a loud thump. The two men looked at each other, until they heard a muffled curse.

"That voice!" yapped Lockie, through his loosely flapping lips. "It sounded like Johno, the bleedin' Pommy sergeant. What the hell's he doin' down here?"

Tiny's gruff voice held a note of concern. "Mebbe he's been hurt. Come on, let's go and check up."

The sounds had come from a few yards ahead of them, where another corridor led off at a right angle.

"He's probably been dumped by the bleedin' crew, and left to perish like us. They're getting rid of us one at a time." Lockie's complaints were becoming increasingly bitter.

Snorting impatiently, as he released the reluctant Lockie's arm, Tiny peered round the corner. "Well I'll be godammed! It's him all right. an' there's another Limey with him."

Since losing Luke, the struggling pair had progressed only a very few yards. Now they were perched one at each end of the beam, to rest and regain their breath.

"Mebbe you were right, sarge," gasped Jim. "We're not going to get much further with this bloody thing."

Johno looked at Jim with a reluctant nod of agreement. "You were right about having a go, though. At least it's warmer here than on the bloody boat deck." He explored the contours of his swollen nose with a tender hand. "Jeez! I think there's something broken here," he continued plaintively.

Jim wasn't listening. "Sarge," he said, "I think I just saw somebody."

"It's that bloody imagination of yours." For a moment Johno looked aggrieved at his plight being ignored. Then he turned his head to look along the passage, following the direction of Jim's excited eyes. He was just in time to see Tiny's head appear again.

"I didn't believe in sea-monsters until now," he said slowly, "but nothing else could be so ugly." He got to his feet as the other two men came towards them carefully placing their feet on the unsteady deck. Johno attempted a grin, but gave it up with a painful wince. He stretched out an arm to slap the big man's shoulder. "Tiny, you old fart! How the hell did you get here? And him as well?" The sergeant greeted Lockie with slightly less enthusiasm.

"We was dropped down an elevator," Tiny attempted to explain.

"Helpin' your bleedin' mate we was," Lockie interrupted.

The American gave him a threatening look. "What did I say I'd do if you started your godammed yackin' again?" Turning to the other two, he demanded, "How about you? What are you supposed to be doin' with that godammed thing?"

Tiny listened earnestly whilst they hurriedly gave the reason for their predicament. "Sonofabitch!" he said wonderingly. "You mean they need that godammed thing down below to stop the ship from sinking?"

"That's about it." answered Jim with unfounded authority.

There was a scraping of rough skin as Tiny rubbed his palms together. He spat a squirt of tobacco juice onto the deck, expertly missing Lockie's feet. "Come on, asshole," he said. "Gimme a hand here." He waved at Jim and Johno. "You two can take the other end." He broke off to cough painfully, then wiped his lips with the back of his hand. Jim and Johno hesitated, as they exchanged doubtful glances. Lockie lurked behind the determined Tiny.

"What the hell are we waiting for? Lead the godammed way."

The other two bent to pick up their end. Johno leaned close to Jim's ear. "Better not to tell him yet that we don't know which way to go," he advised in a worried voice.

There began a grim struggle as the four of them tussled with the awkward object, moving it for a few short steps, before dropping it to rest aching muscles.

"Don't know why we're bleedin' doin' this. We ought to be up there, near the bleedin' lifeboats". Lockie's assistance was of such a low order, that he had breath to spare for his discouraging comments.

"What sonofabitchin' boats?" snarled Tiny. Lockie's querulous voice fell silent as he recalled the bleak prospect of the upper decks.

Tiny was wheezing noisily as they stopped to rest. His shoulders heaved with the effort to fill his wasting lungs with air.

"Our only godammed chance is if this tin-can stays afloat." He broke off with another bout of noisy coughing. "There ain't no godammed boats," he finished with watering eyes.

Jim's eyes brightened. "That's what I've said from the beginning," he panted. "Come on we'd better get going."

"Keep moving towards the sharp end," Johno muttered to Jim. "That's where the trouble is."

They had laboriously angled their unwieldly load round another corner. Now they thankfully dumped it on the deck again to take another breather.

"We're bleedin' lost again, ain't we? You two bloody drongos don't know where the hell we are, do you?" Lockie's nose and chin were almost in collision as he stared aggressively at the leading pair.

Johno and Jim exchanged meaningful glances. For once Lockie was right. It was impossible now to know which direction they were taking. The wallowing ship was moving neither forward nor backward.

"All very well to say we'll head for the sharp end," grumbled Jim to Johno. "But where the bloody hell is it?"

Johno scratched his head desperately as he struggled to think. Their surroundings were becoming increasingly different. The floor of the passageway felt warm. Hardboard-covered walls had given way to rough red-painted plates.

"We've got to keep going this way," he gasped worriedly to Jim. "We can't turn that bloody corner again!"

Jim, for once. didn't argue. The corner had been a problem. The wrenching and lifting had become almost manic as they had struggled to manoeuvre the roughly-hewn beam around a right-angled bend in the too narrow passage. Once it had slipped from somebody's grasp when Lockie's head had been very close, but no one owned up to being the culprit.

There was a sudden squeal of protesting metal hinges, from further down the passageway. A steel door set into the wall was being pushed open. The heavily built figure of a man appeared. He clung to the handle for a moment to prevent the door from swinging back as the ship heeled violently. He finally slammed it with a noisy clang. His back was momentarily turned to them. He pulled a piece of rag from a pocket in his grimy overalls and started to mop the sweat from his face and neck as he walked away.

The sound of Tiny's cough drew his attention to the ill-assorted group around their cumbersome charge.

"What the hell's going on here?" He was now walking towards them, wiping his hands on the oily rag. There was a puzzled look on his pug-nosed face. "What are you guys supposed to be doing?" He sounded incredulous as he took a longer look at the strange object they were sitting on. His tired features gradually relaxed into a broad smile.

"Holy mackerel!" he shouted. The smile became a guffaw as he looked at the disconsolate men. "Are you plannin' to launch that thing or somethin'?"

Tiny was still breathing hard, but as he got to his feet, he managed to find his voice.

"No we're not," he growled. "But one more crack like that from you, and we'll shove it right up your godammed butt."

Johno watched as the man's expression changed. His own

140

swollen nose flashed out urgent warnings as the man's free hand balled up into a huge fist. Tiny and the crewman glowered at each other. Tempers were running very high. The crewman pushed back the peak of the baseball cap he wore. He snorted impatiently as he turned away, but then he halted, to point a grease-grimed finger at the massive piece of wood.

"Get the hell out of here," he ordered. "And take your godammed life-raft with you. You're blockin' this passageway."

Surprisingly, it was Lockie who intervened. "Look, mate," he said in his most wheedling voice. "We're trying to get this into some bleedin' place where there's supposed to be some trouble. It can't be far from here. We've been carryin' it for bleeding hours. We can't take it back. It's too bleedin' heavy."

The crewman earnestly scrutinised the hideously smiling Australian. "You with these Limeys?" he asked curiously. "I heard they was a bunch of screwballs."

"No! I'm bleedin' Australian," the indignant Lockie was spluttering, when Jim broke in.

"It's right what he told you," he said urgently. "There was a call for the crew to take these things to a hold where there's some trouble. I gave somebody a hand."

"Then we lost him," Johno continued.

Jim nodded. "But before that, we'd missed a turning somewhere, and didn't know where we were."

"Then they bleedin' found us," came Lockie's shrill voice.

The crewman almost exploded. "For Chrissake shut up!" he shouted. He turned fiercely to the scowling Tiny. "And you, you big jerk! How the hell did you get to be here?"

As Tiny drew a ponderous breath, the crewman stopped him. He held up a hand. "I think I'd rather not know," he said sarcastically.

Jim was about to say something else, but Johno nudged him. "Quiet." he said in a low voice. "He looks as though he's thinking."

The overalled man seemed suddenly to make up his mind. He gave a huge sigh, as though he'd concluded he was a victim of fate.

"OK" he said. "It's time you guys were told. There's flooding in Number 1 Hold. The ship's already down by the stem"."

"He means sinking at the sharp end," Johno whispered

141

importantly in Jim's ear.

The sailor glared in Johno's direction. "The bulkhead between Holds One and Two is holding," he continued. "But only just. The guys down there are doin' what they can. If No. Two floods, the bows may go under." He looked at the ill-assorted group significantly. Then he shrugged and said, "So what the hell! Take 'em your piece of godammed cordwood if that'll keep you quiet." Suddenly he smiled and clapped Tiny on the shoulder.

"Come on you ugly bastard. I'll show you guys a possible way through." He turned serious again. "I warn you, it ain't going to be easy though." He looked doubtfully at the under-nourished bodies of the four listening men. "Right!" he said, in a suddenly hoarse voice, that was somewhere between laughing and crying, "Come on then, follow me."

A blast of hot-air and sickening oily fumes came from the open door. There was a deafening, high-pitched whine from enormous blowers, which fed air to the oil-fired boilers.

"Holy Cow!" muttered Tiny. He let go his grip on the end of the beam. so that it fell with a loud thud, narrowly missing Lockie's toes.

"Clumsy bastard!" Lockie yelled. "That's twice you've nearly done for me."

Ignoring him, Tiny stuck his head through the doorway to look inside. The other three crowded behind.

"Hell's bells!" breathed Johno, in an awe-struck voice. "What's going to happen here?"

They were standing on a narrow steel catwalk with a shiny hand-rail and a latticed steel walkway, which encircled the deep well of the boiler room. A little way to the right was a landing with a metal ladder, which descended about half-way. Here it reached a similar cat-walk, before leading down to the black painted deck plates.

Their new helper, whose name was Mac, was standing near the top of the ladder. He was bawling down to two other overalled figures, far below. One of them cupped an ear with one hand. Mac, who appeared to be in charge, bellowed again. "I want one of you guys to grab a length of rope and haulass it up here. Come on now, move it!" His shouts were becoming angrier, as the two men appeared to be arguing. He turned to the others, who were waiting with some apprehension, to find out what the plan was.

142

"Right. Lemme give you a hand," he said. Lockie immediately relinquished his position. "OK Let's get it through the door."

Jim was already bending to pick up his end with Johno.

The other pair heaved and snorted until the awkward length was turned sufficiently for them to rest it on the steel handrail of the cat-walk. With a little more pushing and a great deal more swearing, the beam was moved still further until about a third of its length overhung the space below.

One of Mac's men had appeared with a large coil of rope. He was smallish, with a round good-humoured face, which glistened with sweat and oil. "Here y'are, chief," he puffed as he handed it over. "It was all we could find down there." He nodded at the four watching men as he used a sweat-rag on his face. "Hi, you guys. I guess you must be some of them passengers I heard we took aboard. From China wasn't it?"

Jim and Johno exchanged glances of bewilderment. The happy looking engineer didn't seem to know where the ship had been, nor - presumably - where it was going. It was only from hearsay that he knew it carried some passengers.

"That's right," Johno answered. "We boarded at Dairen."

The engineer seemed not to hear. He was gazing down anxiously at the pair of steam-squirting monsters at the bottom of the well-like shaft.

"Wish the ship could get movin'," he muttered. "Those babies o' mine don't care for bein' shut down too long."

"Perhaps we'll be under way, again soon." Johno tried to sound reassuring about the welfare of the little man's boilers.

But the engineer shook his head. "I hope not yet awhile," he answered dolefully. "Not till them plates up front are fixed. If they're not strong enough, these fire-eatin' beauties would push her right under." He suddenly reverted to his cheerful smile. "Like a godammed submarine," he added proudly.

Jim and Johno wrenched their minds away from the cheerful sailor's alarming image as they heard Mac's voice.

"OK you guys. Come on over here. We need all hands." He had lassoed the out-jutting end of the beam and was pulling it tight as he called the others. "You guys take hold of the rope," he ordered, "and hang on when we push the sonofabitch over."

He and Tiny had manoeuvred the beam until it was balanced

143

across the handrail. The others grasped the rope as tightly as they could. "Here we go!" boomed Mac.

The rope jerked and juddered in the trio's hands as the heavy length of wood bounced and swung in mid-air.

"It feels like a hanging in Dodge City," Johno grated from between clenched teeth. The beam was swinging wildly with the rolling of the ship. It crashed several times into the lower cat-walk, before descending with a rush, to bounce on the floor of the boiler room.

Mac was already half-way down the ladder. The rest of the party followed more cautiously. They descended into an inferno of fumes and heat and rushing, steamy air.

"Which way now?" Jim was already tugging at the looped rope. He had to shout to be heard. The big engineer gestured towards the far wall. It was easier now, with Mac and his mate helping, as they carried it towards the far bulkhead. When they reached it there was a short wait until Mac made a phone call. "I'd better check what's goin' on for'ard," he said.

Whilst they were waiting, the smaller man came up to the half-naked Johno, to hand him something – a seaman's bulky jersey. "Here, take this, Slim," he shouted. "You might be needing it."

Mac still waited by the telephone. He was having difficulty contacting someone. Finally, there came a reply. They could see his mouth working in short, jerky sentences. When he returned he was looking serious.

"What's the score?" Tiny asked.

The man pushed his cap back from his sweating forehead.

"No change," he replied. "Number One's flooded; Number Two's holdin', but only just. They daren't risk getting her under way. The whole godammed thing might cave-in."

"Are we gonna make it? Tiny wanted to know.

"Just mebbe." Mac answered. "That's if the godammed sea gets no worse."

"Come on then!" Jim burst out. "What the hell are we waiting for?" The light of battle had re-kindled in his eyes. The others could almost hear the bugles sounding in his brain.

"Hold on a minute." Gripping Jim's arm, Johno leaned forward, to hear what the engineer was saying to Tiny.

144

Mac was pointing out a small steel hatch set into the thickness of the main bulkhead, which spanned the boiler-room.

"I'll let you through here," he was saying. "But then I'll have to close it again. I can't take any chances with floodin' in this place. After that, you guys are on your own."

Tiny's craggy face was set in hard, determined lines. Beneath the loosely fitting shirt, his ribs rose and fell in rapid shallow movements.

"Which way?" he panted.

"Through there," Mac shouted, so that the others could hear also. "There's a passageway runnin' crosswise, and another door, right opposite, which goes into the main food store. There's a hatch on the other side of the food store which gives into Number Two Hold." He was already working on several steel handles. He put his weight on the heavy door, to push it slowly away from him. "Quick as you can, fellas. That's the way." He pointed to the door facing them, on the other side of the steel-walled corridor.

Tiny lumbered across to open the store-room door. He stooped with Lockie to haul on the battered beam, whilst Jim and Johno pushed it from the boiler-room end. Its clumsy bulk bridged the passage, moving in reluctant jerks as Tiny and his half-hearted helper disappeared into the store-room. Mac was using his weight to hold back the bulkhead hatch, whilst Jim and Johno struggled through the small opening.

"Good luck, fellas!" the engineer shouted as they wobbled across the passage, bent almost double over their burden.

There was something very final in the sound as the solid metal slammed behind the engineer, and the long handles of the bolts were slammed into place, one by one.

Chapter 11

The Dakota circled for the second time over the barren-looking stretch of scrubland.

"Guess it might be OK," the pilot spoke to his colleague as he peered through the open perspex panel.

"Could be," the other man answered doubtfully. "Just look out for them rocks. Some of them look pretty damn big."

"We've gotta try it," the pilot answered. "We've searched around and there ain't no better place. We've gotta get 'em as close as we can to that chemical joint. How far do you make it from here?" he asked

The other man glanced at the pad on his knee. "I've had no identifiable fixes," he grumbled, "but I make it eight to ten miles."

"Right then, We'll go in. Make sure they're all belted up back there."

The navigator turned to look down the fuselage, at the passengers ranged down each side on their rough canvas seats. He signalled with his hands for them to check their safety belts. One wing dipped as the pilot made a smooth turn before steadying the plane for its approach.

With his shoulders uncomfortably braced against the aluminium shell of the fuselage, Schroeder watched the earth and sky exchanging places through an opposite window. He found himself holding his breath as the engine note changed and the wings were buffeted noisily by the bumpy air. He glanced at his companions, each of them now silent, waiting tensely for the thump, or the cart-wheeling crash, when the wheels touched the boulder-strewn ground.

It was about ninety minutes since they had boarded. He felt uncomfortable in the Russian uniform. It was a used one. Mulholland had decided it was less likely to arouse suspicion. Schroeder wondered grimly who its previous owner had been. Sergei Petrokov had roared with laughter, whilst telling him he should have more medals. The doctor had said nothing as he climbed aboard. In the chill of the pre-dawn air his face was pale and his nose pinched-looking. Unsmiling, Tatiana Chokovska had nodded, as she pushed Stefan Gregoravitch up the steps, ahead of her.

Dum-Dum and Dead-Eye would have been rough-looking soldiers in any kind of uniform. Dead-Eye had volunteered for the

146

mission because Tatiana still had his glass eye. Dum-Dum had thought he "might enjoy the ride." He had carefully checked each round of ammunition before slamming the magazine back into place. "I ain't never tried out these Russki machine pistols," he had mused.

"Don't try it!" Schroeder had warned. "This is going to be a peaceful mission."

He found himself wondering about Naguchi, who was sitting almost directly opposite. The past forty-eight hours had visibly taken their toll. Lines of weariness were deeply hatched down each side of his face. His pouched eyes were seldom still, but unseeing, as though they were searching inside his own head.

"Poor bastard," thought Schroeder. "He's had no rest for two days". The interrogation of the Jap scientists, the arrangements with the two agents in Pingfan, the interpreter had played a vital role in every part of the operation.

There was a warning shout from the pilot, then a crash and a spine-jarring jolt as the wheels of the sturdy machine hit the ground.

Dum-Dum's ugly face broke into a pleased smile when he felt his arm being gripped by Tatiana Chokovska. He was about to give her knee an encouraging squeeze when the seat belt cut painfully into his flesh. As the racing wheels hit a protruding edge of rock, the plane bounded skywards again. It tilted slightly, the tip of one wing almost scraping the ground, before recovering. Hydraulics shrieked as the under-carriage took the shock of a second landing. Loose stones battered the under-side of the fuselage whilst the plane careered madly over the pitted ground. With both legs braced, the pilot clung grimly to the juddering control-column, before bringing the Dakota to a slithering halt.

The clouds of dust were beginning to settle as the navigator opened the door to drop the short ladder for the shaken passengers to scramble down. As they moved rapidly away from the machine to escape from the dust, the pilot jumped down behind them.

Schroeder looked quickly round the empty landscape, before producing a crude map from his pocket.

"Watch out for sight-seers," he warned Dum-Dum and Dead-Eye.

The two men nodded, taking up positions where they had good views of the surrounding terrain.

147

He showed the map to the pilot. "Can you pin-point our location?" he asked.

The young man shook his head doubtfully. "There doesn't seem to be a landmark worth a shit round here," he observed. "All I can tell you is that there appears to be some kind of road about a mile or so west." He placed a finger on the map. "There it is."

Schroeder nodded as he looked at the thick straight line.

"That should be the main road to Harbin." He looked over his shoulder as Yukovlev and Petrokov moved up to stand behind him.

Petrokov spoke briskly. "This road runs roughly north and south," he pointed out. "Pingfan is further to the west. I remember a connecting road from this one to Pingfan, but the turn-off could be anywhere north or south of here."

"In that event," the pilot said, "I'd advise you to head north. I sure as hell saw no other road on the way up. It looked like the godammed Gobi Desert."

"How far from the turn-off is Pingfan?" asked Schroeder.

Petrokov looked vague, then gave a slight shrug. "I think about fifteen kilometres," he ventured.

Schroeder looked quickly at his watch. "It's a little after seven," he said to the pilot, who was showing signs of impatience. "We want you back here at 18.00 hours. Do you think you'll be able to find the place?"

The pilot grinned. "We'll sure as hell give it a try," he answered. "We used dead reckoning to get here, we'll do the same comin' back. It'll be a big help if you can put up some smoke though."

Schroeder nodded. "OK We'll do our best."

The navigator had a sudden idea. He turned to climb swiftly into the plane. "If you should run outa matches, try using this." He leaned out to toss a Verey pistol to Schroeder. The pilot was already re-starting the engines as the young man gave a cheerful wave. "See ya later," he yelled.

They watched for a few moments, as the plane was turned to face into the wind before the throttles were opened. Those watching protected their faces from the dust as the machine gathered speed over the dangerous ground before taking to the sky in a swift climbing turn, to head off in a southerly direction.

Schroeder looked critically at the small party, huddled together

148

in the bleak half-light of an early-autumn morning.

"For Chrissake!" he called out, "Let's stop dragging our asses and get movin' We'll be heading due west until we reach the road." He joined the Russian officers as the party plodded over the rough ground at a normal walking pace.

"You going to be OK Captain Yukovlev?" he asked the pale-faced man. With a wry smile, the Russian nodded his head.

"We're goin' to have to rely a lot on your help," Schroeder continued. "It's lucky, that as a doctor, you, at least, have a permit to enter Pingfan."

The other man's skin looked clammy. As he spoke, he had to pause frequently, between deep irregular breaths. "That is true," he agreed. "Nor would it be unusual for me to be accompanied. On my previous visit, I took my friend Sergei Petrokov."

"Yeah, I know we have already talked about this, but won't you be taking a big risk?"

"Not as big as you, my friend." Again Yukovlev showed his sardonic smile as he answered. "Besides, as you Americans might say 'What have I got to lose'?"

Schroeder avoided the speaker's sidelong glance by looking straight ahead. "If this crazy plan comes off, doctor, we'll never be able to repay you."

The doctor's reply sounded very odd to the American. "I think what you say may be very true," he answered in a dry, hard voice.

"Say, miss. I hope you're takin' good care of that little object you're keepin' for me." Dead-Eye, wearing a black patch over the empty socket, directed his remaining eye at Tatiana as she strode easily along at his side.

"Not a chance of you gettin' your godammed hands on it," grinned Dum-Dum from the other side.

Tatiana gave a contemptuous sniff as she glanced at the villainous looking Dead-Eye. "I think you are better with the cover over," she said in a serious voice.

"Gee did ya hear that? I told you she liked me!" The jesting Dead-Eye passed a playful arm around the woman's waist as though helping her on her way.

"Niet! Niet!" Dead-Eye and Dum-Dum whipped their heads around as the angry voice came from behind them. A red-faced

Stefan Gregoravitch gestured with his rifle for Dead-Eye to remove the offending arm. With a look of mock terror on his face, the American did as he was told. "Sorry kid. No offence meant," he said abjectly.

Dum-Dum was looking surly. "Who's that godammed school-kid think he is?" he demanded.

Tatiana had a broad smile on her face however. Looking over her shoulder, she spoke a few words to the young soldier in a relaxed manner, as though explaining something. He nodded and hung his head as they continued walking. She held out both hands in an appealing gesture to the Americans. "It is the eye. Perhaps he thinks you try to steal it," she explained.

"Say, look! Over there! I saw something shinin'," Dum-Dum was pointing straight ahead.

Everyone in the party instinctively crouched low as their eyes followed the direction of Dum-Dum's pointing finger. Sure enough, something glinted as it caught a feeble ray from the sun, which was low in the sky behind their backs.

The flash of light disappeared, to be followed by another. Then came several others, accompanied by a familiar sound.

"That must be the road," Schroeder snapped. "A convoy of vehicles just went by."

Sergei Petrokov ran a finger round the collar of his tunic as he placed a hand on Naguchi's arm. "Good!" he panted. "Perhaps now we will be able to ride."

Naguchi shook his head doubtfully. "We'll have to be careful," he warned.

"But fifteen kilometres! We cannot walk." Petrokov's voice was pleading. He spread his arms expressively.

Schroeder walked over to where the two men were standing. He looked at them both with careful eyes. Petrokov was jesting, he decided, but Naguchi looked ill.

"Do you think we could risk stopping a truck?" he asked the Russian.

Petrokov raised his eyebrows with astonishment. "Why not?" he asked. "We are Russian officers. Our vehicle has broken down. We could not be seen walking along the road."

Schroeder turned to Yukovlev. "What do you think?" he asked.

The Russian nodded agreement. "I think my friend is right," he replied. "I shall explain that we are a medical team on our way to Pingfan."

Schroeder indicated Dum-Dum and Dead-Eye. "It'll be hard to convince anybody they are doctors," he pointed out.

The two men looked hurt. "Why the hell not?" queried Dum-Dum.

Petrokov interrupted. "All kinds of people ask for rides," he insisted. "In a country like this there is no other way."

Schroeder looked round the group for any signs of disagreement with Petrokov's plan. "O.K! What the hell!" he announced. "Let's try it."

For the first time he was appreciating the soundness of Mulholland's order when he had insisted on the Russian uniforms.

"I only hope the borrowed Russian papers hold up," he muttered to himself.

The party stopped again to confer about two hundred yards from the road. It had seemed to Schroeder, during their approach, that there was a fairly regular flow of traffic in both directions. If anything, the southerly flow had seemed the greater.

"I guess we had better take the fly-boy's advice and head north," he said to Naguchi. "We don't know how far we are from the turn off to Pingfan, but if we can get a friendly driver, maybe he'll put us right.

Naguchi had agreed. Now as the party crouched behind a low mound, Schroeder handed his binoculars to the interpreter.

"Looks like they're mostly army trucks," he commented. "I spotted an occasional armoured troop carrier and a few jeeps. I've also seen a few large limousines. Staff cars I expect. We've got to avoid those at all costs."

Naguchi passed back the binoculars. "Sure," he said. "It'll have to be a truck."

Schroeder leaned on an elbow to look directly at the man by his side. "Are you going to be OK?" he asked. "Because from here-on it won't be easy to turn back. Not till the job's done."

"I'm just tired, I guess. Don't worry. I'll be OK"

Naguchi's eyes remained fixed on the road as he spoke.

Schroeder felt the interpreter was being evasive for some

reason. "He's also godammed worried," the lieutenant concluded. "Those buddies of yours," he went on, "They should soon be outa there. You arranged a place for the pick-up didn't you? You'd better tell me again."

Naguchi's reply was tense. "Sure, there's a hole in the wall on the north side by some demolished storage tanks. They'll be there at noon."

Shroeder swore softly to himself as he shoved the binoculars back into their case. "What the hell has got into Naguchi?" he wondered. "The man isn't scared. He has the same contempt for those who fear death, as the enemy he has been fighting." But so far on this mission, Shroeder had sensed an unusual hesitancy on Naguchi's part, which made him feel jumpy. "Had the interpreter learned something from the scientists which Mulholland had forbidden him to talk about?" Shroeder tried to shrug away the worrying thought. "Mulholland's so damm devious." He remembered the major's cynical comment about the Russians being America's allies. "Only a bastard like him could have worked out a deal like this," he told himself bitterly. Now the so-called allies were being treated like the enemy, whilst those slimy Jap scientists were being smuggled to safety. Meanwhile, the lives of those guys, on that ship, depended on himself and some Russian friends, who were expected to double-cross their own countrymen. "Is there some godammed special place," he wondered, "where guys are bred with minds like Mulholland's?"

Dead-Eye was lying comfortably on his back. Dum-Dum toyed lovingly with the breach of the weapon he carried. The small group of Russians were squatting in the shelter of the knoll, waiting for Schroeder's decision.

"O.K!" he said finally, "We'll do as Petrokov suggests, and try to hitch a lift."

Petrokov nodded approvingly. "There will be no trouble," he announced. "I will do the explaining."

Schroeder shook his head. "I'd be happier," he said, "If Captain Yukovlev did the talking. Remember, we are supposed to be a medical mission."

Yukovlev nodded slowly in agreement. "Very well," he said. "There will be no talking from anyone else, unless it is unavoidable."

Tatiana Chokovska marched briskly to Schroeder. "I," she said, "Will make the driver stop."

Schroeder was surprised to find himself grinning. "What the hell," he replied. "It always works better in the States if you can get a dame to do it!"

They stood discreetly by the edge of the road until a large truck appeared. Whilst it was still in the far distance, Tatiana tugged at her tunic and straightened her cap, before stepping onto the road into the path of the heavy vehicle. Her set features and upraised hand remained unchanged.

"Not exactly a sex-trap!" reflected Schroeder.

The moon-faced driver, who was accompanied in his cabin by a gap-toothed guard, dropped the window with an ingratiating grin. It disappeared promptly, when she spoke sharply to the two men, demanding to see their papers. Stefan Gregoravitch was now by her side, whilst Dead-Eye and Dum-Dum provided a daunting back-up.

The driver, now looking anxious, talked rapidly, whilst producing his papers. He was "from a Service Regiment" he told them. "On the way to Mukden to pick up supplies."

She returned the man's papers with a flourish, and then demanded to see the surly guard's. The harassed driver's eyes opened even wider, when she stepped back to indicate the group of officers, who were standing quietly near the rear of the truck.

Schroeder touched Yukovlev lightly on the elbow. "Mebbe it's time for us to help out," he whispered.

Yukovlev nodded, so together, they strolled towards Tatiana. She was haranguing the driver, whose ruddy cheeks were now almost drained of colour. He was shaking his head vigorously. "Pingfan, niet! niet!" The others could hear him repeating the words in a voice which had the urgency of terror.

Tatiana turned to salute as the officers approached. The driver's voice tapered away to silence. Yukovlev looked at him thoughtfully for a moment, then with one finger indicated that he should get out of the cab.

As the man stood to attention, Yukovlev, in a quiet voice, patiently explained.

"I am a doctor," he said. "I and my medical team have work to do at Pingfan. It is your duty to get us there."

For a moment, Schroeder thought the terrified soldier was about to burst into tears. Then, in amazement, he realised that the torrent of words was explaining a dreadful and totally unanticipated situation. "People in the Pingfan area are dying of the plague. The whole place is in quarantine. The army is under orders to allow no one in or out." The man suddenly stopped talking. He looked confused. His expression was saying quite clearly that surely the doctor must have known about that. He shot a furtive glance at the guard, who was now by his side. The guard made an involuntary gesture with his rifle, then froze when he heard a click from Dum-Dum's pistol.

The doctor quickly collected himself. He forced a note of outrage into his voice. "You fool!" he snarled. "That is why we are needed. Take us to the nearest outpost immediately."

Petrokov's jovial laugh relieved the tension. Schroeder and Yukovlev turned their heads as he sauntered towards them.

"Some interesting things you have in the back." His cheerful voice held not a vestige of threat, but the driver and his companion appeared suddenly to quail. "Japanese cigarettes, saki, bags of rice, winter clothing." Petrokev's smile remained unchanged, but his voice had hardened dangerously. "Black-marketing is a very serious offence," he continued.

Yukovlev broke in as the quivering driver seemed to hesitate as though considering the doleful option of death for black-marketing or death from bubonic plague.

"I am requisitioning this lorry," the doctor said impatiently. "We have wasted too much time. You will take us to Pingfan."

With a sickly smile, the sweating driver gave a fumbling salute, before turning to open the door of the heavy truck. As the Russian guard made to enter the opposite side, a tap on his shoulder made him turn his head. Dum-Dum's ugly face confronted him and Dum-Dum's thumb indicated that he should sit in the back of the truck with the others. The disguised American clambered aboard, to squeeze on to the bench seat alongside the driver. Leaning out, Dum-Dum then stretched out a hand to assist the doctor into the cab, where he could sit next to the window.

The authority of Tatiana's upraised hand was sufficient to halt the few vehicles that came along as the driver laboriously turned the truck in the road to retrace a part of his route.

The turn-off to Pingfan was only two or three kilometres further north. As they approached it, rough wooden boards appeared on the roadside, showing black crosses and crudely painted death's heads. Lettering in both Russian and Chinese forbade entry into the plague zone.

As he slowed to make the left-hand turn, the driver's podgy cheeks were glistening. There was a surprising absence of guard-posts as the reluctant man lumbered his heavy vehicle along the narrow road.

Schroeder had rolled up the stiff flap at the rear of the truck so that he could see across the deserted landscape. Nothing appeared to be moving. Perhaps the threat of this vilest of deaths was in itself a sufficient deterrent. There was not a sign of human life, yet something in the air was causing his skin to prickle. He sniffed, aware only of the reek of hot diesel fumes. Then, suddenly, he understood. As the occasional scurrying breeze swept away the oily smoke, it carried with it the cloying smell, which when recalled, could still make his stomach heave.

It was after the fighting on the island of Luzon, when the Japs had been thrown back, after their final attempt to take the airfield. They had fled, leaving behind them hundreds of unburied dead. For days the American had been forced to breathe the odorous miasma from the rotting human bodies. It had hung around them wherever they were. It rose in bubbles from the swampy soil. It was trapped in the fleshy leaves and hollow oozing stalks of the decaying vegetation. It clung to their clothes and blankets. They tasted it in the food and in the water they drank. For a long time afterwards, Schroeder had been aware of it in his uniform, even after several launderings. He imagined it had crept into his skin. He became obsessed with hot showers. His shoulders and chest developed sore patches where he constantly scrubbed them.

Now as he knelt to look over the tail-board at a flock of fluttering carrion crows, his nostrils twitched involuntarily. It was unmistakable. Death was in the air as they approached Pingfan.

"Hey, would ya just look at that!"

He was startled from his morbid train of thought by Dead-Eye's voice.

He was pointing towards a large dog which had bounded into view from a slight dip in the ground, about twenty paces from the edge of the road. It was followed by two others. They ran for a short distance, then paused to lick their chops as they stared after the lorry.

Schroeder pounded on the back of the cab. "Hold it for a minute," he shouted. "I want to check something out."

As the truck slowly came to a halt, he started to climb over the tail-board. Dead-Eye pulled him back. "Hold it, lootenant. Let me go. You ain't looking too good."

A few moments later he returned. His leathery face was grim. He banged on the cab for the driver to start as he slowly settled back into his corner. His single eye blazed fiercely, whilst he groped into a pocket for a cigarette.

Schroeder and the others were watching him. "I guess I was right, then." Schroeder's voice sounded harsh.

Dead-Eye nodded briefly. "Sure," he said, as he dragged on the cigarette. "It was a dame. She'd had a kid with her."

Tatiana clutched Schroeder's sleeve. "Wild dogs," she muttered. "They hunt together. There are many of them here."

It was but few minutes later when they encountered the first army road-block. A rough wooden barrier halted their progress. At each end stood an armed sentry. Their faces were partially obscured by white cotton masks of a type much favoured by the Japanese. One of them pulled down his mask. He approached the driver to question him about his documents. The other man ambled over to where Yukovlev sat silently with an arm resting idly on the sill of the door. Upon seeing his rank, the guard's attitude changed. He saluted briskly and politely asked Yukovlev the reason for their being in the area.

"This is it," thought Schroeder, listening anxiously in the back of the truck. "Will Yukovlev be able to bluff it out?"

He next heard the click of the cab's door latch, as Yukovlev opened it, then a stifled gasp as the doctor stepped painfully down to face the guard.

Schroeder realised that he was sweating slightly as he strained his ears to catch what Yukovlev was saying. He was demanding to see the N.C.O. in charge of the guard. By squinting through some lace-holes in the side covers of the lorry, Schroeder discovered that he could see what was happening.

The guard appeared to be arguing. Then, as Schroeder heard Yukovlev's quiet voice being slightly raised, the truculent soldier trotted off towards a nearby wooden hut. Schroeder observed grimly that the door and wooden shutters were tightly closed.

There was a chuckle from Dead-Eye, who was using his single eye to good effect peering out of the opposite side.

"I don't think this sonofabitch knows how to read." He was watching the beetle browed Russian soldier as he thumbed stolidly through the driver's papers, scrutinising each one carefully, before placing it at the bottom of the pile.

"I guess these guys must be the assholes of the Russian Army, to be posted to a dump like this." Dead Eye's rough voice sounded disgusted. "Sweet mother, just take a look at it! and the smell of the godammed place!"

Schroeder looked. By moving around in the back of the lorry, he could see that on each side of the guard post triple coils of barbed wire extended across the barren soil as far as his limited vision could see. The woman and her child must, somehow, have got through. "Was it the plague, or the wild dogs that had finished them off?"

Schroeder suddenly made a decision. "Come on you guys," he said. "Drop that tailboard. We're getting out."

He had heard the slam of the guardroom door and knew that a search of the lorry was inevitable. As they dropped to the ground, they made a formidable group. Schroeder warned them, however, to behave as if they were relaxing after a long trip. Accompanied by Petrokov, he strolled over to join Yukovlev. The doctor was showing his documents to a bleary-eyed sergeant, who had emerged from the hut. Yukovlev's bowed shoulders straightened somewhat as the other two officers joined him. He introduced them to the sergeant, who seemed afraid to remove his thick cotton mask. The N.C.O. saluted, then asked, in a muffled voice, to see their papers.

Schroeder sighed with relief as the man handed them back after a perfunctory glance.

"I was explaining to the sergeant," Yukovlev said, "that we are a medical team, sent here by the army to help those who are sick."

"That is very true," Petrokov added. "We are also carrying a few small comforts for those most in need."

Dum-Dum, still sitting inside the cab, dug a little harder with his partly concealed pistol, as the driver made an indignant move. The guard commander's shifty eyes showed sudden interest. He walked unsteadily to the back of the truck, where he rested his hands on the dropped tail-gate, whilst he took a good look at the carefully arranged rows of crates and sacks which took up half of the space.

Dead-Eye was smiling pleasantly as he stood beside the truck driver's ugly comrade, who had an expression of hatred on his face.

"Of course," Petrokov's smooth voice was saying, "these comforts are also for the brave men who protect the unfortunate ones who must stay here."

A few minutes later, the two Russian guards were pulling away the barrier. Tatiana, who had been stooping near the guard-room to tie a shoelace, moved hurriedly to climb aboard as the engine was violently started. The sergeant waved them through with gusto. His eyes were directed obliquely on the two cases of saki and a large crate of cigarettes by his side.

"Stroke of luck, that," grinned Schroeder to the others, as the truck ground slowly on its way. "Having those things aboard, sure was a big help."

Ignoring the black looks of the lorry's former guard, he continued swiftly, in a more serious voice. "We've gotta hope that he doesn't decide to check up and phone through to his garrison headquarters."

Tatiana interrupted suddenly, "The telephone line," she said. "It is broken."

"How the hell do you know that?" Schroeder looked puzzled as he asked her the question.

She shrugged and raised her eyebrows. "It was from the guard's room, under the ground." She produced a large clasp knife from her pocket. "It was broken when I tied my shoe."

There was a roar of laughter from Dead-eye, who tried to give her an appreciative hug.

"If that doesn't beat everything," he wheezed as he recovered from the jolt delivered by her elbow.

Schroeder's mind was busy revolving round the scraps of information they had picked up at the road block. There was, it seemed, some kind of temporary hospital, which had been set up for the plague victims. The frightened sergeant had told Yukovlev that when the Japs had destroyed the Pingfan buildings, they had released thousands of plague-carrying rats into the surrounding countryside. The peasants who had lived nearby were being infected and were dying in large numbers. No one was allowed to leave the area. In addition to the manned road-blocks, the wire fence was constantly patrolled by guards in scout cars.

The American looked over the tail-board at the eerie desolation of the landscape. Brooding clouds hung heavily over the colourless scene. He looked with revulsion at the shadowy shapes of the dogs, who flitted from time to time between distant hummocks, half-concealed by the contours of the ground. The bile rising in his throat, made him gag as the smell of putrefaction again assailed his senses. It was becoming stronger. He leant over the rear of the truck to see better as he tried to discover the reason.

Some way ahead of them, he could now see, there was a large area, where patches, coloured a deeper brown, were scattered in irregular clusters on the mottled earth. Petrokov had joined him. They clung to the tailgate, straining their eyes to see through the dust.

"That, my friend," said the Russian in a grave voice, "is a tented army hospital. It is a very large one. There must be many sick people."

There were more barriers they had to pass through, but the worried-looking guards barely glanced at their papers, which had been stamped at their first stop.

"Seems to me, they're more concerned with keeping people in," Schroeder muttered as the heavy truck rumbled on its way.

Petrokov's normally ruddy cheeks were pale as he looked at their sombre surroundings. "All this," he said, indicating the acres of dun-coloured tents and marquees, "It was not here before,"

Sitting in the cab, by the passengers' window, Yukovlev pointed out a patch of packed earth to the driver.

"Park over there," he ordered.

With a hang-dog expression the driver turned the truck off the road, where it bounced across a stretch of uneven ground before he brought it to a halt alongside two dirty, open-topped lorries.

"For the love of God, move it further away." With his face contorted with horror, Schroeder clambered down onto the ground. He rushed ahead to bang on the driver's door. The stench from the two parked lorries was overwhelming. From where he had been standing, Schroeder had been able to see what they were used for. Their uncovered decks were discoloured with dark patches. Remnants of filthy clothes clung raggedly to smears of dried pus and excrement and trailed over the hanging tailboards. With a hand held firmly over his mouth and nose, Schroeder waved frantically at the alarmed driver.

159

Urged on now, by Yukovlev, who had realised the situation, the man ground the gears into action. The gasping Schroeder stumbled after the vehicle, aware that buzzing behind him were myriads of bloated blow-flies. He clung to the sill of the passenger door as the truck came to a halt again. Yukovlev's burning eyes looked down at him. "It would seem," he gasped in a deep troubled voice, "that we are nearing our destination."

Tatiana grudgingly took Dead Eye's proffered hand as she and the others leapt down from the back of the truck. She tugged at her tunic as she gazed with disgust at their surroundings.

The largest tents had been arranged in several uneven rows. Many of them sagged, their canvas walls flapping forlornly where untended guy ropes had lost their tension. The trodden earth between them looked scuffed and treacherous, with patches of mildew in shaded places, where sunlight never reached.

"At least it looks like they've got some chow here." Dead-Eye gazed hungrily at a roofless enclosure some distance away, where smoke curled from the tin chimneys of a row of field stoves.

"Holy cow! How can you think of eating in a dump like this?" Dum-Dum's wary eyes narrowed as a blanket-clad figure stumbled towards some canvas screens which concealed the unroofed latrines.

Schroeder was conferring with Naguchi and the Russian officers. They were puzzled by the lack of interest in their arrival. "Remember that we are in a quarantined plague area," Yukovlev muttered. "Visitors will not be expected."

Schroeder looked anxiously at his watch. "How far are we from the main place,?" he asked. "Where the bastards worked, those who started all this."

"About two kilometres," Petrokov explained. "This is where the village was. Look, some of the houses still remain."

Schroeder looked about him, feeling helpless. As he stood considering, he became aware of other sounds. They were muted, distant. muffled by the heavy thicknesses of canvas, but they held an indescribable melancholy. The wails of children, pain, grief, unbearable sorrow. The lamentations of a host of frightened people, whose only crime had been to live near Pingfan.

"Mebbe we'd better take a look around," he said reluctantly.

Naguchi nodded. "Yeah," he agreed. "Let's find out what's going on."

160

Schroeder looked at him sharply. The interpreter's voice had been almost a snarl.

"OK" Schroeder grunted. "Just you and me and Doctor Yukovlev. The rest of you stay with the truck."

"I shall come also." Tatiana's voice was determined.

"Say hold on babe. There's no point in sticking your neck out," protested Dead-eye.

Tatiana showed her teeth in a scornful smile. "Mind your own godammed business," she replied.

Dead-Eye's face creased into a huge grin. "Well if that don't beat all!" he roared. "Don't forget," he called after her, "I still got my eye on you!"

They skirted the first of the larger tents, making their way carefully through a confusion of guy ropes. The mushroomed heads of angled tent pegs leaned dangerously out of the slippery earth.

"They must have sprayed the soil with disinfectant," Yukovlev observed. Schroeder nodded dumbly. He took a handkerchief out of his pocket to hold over his face as they approached the open flaps of a second tent. It was the size of a large marquee.

Yulovlev held up a cautionary hand as he stopped to look inside. The other three, in various stages of increasing nausea, held their breath or covered their nostrils as they followed him into the gloomy interior. The sickly stench enveloped them with the claustrophobic intimacy of a shroud. Schroeder discovered that, despite the semi-darkness, his eyes were refusing to open fully. From time to time, he realised they had closed completely as if to shut out the horror of the scene around him.

There was a piteous moaning from many of the semi-naked figures sprawled in ungainly postures on stained straw mattresses. Some of them were alone, making hideous choking noises as if pleading for help which would never come. There were others in the centre of small family groups who wailed and pleaded as the small party stepped carefully amongst them.

Tatiana stared at the scenes with a look of disbelief in her eyes as she covered her mouth and nose with one hand.

Schroeder looked down in alarm as he felt a hand clutching at his booted ankle. His eyes met those of a woman, who held out her arms in a despairing gesture. She was showing him the naked shape of a young girl, by whom she was crouching. The slim adolescent body was pitted with pus-encrusted ulcers which stretched from her belly to her small, pathetic breasts. Her face was grotesquely distorted by bulbous swellings. Blood and pus seeped through ragged dressings tied roughly round weeping abscesses in groin and armpits. The child was still breathing. A white rime clung to her dark eyelashes where undried tears still trembled.

Schroeder felt suddenly weak with shock and pity. Ignoring the filth around him, he dropped to his knees. There was an unaccustomed prickling behind his eyes. He looked helplessly at the woman's grief ravaged face. "I'm sorry," he said, "but there is nothing I can do." The woman seemed to understand. She dropped her head and wrapped her arms around her chest, whilst her body shook with sobs.

He felt a tap on his shoulder. Yukovlev was standing behind him, grimly shaking his head. Schroeder rose to his feet as the doctor moved past him to bend over the girl. He had in his hand a pack of morphine syrettes. He removed one, then gently slipping the needle into the girl's arm, he squeezed the tube. He took another and injected that also. Returning the pack to his pocket, he rose to his feet, to stand beside Schroeder. "She will know no more pain," he told the weeping woman.

The American turned away to stumble wildly into the open air. He was breathing hard. His fingers were shaking as he pulled a cigarette out of a pocket. "The bastards!" He choked as he fumbled with a match. "The bastards who did this! I'll kill every mother lovin' sonofabitch I can lay my hands on!"

The others joined him, looking pale and shaken – except Yukovlev, who was wiping his hands on a handkerchief.

"Be careful," he said to the raging American. "Sentiment can be very dangerous. It can make you take unnecessary risks. Remember," he went on, "why you came here. It was in those laboratories that this devilish work was planned. If you do not discover the names of those prisoners, this could happen in your own country, and in Great Britain or Australia, at any time, in any place."

Schroeder nodded. He ground out the cigarette with the heel of his boot. "Thanks," he said shortly. "I'll remember that." He hesitated before turning away. He pushed back his cap, looking embarrassed. "Thanks for helping that kid. It's lucky you had the stuff with you."

Yukovlev's tight lips had an ironic twist. "Sometimes I use it myself," he replied.

Schroeder's face turned crimson. "Godammit!" he cursed his own lack of tact. "Why can't I keep my godammed mouth shut?" He bumped clumsily into someone who had rounded the corner of another tent. They both halted to look stupidly at each other. The man, Schroeder saw, was a Japanese soldier. The American's hand moved swiftly to the automatic weapon slung over his shoulder, but, before he could unhitch it there was a click from behind him.

"Don't move!" The simple order rapped in Japanese, held the threat of sudden death. Schroeder instinctively froze, but the Japanese soldier almost fainted with terror.

The American relaxed with a sigh of relief, as he realised the voice was Naguchi's.

"OK Sergeant," he gasped to the interpreter. "This guy can't do us much harm. He's got no weapons."

Naguchi reluctantly lowered his machine pistol.

Schroeder looked curiously at the cowering Jap soldier. His unbuttoned tunic was filthy. His breeches, with their tightly-wrapped puttees, were caked with layers of dried slime.

"I guess he's one of the Jap P.O.Ws." Schroeder's voice was thick with menace. "Ask him what he's doing here."

Naguchi rapped out the question in a bullying voice.

The frightened man immediately replied with a guttural volley of explosive words, whilst describing with his hands how his duties involved the removal of the dead from the tents.

Naguchi looked stonily at Schroeder as he gave the lieutenant a rough translation.

"I guess you got the message. He is a prisoner. He helps out around here."

Schroeder was losing patience. "Helps who - godammit? Who the hell's in charge for Chrissake?"

The interpreter's face was impassive as he answered. "He's already told me. The doctor in charge is Japanese. The place is being run by P.O.Ws."

Yukovlev interrupted with a grim chuckle. "I should have guessed," he said. "My people sometimes have a simple sense of

163

justice.

Schroeder sounded worried as he looked at his three companions. "Mebbe we should just get the hell out of here and leave them to it."

Naguchi nodded. "Those two guys of ours will be expecting me in about an hour. You still have to get into the place and find those papers. There's a hell of a lot to be done, before the plane comes back to pick us up." He brushed away the hordes of flies with a quick nervous gesture, whilst waiting for Schroeder's reply.

"I would first like to see this Japanese doctor." Addressing Naguchi, Yukovlev pointed at the miserable looking prisoner. "Please tell him to show us the way."

"We'll have to be quick," Schroeder told the Russian as they followed the beckoning Jap. "What is it you're wanting to know?"

"My fellow-countrymen will be guarding the laboratories," Yukovlev commented drily. "Perhaps this doctor will tell us something about them."

Their guide had stopped outside a small dilapidated tent. Its mildewed roof sagged dismally. The canvas walls leaned at drunken angles. Inside was a desk, a camp-bed and some up-turned boxes. The figure of a man was sprawled across the desk with his balding head resting between outspread arms. He rose unsteadily to his feet in slow frightened movements, as the small group, wearing Russian uniforms, entered the tent.

"Why are you sleeping?" Yukovlev's quiet voice was almost gentle.

As the terrified man hesitated, Schroeder stepped forward, his hand on the butt of his pistol. The man's unshaven face crumpled with fear. He bowed repeatedly from the waist as he answered, keeping his eyes directed at the ground.

Naguchi listened intently to the jabbered staccato sentences. The Japanese doctor's stream of words was slowed from time to time as he sucked in flecks of spittle which formed at the corners of his mouth. When he had finished speaking he looked at them furtively from under his downcast eyelids.

"Well, what the hell was he saying?" demanded Schroeder.

"He was asking for mercy. He thinks we've come to shoot him." There was a tight controlled smile on Naguchi's face as he looked at Schroeder. "He says he is sorry the patients are dying, but he has no medicines for them."

Schroeder looked baffled. "Well mebbe he isn't the best doctor in the world, but why the hell does he expect to be shot?"

"He says the Russians call in once in a while."

"Yeah, go on," urged Schroeder, as Naguchi hesitated.

"He says if more than fifty people have died since their last visit, they shoot the doctor." The interpreter's voice remained cold, his smile had disappeared. "He's trying to explain that he doesn't think they've quite reached fifty yet. It seems the Russians kept their word with some others before him."

"Well I'll be godammed!" Schroeder stared at Yukovlev. "What the hell do you make of that?"

Yukovlev's reply was business-like. "It means," he said, "That, so far, we are the only Russians here, therefore, it should be safe to continue on our journey."

Tatiana was looking bewildered as she listened to the interchange. "Then sometime this doctor will be killed?" she asked.

"I guess it looks that way," was Schroeder's laconic response. He made for the door of the tent. "Come on, Let's get moving." He turned and spoke to Naguchi. "Tell that bastard we'll be back later. Just to keep him quiet," he added as they left.

Tatiana shook her head. "This is a place of hell," she said in a troubled voice.

Schroeder overheard her. "I guess you mean a helluva place," he rasped. "You couldn't be more right."

The rest of the party they had left with the truck were getting uneasy by the time they returned to join them.

"O.K! Climb aboard," Schoeder ordered. He looked around for the Russian driver and guard.

"What the hell happened to 'em?" he demanded. Schroeder sniffed as he moved closer to the back of the truck. The unmistakable smell of strong alcohol drifted from its gloomy interior. He swung round with a threatening stare to gaze at Dum-Dum and Dead Eye. "Say, have you guys been drinkin'?"

They both looked indignant. It was Dead Eye who explained.

"Nope, we ain't been drinkin' lootenant," he said in a hurt tone of voice. "But we thought it might be a good way of keeping the

165

Russkis quiet."

"It's their godammed saki anyway," added Dum-Dum magnanimously.

Schroeder suppressed a grin when he saw the snoring figures reclining untidily on the floor-boards.

"We even made sure they drank it." Dum-Dum was stubbing out a cigarette as he spoke. "A whole godammed bottleful right down their gullets."

"Nice goin'," Schroeder answered briefly. He clambered up into the back of the truck to seize one of the unconscious men under the arms. "Let's get 'em out of here."

The others reached up to lower the prostrate forms to the ground. "Stick 'em in that old hut over there."

For good measure, the Americans used the mens' belts to fasten their arms after dumping them in the scant shelter of the deserted dwelling. "That should keep 'em quiet for a while," said Dead Eye with satisfaction.

Dum-Dum's expression was grim. "Till we're back on that godammed plane, I hope." He patted the bound men on the head as they heard Schroeder's voice calling them to hurry.

"You drive," he shouted to Dum-Dum. "Stop over by that kitchen on the way out."

With Yukovlev in the window seat, the others jumped hastily into the back as Dum-Dum gunned the engine. He swerved the heavy truck onto the dirt track, to halt in a cloud of dust by the battered looking field stoves. A few Chinese cooks ran out from beneath a rough canvas shelter, their mouths open wide with their shouts of alarm.

"OK! Dump the godamm lot." Schroeder was already dragging a sack of rice to the tail-gate. The rest of them joined in with frenetic haste. The astonished cooks watched with disbelief as cases of saki and cigarettes were dropped alongside the bulging rice bags, together with bales of winter clothing.

Petrokov held up a hand as Dead-Eye and Naguchi reached for the last two cases. "One of saki and one of cigarettes," he pointed out. "Perhaps we should keep them. They might be useful."

Schroeder nodded curtly. He leaped into the cab to squeeze between Dum-Dum and the doctor. "O.K!" he shouted, "Lets go."

166

He clung to the dashboard as the wheels spun viciously.

"Take it easy!" he jerked out breathlessly, as Dum-Dum's large feet hit the pedals again. Hearing Yukovlev vainly attempting to suppress a groan, Schroeder looked furiously at the determined driver and shouted: "Slow down for Chrissake!"

"That flea-bitten dump sure gave me the creeps." Dum-Dum's scowl relaxed as they reached the road. Its pot-holed surface still caused the lightly laden truck to bounce uncomfortably. The white faced doctor was fumbling inside his tunic. From an inner pocket he produced the pack of morphine syrettes. His hands were shaking as he pushed back a sleeve to expose his forearm.

"Schroeder suddenly tapped Dum-Dum's shoulder. "Head off over there," he yelled. His finger was pointing to the right, where the skeletal frames of some wooden buildings stood starkly against the skyline.

The driver grunted and turned the vehicle towards them. It lurched drunkenly over the hummocky ground, before coming to a halt. The remains of a fire blackened wall gave it partial concealment. Overhead some loose sheets of corrugated iron were hanging precariously from half-burned beams.

"Must have been some kind of barn. What a helluva stink." Dead Eye sniffed noisily as he descended from the back of the lorry.

Schroeder waited until Yukovlev had pushed the needle into a vein. The Russian tossed away the empty tube. He breathed deeply as he rested his head against the back of the cab.

As he jumped to the ground, Schroeder motioned urgently to the others who had gathered around. "Spread out and keep your eyes open," he told them. "Pass me the word if you see anyone."

As the party scattered, he called for Naguchi to join him. He took from his pocket the plan of Pingfan, which the interpreter had obtained for Mulholland.

"Seems to me," said Schoeder, "that from hereon anything might happen. The Russians are staying clear of the village and the hospital, but security's certain to be tighter around the plant itself."

Naguchi nodded. "I guess so," he said hesitantly. "On the other hand, why the hell should they feel that it's necessary? Nobody's goin' to come within miles of here, unless they have to."

Schroeder looked grim. "Sure," he said. "There's nothing like a plague for scarin' people off, but they wouldn't leave it unguarded.

Anyway," he continued sharply, "You had the word from your two friends that the Russkis were really goin' to town in the godammed place."

Naguchi gave a helpless shrug. "That's right," he agreed. "But what they learned was mostly from rumours among the P.O.W. labour-gangs. The Russians spent a lot of time questioning everybody. They'd sure give a lot to get their hands on those scientists." The interpreter's thin lips curled back in a cynical smile.

Schroeder shot him a questioning glance. "Didn't they say anything about the outbreak of plague?"

Naguchi hesitated. "Well, some," he answered, "but not a lot. I thought maybe it was just the P.O.Ws who'd got it, from working inside the joint."

Schroeder's voice expressed disbelief. "That sounds like a loada crap," he retorted. "I reckon you must have known all along what the conditions were like here."

Naguchi's face was the colour of old ivory, his voice cold and distant. "They were transmitting in morse," he answered. "They had only a very short time on the air. Most of it was in code which only Mulholland could decipher."

Schroeder kicked out at a scorched piece of wood which lay near his foot. "That sonofabitch Mulholland!" he exploded. He slapped the smaller man on the shoulder. "Sorry!" he said. "I should have guessed."

The interpreter relaxed. Taking out a cigarette, he offered the pack to Schroeder, whose attention turned once more to the map. "We'd better take another look at that piece of paper."

Naguchi shook his head, after glancing at it briefly.

"It's just a ground plan of one of the main buildings," he pointed out. "Mebbe it'll help you guys if you can get inside, but it's no damn use to me."

Delving into a pocket of his tunic, he pulled out an aerial photograph. He pointed to the demolished storage tanks near an outside wall. "This is where I have to meet up with our men." He glanced anxiously at his watch. "In half an hour, for Chrissake!"

Schroeder pulled of his cap to scratch his sweaty scalp. His eyes searched swiftly to check that the others were still at their posts.

"Listen!" he said to Naguchi. "Now's a good time to split, the

168

way we agreed. You, Petrokov and Dum-Dum can make for the place where our guys should be waiting. Keep under cover as much as possible. If anyone spots you, let Petrokov do the talking. Remember you are all in the glorious Red Army." Schroeder gestured impatiently as Naguchi was about to speak. "The rest of us will make our way in the truck, and hope that Yukovlev can think of some kinda story. When you've found those two guys," he added, "keep your heads down and stay outa sight 'til we come and join you." He paused to look at his watch. "We'll be aiming to reach you not later that 16.00hrs. If we don't make it by then, you get the hell outa there, and make for the landing place the best way you can. That's an order." he said with finality.

There was a sudden cry from Dum-Dum. His craggy features were a coppery green hue.

"Jesus Christ!" he shouted. A pointing finger was shaking as it indicated several scurrying black shapes. There was a sudden rustle from a heap of rotting straw, near which he had been kneeling as some more leapt out to follow the others across the rubbish-strewn floor.

The shocked faces of the raiding party saw the horrified Dum-Dum beating savagely at his gaitered legs. "Rats," he was shouting. "The godammed place is crawling with 'em. Look at the bastards."

Schroeder felt suddenly cold. "Cut that out!" he shouted. He strode over to the wildly cursing man. "Quit that." he ordered in a more normal voice. Schroeder's gaze was darting around the earthen floor. As he was looking, a shriek from Tatiana spun him on his heels. She was gazing with wide eyes at heap of mouldering sacks. Schroeder briefly glimpsed the pink-edged claws before they disappeared. There were squirming undulations between the layers of rotting hessian.

In frozen silence, those watching clearly heard the slithering of small bodies as they landed amongst mounds of charred grain.

It was Petrokov's robust voice which broke the spell.

"This is not a good place to stay," he said. "We should leave it as quickly as possible.

Schroeder tried to ignore the icy needles which were prickling beneath his heated skin. He heard himself gulp noisily before he replied. "Sure," he gasped, "Let's get goin'."

The small group looked furtively at each other, whilst they made hasty preparations to leave. Each was afraid to voice his

169

thoughts as they imagined the legions of plague-infected fleas being carried by the hordes of fat-tailed rodents.

Naguchi checked the magazine in his automatic, before sliding the gun back into its holster. Petrokov and Dum-Dum waited impatiently near the rear of the lorry. Dum-Dum was licking lips that had gone suddenly dry as he nervously scanned the filth encrusted ground. "Come on, let's get outa here." he called to Naguchi.

Schroeder nodded. He turned to Naguchi and his two companions. "OK" he said. "Beat it you guys. And good luck."

The interpreter gave Schroeder a quick side-ways look. It seemed that he was about to say something, but then changed his mind. "So long. See you later." He stopped to look over his shoulder as Schroeder called after him

"Remember the Verey pistol! It's hidden under some rocks, near where we were hiding."

Naguchi signalled his understanding of Schroeder's message with a nod and a grim smile. The next moment, bent almost double to prevent their profiles being observed against the skyline, the trio were moving swiftly across the broken ground.

Schroeder went over to the cab, where Yukovlev had remained in his seat. "How are you feeling now?" he asked the white-faced man. The Russian made no reply, but after a few moments he slowly opened his eyes. He looked amused at Schroeder's expression of relief.

"As you see, I am still alive," he answered. He pulled from a pocket a small metal flask. His fingers fumbled stiffly with the screw cap before he raised it to his lips. The familiar smell of cognac reached Schroeder's nostrils. The doctor offered him the flask, but the American shook his head.

"Come, then, my friend. We have work to do."

Schroeder marvelled at the change for the better as Yukovlev returned the flask to his pocket. How long would it last he wondered? Shrugging off his doubts, he called to the others.

Dead Eye, with Tatiana and her limpet-like escort came over to join them. "We'll be making our way towards the main buildings," he told them. "We're sure to encounter some guards. Captain Yukovlev will explain that he's here to confirm some observations from his earlier mission."

170

"Do you think the Russians will buy that, lootenant?" Dead Eye's jaws were working rhythmically on some gum as he asked the question.

Schroeder sighed despairingly, "In your case," he told the earnest-looking soldier, "They'd have to be crazy to believe that you are anything remotely medical."

He looked towards the cab as Yukovlev's voice interrupted. "All our vehicles carry a guard," he reminded them.

Schroeder scowled at Dead Eye. "Then throw that godammed gum away," he ordered. He reached for the driver's door. "OK Let's go," he said with a swift glance round at the others. As he climbed into the cab, another figure followed closely behind. He found that he was being dislodged from behind the wheel, as Tatiana gave him a push and signalled him to move along.

"An officer does not drive a four-ton truck," she explained in a firm voice.

Wedged between the two Russians, Schroeder was aware of his quickening heart beat as the engine burst into life. When the truck drew away from the crumbling barn, he had the feeling that hundreds of tiny eyes, blinking with sinister malevolence, were hungrily watching their departure from among the thick swirls of brown dust.

Under Tatiana's firm guidance, the large vehicle jolted steadily towards the narrow strip of concrete road. She slowed down and expertly changed gear as the tyres met the smoother surface.

"There it is, the gateway to hell!" Yukovlev's breathing was laboured. He was staring directly ahead through the windscreen, as the lorry reached the top of a small rise.

Schroeder was staggered by the immense scale of the complex; and also by the destruction which had been carried out.

"You sure weren't kidding," he breathed, "When you told me the Japs had knocked out the whole godammed place."

The Russian's expression was ugly with hate.

"They wished to leave no trace of their devil's work," he snarled. "I will not allow myself to die," he went on with terrible emphasis, "Until I know that justice has been done."

Schroeder was shaken by the chilling ferocity in the voice of the quietly spoken man.

171

"There are soldiers following behind us." Tatiana's urgent words intruded into Schroeder's guilty recollection of Mulholland's duplicity.

Almost as Tatiana finished speaking, they were overtaken by a jeep-like vehicle which carried four armed men. Its klaxon blared repeatedly as it pulled ahead of them before swerving to a halt by the edge of the road. Its occupants climbed hurriedly out. They advanced towards the stationary truck, with rifles held threateningly at the ready.

Dead-Eye, his single eye fixed firmly against a chink in the cover at the back, spat contemptuously as he recognised their weapons. "Godamm Jap army pea-shooters!" he exclaimed to his young companion.

Stefan Gregoravitch patted his own heavy weapon and grinned with anticipation as the four soldiers drew close enough for the two of them to recognise the Japanese style of headgear.

One of the soldiers hammered with his rifle butt on the door of the cab, and motioned for Tatiana to step down.

Tatiana glanced at Schroeder, who nodded. "Go ahead," he whispered. "I'll follow."

Yukovlev grasped his arm before he could do so. "Those men," the Russian said quickly, "Are Korean. The Japanese used many of them for police work and as guards. They must have been kept on. Take care. They can be dangerous."

"Thanks," muttered the American. He followed Tatiana with deliberate slowness, so that he could take a good look at the guards. Apart from their distinctive green caps with the yellow star insignia, their uniforms consisted of green, one-piece overalls, tightly fastened at the cuffs and ankles. Over the lower part of their faces they wore the inevitable surgical mask.

Their leader was heavily built, with piggy eyes, which glittered aggressively above his mask. He shouted in a bullying voice for Yukovlev to join the other two. The Russian doctor slowly opened the door to lower himself carefully out of the cab. His voice was cold as he addressed the oafish leader.

"Who are you?" he demanded. "And why do you stop a vehicle with two Russian officers?"

The man looked suspicious as he examined Yukovlev's papers. He explained in a surly voice that he and his men were responsible

172

for checking all movements of people within the wired-off area.

His explanation was partly drowned by shouts of coarse laughter from two of the other Koreans. One of them was attempting to hold Tatiana's wrists, the other was taking his time in fumbling with the breast pockets of her tunic. He shot back with a shout of rage as her knee just missed his groin, but was followed by her shoe coming down heavily on his lightly shod foot.

Forgetting the fourth guard, who had a rifle pointed at his stomach, Schroeder made an instinctive movement towards the small group. His action was halted by a bellow from the leader, who directing a stream of obscenities at the pair of darkly cursing men, ordered them to search the back of the truck.

Schroeder was trying to identify the language he was using between the profanities. "Some kind of army jargon," he decided. "A bastardised mixture of Japanese and Russian".

At the rear of the truck, the two grumbling guards pulled back the heavy flaps, to stare goggle-eyed at Dead-Eye's short barrelled machine rifle and Stefan's formidable rifle.

The villainous-looking Dead-Eye shook his head slowly. He placed a finger against his lips with a sad patient smile. Then he motioned to the youthful Russian, who slipped silently over the tailgate to take the weapons from the gaping Koreans.

Whilst the fierce-eyed young Russian held the two men at gunpoint, Dead-Eye slid, with astonishing stealth along the side of the dirty vehicle.

As the brutish N.C.O. looked closely at his false papers, Schroeder feigned anger and impatience. Inwardly he was wondering what their chances would be if this man should attempt to arrest them. The Korean leafed noisily through the documents. He shot frequent glances at Schroeder's set face, whilst the remaining guard kept his rifle pointed menacingly at the disguised American.

As Schroeder's gaze shifted warily in the guard's direction, he saw a look of sudden surprise appear in the man's eyes. Then the Korean's body stiffened, as though a hard object had been pressed against his spine. With perfect timing he turned his head so that his jaw met the metal-clad butt of Dead-Eye's weapon.

As the startled leader watched the guard's knees buckle, Schroeder moved swiftly. His automatic was already pointing at the man's stomach, as with a guttural oath the N.C.O. reached for his pistol. The man's baleful eyes almost disappeared beneath mounds of

173

flesh as his features contorted with rage. He half crouched as though about to spring, until Dead-Eye moved forward threateningly.

"Nice going', take his pistol!" Schroeder panted.

The bulky Korean was breathing noisily through the thick gauze of his face mask as the hard-faced American reached forward to remove the weapon from its holster   The N.C.O's curling fingers swept downwards to forestall him, but Dead-Eye thrust forward with his own gun-barrel and smashed it against his opponent's chest.
With a howl of pain, the enraged man   staggered backwards. The watching Tatiana placed a foot neatly between his ankles.   His heavy body hit the ground head first with an audible thump. Tatiana and Dead-Eye exchanged approving glances when they saw that he was unconscious.

"What   about   the   rest?"   Schroeder   was   scanning   the surrounding landscape as he rapped out the question.

Dead-Eye, who was disarming the other prostrate guard, motioned with his thumb at the grinning young Gregoravitch, who had appeared from the rear of the truck. The two prisoners shuffled reluctantly ahead of his pointing rifle, to stare with sullen eyes at their groaning comrades.

"OK" said Schroeder. "Take their clothes off, then truss them up with their belts. Look in the jeep," he added, with a sudden afterthought.   "They might have been carrying handcuffs."

Yukovlev, who had been watching the proceedings anxiously whilst staying close to the front of the truck, looked questioningly at the American officer.

"Sorry Doc."   Schroeder was busy tugging the overalls off the beefy guard. "But now that we've got so far, I think this might be a good time to change our plans."

The Russian officer's eyes were unusually hard as he stared at Schroeder. "You plan to go in dressed as Korean guards?"

Schroeder ripped at the N.C.O's shirt for some material to make a gag, which he stuffed into the man's mouth as he began weakly to protest.

"Yes, that's the idea," he answered briefly. "It should make the job quicker."

"It is madness," Yukovlev protested. "You will be recognised."

"We'll have to take that chance." Schroeder pulled the guard's arms behind him, and snapped on a pair of handcuffs.

He stood up to face the angry doctor.

"Listen," he pleaded. "You've done as much as can be expected. From hereon you could pretend you never saw us, and start taking care of yourself." He looked earnestly at Yukovlev's waxen cheeks and burning eyes as he spoke.

The doctor fiercely returned his gaze. "I have promised myself," he said, "That I shall live until this task is finished." He drew a pain-filled breath as he pulled back his shoulders.

"Very well," he admitted. "Perhaps if I remain with you I shall be a hindrance."

"That isn't what I meant," answered Schroeder, flushing hotly. "But if you are still set on seeing it through, you could wait somewhere outside here 'till we get back."

He broke off, to call over to Dead-Eye and the two Russians, "Stick these guys into the back of the truck and change into their overalls. Go on. Move it!" he shouted as Tatiana hesitated.

Schroeder glanced quickly at his watch as he turned to face Yukovlev again. "We've got just three and a half hours before we meet up with Naguchi again." He lowered his voice, to sound more convincing. "Don't you see that dressed as guards we can mebbe slip in and out without arousing suspicion. If you have to persuade whoever is in charge, it could take up more time."

As the Russian doctor remained silent, the American pressed the point farther. "I was thinking," he continued, "That we could take the truck and the prisoners back there, where we just left." He indicated, with a thumb over his shoulder, the ruined farm buildings.

Yukovlev smiled grimly. "Your plan is that I stay with them? To protect them from the rats, perhaps?"

Schroeder looked at him, then gave a hopeless shrug. "Well, yes, that's about it I guess. But if you don't agree, it's got to be just you and I who go in. The others stay outside. The way I see it, that gives 'em more of a chance."

"And if I do agree?" The doctor's question had a caustic irony.

"Then, like I said, wait over there, 'til we get out. We'll pick you up on our way to meet Naguchi."

The doctor's smile was brief and bitter. "I had expected my role to be different," he answered.

175

As he slowly turned to move away, Schroeder grasped his arm.

"Believe me, sir. We could not have made it this far without your help. Besides," he went on, "I'd like to leave young Stefan in your care. There's no sense in risking his neck. He's just a kid."

The doctor's shoulders slumped as he replied in a heavy voice. "Very well. It shall be as you wish."

"Thanks," said Schroeder, sounding relieved. "One thing more," he added quickly. "If for any reason we don't make it, then use the truck to meet up with Naguchi at 16.00 hours. There are the remains of some storage tanks about half way along the northern wall. That's where he'll be."

Yukovlev looked up as though with a sudden recollection.

"Yes, I remember them," he said. "They were very large. I have often wondered what they had contained."

His words added further to Schroeder's increasing forebodings. Here, he felt, the greatest dangers were the ones they couldn't see. He fought back a growing sense of doom as he recalled the scenes in the hospital; the obscenely bloated rodents and the blood-sucking insects whose microscopic jaws passed on such hideous death.

Yukovlev had walked away with shoulders slumped.

A voice from behind made Schroeder jump.

"How about this lootenent?"

He whirled around, thankful for the interruption to his rioting imagination.

Dead-Eye was uneasily moving his shoulders beneath the tightly fitting overall. Behind him was Tatiana, almost unrecognisable in the similar unfamiliar garb. She looked hot and unusually flustered as she fastened the buttons up to her chin. The lieutenant gave an approving nod. He discovered he was trying not to smile at Tatiana's flushed cheeks.

"Has young Stefan changed yet?" he asked them.

Tatiana shook her head, avoiding Schroeder's eyes. "No," she said with an angry gesture. "This man," she flung a furious glance at the poker-faced soldier, "told him to wait until we had finished."

"OK I'll tell the youngster not to change. He won't be coming with us."

Ignoring Tatiana's start of surprise, he brushed past them to climb into the back of the lorry. "Hope you've left a change of clothes

176

for me," he grunted.

Then, as though remembering something, he suddenly turned to face Dead-Eye. "Say," he drawled, with an exaggerated note of approval, "I see you've got your eye back."

A smug smile spilled itself across the man's unlovely features. "That's right, lootenent. I won it back in a fair fight," he asserted.

Schroeder didn't wait to hear any more.

Whilst the four bound guards, now all fully recovered, squirmed and made choking sounds through their gags, he explained the change in their plans to a mutinous Stefan Gregoravitch.

"It's like this," he told the indignant young soldier. "Captain Yukovlev is a very sick man. He can't come with us, but we can't leave him alone."

Schroeder was dragging on the clumsy garment left for him as he spoke. "We'll be depending on you to look after him 'til we get back."

The hot-eyed youth looked slightly less hostile.

"But Sergeant Chokovska. You will take care of her?" he snapped.

"With my life." Schroeder promised solemnly. Somewhat to his own surprise, he realised that he meant it.

"The other American soldier? What about him? Sometimes he makes her angry."

"No use explaining about the course of true love," thought Schroeder, as he tried to suppress a smile. His voice was perfectly serious when he replied, "He, too, will promise to protect her."

There was a pause of several seconds whilst the young Stefan appeared to be thinking deeply.

"Very well," he grudgingly agreed. "I will stay with Captain Yukovlev. Until you come back with Sergeant Chokovska," he added firmly.

Schroeder slapped him on the shoulder. "Great stuff, kid," he added in American. With a sudden afterthought, he reverted back to Russian. "Can you drive a truck, by any chance?" he asked.

All lingering traces of resentment abruptly disappeared from the smooth young face.

"Yes, I can," he replied eagerly.

177

"Very well," Schroeder told him with heavy authority. "You will be responsible for this vehicle and the safety of the doctor."

He shook his head as he grinned inwardly.

"Nothing like putting a kid behind a wheel to make him happy," he was thinking.

A few minutes later, after several false starts, the truck lurched off the road, with a horrible grinding of gears. The unfortunate Yukovlev clenched his teeth and gave thanks that the burned out buildings were but a few hundred yards away.

The red-faced Stefan Gregorvitch kept his eyes firmly on the small square scout-car as it bounced ahead of them, carrying his three comrades. It came to a halt in the same broken down barn. Schroeder slid his legs over the low door of the car to race back to the steaming lorry. "Great stuff soldier," he complimented the perspiring driver, as he grabbed the side of Yukovlev's door.

"We'll have to leave you here," he called up to the white-faced doctor. Schroeder moistened his lips as he looked around. "Mebbe it'll be best for you to stay in the truck."

He returned hastily to the jeep when Yukovlev made no reply.

"See you later," he yelled. "Come on let's go," he muttered to Tatiana in a much lower voice.

In the rear seat of the open vehicle, Dead-Eye twisted his body for a parting backward glance as they left their comrades to their eerie vigil.

"Nice little place for a motel," he was about to say, when Tatiana's voice forestalled him.

"Look over there," she was saying. "There is something else coming."

They had not yet reached the narrow strip of concrete. Tatiana's finger was pointing to a cloud of dust approaching the road from the opposite side.

"Slow down," Schroeder told her. "Let them get there first."

They could see, now, that it was a scout car like the one they had borrowed. Their own vehicle was moving quite slowly as Tatiana obeyed Schroeder's instructions. The other car was braking also. They saw it bounce slightly as its front wheels encountered the raised edge of the road. Its four occupants waved in their direction before the note of the engine changed again.

"Wave back!" Schroeder said quickly. "Use both arms. Make

178

'em think there's four of us." He sat back in his seat. "Right," he told Tatiana. "Follow behind them, not too closely."

The direction the other car had taken was towards their own target - the factory and the research laboratories.

"Mebbe they're just returning from patrol." Schroeder spoke quickly to his pair of helpers. "We'll try following them in."

They had reached the length of pitted concrete. Tatiana's hand moved quickly as she leaned forward to change gear.

"Sure as hell hope hope you're right, lootenant. Dead-Eye's expression was wary, as he craned his neck to scan the drab landscape. He fingered the Japanese rifle he was holding, and checked that the machine pistol was safely hidden under his seat.

"We are coming to it." Tatiana indicated the break in the skyline ahead of them with a nod of her head.

The car they were following was slowing down. Tatiana braked slightly to keep the same distance between them.

Schroeder rested one hand on the dashboard as he peered over the low windscreen to get a better view of the place they were approaching.

"Hell's teeth! It looks like there's been a godammed earthquake." Dead-Eye's voice was awed as they drew nearer. Schroeder felt increasingly hopeless as he looked at the tangles of twisted steelwork rising from massive slabs of shattered concrete.

They were half a kilometre from the ruin, but even so, the remaining walls of the three storey buildings could be seen to lean at precarious angles.

"Yukovlev told me that they exploded four ton trucks filled with dynamite around the godammed place." Schroeder's eyes were searching for possible clues to identify the buildings.

Tatiana'a face was tense as she pointed with one hand to the car ahead of them. "Look they have stopped."

The lieutenant reached into a pocket to pull out a grubby square of gauze with tapes attached.

He sounded sick when he spoke to the others. "OK We'd better get them on," he said.

They were moving very slowly now, as they waited to see what was happening at the guard post where the other car had halted.

Tatiana took off her cap and pulled the tapes over the top of her head, with an expression of disgust.

"This," she said, "is the worst thing that I do."

"I'd settle for that." Dead-Eye dried his nose with the back of his hand before pulling the mask into place. "Jeez," he spluttered. "This guy must have been eatin' garlic."

179

Schroeder sat with muscles tightly bunched as the Korean guard held up his hand at the barrier. The other car had driven off. Tatiana followed it with narrowed eyes to see which direction it had taken. The road they had been following joined up with another,which ran off in both directions, to encircle the partially demolished outside wall, which had originally protected the site.

The boundary road was on the other side of the guard-post. She noticed that the scout car and its occupants turned off to the right.

Giving a mumbled reply to the guard's greeting, Schroeder held out their passes for inspection.

"Hope to God he doesn't look too closely at the driver," he was thinking.

Tatiana's generous curves were reasonably well covered by her shapeless overall. She had leaned forward in her seat to examine the dials on the dashboard, as Schroeder handed over the three passes they had "borrowed" from their owners.

The guard was apparently relaxed. He continued a conversation he had been having with his comrade on the opposite side as he scanned the roughly printed cards. He checked the details with those on the white armbands which were pinned to their overalls, before handing them back with a brisk nod.

"Where's your comrade?" The man's slanted eye's looked at Schroeder with a questioning stare, as he indicated the empty place in the back of the car.

The mask he was wearing muffled the American's voice as he strove to imitate the strange Korean inflections.

"He was taken sick." Schroeder shrugged and returned the guard's gaze, as though the man should have known. He pointed expressively towards the empty landscape behind them, back to the guarded area beyond the wire fence. "He became sick soon after the patrol started. We took him back to the other guard-post." Schroeder pointed over the guard's head in the direction where he thought the road would continue as it left the wreckage of the fenced-off site.

The man's easy manner was changing. He sounded suspicious. "You should know the other entrance is forbidden to all but the NKVD."

An ice-cold chill spread its tentacles inside Schroeder's brain. Yukovlev had mentioned them, but hadn't been too sure. Now this man's words confirmed it. The NKVD, the dreaded Russian secret police, were operating here.

"It was urgent. The other post was closer." Schroeder tried to sound convincing, but the guard was clearly not satisfied.

With a peremptory gesture, he ordered them to remain where they were until he made a phone call. Tatiana and Dead-Eye waited for Schroeder's reaction as the man disappeared inside the small hut.

As Schroeder slid easily out of the car, the remaining guard reached for his rifle sling. He relaxed, however, as the disguised American squatted on his haunches to examine a rear wheel. Schroeder's eyes had a worried look as he shook the wheel and pointed to the brake drum. As the guard left his post to crouch beside him to take a closer look, the kneeling officer gave Dead-Eye the briefest of nods.

The butt of Dead-Eye's pistol swung in a short but violent arc. The guard subsided into Schroeder's waiting arms with a scarcely audible gasp.

"Get him aboard." Schroeder had the collapsed man by the shoulder. Dead-Eye needed no urging. He leaned over to grasp the limp body and haul it into the seat by his side. Schroeder moved forward swiftly to raise the counter-balanced arm of the barrier.

At his signal, Tatiana slid the car into gear to move it quietly past him. He swore as the arm came down too quickly when he relaxed his pressure. By crooking his elbows beneath it, he prevented it from crashing noisily into the metal cusp.

"Keep goin'," he told Tatiana as he swung himself over the door to land by her side. "Turn left when you hit the other road." He was slightly breathless as he gave her the instructions. "Don't drive too fast, we don't want to attract attention."

"I think we'll soon be gettin' some," grunted Dead-Eye. He was looking back at the guard post, where the other man had appeared suddenly from inside the hut. Dead-Eye continued to watch as the man dashed across the road to search for his vanished comrade.

Pushing the sagging body upright, Dead-Eye gave a villainous chuckle. "At least there's four of us now!" he said.

Tatiana was driving carefully. "The first car, it went the other way," she told them.

"Yeah, I know," Schroeder answered. "That's why we're goin' this way." They were now passing people and other vehicles moving along the strip of narrow road. About fifty yards to their left was the newly erected fence. Its straight metal posts had strong steel mesh stretched between them. At a similar distance on their right were the blasted remains of the original walls.

"The poor bastards!" whispered Dead-Eye.

They were approaching gangs of dust-caked labourers who were toiling between heaps of debris and lines of standing lorries.

"They're Jap P.O.Ws," replied Schroeder, speaking over his shoulder.

Dead-Eye's single eye hardened. "In that case I take back what I said," he grated.

"Drive more slowly," Schroeder told Tatiana. "Let's try to figure out what's going on here."

He knew that by now the alarm would have been raised. His hope was that among this activity their chances of being spotted would be lessened. The trio noticed that at intervals along the remains of the wall, gaps had been enlarged and reduced to ground level. It was through these spaces that the gangs of workers carried the rubble and broken masonry from the collapsed buildings.

"Looks like they're tryin' to clear some roads through all that godamm mess." Dead-Eye broke off, as the sagging man by his side began to moan. "This guy's coming' round, lootenant."

"Try to keep him quiet. If be gets too noisy, you know what to do," Schroeder answered.

He was becoming increasingly confused as he tried to check their position. The drawing was still in his pocket. He struggled to recall its sparse details, and to relate them to the scene around him.

From time to time, Tatiana had to slow the car, to crawl round obstacles, as debris from the spoil heaps spread into their path. Overloaded lorries, spilling their contents, rumbled past them, leaving their thick oily smoke to mix with the dust which was flung up by their wheels.

Schroeder strained his eyes to see beyond the gangs of labourers. About a hundred metres into the remains of the site, he thought he could make out the outline of a large central building. It was little more than a rectangular heap of rubble, where fragments of broken walls were tilted at odd angles, by the weight of twisted steel girders. The remains of other buildings of varying sizes which had been set up around it showed the same horrific devastation.

Schroeder grasped the top of the windscreen with one hand to support himself when the tiny car bounced to a halt again. The way ahead was blocked by a slow-moving column of workers.

"Sonofabitch," he breathed. "The godammed basement I'm supposed to search must be buried beneath all that crap."

He gave a sudden start when he heard Dead-Eye's voice.

"Watch out lootenant," he was saying, "that slope-headed guard is losin' his temper."

A Korean guard was waving his arms angrily, telling them to get out of the way, as a laden lorry on the hard-pounded verge beside them, noisily revved its engine, waiting to move out in the opposite direction.

Tatiana glanced at the lieutenant and pulled her cap further over her eyes before engaging gear. She rolled the car slowly forward so that the straggling gang of Japanese labourers had to form a single line for them to pass.

Schroeder watched the prisoners' stolid peasant-faces as they shambled along listlessly, swinging the large wicker baskets they used for carrying rubble.

"Could these guys have known what was going on here?" he wondered.

The two Korean guards, one at the front and the other at the rear of the column, shouted at the men in their charge to keep moving, as they paused to stare at the almost stationary car and its occupants.

"You watch out at the back," Schroeder called to Dead-Eye. The one-eyed American's companion slumped untidily at his side. The Korean's jaw now had an ugly swelling.

"Godammit lootenant! I can't get this guy to sit up straight," Dead-Eye grumbled.

Schroeder swore impatiently as the car had to stop again. A battered bulldozer had broken down. Its enormous shovel took up most of the road. The Japanese driver was being savagely beaten by another armed guard, who turned as the scout-car stopped close behind him. He advanced on Tatiana with an ugly expression in his eyes.

"What are you doing here?" he shouted. "This is a working area. Patrol-cars should go the other way." He bent down, as he spoke, to make his voice heard above the clatter of the bulldozer's engine, which had suddenly restarted.

"Watch out!" Dead-Eye suddenly growled in Schroeder's ear. "There's another car coming up behind."

Schroeder swung round in his seat to see the other vehicle weaving its way towards them, through the obstructions they had just negotiated.

The Korean guard leapt backwards to unsling his rifle when he heard Dead-Eye's voice. The American reached down to grab his machine pistol, but was hampered by the slack body of the man by his side.

"Get movin'!" Schroeder spoke sharply to the driver. Tatiana didn't hesitate. The car shot forward. It caught the guard on the hip, spinning him round as he levelled his rifle. There was a shriek as the rear wheels lurched over something hard. Another guard loosed off a shot as the car bounded past him. He aimed again as

Tatiana stopped where the bulldozer blocked the road. The gang of Japanese prisoners scattered with warning shouts as Dead-Eye's automatic weapon stuttered briefly at the pursuing vehicle which had slowed again to veer round a spillage of masonry. It stopped abruptly with a squeal of brakes as Dead-Eye's bullets flung the Korean backwards to thud against the radiator.

"Go round it," Schroeder yelled, pointing towards the bulldozer.

Tatiana's eyes narrowed as she pointed the scout car towards the enormous mound of piled-up rubble alongside the massive machine. The bulldozer started to move as the driver tugged wildly at its controls. His mouth opened wide in a cry of alarm as the front wheels of the stolen car climbed slowly above his head. He flung himself sideways to leap into the back of the lorry he had been loading, whilst dislodged lumps of steel-reinforced concrete bounced onto the driver's seat.

Whilst the wheels of the scrabbling scout-car spun in short bursts, Schroeder was standing as though to urge it on. He flung a glance over his shoulder. He had a glimpse of olive green uniforms leaping out of the stranded car, and of the rusted old earth-mover rumbling steadily towards it. The grin froze on his face as he recognised the yellow shoulder-boards on the mens' tunics.

"Those bastards are NKV," he shouted to Dead-Eye

"That godamm ole machine don't give a shit about that," Dead-Eye roared. He broke off as the air exploded from his lungs.

The front wheels of the scout-car shrieked noisily when they encountered empty space. Above the stifling mask, the sweat shone on Tatiana's forehead. She clung to the steering wheel whilst her feet jabbed at the clutch and brake pedals. The front of the car hovered for a stricken second before dropping with a crash amongst the crushed fragments and tumbled chunks of concrete on the other side of the spoil-heap.

"Jump!" yelled Schroeder as the car began to slide. He tried to roll as he hit the lumpy surface, but a length of jagged metal ripped into the sleeve of his overall. Staggering to his feet, he stared with dismay at the blood which welled from a deep gash in his forearm.

"Holy mother! Tatiana?" The cry broke from his lips as he saw Dead-Eye stumbling towards the car, which was lying on its side.

The loose rubble caught at Schroeder's feet as he slithered to the place, a few feet away from the wreck, where Tatiana was gasping, as she struggled to stand upright.

Dead-Eye reached for the weapons which had been flung out when the vehicle had rolled. Petrol was flooding from its damaged tank. He looked round when his quick ear caught the thin crackle of high-voltage sparks.

"Look out!" he yelled. "She's gonna blow."

Schroeder pointed to the stumps of broken wall, a few yards away.

"Get behind there!" he shouted.

His fingers were slippery with blood as he grabbed Tatiana's hand. Dead-Eye, with a pair of machine pistols clumsily slung, pulled her other arm around the back of his shoulders.

"Come on, get started!" he called

As they collapsed in the partial shelter of the ruined wall, the leaking petrol tank ignited. There was a muffled roar, followed by a blast of heat from the gush of red-tinged yellow flames.

They looked at each other breathlessly for a moment. Then Schroder panted, "We've got to get away from here." He was groping for the emergency dressing in the pocket of his borrowed overall. He gasped with relief when he found the rectangular pack. Tatiana, white-faced took it from him.

"I will do it." she announced in a voice which was regaining its strength.

Whilst she swiftly bandaged the raw-edged gash, Schroeder strained his eyes to see through the pall of black smoke given off by the blazing car.

"Look over there." He pointed with his free hand to the wire fence on the opposite side of the cluttered road.

As his single eye followed the direction of Schroeder's finger, Dead-Eye nodded. "Sure," he said. "There's some more wrecked buildings over there. The fence bends back to go round them."

Tatiana held on to Schroeder as he attempted to pull his arm away.

"Look!" he protested. "Now is our best chance. If we go whilst the smoke's so thick, we can get some cover in the ruins over there."

She finished tying the bandage, then reached out for Dead-Eye's spare machine pistol. The blood from Schroeder's arm left a smear across her chest as she wiped it with her sleeve. With an impatient tug, she pulled down the grubby mask so that it revealed the determined thrust of her chin.

"What are we godammed waiting for?" she snapped.

A few excited Jap workers had gathered around the blazing car, maintaining a safe distance, for fear of further explosions. Two more Korean guards came running towards them from further along the road. They waved angrily at the excited prisoners, aiming blows at their heads as they screamed at them to carry on with their work.

The guards appeared puzzled by what was happening. One of

them started to follow the car's skid marks to the top of the mound. Before they reached the top, two heads appeared from the other side. They were wearing the shiny-peaked caps of the NKVD. One of them shouted for the other Koreans to start searching the area.

The crackling flames of the burned-out car had now almost died away. The clouds of smoke were rapidly thinning as the three raiders, each choosing their moment, darted across the road.

The heavy metal gate, by which they entered the separate compound, had been left open for use by the labour gangs. Taking what shelter he could among great slabs of concrete and the remains of damaged walls, Schroeder motioned urgently for the others to follow him. They came to the edge of a massive crater, into which they scrambled to lie uncomfortably on their stomachs and peer cautiously over the edge.

Dead-Eye's expression was tense. He was breathing hard as he looked sideways at his officer.

"Can you see if they're coming after us?" he asked.

"They're starting to search," Schroeder replied. More guards had arrived. The two NKV men were shouting and pointing in various directions, as they ordered the Koreans to spread out. Most of their efforts were directed to the other side of the road, where the skeleton of the car still smouldered.

"Mebbe they'll think we didn't get out," offered Dead-Eye.

"Like hell they will," Schroeder began, when, suddenly, he ducked below the rim of the crater.

"Keep down," he grated. "One of those NKV pricks is pointing this way."

He edged back up to take another quick look. Half a dozen guards were fanning out towards them from the gate where the Russian stood shouting directions in a furious voice.

Schroeder rolled over to speak to Tatiana. The movement caused a tearing pain in his injured arm. He heard the sound of someone scrambling towards him as he tried to suppress an involuntary groan. There was concern in her eyes as she flung herself flat by his side, but her voice was sharp.

"Your arm," she said. "You must take care or it will be very bad."

The American managed a wry smile. "Thanks a lot nurse. Just find me a hospital bed."

He realised she had hardly listened to him. She was pointing to the bottom of the crater, where she had been exploring.

"Down here," she was saying, "there is perhaps a way."

Schroeder followed her as she slid quietly back to the base of the saucer-like depression.

"Tell us if they get any closer," he called back to Dead-Eye in a low voice.

Tatiana was urgently indicating a roughly rectangular opening. It appeared to lead downwards from a position in the crater wall only a few yards from the bottom. The American ducked his head to peer inside, but the pit-like entrance was partly blocked by several lumps of concrete which had tumbled down from a higher level.

With Tatiana's help he scrabbled at the obstructions. He could feel the bandage on his injured arm becoming soggy, as his efforts opened up the wound.

The woman was breathing heavily as she grappled with a steel-reinforced slab almost the size of a house door. She finally stood upright to shake her head. Her face was crimson from her efforts, but now there was sufficient space for Schroeder to get a better look inside.

"I think there's some steps down there," he told her excitedly. "Let's get Dead-Eye."

As he spoke, there were two single shots from above the rim of the crater. They both instictively ducked. Schroeder cursed under his breath.

"They must've spotted something. Hang on," he told her. "I'll see what's happening."

He squirmed painfully up the crater wall to lie beside Dead-Eye, who was carefully aiming his automatic weapon as he squinted over the rubble strewn ground.

"The shots weren't aimed at us, lootenant. They musta seen something else."

The officer could see the half-dozen guards who were hunting around among the wreckage of the building, a short distance away to his left.

"Get down there and help Tatiana," he whispered to Dead-Eye. "Get going dammit!" he exploded from between set teeth as the soldier seemed to hesitate. "There may be a way out."

Dead-Eye nodded, then slid carefully down the slope to join her.

The lieutenant unslung his own gun. His injured arm was throbbing with a fast, sticky rhythm as he dragged the heavy strap over his head. The bandage squelched as he rested it on the parapet. He sucked in his breath in an effort to steady the weapon, and painfully slid a finger through the trigger guard.

A quick look behind showed Dead-Eye and Tatiana tugging frantically at the embedded slab. Schroeder carefully aimed his

187

machine pistol at the nearest of the two Koreans, who were cautiously approaching the place where he lay concealed.

He could see one of the guards turning his head as he called to the other. They were getting very close. The barrel of Schroeder's pistol moved imperceptibly as he realigned it on the slowly moving man. The Korean must have seen it. He gave a quick warning shout, and loosed off a shot in the American's direction.

The echoing crack of the rifle almost prevented Schroeder from hearing Dead-Eye's sudden call. The two guards leapt to seek cover among the ruins, as Schroeder's finger squeezed the trigger. A short burst of gunfire ricochetted around their heads whilst the American risked a quick glance behind and across the crater to where Dead-Eye and Tatiana were beckoning wildly.

His machine-pistol rattled again, causing several other Koreans to rush for shelter. Before they could recover, Schroeder flung himself down the slope in a welter of grey dust and clattering concrete fragments.

Dead-Eye's gun sprayed the lip of the crater, as the officer's feet gained a tottering hold. Several more Koreans ducked hastily as the bullets swept through the air above their heads.

"Come on now, through here lootenant."

Between quick bursts of fire the enlisted man was indicating with his gun the cave-like opening behind him.

Grabbing for his fallen gun, Schroeder scrambled across the few intervening yards. With a helpful push from Dead-Eye, he stumbled through the opened gap into the semi-darkness beyond it. He heard Tatiana's breathless voice urging him to follow her. There was a short flight of uneven steps. His clumsy weapon scraped along the wall of a tunnel. A few more sharp bursts from Dead-Eye's gun, were followed by the clatter of his feet down the steps.

Schroeder winced at the sharp stab of pain which ran down his injured arm as Tatiana grabbed it.

"Through here, quickly," she was shouting.

She half-led, half-dragged him over a heap of fallen debris. An eerie finger of light crept into the tunnel from the cracked roof immediately above.

There was a gasp from Dead-Eye as he squirmed his way past the protective mound to join them. "Sonofabitch! That was close," he panted.

"Is there any way through?" Schroeder broke off as a volley of rifle shots filled the stagnant air with noise and the reek of cordite.

"I think I saw a door," Tatiana coughed as spurts of dust were thrown up from their barricade, by another fusillade of bullets.

"Good thing only one guy at a time can stand in that opening. Go back there and check out that door." Schroeder spoke rapidly to Tatiana.

There was a yell of pain from the figure outlined at the entrance, as Dead-Eye fired a short burst, which was deafening in the confined space. The ringing in Schroeder's ears shut out the sound of Tatiana's voice for several seconds, but she continued tugging at his good arm and pointing backwards. "Come and see," she was shouting.

"Keep 'em out while I take a look." Schroeder flung the words to Dead-Eye as he stumbled after Tatiana's dimly-seen figure. She stopped and pointed to a heavy wooden door with a barred grille at eye-level.

"It is fastened," she panted.

"Stand back!" Schroeder pushed her behind him as he stood back and pointed his gun at the lock. The woodwork splintered, and flew around their ears, as the snub-nosed weapon jerked in his hand. Its hammering stopped after the first few rounds. There came a harmless click from the breach.

"Jesus Christ! it's out of ammo." Schroeder kicked furiously at the shattered woodwork around the lock, but the door refused to open. "Dead-Eye has some spare magazines," he shouted.

There was no time for Tatiana to run back. They could hear Dead-Eye yelling. The Koreans had forced their way through the opening. Schroeder suddenly remembered the Korean guard's pistol. He tugged at the flap of the holster with fingers which were sticky with blood. Tatiana pushed him roughly aside as she aimed her own pistol at the stubborn lock.

They each protected their eyes with raised forearms as the wood and metal sang around their heads.

"Come on! Try again." Schroeder's boot crashed against the shattered metal, whilst Tatiana flung herself at the studded planks.

The door suddenly gave before their combined onslaught. It crashed back against the wall as they staggered through. Schroeder turned swiftly to call for Dead-Eye, who was moving backwards, squeezing himself as closely as possible to the wall for protection. From time to time his gun chattered in quick bursts at the Koreans who crouched on the other side of the spilled rubble.

Tatiana reached out to drag the sweating man through the doorway, whilst Schroeder used his pistol to make their pursuers duck for safety again.

With Tatiana's help, Dead-Eye leaned his weight against the battered door, to close it with a heavy thud. There were thick iron bolts on the inside, which Schroeder slammed into place.

"Sonofabitch! If that doesn't beat everythin'." Dead-Eye was breathing hard as he wiped the dust and sweat from his weatherbeaten cheeks.

A rifle shot whined past their heads, as a guard pushed the barrel of a rifle through the small grille near the top of the door. The butt of Schroeder's empty weapon swung upwards to dislodge it. There was a scream of pain from the other side as Tatiana stepped forward to fire her pistol between the bars. They heard the Korean's rifle clatter to the floor.

"Come on," grated Schroeder, "We've got to keep goin'."

Beyond them the tunnel was completely dark. The faint light which had leaked through from the grille rapidly faded as they stumbled into the blackness. The air became more foetid. Dead-Eye, who was leading, suddenly halted. Through the darkness, Schroeder could hear his laboured breathing

"Jesus," wheezed Dead-Eye, "there's something smells like godammed poison gas."

Schroeder, too, was now coughing as acrid fumes caught at his throat. Behind him, he could hear Tatiana vomitting.

"Cover your mouths and noses," he gasped. "Use the masks, anything you've got." He reached behind him to grasp Tatiana as she partially recovered. "Move slowly," he told the man in front. "Try to breathe as little as possible." His eyes were becoming more accustomed to the darkness. He could dimly see the walls of the tunnel stretching ahead as they moved cautiously forward. He suddenly froze with an involuntary cry as something scampered over his feet. He heard Tatiana scream. There were rustling sounds all around. The paved floor of the tunnel felt to be moving as a horde of squealing rats swarmed past them in tumbling slithering confusion.

He held on to Tatiana's arm for a few more moments as the sharp-toothed pack disappeared along the tunnel. He could feel she was trembling. His feet slithered on something sticky as he tried to support her.

Dead-Eye was calling back, his rasping voice sounding unnaturally loud as it echoed from the brick walls.

"Do I keep movin', lootenant?"

"You sure as hell do!" There was no doubt in the officer's mind. "But try saving your breath." A sawing sound was coming from his own lungs as his voice tailed away. "The godamm smell's getting worse," he choked. He could still faintly hear the banging on the door behind them. "If the sonofabitch rats can stay alive, then so can we," he told himself. "Watch your step," he tried to warn Tatiana.

"The floor's getting slippery."

She nodded weakly as she stumbled after him with one hand held over her mouth.

Another gasped warning from Dead-Eye brought them to a halt again.

"Watch out on the wall," he began. "We're comin' to some doors." His voice abruptly thickened, as though a gag had been thrust down his throat. Schroeder rushing forward, caught the veteran soldier as he lurched against the open door of a cell. There was a splashing sound as a stream of vomit spattered on the floor. Schroeder felt his own stomach heave as he skidded on the slimy paving. The stench of putrefaction caught him by the throat, to turn his saliva into thick, cloying mucus. He turned back to stop Tatiana, but found himself retching as he hung on to her shoulders. She stood rigid as she looked into the cell with eyes which had become adjusted to the darkness

Dead-Eye swallowed as he joined them, wiping his lips with the back of his hand. "I kinda pushed against the door and the godammed stink hit me." He was still panting, his voice sounding apologetic.

Schroeder was thankful for the extra darkness, which shrouded the bloated corpse as it lay obscenely in a pool of liquid putrescence. The vile mixture had oozed beneath the door to form a dark pool on the floor outside, where it now lay mixed with Dead-Eye' vomit.

Schroeder remembered with a shudder, the slippery feel of the floor further back. "Carried by the feet of the rats," he decided. He found he had his good arm around Tatiana's waist. He released her, to hitch the gun over his shoulder.

"O.K! Let's keep going," he whispered thickly.

Now, there were cells on each side of the tunnel. Doors were open or closed haphazardly. Some of them held the hideous remains of their occupants; others were empty. Pockets of the pungent gas still tore at their throats as they fought off the waves of nausea.

"They must have gassed the poor bastards in their cells." Schroeder coughed harshly during a brief pause for breath.

"I wonder where this godammed tunnel goes to?"

For a moment, Schroeder ignored Dead-Eye's question. He was listening intently. He fancied he could hear the faint sound of voices far behind them.

"We'll soon be finding out," he answered grimly, as they moved off again. "We sure as hell can't go back."

Tatiana was now behind Dead-Eye. Schroeder, bringing up the rear, was straining his ears for sounds of pursuit.

191

"Those bodies," she was saying in a low, shaky voice, "were prisoners. Where would they be taken from here?"

The succession of ghastly events over the past few minutes, had left Schroeder feeling dazed. Straining his eyes to pierce the darkness, he could vaguely see that other galleries angled away on either side. "This must be the basement of the prison block," he whispered. "The part of it above ground was flattened like the rest of the site." He swallowed hard as the taste of vomit remained sour in his throat.

"Hold on!" The trio paused again as Schroeder turned his head to listen once more. He tried to close his ears to the squealing and scuffling sounds from scurrying rats as they were startled from their gruesome meals. The sounds of pursuit which he thought he had heard seemed to be no longer there. But he felt that the foul air could be muffling the tread of stealthy feet.

"There's got to be a chance," he told them in a hoarse voice, "that the tunnel connects with the main building. There's probably a network of tunnels under the whole site."

"Those godammed guards," Dead-Eye muttered suspiciously, "Maybe they've gone to find another way in?"

Schroeder nodded. He could just make out the bulk of Dead-Eye's shape outlined against the deeper blackness.

"Could be, but they might have trouble. Everything's buried up there. I feel like I'm suddenly a mole!" A hollow laugh had risen from Schroeder's heaving chest, but it came out as a strangled cough. "So long as we're underground," he continued, after recovering his breath, "we might have a chance."

Tatiana had been half-bending, with both hands pressed against the clammy walls, as she fought to suck life from the tainted air. "That room," she panted, "on your plan, it was below the ground."

The officer nodded his head.

"Good thinking," he panted. "Come on. let's go."

He flung himself violently against the opposite wall as a bullet struck sparks from the brickwork just above his head. It was followed by the whip-like cracks of several more shots.

"Jesus Christ! They're here. Get down!"

The sudden yell exploded from Schroeder's lungs as he dropped flat on his stomach.

There were guttural voices now shouting excitedly, and torches stabbed their beams through the darkness behind them. He rolled over to drag round his automatic weapon. It stuttered with a deafening roar, as his finger closed on the trigger. The shouts turned

192

to screams. There was a horrid gurgle, and the sound of thrashing limbs, which ceased abruptly, as the victim's lungs filled with blood.

Schroeder had closed his eyes before firing, to avoid being dazzled by the gun flash. When he opened them, the light had disappeared. He jumped, as a stealthy form crept up by his side. It was Dead-Eye. "Do you think you got all the bastards?" he panted.

"Can't tell. They've gone kinda quiet."

Despite their predicament, the officer could have cried out with relief. The iron band which he had felt clamped around his chest had been removed. He was breathing more freely. The oozing slime sucked at his clothes. The stench was indescribable, but the suffocating gas had not reached this level. "That accounts for the rats," he was thinking, as another burst of rifle fire stuck shards of stone from the paving close to his head. With a curse, he raised the gun again to rest the barrel on his injured arm. Before he could pull the trigger, Dead-Eye thrust out a warning hand. Without a word he squirmed back into the darkness. A second later a beam of light from a torch held close to the ground, outlined the startled figure of a guard with his back pressed hard against the wall.

"Shoot the bastard," yelled Dead-Eye.

The Korean's body jerked and twisted, and his rifle was flung into the air, by another burst from Schroeder's gun.

Dead-Eye crouched on his haunches to flash the torch quickly round the tunnel. There was no sign of life. "Three of the sonsabitches," he grunted. "Nice goin', lootenant!"

Schroeder's head sagged briefly onto his arms to still the drumming of his ears. When he raised his head, he looked at the one-eyed soldier. "Holy jeez," he breathed, "how did you see the sonofabitch?"

The man's crooked mouth split in an embarrassed grin. "Can't say I did, lootenant. I heard him. But before then," he added quickly, "I'd heard the other guy's torch fall on the ground."

Schroeder rolled to a half-lying position, staying as close to the slimy paving as he could whilst he spoke.

"It seems like there's no one else followin' us right now," he said. "Mebbe the others turned back to find another way. Mebbe they suffocated in the tunnel – if it leads to the main building like we think." He paused for breath, his heart was pumping harder again. "It can't be much further," he went on. He looked at the other two ghostly shadows crouching near the ground. "Do you both agree that it's best to keep on goin'?" he asked them.

They both nodded affirmatively. "There ain't no other way I can think of, lootenant. By now the other end will be blocked off."

Tatiana, breathing heavily, nodded again with dogged determination. "We must find this place," she replied. "Those guys on the ship. They should not be broken off."

Dead-Eye shuffled foreward on his knees, to take her by the arm. "Not quite right, babe, you mean 'given a break' but you got the message. We're ready, lootenant."

"OK" said Schroeder. "From hereon, we'll crawl on our bellies. I'll go first. You at the back," he told Dead-Eye.

They squirmed their way slowly along the festering floor, where pockets of gas remained in some places to
tear their raw lungs. Schroeder's stomach convulsed repeatedly as his fingers clawed through patches where protesting rats scuttled away from shredded mounds of decaying flesh. From time to time, he stopped to ease the gun across his aching shoulders. Behind him he could near Tatiana swearing. The stream of Russian oaths struck sparks in Schroeder's mind. Translating her picturesque vocabulary helped him to fend off his own weakness.

"Pingfan is a place where glimpses of hell make men afraid to die." Garbled versions of Yukovlev's words spun round and round inside his brain. A strangled moan escaped his lips. His lungs were pumping. Stabbing pains seared through his injured arm. The darkness became absolute.

"Lootenant! Lootenant!" It was Dead-Eye's voice which roused him. Opening his eyes made little difference. There was darkness, only darkness, the deepest, deepest darkness, and death, and the stench of total degradation. Mans' ultimate mortality revealed in pools of stinking slime.

He heard himself groaning and Dead-Eye's panting voice again. "Holy cow! I hope the sonofabitch ain't gonna die,"

A muffled scream tore itself from Schoeder's throat as Dead-Eye unthinkingly grasped his wounded arm. The blackness in his conscious mind became a trembling red haze. He tried to raise himself. His lungs were rasping as he fought for breath. Then he heard the woman's voice. It sounded close to his ear. It was making soothing sounds. Her arm was supporting his shoulder. She was stroking his cheek. For a few miraculous moments in that terrible place, he experienced a feeling of contentment unkown since his childhood. He felt himself drifting.

She drew away quickly as he struggled to rouse himself.

Dead-Eye was sounding panicky. "Come on, come on, lootenant. We gotta get out of here."

He would have shaken the injured arm again, but for Tatiana's angry intervention.

"OK! OK! What's the godammed fuss about?" The lieutenant flicked his bloodshot eyes towards Dead-Eye, who was lying on his belly near him.

"Thank Christ you're OK lootenant." There was an audible sound of relief in Dead-Eye's hoarse voice.

"Sure I'm OK" Schroeder gasped painfully. "What the hell do you take me for soldier? I just blacked out I guess?" His voice tailed off with a sudden groan.

In the darkness Dead-Eye flung the officer a worried glance. He ignored Schroeder's outburst. An excited note crept into his voice.

"I think we might be nearly there lootenant. There's a crack of light from someplace way ahead of us."

Squirming over onto his belly, and lying flat alongside Dead-Eye, Schroeder wheezed, "OK." The mucous was gathering again in his throat, "Lead the way you bat-eyed sonofabitch."

The three of them dragged and pushed themselves with their knees and elbows to reach the place where Dead-Eye stopped. The scabrous floor of the tunnel had led them to another wooden door. The faintest crack of light was filtering through the edge, where it had not been fully closed.

"Holy mother! I was right," panted Dead-Eye. "What do we do now, lootenant?" He turned his head to look questioningly at the officer who had crawled his way forward to join him.

They pressed their ears against the wood to listen. Apart from their own ragged breathing they could hear no other sounds.

"The sonsabitches might be waitin' out there." A note of caution had crept into Dead-Eye's voice.

"I guess we'll have to take that chance." Schroeder breathed deeply several times, inhaling the fresh air from the faint draught. "I'm goin' to take a look," he told the listening soldier. "You cover me when I get outside."

He placed his hand against the door and pushed at it carefully. At first it resisted. He pushed again, harder. He felt a pain in his lower lip as his teeth bit into it. The door gave slightly, its bottom edge scraping against a thick layer of dust and plaster. He found he was blinking, as the thin grey light beyond the door broke against his eyes. The door would move no further. It was jammed against an unseen obstacle. Clutching his gun across his chest, he rose clumsily to his feet. As he stumbled through the narrow gap, he braced himself, waiting for a fusillade of shots.

The watchful Dead-Eye sidled after him, his finger curled tightly round the trigger of his pointing weapon... They both

195

relaxed as they looked around the circular chamber. The shadowy openings of several corridors were spaced around its circumference. It was silent and closed off. Above their heads, steel girders were bent beneath the weight of the demolished building.

Tatiana had scrambled through to join them, her red-rimmed eyes were wide open as she gazed at the sight of the slime-soaked, foul-smelling men. Her face was a pasty white, but it broke into a rueful smile as she looked down at her own soggy boilersuit.

Schroeder signalled for them to keep quiet. Dead-Eye crouched beside the closed tunnel door, his head turning watchfully from side to side, as he squinted into the gloom.

The light in the underground chamber, which had seemed so bright as they emerged from the tunnel, was weak and dust-hazed. It crept through countless tiny crevices in the mountain of shattered concrete above them, before spending itself on the cellar floor.

At a nod from Schroeder, they moved off silently in different directions round the circular room to examine the other entrances. Before Schroeder reached the first passage, he found a door set in the wall. He quietly pushed it open. As his eyes probed into the semi-darkness, he made out the shape of a large piece of machinery. It had been dislodged from its concrete bed, but was recognisable as a generator and pump with an auxiliary engine. As he came out he saw that Tatiana was opening a similar door on the other side of the tunnel.

The corridor into which Dead-Eye peered had a crazily fissured ceiling, through which, chest-high drifts of rubble had poured. To force their way down that passage for more than a few yards, they would have had to climb over, or dig their way through the debris.

Dead-Eye tentatively turned the knob of a door that could still be reached. When he cautiously opened it to look inside, his nostrils wrinkled with disgust. Before he slammed it shut again he had had a glimpse, through the semi-darkness, of batteries of wire cages. In them were the maggot-riddled bodies of hundreds of rats. The musty air, thick with the smell of rotting flesh and fur, had been filled with the busy drone of hordes of flies.

Schroeder was gulping when they met in the outer room.

"Did you find something, lootenant?" Dead-Eye asked him anxiously

Schroeder turned away quickly. "There was a kinda museum," he replied. "A lot of things in glass jars on shelves. Most of 'em were broken." He turned towards Tatiana, who appeared from a room on the other side of the tunnel. "Is there anything in there?"

She gave a tired sniff as she shoved her pistol back into its holster. "Only things for an office," she replied.

Glancing over her shoulder the lieutenant could make out the outline of metal cabinets and jumbled furniture. Half supporting himself with one hand, which he trailed along the wall, the exhausted man stumbled along towards the generator room.

"Come over here," he called to the other two. "Look around in this room and see if you can find any gasoline. This godammed machine must have run on it," he added, when Dead-Eye looked surprised. Schroeder's eyes followed them thoughtfully as they left him. As he was speaking, he tugged deliberately at the sodden flap of his boiler suit pocket. His fingers groped clumsily inside to produce a tattered piece of paper. Standing beneath a weak glimmer of light, his filthy hands trembled as he strove to unfold it. The wet paper tore before he had finished. The pencilled lines were blurred and stained, but he could see enough to be convinced.

"The strong-rooms," he breathed. "They're the strong rooms down one of those passages. He peered more closely, trying to make out which corridor led to the rooms they were seeking. The soggy paper fell apart into two separate halves, but he had seen all he needed to see.

He turned quickly as his two accomplices staggered out of the generator room. Dead-Eye's voice sounded triumphant.

"We found some gas, lootenant." The liquid gurgled in the two jerry cans as he dumped them on the floor. Tatiana was close behind him, her shoulders bent beneath the weight of the two other heavy containers.

"That thing in there was fixed to some air-ducts," Dead-Eye told him.

Schroeder nodded. "Yeah," he said quickly. "They'd need to ventilate the underground rooms." Before Dead-Eye could say anything else, Schroeder showed him the remains of the diagram. The pencilled lines were almost invisible in the feeble light, but Schroeder was explaining them in a low excited voice. "One of these corridors." he said, "is where the strong rooms are, the rooms where all the records were kept."

There were two heavy thuds as Tatiana deliberately set down the two cans. The impact caused the thick dust to rise in cloud.

"Where is it?" she demanded.

Schroeder nodded towards one of the shadowy spaces. "Down there," he told her cryptically. "The last door but one, on the left."

The three of them suddenly started as a thin trickle of fine powder and hard, tiny fragments spattered on the floor, close to where they stood. Their eyes swept upwards to the pyramids of

197

wreckage supported by the bare steel girders which protected the basement.

"I can hear some hammerin'." Dead-Eye's husky voice had sunk to a cautionary whisper. Schroeder fancied he could see faint shadows blocking off some of the daylight which had squeezed itself through the tumbled blocks of concrete.

"The bastards have caught up with us. They must have worked out where the tunnel ended."

As Schroeder was speaking, Dead-Eye shot a swift glance at the closed door of the tunnel, "Do you think they'll try comin' through there again, lootenant?"

"Sure to," the officer answered briefly. "They're probably getting ready right now. Mebbe they'll have gas masks this time." He was busy unfastening the cap of a jerry can, grunting occasionally with the pain in his arm.

"Open that door." He spoke rapidly, urging them to move fast.

As Tatiana rushed to grapple with the bolts, Schroeder picked up one of her heavy containers. Shouting to Dead-Eye, "Come on, bring the others," he lurched one-sidedly into the mouth of the tunnel. The gas fumes tore at his throat after the first few yards. He staggered a little further, holding his breath. The gasoline gurgled noisily as it gushed out of the can. He swung it around to drench the walls and the floor, before flinging away the empty can. Dead-Eye and Tatiana were close behind with the others.

"Go ahead, as far as you can," he rasped, as he ducked past them to refill his protesting lungs.

When the three of them were back in the underground room, Schroeder leaned his weight against the door to close it with a heavy thud.

"If there's any trouble now from in there," he panted, "all we'll be needin' is a match.

Tatiana was coughing as she recovered her breath. "Stay here, near the door," he told her. "Listen for anyone coming through the tunnel.

He and Dead-Eye moved quickly across the cellar floor to the corridor where the strong rooms were. At the entrance, Schroeder held out an arm to prevent the other man from following. "I'll go in first and see what it's like. We need you here to watch out up above."

Dead-Eye nodded reluctantly. "OK lootenant. I guess we'll have to work fast. It won't take 'em long to find a way in here." He was already looking upwards, but there was no visible sign of movement. "I don't like it, lootenant. The bastards are up to something," he muttered uneasily. But Schroeder had already left him.

He passed two doors, one on each side of the corridor, before encountering the first roof-fall. The gap in the ceiling through which it had poured, allowed a sparse sprinkling of light to filter through. The powdery grit was piled against both walls, in a cone shaped heap. Quickly unslinging his gun, he dug the toes of his booted foot into the loosely packed rubble. He snorted to clear his nostrils, as he heaved himself painfully to the top. The cloud of grey dust settled on his eyelids, making him blink as he tried to see through the murky darkness on the other side. A few yards further along, the ceiling had again been split open. An enormous slab of masonry, which had ripped its way through, completely blocked the whole width of the corridor.

Its upper end leaned uncertainly against the edge of a rusting girder. Its lower end was buried in the floor of the passage.

He allowed himself to slide slowly back, his mind dazed with the shock of his bitter disappointment. It seemed clear the remainder of the corridor was completely blocked. It would take a team of miners to burrow a way through.

The breath exploded from his lungs in a great sob of rage as he reached for his gun. His task now was to get his team back, so that people could be told about Pingfan. As for the poor devils on the ship, they'd either die, or be treated as pariahs for the rest of their lives. Each man would have to be treated as a carrier of the deadly plague until the day he died.

He jumped as a shout from Dead-Eye jolted him back to their desperate situation.

"Lootenant, See there! The bastards are breaking through."

Dead-Eye was staring at a spot, far above, where a tiny gap in the ruins showed signs of widening.

"Don't do anything yet. They can't be really certain that we're here," Schroeder warned.

On the opposite side of the cellar, Tatiana's back was pressed against the wall by the side of the tunnel door. Her ear was close to the small metal grille, but her eyes anxiously followed the gaze of the two men.

They could hear the thud of heavy hammers. Streams of powdered cement fell about their feet in sudden spurts, as crowbars levered aside the larger blocks.

Schroeder looked desperately around at the other passages.

"Go round and check 'em all out," he whispered to Dead-Eye. "See if you can find one that isn't blocked."

Dead-Eye shot him a swift enquiring glance. "The one you've come out off, lootenant? I guess there's no way through there?"

Schroeder shook his head grimly.

For a split second Dead-Eye's chin sank to his chest, but a moment later he had slid quietly away to do Schroeder's bidding.

Schroeder continued to watch and listen. He could hear the shouting more clearly now. They were rapidly breaking through.

Tatiana was no longer looking. Her voice was taut with uncertainty as she called across the the cellar. "I think there are voices inside the tunnel."

Dead-Eye reappeared at Schroeder's side.

"Not a chance in hell of findin' a way out," he said hoarsely. "As far as I can tell, them passages are all plugged tight." He fingered his gun nervously, his gaze fixed on the mounting pile of debris. It was steadily being added to by clattering flurries falling from the widening cracks as massive blocks of concrete were prised apart.

"The whole godammed lot could come down on top of us." He hugged the wall as another fall kicked up the thick dust already on the floor.

Schroeder ignored him. "Get over there by Tatiana," he barked. Another rush of falling masonry followed the soldier as he took a few quick strides across the underground room.

The confused voices from the men above changed to shouts of triumph. One of them must have spotted the movement. Schroeder ducked as several quick shots bit into the walls from a rifle thrust through a gap. He stumbled across to join Tatiana and Dead-Eye by the tunnel door. He heard a metallic rattle from the grille at head-height.

"Stand back!" he screamed to the others. He flung himself sideways as the sub-machine gun stuttered from the far side of the door. He had a wild glimpse of goggled eyes illuminated by the blinding flash which instantly followed. There was a thunderous roar from inside the tunnel. The door burst open as iron bolts were wrenched from their sockets. A tongue of black-edged fire boiled across the room to expire almost immediately against the solid concrete walls on the other side.

Tatiana clawed herself to her feet, her fingers slipping on the oily film left on the wall by the thick smoke which swirled around the cellar. She could hear Dead-Eye coughing and cursing, then the smothered sound of Schroeder's voice.

"That's our way out, back through the tunnel," he choked.

There were more shots from the snipers above ground level as they fired blindly through the billowing smoke.

"Quick follow me, before it clears!"

Schroeder's boots crunched over the fallen door. He gave a warning shout to the others as his feet caught against a bundle of charred rags. Wisps of flame still fluttered from two more which he narrowly avoided. There was a smell of burning rubber. Dead-Eye kicked aside the melted gas-mask still glued to the remains of a hairless skull.

The walls of the tunnel were too hot to touch. Schroeder lurched from side to side with short uncertain steps as he clutched the gun across his chest and peered into the darkness. The blast of heat and the explosion of the air had cleared the tunnel of the asphyxiating gas. His breathlessness came from exhaustion and fear.

The sides and floor of the tunnel very soon became cooler. He found he could feel a faint stirring of the air against his cheeks.

"Halt here for a while," he called back in a husky whisper. Whilst the others pressed their bodies flat against the brick-lined wall, Schroeder sidled further along, following a gentle curve. He stiffened in alarm as a wand of weak light swept over the opposite wall. It moved in rhythmic jerks as though its source was moving at a slow walking pace.

Cursing under his breath, he moved slowly backwards. He could hear the sound of voices getting closer. They sounded smothered and unreal. He heard enough to tell him they were nervous of the possibility of a further explosion.

He reached the place where the others waited.

"Scram!" he whispered. "We've gotta hide. We'll use that last pair of cells we just passed."

The moving patch of light was becoming stronger as the guards drew closer to the place where the tunnel curved.

The crouching trio retreated swiftly until they reached the door of a cell. It was hanging partially open. At a signal from Schroeder, Tatiana and Dead-Eye slipped quietly inside.

Schroeder took two quick strides across the tunnel to hide in the cell opposite. The door was firmly closed. He pushed harder, but it still refused to move. With a rapid intake of breath, he spreadeagled himself against the brickwork, as the beam of the torch fanned round the bend. It moved slowly over the walls and the roof, until it was pointing towards the floor. Schroeder scuttled, crab-like, further back to the entrance of the next cell. The door was open. Silently he slid into the squalid blackness. Edging his shoulder close to the blistered woodwork, he watched carefully as the guards approached. There were three of them in single file. The outline of

201

their faces showed as elongated snouts. Their eyes were wide, glistening circles, reflecting the beams from their torches.

"Gas-masks!" The reason for his not hearing their voices clearly.

The man in front was concentrating on showing the way through the tunnel. Those behind were checking the cells on either side. They were not enjoying the task. Their grumbling voices came thickly to Schroeder's ears. He waited breathlessly, as they approached the cell where Dead-Eye and Tatiana were concealed.

The leading guard walked slowly past. The one behind him pointed his torch at the door which Schroeder had failed to open. The guard first tried the handle, then struck at it several times with the butt of his rifle. When the man in front heard the noise, he turned his head in sudden alarm. The third guard added his weight to that of his irate comrade, as he lunged at the door with his shoulder. The door flew open with a crash. As the pair of them disappeared inside, Schroeder stepped out from his hiding place. The leader must have heard him; he swung round to face the sudden danger, but Schroeder's pistol was already nudging his ribs. The American's voice was cold. "Don't move," it warned.

Dead Eye and Tatiana, who had been watching as the first two guards lost their balance, moved swiftly across the tunnel into the cell. The Koreans dropped their rifles with a clatter at the sight of the filthy apparitions with their pointing guns.

Dead-Eye was bad tempered as he watched their three pursuers take off their overalls.

"We'll soon have undressed their whole godammed army!" he said with a sour expression.

"Stop whining," Schroeder told him in a tired voice. "We all smell so godammed bad we'd be identified at a hundred yards."

Tatiana was holding one of the torches. The charred remains of a straw mattress rustled under her feet as she walked round the three sullen prisoners. She stopped in front of one of them. "This will be right for me," she said firmly. The two Americans exchanged a glance.

"Just like a woman to chose the best fit," Dead-Eye grunted.

The guards had been carrying water bottles. Dead-Eye smacked his lips after taking a long drink. He wiped his mouth with the back of his hand as Schroeder urged the two of them to hurry.

"We'll have to take their rifles," he was saying. "Ours are nearly out of ammo anyway."

The Koreans were trussed and gagged, then left in a corner of the cell, as the trio prepared to leave.

The cell door was closed.   Schroeder shone a torch briefly so that the light reflected from a wall.   It showed the red-rimmed eyes and slime streaked faces of the other two.

"I guess it's just as well we can hide 'em," he said with grim humour.   Swiftly gathering up the gas-masks, he tossed one to each of his weary helpers.   "Get 'em on as fast as you can," he told them.

With pursed lips Tatiana pulled off her cap and tugged the straps over her tangled hair.

Dead-Eye was about to protest, when a quick word from Schroeder shut him up.

"Get the damm thing on," he flung at him.

Stretching out his good arm, the lieutenant leaned against the wall, before putting on his own mask.   He checked that they each had a rifle and a torch.

"I think it's best if we go back to the cellar." He tried to control the uncertainty in his voice.   There was a muffled comment from behind Dead-Eye's mask.   Schroeder ignored him.

"Either way," he continued, "We're going to be shot to hell if we're underground.   We do know that these guys were going in that direction."

He looked quickly at the three figures on the cell floor, tightly bound with discarded belts and bandoliers.

"Mebbe if the others have broken through into the cellar, they'll be expecting somebody else through the tunnel, especially as the first three had such a sticky end."   His voice became distorted as he struggled to adjust his mask with one hand.

He glanced quickly both ways along the tunnel, before moving out of the cell and motioning the others to follow him.   Dead-Eye was the last to come out.   He pulled hard on the door handle to jam it tightly shut again.

The shadowy shapes of Schroeder and Tatiana were already several yards further along.   His own breathing sounded noisy as he hurried after them.   When he drew nearer he could hear the slapping sound of their gas-mask valves.   Schroeder was crouching slightly, straining his eyes to peer ahead. Tatiana followed closely, whilst Dead-Eye trailed a little way behind. They carried the torches, but were not using them. Their eyes were so accustomed to the darkness, that when a a flicker of light appeared, they were startled by its brightness.

Schroeder raised a warning arm, and moved closer to the tunnel wall, reducing his pace to a stealthy crawl.   The others followed suit, until, finally, the lieutenant stopped.   He turned to

203

look at them, with a puzzled shake of his head.   The crack of light was now larger, and rectangular.

Dust was settling on Schroeders goggles.   He rubbed a dirty thumb across them.   Hazy silhouettes of men could be seen crossing and re-crossing the space where the door to the cellar had been. Except that it was no longer a cellar.

Schroeder reasoned it out. The cellar roof must have finally collapsed.   Perhaps from the blast, perhaps the result of the efforts of the guards as they strove to smash their way through.

The air buzzed into his gas-mask as he took a deep breath. He tugged the mask slightly away from the side of his face so that the others could hear his voice, whilst he explained what he thought had happened.

"If those guys are down there," he said, with a surge of hope in his voice, "it must mean there's a way out.   Whatever happens," he added, "stick close together, and keep these godammed masks on as long as we can. I wish I understood the Korean lingo better," he grumbled as an after-thought.

Tatiana pushed her mask close to his, so that he could hear.

"Sometimes I can understand," she told him.

Their faces were running with sweat behind the smothering masks, but he could make out her earnest eyes.

"Honey, you're a treasure," he replied. "Try to keep me posted."

He didn't see her worried expression, as he moved off towards the exit.

"Posted?" she was saying to herself as she followed.   "How do I godamm post him?"

The exit from the tunnel must have been completely blocked by the roof fall after their escape.   Now, as the masked trio emerged, they had to squeeze their way between broken chunks of concrete, which had been shoved aside haphazardly to clear a way.

Above their heads was a murky sky where the remains of the roof had been. Ugly stumps of fractured steel girders stuck out from the mass of wreckage, which almost filled the cellar. Clouds of dust hung around the labouring shapes of a dozen or so Korean guards. They were straining noisily at some larger sections of concrete. Streams of displaced rubble clattered from under their feet as protruding slabs were hauled aside.

As Schroeder and his small team appeared, the man in charge turned to stare.   His eyes blinked several times.   Behind his gauze mask his mouth hung slackly open. He lowered his gaze to look blankly at the three incinerated corpses which had been carelessly dragged out and dumped near the tunnel exit.

The sight of the gruesome remains still lying there apparently reassured him. He recovered his voice to bawl a question, whilst removing his cap to wipe a sleeve across his forehead.

"I guess he's asking if we found anything?"

Tatiana nodded a reply to Schroeder's scarcely audible question. She called something back to the overseer. Her voice was deep and distorted by the gas-mask. Schroeder and Dead-Eye shook their heads vigoruously, making sweeping motions with downturned palms.

The man seemed to understand. He turned back to his men, urging them to work faster. There was an added urgency to his gestures, as he pointed out different places for them to concentrate their digging.

"They must think we are under there." With his gas-mask pushed up to rest on his forehead, Schroeder spoke quickly to Tatiana, who was fumbling with her head-straps as though having difficulty. "Dead-Eye is going to faint," he warned her.

The tough G.I. whose mask was also half-off looked at him in amazement. "I feel OK lootenant," he protested.

"That guy is sure to come and ask some more questions." Schroeder nodded towards the Korean who was shooting suspicious glances in their direction. "Before he does, you're goin' to collapse, and we'll have you up that thing to get some air." He indicated a short rickety ladder leaning dangerously against the jagged edges of the cellar ceiling. The foot of the ladder was wedged precariously into the heaped-up rubble.

Dead-Eye was looking mutinous. "It's dames that should do the godamm faintin'," he argued.

"I'm ordering you to faint, soldier," Schroeder snapped. As he spoke he glimpsed the guard picking his way towards them across the fallen wreckage.

"Come on godammit!" He grabbed the flustered Dead-Eye around the hips. Reluctantly the soldier allowed his body to flop across Schroeder's shoulders.

"Go on get over to the ladder," he gasped as Tatiana picked up their rifles. "First tell that guy we don't need any help, our comrade 's only fainted."

Tatiana had found the mandatory square of gauze in the pocket of her overalls. Holding it over her nose and mouth as though being choked by the dust, she called back an explanation to the guard.

The Korean stopped. He made a derisory gesture as though disgusted that a man should be so weak. Dead-Eye, watching from his upside down position, turned purple with rage.

205

Schroeder's boots caused minature land-slides as they scrabbled for toe-holds in the loosely packed mass. When he reached the ladder where Tatiana waited, his chest felt as though it were caving in. "You get up there and pull," he wheezed. "I'll push him from behind."

Tatiana slung the three rifles across her back. As she mounted the first rungs, she gave a hasty glance towards the guard, who had turned to stare at them again.

Schroeder slammed Dead-Eye's body hard against the ladder. "Go on, you stupid bastard! Reach up and grab her hands." He could feel the fresh blood dripping from his hand as it ran again from his re-opened wound.

The suspicious Korean must have spotted it, too. He made a determined move towards the ladder.

The affronted Dead-Eye saw Tatiana's arms reaching down. He clutched at her wrists to drag himself over the ragged concrete edge.

There came a yell of alarm from Schroeder as the ladder slithered from under his feet. Dead-Eye lunged forward to grab his shoulders. Schroeder hung there for a moment, until Tatiana hooked a hand under his belt. Between them, the man and the woman hauled him over the top.

* * *

Nicolai Yukovlev had watched them leave the ruined barn with a thoughtful expression in his deeply set eyes. He knew how slight was the hope of their accomplishing their hazardous mission.

He spoke curtly to Stefan Gregoravitch. The boy's rebellious gaze was fixed on the small car as it jolted towards the ribbon of road.

Yukovlev ordered him to check the prisoners in the back of the lorry. He realised how sharp his voice had been as the young soldier moved smartly towards the tail-gate.

The gaunt-faced officer's body was bent slightly forward. He pressed an arm against his stomach as he walked slowly back to the door of the cab. He hesitated taking a deep gulp of air, before gripping the edges to pull himself painfully up to the passenger seat.

Stefan Gregorovitch peered over the tail-gate at the trussed figures of the four Korean guards. Clad only in singlets and underpants, they were squirming where they had been dumped on the rough wooden decking of the truck. Lowering the tail-gate, the boy climbed up and perched on the boards, his legs dangling over the edge. His uneasy gaze switched from place to place around the layers of filth on the floor of the barn.

The rats were becoming confident again. Their squeaking and scuttering raised goose-pimples on his skin. Gripping his rifle between his knees, he searched his pockets for a cigarette. His brow puckered with frustration when he found only an empty packet. It cleared when he remembered the sealed cardboard box they had kept back, along with the crate of saki.

He lodged the rifle carefully against a mudguard before clambering forward to where the boxes had been left beneath a tarpaulin. From above his gag, the bulging eyes of the Korean N.C.O. followed him as the young Russian opened the cardboard flaps to pull out a waxed-paper carton. There was a clonking of glass as he also reached for a bottle of the saki.

Stepping over the curled-up limbs of his prisoners, the boy weaved his way back to the open end of the truck. Sitting on the scuffed wooden boards at the tail, he stretched his legs across its width and leaned his shoulders comfortably against the raised side. There was a pleased grin on his face as he lit a cigarette. He prised off the cap from the saki bottle with the handle of his bayonet.

He roused later with a startled gasp when a pair of booted feet were shoved hard against his ankles. He looked around in a semi-stupor for his rifle, before remembering he'd leaned it against a wheel.

The N.C.O. had squirmed along the floorboards to attract his attention. The man's piggy eyes above the gag were focussed on the young Russian with an expression of desperate entreaty. With a convulsive movement the Korean arched his massive body, his choking curses half-smothered by the dirty cloth wrapped around his mouth.

The boy's sudden movement of alarm dislodged the empty saki bottle. It rolled off the edge of the platform to fall amongst the scattered cigarette ends on the ground. His fingers were clumsy as they fumbled with the knots that held the man's gag. The Korean's legs were flexed, his knees drawn up to his chest. He spat out the spittle-soaked rag to plead in an agonised voice,

"I want to piss. My belly's bursting. I have to take a piss."

Stefan looked angry. "Why don't you piss on the floor?" he belched.

The guard's ugly face was ridged where the cloth had pressed into his cheeks. "I can't," he slobbered. "I have to stand. Help me for just one minute please."

Grumbling, the boy yanked the distraught man by the legs to swing his bound feet over the edge of the floor-boards.

The Korean rolled onto his stomach as he half-fell onto the

ground, his hand-cuffed wrists thrust stiffly out behind his back. "Unfasten them, or you will have to help me," he screeched.

The boy was sober enough to shudder at the thought of holding the ape-man's dick for him. He reached into his pocket for the handcuff key.

Sitting alone in the driver's cab, Yukovlev hunched his body to ease the pain. His morphine clouded senses drifted in and out of consciousness. He struggled to suppress his groans each time the tentacles inside him tightened their grip. Carefully turning back the cuff of his tunic, he looked at his watch once again. There were three hours to go before Schroeder was due. He locked his fingers together, as another spasm made him gasp.

He had used the last of his morphine. Schroeder had been right to change the planned operation. Yukovlev knew that now. His mind was wandering again. He thought wryly of the morphine he had used on the child in the hospital. He remembered Schroeder's grateful stare.

Somewhere deep inside his brain there were tiny signals alerting him to a sense of danger. There were vague noises behind him inside the truck, someone shuffling and then calling, pleading in a strangled voice.

Yukovlev's forehead felt clammy. He remembered the captured guards and the boy. With shaking fingers he drew his pistol from its holster and reached for the handle of the cab door. He dropped to the ground as it fell open. As he did so, a wild-eyed Korean swung savagely round to face him. The man's blood stained hand clutched the hilt of a bayonet. It protruded from beneath the young Russian's chin.

Yulovlev clung to the side of the truck with one hand as the half-crazy guard tugged at the embedded blade. The boy's lifeless body sagged to the ground as he finally wrenched it free.

The pistol felt heavy in Yukovlev's grip. Its muzzle wavered as he managed to raise it. He could hear the guard shouting obscenities as the bayonet came over to slash at his head. Bracing himself, the doctor squeezed the trigger. The man's shouts became a choked-off scream as the bullet shattered his shoulder. The bayonet arced through the air from his outflung arm. Holding the pistol now with both hands, Yukovlev fired again. The guard's body quivered after hitting the ground, then became perfectly still.

Yukovlev's wasted frame was drenched with sweat, as, with the pistol hanging from his fingers, he staggered to where his young comrade was lying. A cursory glance at the gruesome sight was enough to confirm there was nothing he could do. He fell to his knees, suddenly whimpering as the cancer gnawed again at his guts. He crawled on all fours to rest his back against the rear wheel of the truck. Through the floor boards above his head, he could hear the bumping and scraping of the tied up guards as they struggled to free themselves.

The stricken man alternately sweated and shivered as he rocked from side to side. The intervals between the attacks of pain were rapidly diminishing. During one brief spell of relief he looked at the pistol still in his hand, then raised it to his temple. Then, recollections of his vow swam weakly to the upper reaches of his tormented mind.

Snuffling and grunting like an unwilling beast, he dragged himself to his feet. The three trussed guards promptly stopped their struggling when they saw the pointing gun. Their staring eyes rolled cautiously over the panting, dishevelled officer.

"Get out," he gasped.

The men exchanged glances, but a click from the revolver made up their minds. One by one, they half-slid half-tumbled from the back of the truck. The filth-encrusted earth floor onto which they fell was soft and muddied with runnels of blood from the two corpses. It formed puddles which the cursing guards tried to avoid as they rolled around amongst the rodent droppings.

Yukovlev ignored their stifled cries. Staggering to the driver's door, he took several deep breaths before placing a foot on the step. He was sobbing with pain and rage by the time he fell into the seat and switched on the engine. With the part of his mind which still functioned, he concentrated on turning the lumbering vehicle in the direction his comrades had taken.

The guards at the gate were in an ugly mood, when the slowly moving truck creaked to a halt. The nearest one leapt onto the driver's step, whilst another watchfully levelled his rifle. The first one called urgently towards the guard-house as he opened the door to examine the slumped figure.

Two more men emerged from the wooden shed. The Korean officer who was leading, had a deeply-set scowl on his face. When he saw Yulovlev's unconscious body, his expression changed. The badges of rank and the medical insignia were clearly visible on the dusty uniform.

The officer nervously adjusted his mask whilst his eyes flickered over Yukovlev's face for symptoms of the plague. Remaining at arm's length, his fingers sought in the helpless man's pocket for evidence of identification. The Korean's slitted eyes turned thoughtful as his fingers flicked through the lengthy records of the

Russian doctor's service.

Remaining outside, on the step of the cab, he called to one of his soldiers. The man nodded his head, after a perceptible hesitation, when the officer ordered him into the driver's seat.

Yukovlev's skin had a yellow sheen. There were flecks of dried saliva at the corners of his lips. He was breathing noisily, in short irregular bursts. When the guard tried to move him from behind the wheel, Yukovlev's eyes jerked suddenly wide open. He spluttered and coughed as he smothered a cry of pain. His spittle sprayed the officer, who hastily retreated from the open cab window.

With one hand firmly holding the mask in place over both nose and mouth, he shouted muffled instructions to the reluctant driver. As the panicking man pressed the starter, Yukovlev's bloodless lips relaxed in the ghost of a smile. His mind had been more alert than the Korean guards had realised. His plan to enter the site had been based on the desperate hope of there still being a Russian-manned casualty station. He had also deliberately counted on the Asian fear of plague. Without treatment for the pain which was killing him, he knew he would lose his mind completely.

The convulsion which stiffened his limbs and threw his body forward, was not feigned. The driver shot him a frightened glance as he listened to the rasping breath of his passenger. With little regard for safety, he spun the lorry in a tight turn off the perimeter road, stopping sharply beside a Quonset hut. Jumping down almost before the truck had stopped, he rushed across a small compound. After hammering on the wooden door and gabbling his message to the tousle-haired man who appeared, he departed with all possible speed.

With a puzzled expression on his pug-nosed face, the man walked quickly over to the standing vehicle. He reached for the door on the passenger side. When he pulled it open, a dust covered body, in a foul-smelling Russian uniform almost fell on top of him.

The young man's mouth opened with a startled exclamation.

"My God!" he gasped. "Nicolai Yukovlev! What the hell has happened to you?"

There was a glimpse of pale light as he rose slowly to the surface of a dark pool. He could feel the fronds of willow brushing gently on his face as he floated drowsily towards the shore.

"Comrade. comrade, wake up. You will be all right." The deep voice was insistent. There were fingers tapping his sunken cheeks.

Yukovlev opened his eyes abruptly, blinking hard to clear away the soreness which rimmed them. Groaning faintly, he turned his head to locate the voice.

"Nicolai Yukovlev," it was saying, "wake up. It is I, Boris Lytynski." There was an encouraging smile on Lytynski's rugged face, but Yukovlev could not fail to see the pitying expression in his eyes.

Yukovlev licked his dry lips. Thankfully, he realised that the tearing pain was abated. He took a sip from the tumbler, which the other man offered to him. Gradually, he began to think more clearly, but to give himself more time, pretended to be still confused.

"Lytynski." He recalled the name. As a junior lecturer in the Medical School in Leningrad, Yukovlev had taught the second year student some anatomy. After the outbreak of war, their paths had crossed several times on various battle-fronts. They had come to know and respect each other, but apart from their shared field experience, had little in common. Yukovlev was the withdrawn academic, Lytynski the amiable, extrovert sportsman.

"My friend," Yukovlev breathed. "It is good to see you." He looked around to get his bearings. He was lying on a trestle bed in the room which had been equipped as a surgery. "What is the time?"

As he asked the question, he lifted his arm to look at his watch. He was startled. It was ninety minutes since he had left the barn. He remembered little of events since then.

"The time comrade? Why should it matter?" Lytyinski laughed as he answered the question. Then his face turned suddenly sober. "I am sorry, my friend. Perhaps it is of importance to you." He looked steadily at Yukovlev before he continued. "I am sorry that you are so sick."

He hurriedly held out an arm to offer support as Yukovlev raised himself, before stiffly edging his feet off the bed.

"You must be careful." There was alarm in Lytynski's voice. "You should rest," he added vehemently. Suddenly he sounded perplexed. "How did you get here comrade? Why did you come?"

Yukovlev shrugged, as he shakily reached for his stained tunic, which had been removed. "I thought that would have been obvious." He managed to sound a jocular note. "Even to a bone-headed student, who couldn't tell a scalpel from a trowel!"

He watched furtively from the corner of his eye for the other man's reaction as he went on. "I was in pain. I ran out of morphine on the way to Harbin. This was the nearest place."

Boris Lytynski pushed back a lock of hair as he shook his head wonderingly. He pointed to Yukovlev's uniform. "But you are in such a hell of a state," he burst out. "Besides this place is out of bounds. The plague, the guards, the security." He looked baffled.

Yukovlev showed his teeth in a ghastly smile.

"My dear Lytynski," he said in a gentle voice. "It was to be my last journey. There was a hospital bed waiting in Harbin. I called in at some interesting places on the way from Dairen. I even managed to lose my driver," he added apologetically.

Lytynski looked incredulous. "Sickness does strange things to a man," he said at last.

There was a trace of mockery again in Yukovlev's voice.

"Some students! They don't ever learn! You should know it is the effect of the morphine! Thank you for your treatment," he added soberly. "I would welcome a supply for the remainder of my journey."

"I should not allow you to leave. You do understand," he burst out, "you could die at any moment?"

With unsteady fingers, Yukovlev finished buttoning his tunic. "I would prefer not to die here," he said simply. Behind his professional arguments, Yukovlev's mind had been racing. He had to leave before the bodies of the guards were discovered in the ruined barn. There was also some kind of furore outside in the wreckage of the factory buildings. Guards and vehicles were scuttling around. He thought he had heard the sound of shooting. He was gazing through the window as he asked Lytynski, "Is there some trouble?"

Lytynski's lips twisted scornfully. "There is always trouble! Starving peasants, escaping P.O.Ws., Jap troops who won't surrender, Manchous after revenge, plague, torture, the NKVD. This place is hell on earth."

"Were you posted here as a punishment?"

The question was asked in a bantering voice.

Lytynski nodded ruefully. "Some little trouble with a colonel's wife."

"And a little too much vodka, no doubt?"

The other man nodded again, as Yukovlev glanced desperately at his watch. Suddenly, he seemed to remember something.

"There are some bottles in the truck which might interest you – only saki," he added hurriedly, as the downcast man raised his head. "But perhaps it will help to cheer your exile."

An interested gleam came into Lytyinski's eyes. His doleful expression slowly cleared.

"This place is run like a jail," he confessed. "Those NKV swine won't allow liquor into the camp. They're afraid of the Koreans running amok." He broke off.

Both men ducked their heads in sudden alarm as the sound of a muffled explosion rattled the windows. When they looked up they saw a cloud of black smoke. It was spreading in oily festoons as it writhed from a myriad crevices in the wreckage of the central building.

Yukovlev sat down unsteadily as the blood drained suddenly from his brain.

Boris Lytynski strode quickly over to a locked cabinet on the wall. Unlocking it, he took out some ampoules and a syringe. Thrusting them into Yukovlev's shaking hands, he said, "Take these, comrade, and leave this place." He scribbled on a pad which he took from a drawer. "This tells the guards that you came here for emergency treatment."

"The stuff in the truck, I'll leave it with you." Yukovlev's voice was unsteady as he rose to face the other man across the desk. He was desperately playing for time. He felt that Schroeder and his team were in terrible trouble. If they had been caught in that explosion, they would be dead, or trapped underground.

There was a sudden draught as Lytynski opened the outside door. "Thank you for the offer of the saki," he was saying. "I'll pick it up from the truck."

Yukovlev's legs felt heavy, as he followed his colleague across the yard. The younger man had climbed aboard by the time he reached him. A pleased smile lightened Lytinski's face as he looked at the crate of bottles.

"The cigarettes, take those too," Yukovlev urged. He was watching the scene beyond the remains of the perimeter wall as he spoke. There were shouting men climbing around the jungle of wreckage where the central block had once stood. Some of them were using hammers and picks.

Lytynski looke worried as he carried the crate back to his office. He was sniffing the still air when he returned to the truck a few minutes later. "Smells like a gasoline explosion," he remarked, thoughtfully. "I wonder what the hell's going on."

"Surely you'd be told if there were casualties?" Yukovlev questioned.

"Sooner or later," the young man replied, with a grim smile. "These people don't give a damn about who gets hurt."

He climbed quickly into the truck again as he was speaking, his eyes on the large box of cigarettes, when a cry from Yukovlev made him turn.

The sick man was looking at the ground with a startled expression. "I felt it tremble."

Lytynski wasn't listening. His gaze was on the place where the guards had been digging. The contours of the ruins seemed to have changed. The two doctors thought they had heard a faint rumble.

213

Some of the guards were no longer visible. As they watched, the remainder of a standing wall seemed to totter. A cloud of dust rose as it slowly crumbled. They thought they could hear the sound of screaming.

Lytynski set down the cardboard container he had been carrying. "It looks as though there's been a cave-in," he told Yukovlev. "There is a warren of cellars and passages under the ground here."

Yukovlev swallowed to ease his dry throat. He became aware of Lytynski shaking his hand. "Good-bye, comrade," he was saying. "I'll have to find out what happened."

He was already moving, when Yukovlev grasped his elbow. "The truck," he urged. "Why not take the truck? I can come with you."

The other man shook him off with a sympathetic smile as he ran towards the surgery. "This is no place for you, comrade," he called back. "You said it yourself."

When Lytynski emerged, carrying a heavy bag, Yukovlev had already struggled into the driver's seat. His voice was weak, but Lytynski could hear the panted words, "Come my friend, this truck will be quicker. It will carry the injured."

With an exasperated oath, the young doctor swung his bag up to the passenger seat, before clambering after it.

The engine turned over with a clatter as Yukovlev leaned on the starter. He was already sweating beneath his heavy tunic.

"Are you sure you can manage this thing?" Lytynski sounded apprehensive as the truck narrowly missed a gatepost.

Yukovlev nodded. He was fighting to retain his reeling senses. He could no longer feel the killing pain, but he knew that it was there, still probing with insistent malevolence.

"Go more slowly," Lytynski warned. "We have to turn off down that road the Jap P.O.Ws have cleared across the wreckage."

The truck lurched as it turned through the gap in the wall. Yukovlev was blinking to clear his vision as he hung on to the wheel. He realised with dismay that his body was responding with increasing reluctance to his drugged mind's tardy messages.

"You shouldn't be here," Lytynski snapped angrily.

"I must find out if you have learned yet how to use a scalpel."

Yukovlev's laboured joke was missed by the younger man, who pointed to a small cleared area.

"Stop here," he directed. "We can't go any further."

Not far away, a group of Koreans were removing large sections of a freshly collapsed wall. Beneath it, one of their number was trapped by his legs. He was crying out as the cursing gang heaved aside the huge lumps of concrete.

Lytynski had his door open before the truck had stopped. Grabbing his bag, he leapt down and ran towards the dust-covered workers.

Yukovlev watched him as he crouched beside the injured man. Then he turned his heavy eyes towards the other groups who called to each other as they sweated with picks and crowbars in what had been a cellar. The strong smell of gasoline, and the black smudges seared into the surrounding grey rubble, identified it as the site of the explosion he had heard.

The sick doctor clung to the steering wheel as his body started to shake. His hands were clammy. He fumbled with the window to let in some air. The sounds outside came to his ears more clearly. A bullying voice was urging some men to dig more quickly. He gulped back a wave of nausea. If his instincts were correct, and his American comrades had been involved, there could be little hope for them now.

There must have been casualties. Two figures who had scrambled out of the pit were reaching down to help another. Most of the guards were climbing around amongst the wreckage, following instructions from their bawling N.C.Os. This trio looked exhausted. Their uniforms were almost black, as though covered with soot. They seemed, somehow, to be apart from the rest of the activity.

He continued to watch them as they rose to their knees, looking round as though to identify their surroundings. A ridiculous thought was stirring inside his fogged brain. Something familiar about the way one of them cocked his head as though looking sideways. Another one, smaller, but robustly built, raised his hopes still further.

He discovered that his finger was on the starter button. The engine revved noisily, attracting curious stares. Yukovlev prayed for strength as he struggled with the gears to reverse the truck and face the direction from which he had come. The whites of his eyes showed as he tugged at the heavy wheel. An N.C.O. came towards him with a questioning glare, but turned away when he recognised the officer's uniform. Yukovlev straightened his peaked cap carefully before lowering himself from the cab. Placing his feet with great deliberation he walked steadily to face the three staring figures.

"I think you are hurt," he said calmly. "You had better come with me."

"Holy Mother!" breathed Dead-Eye.

215

Schroeder pulled himself from a kneeling position, to stand upright before the waxen-cheeked speaker.

"Thank you, comrade doctor," he croaked.   "We shall be grateful for your help." He was glancing from side to side as he spoke. Tatiana and Dead-Eye kept watch from where they crouched, their rifles unslung and close to their hands.

An expression of bewilderment came over Dead-Eye's blackened face, when Schroeder's foot gave him a hearty nudge.

"Well come on, soldier. You're the guy who fainted."

With Dead-Eye's drooping body supported between them, Tatiana and Schroeder lurched towards the the waiting truck.

Yukovlev had left the engine running.   Schroeder could feel the exhaust smoke hot about his legs as he closed the tail-board behind his two companions. Then, gripping the exhausted doctor by his arm, he helped him into the passenger seat.

Apart from a puzzled glance from the busy Lytynski. there was no reaction when the truck rumbled off, with Schroeder at the wheel.

Chapter 12

Dim, emergency lighting showed up the confusion in the food store where crates of canned and processed food had been dislodged and flung around the room, spilling their contents on the rolling deck. Sides of bacon were trapped between flattened boxes tightly squeezed against a wall. Swinging heavily from hooks in the deck head, giant hams made them duck their heads. Cheeses, the size of mill-stones, shattered tubs of butter, and huge cans of fruit and preserves, menaced their feet, as Jim and Johno, pushing together, almost fell through the doorway.

Johno abruptly stopped and stood upright as the sweat on his back started to crackle. The breath of the men was turning to steam as they paused to get their bearings.

"Nobody told us the bloody place was a 'fridge." Johno's teeth were starting to chatter as he thankfully pulled the seaman's jersey over his head.

The fully-clad Jim said "Don't be bloody soft sarge," before spitting on his hands and renewing his efforts.

They dragged the solid baulk of timber clumsily across the floor, with huge disregard for crushed cans of liquid eggs and squashed giant sausages.

"Come on you guys, not much further,"

Tiny ignored the glowering Lockie, who was chomping his jaws like an unwilling donkey.

The wheezing giant stood upright to point out the hatch in the metal bulkhead. The steel door, with its strong-handled levers was but a few yards from where he stood.

Johno dragged back the sleeves of the jersey which were far too long and hung over his hands.

"Right, you bastard! We'll soon have you where you belong," he viciously addressed the unfeeling beam, before curling his fingers under its rough edge.

Their feet slithered in the mess on the floor, as they pushed and heaved , until Tiny and Lockie had to jump aside as their end slammed against the coaming below the hatch.

Tiny was already reaching for one of the handles.

217

"You'd better watch it," Johno called out. "We don't know what's on the other side."

He was staggering with the roll of the ship, as he used each hand in turn to tug again at the sleeves of his oddly shaped jersey.

Tiny already had an ear pressed tightly against the cold metal, when Johno joined him.

"Sounds like somebody usin' a hammer."

Tiny reamed out his ear with the end of a thick-nailed finger, before applying it again to the door.

"Come on let's get bloody movin'! My balls are droppin' off." Condensed breath writhed around Lockie's head as he blew on his hands.

Johno observed that the bulbous end of Tiny's nose was turning purple as he looked at him again.

"It should be OK to go through. Mac told us he had checked it out."

The four of them huddled together as Johno pondered.

"If the flooding in the hold's got worse, and we open this bloody door, we'll flood this place as well."

"Then we'll be bleedin' drowned," piped Lockie. His shoulders were hunched as he pulled at the collar of his blouse.

"But if the flooding on the other side is real bad," Jim pointed out, "the door won't open anyway."

Tiny looked at him admiringly. "I guess that's gotta be true," he said.

Johno sounded impatient now. "Come on then," he decided. "Let's get the soddin' thing open."

He moved nearer to the hatch, but Tiny stuck out an arm to hold him back. "OK O.K!" he said sternly. "Let's do it nice an' easy now."

His large hand grasped one of the handles. It moved smoothly as he applied some pressure. There were six handles. The last one squealed noisily when it was turned.

The others had to move out of the way while Tiny stepped back to straddle the thickness of the wooden beam. He stood squarely in front of the hatch. A fresh cloud of vapour rose above his head as he took a deep breath before using a shoulder to push against the heavy door.

It swung open quite easily.

Tiny almost fell over the coaming. A gruff cry of alarm tore itself from his throat. He flung his arms wide to prevent himself from pitching headlong. He looked shaken as he pulled himself back and stared at the floor of the hold, some thirty feet below.

"Godamm it to hell!" he shouted. "What kinda stupid sonofabitch builds these rust-buckets with the godammed door near the ceilin'?"

The others were not listening. They were blinking through the glare of the arc lights spaced around the dark pit of the hold.

"Bloody hell!" said Johno at last. "I'm glad I wasn't down there when we hit the mine."

Neatly stacked tiers of enormous wooden crates and giant steel containers had been torn loose and tossed aside in mangled heaps. The jumbled masses of splintered planks, dented metal and spilled cargo stood out like islands surrounded by oily water which swooshed around them with the hiss of breaking surf.

"Look at them bastards. They're making a bleedin' raft."

Lockie's finger pointed down at a gang of oil-smeared men, in a roughly cleared space. They were working around a number of salvaged crates, which had been pushed together to make an improvised platform. Laid out on its surface was a great rectangular frame. It was made-up from baulks of timber like the one they had been carrying.

A large drill was shrieking as two men bored holes to take long steel bolts. Two others were labouring with saws to cut out cross pieces for the centre.

Jim's eyes gleamed with excitement. He craned forward, leaning at a dangerous angle through the hatch. He used one arm to indicate the far side of the hold near where a welded steel bulkhead spanned its width.

"Look it's another of those things they're making."

A complicated criss-crossed wooden grid was rising slowly from the deck, on the end of a block and tackle. The blocks had triple sheaves and the sailors hauling on the chains were working hard, as it swung slowly upwards, a few inches at a time.

"They'll be propping it against that damaged bulkhead, to

strengthen it." Jim explained. "When the ship gets under way again, it'll be taking the full force of the sea."

"Shit!" breathed Tiny, in an awed voice. You mean there's nothing on the other side?"

Lockie interrupted. "'Course not. The front end was blown off by the mine, you stupid drongo!"

Before Tiny's hand could reach Lockie's neck, the heavy door escaped from Jim's grasp. It swung back with a resounding clang, as the ship's bow angled upwards. From below, several pairs of eyes looked sharply in their direction. One of the men using a drill raised an arm to screen off the dazzle of the lights. A startled shout formed on his lips. He gestured with his free hand.

"Get the hell away from there," he bawled. "And shut that godammed hatch."

Tiny stuck his head and shoulders through the opening.

"We've got somethin' for you," he shouted.

The man seemed not to hear him. "Go on beat it," he yelled back. His voice sounded hollow in the vast, gloomy space.

Tiny was breathing hard as he looked at the others.

"Come on, gimme a hand," he grunted.

With Lockie's grudging help, he bent down to lift the end of the beam until it rested on the raised steel ledge.

. "The sonofabitch wanted some lumber," rumbled Tiny. "He's sure, as hell, goin' to get it!"

He peered through the hatch again towards the open-mouthed man. "Stand by below!" he shouted. "There's somethin' comin' down."

The four of them lifted and pushed together, until their burden teetered on the metal step. A final defiant glance by Tiny, then the whole length slid away and bounced onto the flooded deck far below, amidst cascades of filthy water.

Ignoring the outcry from the men in the hold, Tiny cautiously planted a foot on the top rung of the vertical ladder. The others clambered through the hatch to follow him.

"Watch out where you're putting your bloody great feet."

An elongated sleeve of Johno's jersey had coiled itself round a rung. He was trapped as one of Jim's feet descended on it.

220

"What are you two jokers bleedin' arguin' about?" came Lockie's plaintive voice from above.

Tiny, who had arrived at the bottom, splashed his way through the swirling water. He was met by the man who had been doing the shouting. "Who the hell are you guys?" His thick neck jutted forward aggressively. His arms were slightly bent at the elbows, as though he wanted to swing his fists.

Tiny's rib cage rose and fell rapidly.

"My buddies and me were told you needed some lumber down here. And that's what we've done. We brought you some, you stupid sonofabitch."

Tiny's voice sounded gravelly. It turned into a bout of coughing as he finished his speech. He hawked up some green phlegm, which he spat into the water.

The gang leader hastily backed away as it bobbed around his soaked denims. The bridge of the man's nose was flat, and his eyelids were swollen, as though they hadn't been closed for a long time.

"Lumber eh? Thanks fellas." His voice was heavy with sarcasm. "Fact is I've got all the frigging lumber that I can use." He thrust out an angry chin to indicate a stack of giant timbers pushed up against the side of the hold. Then he prodded Tiny's chest. "I sure as hell don't need you guys telling me I've gotta have some more. Look, the godammed things are everywhere."

Lockie's voice was pitched high with indignation. "I've been rupturin' me bleedin' self to carry that soddin' thing down here, and this joker's got millions of 'em."

"No wonder! Look what the bloody things are used for: to separate the rows of cargo when they're stacked." Johno pointed to some tiers of crates and bales which had held up against the storm and the explosion. Turning, he scowled at Jim. "Are you sure you got that message right - about some more being needed down here?"

Tiny and the crewman were still exchanging insults.

"The godammed thing nearly landed on my head, you crazy bastards!" the crewman was yelling. "Go on, get your asses out of here." His tirade was stopped short by yells from the men who were handling the lifting gear.

"Hey, Jake! Over here!"

The weighty frame they were raising swung high above the

deck. Each roll of the ship smashed it, with a self-destructing crash against the strained steel plates of the leaking bulkhead.

"Somebody gimme a hand," Jake bawled. His stubby legs were creating waves as they thrashed through the water. Some of the other men had dropped their tools, but it was Jim who followed closest in Jake's turbulent wake.

The pair of them arrived together by the stack of piled-up timbers. Wrapping both arms round a protruding end, Jake attempted to drag it with him. He almost fell over as the ship's bow dipped alarmingly whilst he strained against the cumbersome length of the beam. Jim floundered among the sloughing wavelets as he stooped to grasp the trailing end, using both arms as a cradle. With his body bent double, he struggled to maintain his balance whilst keeping up with Jake.

They were both breathless when they reached a point directly beneath the gyrating frame. Jim's cry of alarm was drowned by the crashing of wood against metal as the ship heeled and the ponderous object swung again.

"Stand the godammed thing on its end."

Other hands were helping now, adding to the confusion, as they raised the bulky length of wood to a vertical position.

They aimed it unsuccessfully several times at the spaces between the cross-members of the clumsy wooden structure whilst struggling to keep their foothold. Jim and Jake both staggered when the twirling rig was caught and stopped in mid-swing before it could smash yet again against the flaking grey metal.

"Bring some more props," Jake shouted, whilst still holding on to the upright beam.

Johno and Tiny were not far from the stack. With resigned expressions they sloshed through the water towards it, but a hefty seaman was there before them. He reached the beams and heaved the end of one length across his shoulder. He winced as the sharp edge bit into his flesh.

"You guys take the other end," he grated.

Tiny and Johno dragged it from its place. It slipped from their hands, splashing heavily into the water. Their arms and shoulders were submerged as they picked it up. With bent knees and straining backs they staggered behind the burly seaman.

"Try and catch the other end," the gang leader bawled, as they

222

stumbled towards him. With Jim, he was hanging on grimly to the upright support. It tilted dangerously in their hands as the wallowing ship tugged at the dangling contraption, threatening to wrench it free again.

Tiny and Johno thankfully slammed down their end of the extra support. Gasping, they helped the sailor push it upright. Its top end cut vicious patterns through the air. Johno felt giddy as his eyes tried to follow its erratic circles against the background of glaring lights. The three of them clung on, fighting against the heaving deck, until the vertical length of wood reached a point of balance.

"Steady as we go!" the sailor was yelling. "NOW!"

A concerted lift and thrust and the maverick frame was caught at the opposite corner to Jake and Jim's.

"Easy does it now."

Jake was shouting the orders, all his strength and concentration focused on manoeuvring the massive construction to lie flat against the bulkhead. His hoarse voice was now little more than a croak. "I want the sonofabitch right there. Let go some more chain you guys."

Slowly and painfully they eased the ungainly thing forward. It was hanging between them, uncertainly balanced, like a giant waffle between two skewers. One more combined push and the captive load was pinned in place.

Extra hands now came with hammers and wedges to jam the bottom edges of the angled props hard up against lugs in the deck plates. Johno watched the splashes as Jim used his foot to kick one of them more tightly into place.

Now Jim was limping badly as he paddled towards the upturned crate where the other two had flopped. He was panting as he sat down to pull back a soaking trouser leg. Dark blood oozed turgidly from a ragged gash on his shin. It dribbled over his glistening boot and mixed with the oily water on the deck. He fumbled in his pocket and found a sopping bit of dirty rag.

"Sod it!" he gasped. "Just my bloody luck. I can't think how it happened."

"It couldn't be from kicking the hell out of a twelve inch rail?" wheezed Tiny. He was sitting with his head almost between his knees, mouth hanging slackly open.

Johno looked at the sodden sleeves of his mis-shapen jersey dangling over his knees. At his feet, floating bits of debris were being carried by the swirling water.

He turned to Jim with a sour expression. "I'll tell you one thing for sure," he panted.

"Go on then. what is it?" Jim grunted, dabbing at the blood.

"You'll have to tear-up your own bloody shirt if you want to bandage it."

A line of approaching water spouts made him look up. It was Jake, thrusting his way towards them.

"Are you guys all right?" he was shouting. "Where's the other one who was with you?"

The three of them stared at each other. "Lockie?" None of them remembered seeing him since their arrival in the hold.

Jake was already moving away, his arms windmilling to assist his passage through the water. His legs were lifting in short high jerks. He stopped, and as Johno called to him, turned to shout back, "Yeah, what is it?"

The sergeant was paddling towards the impatient crewman.

"Our mate," he said, "Lockie, the Australian, we haven't seen him. Where should we start lookin'?"

Beneath the shiny peak of his cap, the smaller man's eyes looked suddenly very tired. "Just how the hell would I know that?" he replied. He looked significantly at the black water and the half-covered objects over which it ebbed and flowed.

"Take a good look around," he advised.

Jim lurched forward. He pointed to the hatch by which they had entered, high above their heads. "Is that the only way out? he asked.

The crewman shook his head. When he pointed, the small group could see there were other doors in the bulkhead at varying levels. "We have to get in and out as the cargo builds up," he explained. "But they can be dangerous if you don't know where you're goin'.

"We'd better start lookin'." There was a shocked expression on Tiny's leathery face. "I never thought the little sonofabitch would get himself drowned."

As the small party broke up to begin their search, the gang-leader called after them, "Don't none of you guys leave here 'til I can send somebody with you." As he strode away he growled, "Godammed army! Nothin' but a godammed nuisance!"

The trio separated to explore the darkest corners of the hold, wallowing in places against the surge of the water which echoed eerily against the curved steel walls of the hull. After a while, when their hair was soaked and water dripped from their chins from bending to grope beneath the surface, they had to give up.

Tiny's teeth were chattering. Their faces were grimed with streaks of black grease.

"Jesus, I think I'm goin' to die." Tiny's arms were clutched around his bony chest.

Those behind looked up as his gaunt figure came to a sudden halt. His black silhouette elongated against the powerful lights as he towered to his full height.

"You godammed Aussie asshole," he shouted.

Emerging from the shadows to join him, Jim and Johno saw Lockie. He was sitting on the improvised work bench with a cigarette hanging from his lips.

Around him the work had stopped whilst men dipped mess tins into a large container of black coffee.

He waved at the bedraggled trio as they approached.

"Hiya fellas." he called. "I thought you'd got bleedin' drownded or somethin'".

"A fat lot you were doin' about it," Johno replied in a hollow voice. He and Jim restrained Tiny, who, with the promise of murder in his inflamed eyes, was advancing on the grinning man.

Lockie slid down from the comfortable height of the work-bench. An alarmed expression appeared on his squeezed-up face as he splashed hastily away from his enraged friend.

"Hold on, mate." He stopped to hold up a placating hand. "I was only looking around for somethin' hot to drink."

The gang leader smacked his lips and wiped them with his sleeve as he slammed down an emptied mess tin. "The best thing you could have done." He gave the threatened Australian an approving slap on the shoulders. Around them the grateful seamen growled their agreement as they gulped the steaming liquid.

"I guess we was just about all in," one of them said.

Jake sniffed and glared meanly at the thunderstruck trio.

"It's the only godammed time I've known the army do anythin' useful! Come on you guys, let's get back to work."

Tiny stood open-mouthed as, with a final glare, the boss ploughed his way back to the lifting rig, whilst the other men picked up their tools. Lockie was the centre of their attention.

"Are you a Limey?" one of them asked.

The grubby Aussie's indignant denial was lost in the shriek of the drill.

Jim, brushing roughly past the motionless Tiny, picked up a used mess tin. He lifted the lid off the large metal container, to scoop out a helping of coffee.

"There's only the bloody dregs left," he shouted.

"Never mind about that." Tantalised by the fragrant smell, Tiny forgot his rage. He scraped a spare can in the sludgy mess and gave a deep sigh after taking a drink.

"Jeez, that tasted real good." He licked the layer of grit from his lips.

"Glad you enjoyed it, mate." There was relief in Lockie's voice.

Johno shared the muddy contents of Jim's half-filled tin. He gave the Australian a withering look.

"Come on then. You'd better tell us what happened."

Lockie shrugged. "Well, when you lot were buggering about with them pieces of wood, I thought I'd take a look upstairs."

"How did you manage to get out?" Johno looked puzzled.

There was scorn in Lockie's voice when he answered.

"Through that bleedin' door of course." He pointed with the glowing stub of a damp-looking cigarette. It was one of the lower hatches, a few feet above where the water slopped. Metal rungs were set in the bulkhead below it.

"You were bloody takin' off, leaving us down here in the shit," Jim accused.

"Course not!" Lockie looked deeply hurt.

Tiny was trying to follow Lockie's explanation.

"What's on the other side of that door?" he asked.

The crumpled Aussie looked disgusted. "Just a lot more
226

bleedin' ladders," he said. "I thought I'd never reach the top." His grimy face brightened. "When I did, I smelt this coffee," he continued.

The others nodded looking sceptical.

"Go on," Johno told him.

"Well I followed the smell down this long passage and came to this little kitchen where the cook was." A smug expression came over his face as he looked at Jim. "It was that black mate of yours."

Jim sank down on a bale, looking dazed. "You found Luke, back in his galley?"

Lockie nodded triumphantly. "Yeah that was his name, Luke. Grinned all over his face he did when I told him where I'd come from. That's why he brewed this dixie of coffee. He said: 'Your buddies'll probably need it'".

Jim looked at the sandy deposit in the bottom of his mess tin. "Thanks very much," he murmured, in a strangely hushed voice. He rose stiffly to his feet, trailing them in the water as he sloshed towards the platform where the men were working. His lips were drawn back in a fixed grin as he turned to face the Australian with a saw in his hand. "I'm going to help these blokes," he said quietly.

Lockie flinched with sudden fright as Jim's uncanny restraint burst in an explosion of wrath. He waved the saw at Lockie. "Keep out of my bloody sight," he yelled, "or I'll have your bleeding balls off!"

"What's got into him?" Lockie grumbled as Jim sawed furiously at the first piece of wood he could find.

Johno looked dolefully round. He eased himself further back on the lumpy bale.

"I'm pissed off with being down here," Tiny snorted. "Let's tell the little guy to go to hell, and beat it back to the others."

Johno wanted to agree. "I wonder if we could find 'em?" he said.

Lockie looked surprised. "Course we could bleedin' find 'em. They're up there, havin' some tucker. They're using the mess-deck again."

Johno and Tiny stared in disbelief. The screech of a drill drowned Tiny's sudden oath. He thrust a fist under Lockie's nose. "Why didn't you godammed tell us?" he roared.

The smaller man backed away. "I was just waiting for the chance." He gave the threatening pair a furtive glance. "In fact that big bloke, the bo'sun was as mad as hell, asking where you was. Your names were missin' on this list he had."

Johno's shoulders sagged. "Come on," he said to Tiny. "Give Jim a shout and let's go and face the bloody music."

Whilst they waited, he turned toward Lockie, who stood with both hands buried deep in his pockets. "I suppose the bo'sun got your name all right?"

A pleased smirk broke across Lockie's unshaven face. "Course he bleedin' did."

By now the massive frame was in place, firmly buttressed by a web of supporting timbers. The crewmen were screwing the final bolts into the second one. Jim stood looking exhausted, with the saw hanging limply in his hand. He nodded when Tiny approached him, and then spoke to a crewman by his side. As he did so there came a shudder which made the deck plates tremble. From far away they could hear the faint beat of the engines.

Jake came over to hurry the weary workers as they tugged at their heavy construction.

"Let's get that sonofabitch up there alongside the other," he barked. "The captain's gettin' impatient." He looked at Jim and Tiny, and his gaze followed through to take in the other pair. "You guys," he ordered sharply. "Get the hell outa here. I wouldn't want you around if that bulkhead caves in."

As they made for the nearest ladder, he called after them, "Make sure you close the godammed hatch."

Their own log still lay where it had fallen. The rolling water was breaking across it, carrying flotsam from the spilled cargo. The screws were turning slowly as they ascended the ladder. Tiny spat into the water before closing the hatch behind him. "Godammit to hell!" he rasped.

The bo'sun showed no elation when they reported to him.

"You guys should be put on cap'n's report," he told them grimly.

"What the hell for?" The heavy bones made ridges under Tiny's damp shirt as he hunched his shoulders. Slicks of black oil glistened between the patches of skimpy hair on his uncovered head.

The bo'sun licked the stub of a pencil before making some

alterations on a grimy piece of paper. "For not turning up at your boat station."

"But you saw us." Jim broke in.

"Yeah." The bo'sun pushed the tattered papers into his shirt pocket with unnecessary force. "I told you to get your asses back to your boat station. You could have been dead," he snapped.

"How about us going to clean up?" Johno ventured.

"Yeah. Shove off! You look like you need to, but report right back there when you're through." He cocked an eye in the direction of the upper deck.

How about some chow?" demanded Tiny.

Before stalking away, the bosun answered, "Try your luck on the mess-deck. The other guys have already been fed."

The showers were steaming hot. They helped each other to deal with their cuts and bruises. Tiny dabbed around the weals on Johno's back with unexpected care.

"How about this?" grunted Jim, thrusting out his injured leg. It was bruised from ankle to knee. The long ragged wound looked blue and puffy.

"Maybe you should rub somethin' on it," Lockie suggested unhelpfully.

Johno wiped the steam from a mirror. His swollen nose and brightly coloured eye made him jump. "Hell's bells!" he said. "No wonder they bloody laughed."

They found coffee and spam sandwiches in the mess-deck, before crawling painfully back to their boat station. The air in the small room smelled of sweat and bad breath. The usual faces were there, with a crop of fresh lumps and pieces of sticking plaster. About sixty or seventy men: enough to fill a lifeboat – had there been one. Through the haze of tobacco smoke, Johno saw Taffy waving wildly from a corner of the room. As he and Jim made their way towards him, they passed a couple of salt-crusted port-holes. Through them, they caught a glimpse of uncertain daylight. Greyish, white-flecked waves were racing past, to leave the slowly moving ship wallowing in their wake.

Jim was giving short answers to most of the Welshman's excited questions. Johno squatted against a bulkhead, with his knees drawn up almost to his chin. He had questioned Taffy about Pete and been assured that his friend was safely back in the sick bay.

229

He felt drowsy from the heat and the smoke. In his mind he heard the dismal slapping of the water in the hold. He could still see Jake's stumpy figure outlined starkly by the punishing white lights, as he carefully watched those creaking timbers straining against the thrust of the sea. He finally dozed-off.

Around him, men played cards and argued, smoked and yawned and scratched themselves. Jim was sound asleep on the floor. By his side, Taffy sat upright, legs stretched out between other sprawling shapes. From time to time, men stopped what they were doing to exchange nervous glances, when an extra loud screech came from the damaged bow...

"Sarge! Sarge! Come on wake up." Taffy was pummelling his shoulder. When Johno attempted to open his eyes, he discovered the left one remained firmly closed. He turned his good eye balefully towards the excited man.

"What the hell's going on?" he demanded.

"They say another ship's on the way to pick us up."

Johno grimaced at the prospect of a mid-ocean rescue as he felt the lunging motion of the unfriendly sea. Painfully stretching his sore limbs, he looked around for the others, then remembered that Tiny and Lockie were mustered in different groups. He reached out to shake the slumbering Jim, who snorted violently and pulled his arm free. Johno's sour stomach rebelled as he leaned over to try again.

"Come on old son," he belched. "Prepare yourself to abandon ship."

A sturdy mine sweeper from Okinawa stood by to escort the struggling vessel as she clawed her way yard by yard through waves which remained angry and confused from their thrashing by the wind.

The men were allowed on deck as the battered ship edged past the long arm of the breakwater. A number of smaller boats fussed anxiously around, as though to urge her in. There were just a few scattered cheers from the jaded crews of other vessels, as she nuzzled up to a mooring buoy.

It was late afternoon when they first emerged from below, screwing up their eyes to face the unaccustomed daylight. Beyond the harbour, driven by a persistent breeze, banks of dark clouds piled up. Between them, the watery sunlight gleamed, flaking their edges with jasmine and pearl.

"Bloody hell! What a mess."

The softness of the light contrasted with the shambles of the upper decks. Taffy's glazed expression reflected Johno's own incredulity. Jim looked stunned with the shock.

Deck housings had been skewed as though with a giant hand. Loose ladders hung from crumpled upper-works. Taffy's bewildered gaze dwelt for a moment on the remains of the single surviving lifeboat hanging forlornly from its davits.

"Watch your step there, fellas. Stay clear of the rails." Haggard crewmen were busy with ropes, filling in gaps and sealing off damaged areas.

Footholds were uncertain as the deck was tilted sideways in a twenty degree list. It also dipped forward toward the partly-sunken bow. Jagged edges of torn metal could be seen beyond a makeshift barrier.

The small group moved aside to allow one of the crewmen to catch a rope. It was being lowered from a deck above to secure a clanking steel ladder.

"Be safer for you guys down below," he advised. "We've got a lotta things to do up here."

"Too bloody right!" Taffy agreed. "Let's get ready, I don't want to be on her if she bloody sinks."

Johno took a last look at the bridge before they went below. The port wing was sagging as though from a heavy blow. Across the broad sweep of its front there were vertical furrows of red ochre where wind and savage seas had blasted the paintwork.

"How the hell are we going to get off?" The practical Jim voiced the question. "The boarding ladders have been lost, and the bloody ship's leaning too far over to use them anyway."

"There's still a heavy swell," Johno added looking serious.

They fell silent, pondering the possibilities as they gathered together their few belongings.

"Well, I'm getting off, if I have to bloody jump!" declared Taffy with finality.

Soon after first light the following morning, there was open dismay on his face as he took his place in an ill-formed line of unwilling men. Each was waiting his turn to go over the side.

"Bloody hell!" he said. "That doesn't look safe."

The rough-knotted mesh of a scrambling net hung from the broken rails. It dangled clear of the steeply tilted hull, swaying uneasily with the motion of the ship.

"It's like I said," Jim told him with savage satisfaction. "There's no other bloody way of getting off."

"Unless you want to use that." Johno nodded to a sort of cage hanging from the derrick of the mine sweeper escort. It had been used to lift off the casualties.

Taffy gave it a long, hard look. as though considering the possibility.

"Come on, you guys. Keep it movin'."

Johno's arm was grabbed by a seaman who was helping them over the side.

Below the net a small convoy of box-like landing craft bounced around on the choppy water. Johno could smell the exhaust fumes and hear the clatter of their engines, as he clung to the saturated hemp with legs and arms spread-eagled. Taffy was hanging alongside, with Jim next to him, as they waited for the line of men below them to move further down.

Water gushed from discharge ports along the ship's side as the hammering pumps strove to cope with the rising levels in the holds. A strong breeze whipped the spray, saturating their clothes and stinging their eyes.

They clambered down further, as the rows of men below them disappeared from the swaying net. So far, Johno had avoided looking down at the bucking boat, but now he was in time to see it plummeting away in a trough between successive waves.

They took their cue from its coxswain.

"NOW!" the man yelled, as the boat rose again.

The row of men let go. As they scrambled to their feet, some sailors shoved them hurriedly aside. "Keep the deck clear you guys." they shouted.

Everyone ducked as another row of booted feet came tumbling out of the sky. Johno looked around as they were squeezed against the sides of the rapidly filling boat. Everyone seemed to be all right.

"Thank Christ for that!" Taffy gasped.

They braced themselves as the sputtering engine started to

232

roar. From his perch in the high square stern, the helmsman nonchalantly spun the wheel to swing his clumsy craft away from the ship's side. A few more turns and another burst from the throttle took them round the buoy to which the ship was moored. Someone gave a low whistle as they looked at the damaged bow.

"What a bloody mess!" Pointing fingers indicated the rusting edges of the shattered plates, hanging loosely from twisted steel ribs. Deep inside the wedge of darkness, they could dimly see the probing pale-edged waves. The HARRIET L. LANE had not disgraced her worthy American name-sake, but now she looked like a heap of scrap iron, sagging nose-down between her cables.

Turning to view the approaching shore, Johno fingered the strip of plaster across his nose. It had been stuck on by a busy nurse who was hurriedly evacuating the patients. She had allowed him to see Pete briefly. He had been pale, but fully conscious, as he waited for his stretcher to be lifted off the ship. "I'll be off before you lot," he had crowed. "I've heard that the next leg is by air to the Philippines. I'll be waiting for you there."

The men on the boat held on to the peaks of their caps as a stiff breeze billowed their damp denim blouses. A hint of blue appeared between the clouds. An occasional flash of sunlight was reflected from the pursuing waves, as the ungainly craft bucketed towards a strip of sandy beach.

Jim breathed in the clean air deeply. He shifted position to take the weight off his injured leg. Taffy had managed to light a cigarette. With shoulders hunched, he cupped it carefully in his hand, as he sat on an ammunition locker. He looked up eagerly when the engine noise abruptly cut back to a fussy stammer. The bouncing became a slow awkward roll as he stood to join Jim and Johno.

There was a scraping sound as the flat-bottomed craft lurched under their feet and struck the shelving beach. The sailor at the front pulled a lever and the ramp fell forward with a heavy thud. Its edge gouged a deep groove in the wet sand, pushing it into folds, which merged with the glistening ripples left by the tide.

"All ashore, you guys. Let's move it," sang out the cheerful helmsman.

Chapter 12

Schroeder clung grimly to the wheel of the slowly moving truck. He was holding it with one hand. The other, with its blood-soaked sleeve, he rested on the sill of the door.

By his side Yukovlev sat ramrod-straight, returning salutes from the occasional suspicious guard. "The storage tanks are about one kilometre from here," he said in a low voice to Schroeder.

The American nodded. "Yeah!" he agreed. "I think we are goin' the right way."

He had turned the truck onto the boundary road, after leaving the wreckage of the buildings. On their left were the remains of the original wall. To their right was the new wire fence.

"What happened to the kid?" Schroeder asked the silent man.

The Russian slowly shook his head. "The Korean guards, they tricked him. He is dead."

"Tatiana's goin' to be mad," Schroder grunted.

"It was my fault," the white-faced man replied in a toneless voice. "I should have warned him."

Schroeder shot him a sideways glance. "Forget it," he said. "We'll be lucky if any of us get out of this. You probably saved our lives," he added. "by turning up when you did."

Yukovlev appeared not to hear him. He was gazing at the rear-view mirror on the end of its long arm. "There's another truck behind us," he said.

Schroeder's eyes had been fixed grimly ahead. A quick look on his own side confirmed what the Russian had seen. The other truck was overtaking them rapidly. Schroeder cursed under his breath. It was close enough now for him to recognise the NKVD tabs of the man in the passenger seat.

The American's foot went down a little harder. For a few moments the other truck fell further behind. Then, as though the driver had been given an order, it sharply increased its speed. Now with both hands grasping the wheel, Schroeder tried to ignore the pain from his injured arm, as he strove to stay ahead.

Yukovlev was pointing. "There they are."

Schroeder saw the outlines of the giant storage tanks on a

knoll, to their left and just ahead of them. He stamped hard on the brakes. The heavy truck ground along for several more yards before lurching to a halt. The following vehicle swerved wildly to avoid a collision, before stopping in a cloud of dust.

Doors slammed, the pursuer's tailgate crashed down as armed guards leaped from the back. Their guttural voices were threatening as they shouted to the two men to get out of the cab.

"What is the meaning of this?" Yukovlev regarded them with cold eyes as he stepped down. The men backed away, muttering and exchanging glances.

"Perhaps it is I who should ask the questions, comrade doctor?"

There was a sneer on the face of the Secret Police officer as he pushed the Koreans aside. He was dragging the white-faced Schroeder by his injured arm.

"That man is wounded." The haggard Yukovlev faced his gimlet-eyed questioner. "I am taking him for treatment."

"But it is the patient who is driving the truck - and the hospital is in the other direction. How very strange."

He looked thoughtfully at Yukovlev, before shouting some orders in a brisk hard voice.

There was a crunching of heavy feet on the dusty road, as Tatiana and Dead-Eye were thrust through the ring of guards.

"What is your explanation for your other passengers, comrade doctor?"

Yukovlev licked his dry lips. "They were injured in the explosion," the ashen-faced doctor attempted to explain.

At a signal from his officer, a grinning guard slammed the butt of a rifle into the doctor's stomach.

A strangled scream came from Yukovlev's throat. He retched and doubled over, before sinking to his haunches.

Dead-Eye struggled wildly in his captor's grasp. "You bastards!" he yelled. His head rolled from side to side. His eye caught something glinting beneath the storage tanks.

"Get down!" he screeched. He launched himself backwards, taking the guards by surprise and knocking Tatiana over. The hammering sound of a Browning automatic rifle broke into the cries of the startled guards.

As the officer relaxed his grip, Schroeder dragged himself free.

He flung himself face downwards. The Russian's body was spurting blood as it tumbled on top of him. Schroeder rolled him aside, and tugged at the dead officer's holster flap. Dead-Eye had grabbed a fallen man's weapon. He worked his way around to the back of the truck, where some of the guards had taken cover. He grunted savagely to himself as he loosed off round after round.

"Take that, you sonsabitches," he snarled.

Schroeder was shooting from the other side.

The heavy rifle from the storage tanks thudded relentlessly. A few of the remaining guards dropped their weapons and fled. The others lay dead or dying.

Running figures were coming towards them. Still crouching, Schroeder felt giddy with relief. He scrambled to his feet and stumbled forward.

"Sweet Mother! Are we pleased to see you."

He slapped Naguchi on the shoulder. There were savage grins on the faces of Dum-Dum and Petrokov, who accompanied him. The lethal weapon was in Dum-Dum's hands.

"Nice shootin', " Schroeder panted. "I guess you must have been watching."

"You were twenty minutes late," Dum-Dum cracked to the breathless, blackened Dead-Eye. "What the hell kept you?"

"We'll have to get moving," Schroeder broke in. "The guards will be back any second." He saw that Tatiana and Petrokov were kneeling by the gasping doctor. Dead-Eye was keeping a wary lookout across the broken ground. "Where are the other guys?" He flung the question back to Naguchi as he himself moved towards Yukovlev.

"Back there, where we left them."

Schroeder fancied there had been a hesitation before the interpreter replied.

Petrokov's face was unusually grave as he looked at the gaunt features of his friend.

"We must get him into the truck," he told Tatiana.

Yukovlev managed a twisted smile. He was breathing more normally, but his lips had a bluish tinge. "If you will raise me to my feet, I will be able to walk."

Schroeder looked at their bullet-riddled truck.

"We'd better take the other one."

His voice rose to a shout of alarm as several shots came from behind the remains of the wall. The small party crouched in the shelter of the damaged vehicle.

"Keep us covered 'til we move the doc," he called to Dum-Dum and Dead-Eye.

"We can't see the bastards." Dum-Dum snarled. "They're behind the godammed wall."

He sprayed several bullets at the unseen enemy as Petrokov and Tatiana dragged the sick man to his feet.

Dead-Eye ferociously pumped the bolt of his rifle. Between them, he and Dum-Dum forced the Koreans to keep their heads down, whilst the others half-dragged Yukovlev to the guard's undamaged truck.

Naguchi was already behind the wheel. He swung open the passenger door.

"Come on. Get him in", he shouted.

Tatiana clambered into the cab alongside the doctor. Petrokov and Schroeder ran round to the back. The truck was already rolling slowly. Schroeder had to scream above the engine and the gunfire, "OK. Let's go!"

The two G.I.s let loose a fusillade of shots before scuttering back to the moving vehicle.

Dum-Dum flung himself onto the boards. "Holy Cow!" he grunted, "that was close. Let's get the hell outa here."

The truck was quickly picking up speed. The four passengers in the back were flat on their bellies as they sighted their guns on the men who had left the shelter of the wall.

"What the hell!" Schroeder cursed as the truck wheels locked without warning. A cloud of dust obscured their stumbling pursuers, as the vehicle slid to a halt. It had stopped near the damaged storage tanks. Dum-Dum's booted feet scraped on the floor-boards as he knelt to grab a vertical rail. He fell back again, when the truck moved unexpectedly. It bounced several more times as Naguchi slewed it off the road.

Schroeder leaped down and raced to the driver's door. "What's going on?" He broke off and ducked as shots came from ahead.

Further along the road two scout cars had been drawn across nose to nose. Their occupants were shooting from behind them.

"Couldn't have got past." Naguchi's voice was calm, but the skin across the bridge of his nose appeared to have been drawn more tightly. His eyes had a vicious gleam.

Tatiana had leaped to the ground. She reached up to help Yukovlev. The others flung themselves from the back as shots tore through the tarpaulin cover.

They were almost beneath the damaged storage tanks, which had been their rendezvous. The horizontal metal cylinders appeared intact, but the web of metal girders which supported them was partially demolished.

"Take cover where you can," Schroeder barked.

"Sonofabitch!" Dum-Dum spat. He squirmed closer to the ground to rest his heavy weapon on a twisted stanchion. Sparks flew as bullets ricocheted from the tangled metal around him.

"What the hell's in those things?" Dead-Eye squinted with some alarm at the giant tanks above their heads.

Naguchi was exchanging urgent sentences with two men in Jap uniform who had appeared from among the wreckage.

Schroeder's breath caught in his throat. "Jesus Christ!" He'd almost forgotten the men they were here to pick up. He shook his head in an attempt to clear his mind. There was no time for greetings. He signalled to Naguchi, "Are these guys armed?" he rasped.

Naguchi sounded excited. "No", he replied, "But they've done what I told them to do."

When Schroeder shot him an enquiring glance, he pointed upwards to where the huge containers hung askew on their metal cradles.

"They've planted charges of plastic explosive. It was stuff they brought with them when they were dropped," he explained.

Dead-Eye crouched close to Tatiana. She was squinting along the sight of a rifle.

"We can't keep the bastards off much longer." His cracked lips were drawn back from his teeth.

"We will do what we can," she spat. She sniffed and hurriedly drew a sleeve across her sweat-streaked face.

Dead-Eye forced a tired grin. "You're dammed right we will!" he agreed.

His good eye caught a sign of movement in the crumpled steel supports above their heads. He dropped his gaze to fire at a guard who has scuttled across the road to a better point of vantage. He darted another glance at the figure amongst the girders. He glimpsed the wads of putty-like substance to which detonators were being attached. A cold tremor raised the bristling hairs on Dead-Eye's scalp, as he recognised the implications. He nudged the grim-faced woman by his side. "We gotta move," he panted.

Ignoring him, she continued to watch for a sight of the concealed attackers. A hand fell heavily on Dead-Eye's shoulder. He turned his head with a startled curse. It was Schroeder.

"Be ready," he was saying. "We're goin' to get the hell out of here." The officer fell flat as a bullet clanged into some metal-work near his head.

Dead-Eye's face creased further in a hard smile. "Just show us the way, lootenant", he replied. He turned his good eye upwards. "Did you see that sonofabitch up there?"

Schroeder nodded urgently. "Sure. He's one of ours. He was fixing the final charge. We're goin' to blow those godammed tanks."

"What's in 'em, lootenant?" Dead-Eye's gaze was serious.

Schroeder's expression became suddenly harsh. "Some godammed stuff which spreads and burns," he replied. His voice sounded dry and forced. "Hotter and more volatile than anythin' we've ever had." He paused as he noticed that Tatiana was listening intently. "These bastards here were scared of it themselves. They had these tanks specially strengthened."

Tatiana gave him a startled glance. "That is why they were not destroyed?"

Schroeder nodded. "We're goin' to finish the job for them. Listen! I've already told the others. When I leave, you start moving back towards the truck. Keep shooting. Make the bastards keep their heads down. When we are all aboard, Naguchi will throw the switch to explode the charges."

Dead-Eye jerked the barrel of his rifle towards the massive containers. "There's enough stuff there to flood the whole goddamed place."

Schroeder showed his teeth in a hard smile. "Yeah! It'll even take some of their stinking rats."

The party grouped together in a small compact circle as they retreated towards the truck.   They kept Yukovlev near the centre until they reached the tailgate.

Petrokov, Dead-Eye and Tatiana fired frantically whilst the others scrambled aboard.

Naguchi was yelling,   "Come on!   It's going to blow!"

Next to him, Dum-Dum let in the clutch.

In his hand the interpreter was holding a box-like device from which trailed a pair of wires.   The wheels of the truck screeched as the vehicle leapt forward.   Dum-Dum flung up an arm to protect his eyes as he tried to swerve round the stationary cars.   At the same moment Naguchi turned a switch on the box.

Metal plates flew upwards as the tanks disintegrated.   The boom came a split second later.

The stunned Koreans stopped shooting as tongues of blazing chemicals blotted out the sky.

As he juggled the truck's controls, Dum-Dum's face was bleeding, where fragments of glass were embedded.   The vehicle almost stuck between the fence and one of the obstructing cars. With a tearing crash it broke its way through, dragging behind it tangled skeins of barbed wire.

"Great Holy Cow! Would you look at that."

Dead-Eye's voice was awe-struck, as the group in the back stared white-faced at the inferno they were leaving behind. Rivers of fire poured from the remains of the tanks. They spread across the site at breath-taking speed.   Within seconds there were gouts of raw-edged flame erupting and spreading from underground tunnels throughout the whole vast complex.

Still holding a rifle, Schroeder sank back on his haunches. "Well I'll be godammed," he breathed. The reflection from the reddened sky was showing in his eyes as he turned to look at Petrokov who half-knelt at the side of the doctor.   "It looks like you and Naguchi hit on a good idea."

Petrokov's grimy face framed the faintest of smile, as he nodded towards Naguchi's two friends, still dressed as Japanese P.O.Ws "They are the ones who have done it," he said.

Glancing   backwards to where the two exhausted men were

squatting near the driver's cab, Schroeder exclaimed, "Poor bastards! Let's get 'em outa here."

They kept a sharp look-out as the truck sped unimpeded along the ribbon of road. It smashed through the nearest guard post. There was no sign of any men.

Tatiana stared hollow-eyed, across the desolate landscape, where the remains of the abandoned farm stood out against the fitful glare from Pingfan.

"Goodbye Stefan Gregoravitch," she whispered. "I think you have been avenged."

Still panting from their efforts, the escaping raiders looked back sombrely at the ragged hospital standing in wretched isolation as they headed towards the main road.

Traffic was tailing back as Dum-Dum worked the heavy vehicle out of the turn-off, to join the slow-moving stream. The shattered windscreen and the battered state of the truck drew some curious stares, but most eyes were looking towards the distant red-tinged clouds.

Schroeder stepped carefully to avoid the sprawled shapes of the two agents, as he moved forward and banged on the driver's cab.

"Turn off somewhere here," he mouthed, as Dum-Dum glanced through the rear window.

Minutes later, the vehicle was labouring across the bumpy terrain they had previously covered on foot.

Schroeder's watch had long since stopped. "What's the godammed time?" he asked in a weary voice.

Dead-Eye was slouched in a corner. He drew back the overall cuff. "We're fifteen minutes late," he said.

"Watch out for any landmarks."

Schroeder looked round at the other haggard faces. Tatiana and Petrokov were crouching on each side of Yukovlev, who sat on the floor, with legs outstretched.

Schroeder's arm was throbbing as he pulled back the tarpaulin curtain at the rear. The surrounding country looked featureless. As he became aware of Dead-Eye's pointing finger, he had to jerk back his nodding head. He had almost fallen asleep.

"Over there," Dead-Eye was saying. "There's a bit of a hump. There was one near the place where the plane landed."

Schroeder spotted the long low hummock. It was far to their left. The setting sun cast a stunted shadow ahead of the truck. He felt his heart beat beginning to race.

"That could be it. Give Dum-Dum a shout."

He leaned farther out, his eyes anxiously scanning the sky. Far above a tiny dot was circling.

He felt the truck increase its speed as Dead-Eye passed on the message. A few minutes later it slithered to a halt. Schroeder dropped down to stumble towards the place where the Verey pistol was hidden. As he pointed it and squeezed the trigger, two bright green balls arced high over their heads.

His sour stomach lurched resentfully as he clung to the metal-framed seat whilst the shabby aircraft lifted them towards the greyness of the clouds.

"I thought you were never godammed comin'," the fresh-faced pilot grumbled.

"Thanks for waitin'," Schroeder replied. "I guess somethin' must have delayed us."

They had scrambled aboard without further challenge, barely having the strength to scale the short ladder.

The aircraft bounced in the turbulent air, shaking the sprawling passengers. Tatiana was beckoning. He could see her lips moving, but he roar of the engines drowned her voice. Unbuckling his safety belt, he staggered to where she sat, with one arm around Yukovlev's loosely slung body. On the other side, Petrokov carefully supported his comrade's shoulders, preventing him falling forward.

There were tears in the woman's eyes as she turned her grime-streaked face to look at Schroeder. The deep etched creases in the American's cheeks softened as he returned her gaze.

"I'm sorry," he said.

"We must find a place for him." Petrokov's expression was unusually stern as he released the buckle on the dead man's lap.

Between them, they carried the body along the narrow aisle, towards the storage compartment in the tail.

With an embarrassed cough, Dead-Eye stubbed out his cigarette. He pulled himself clumsily to his feet as they passed, and dragged off his cap. Others roused their exhausted frames to follow suit. One of the men in Japanese uniform gave a respectful bow. The other, who was younger, raised his eyebrows when he saw this traditional gesture.

The plane had to use its landing lights, when the pilot dipped its nose towards the Mukden strip.

Chapter 13

As it rumbled to a halt and the engines cut, there were shouts from the ground outside.

"Open the godammed door!" They recognised Mulholland's voice. Someone wrenched at the retaining clamps. As the door opened, Mulholland's voice became clearer. "Bring that godammed ladder can't you?"

There was a scraping sound as a ladder was fixed by someone outside. Seconds later, the bulk of the major's shoulders filled the gap.

Schroeder sank back in his seat, as Mulholland stared down at him. The familiar fish-oil smoke circled from the cigar he held in his hand. The chatter eased off as expectant eyes watched the two men.

Mulholland looked around. "What's the body count?" he snapped.

Schroeder's voice was devoid of feeling. "Two," he replied. "The doctor and the kid."

The major's eyebrows shot up. "Great!" he beamed. "It could have been a lot worse."

Behind him, Tatiana's expression darkened. Getting to her feet, she pushed past the major towards the rear-end compartment.

Mulholland shielded his eyes from the overhead lights as he looked along the fuselage at the passengers on either side. His gaze paused briefly on Naguchi and his two companions, before passing on.

"I'm here to welcome you back," he barked.

"Big deal!" a gruff voice muttered.

Mulholland ignored it. "You'll be taking off for Tokyo as soon as the plane's tanked up."

There were muted cheers, but Schroeder looked startled.

"Why the hell the hurry? I thought we had 'til midnight."

Mulholland chewed savagely on his mangled cigar as he turned towards the exit door. "No point in hanging around," he replied. "We wouldn't want to outstay our welcome."

The weary passengers were shuffling to their feet as he backed out to climb down the ladder.

"There's a chow-truck across the apron," he called. "Grab something, then come back here."

He was waiting on the concrete as Schroeder left the plane. He signalled to one of the mechanics. "Get the lieutenant some coffee and sandwiches."

The younger officer unbuckled his ammunition pouches. He winced as he made to stretch his stiffened arms and shoulders.

Mulholland noticed the blood-stained sleeve.

"Is that goin' to be OK?" he enquired.

Schroeder thrust aside the question. "What the hell's goin' on?" he demanded. "Why can't we shower and change our things? These guys are dead on their feet." He reached out to grab a rung of the ladder, feeling suddenly weak.

"For Chrissake don't pass out now," Mulholland rasped. "We'd better get you back on board."

"Sorry," Schroeder gasped. "Loss of blood, I guess." He looked about him at the surrounding darkness. Beyond the runway and its verges, a ring of lights glowed, marking the perimeter. He could make out the few scattered buildings and the control tower, with its brightly lit turret. The stillness suddenly seemed to contain a vague threat.

He found himself being helped back through the door. He sank onto the nearest seat.

Mulholland was speaking quickly. "That list of names? I guess you didn't find it?"

Schroeder's expression was bitter. He gave a hollow laugh. "Just how the hell would you know that?"

"Never mind! At least you brought these guys back." He gestured with his cigar towards Naguchi and the two other men, still wearing Japanese uniforms, who had followed them into the plane.

Schroeder nodded. He could feel his senses slipping.

"Here drink this, lieutenant," Naguchi was holding a mug to the officer's blackened lips. For the first time, Schroeder was able to take a good look at the interpreter's companions.

The younger one grinned and bobbed his head as Naguchi introduced him. "Kanji Ikari, an old buddy of mine." There was an

245

unusual warmth in the sergeant's clipped voice.

Schroeder stretched out an arm. "I guess we owe you a lot," he said. "You must be the one who fixed those charges to the tanks."

The man returned a self deprecating smile as he grasped the proffered hand. "I was sent there to raise some kind of hell."

Before the lieutenant could speak to the other man, Mulholland's rough voice cut in. "Sergeant Naguchi," he rapped, with cold formality, "I want you to tell lieutenant Schroeder exactly who this sonofabitch is."

The interpreter's face was stone-like. "This is Colonel Yuckio Kikuchi. He was Deputy Director of Research at the Pingfan Laboratories."

Schroeder gaped at him in stunned silence. Then he slowly rose to confront the impassive Mulholland. "You lousy, godammed, sonofabitch," he croaked. "You knew about that from the start. You had us risking our asses to get this bastard away from the Russians."

The major's teeth showed white as he flicked ash from his cigar. "It was either them or us who had to get him, lieutenant. Why shouldn't it be us?"

Before the reeling Schroeder could interrupt, he stabbed a thick finger at the captive scientist. "Just bear in mind, lieutenant, that this guy was Pingfan's number two, the executive, the guy who oiled the wheels, who knew every dammed thing that was going on." He reached forward to grab Schroeder by the arm, but stopped himself in time.

Schroeder backed away, feeling suddenly helpless. He looked around at the tense faces of the other men. The rough canvas seat scraped the back of his legs. He sank down and stared bleakly at Naguchi.

"You knew about this?"

The interpreter looked almost relieved. "Yes, lieutenant. I handled the radio remember." He licked his lips and his eyes flicked nervously towards the major. "But I was under orders." There was a plea in his voice as he turned again to Schroeder. "It wasn't easy, lieutenant, keeping it to myself."

Schroeder looked at him oddly. There was a flatness in his gaze as he asked. "The other guy, your buddy, what happened to him?"

For the first time Naguchi dropped his eyes before Schroeder's questioning stare.

It was Mulholland who broke in. "I'll tell you what godammed happened. The poor bastard died of the plague during their first few days."

He looked around for somewhere to put his dead cigar. Then ground it under his foot. He sat down suddenly in the seat facing Schroeder, leaning forward to add emphasis to his words.

"Listen, godammit!" He was speaking quickly. "Those egg-heads, who gave themselves up, they told me about this guy still in hiding. They told me how important he was. They told me how to contact him. There was a grape-vine through the Jap P.O.Ws."

Schroeder's response was a sarcastic snort.

"So you promised to get him out."

Looking at his watch, Mulholland sounded impatient. He pointed to Naguchi's friend. "Ikari here did a great job. Once he had located this guy, I got him to make a deal."

Schroeder's lips were twisted in a sneer. "So you made a godammed deal? My ass, and all the rest of my squad, in exchange for this valuable commodity." He looked with hatred at the undistinguished Japanese scientist in the floppy private's uniform.

Mulholland remained unperturbed by the outburst. "Not exactly," he answered smoothly. He stopped to nod towards Naguchi, who handed him a sheaf of papers. "He promised to bring these records."

Schroeder looked up. There was something new in the major's voice.

Mulholland flourished the papers under the young lieutenant's nose. "This is a full report of the experiments conducted at Mukden P.O.W camp."

Schroeder hung his filthy hands over his knees, as he allowed his chin to sink to his chest. "Then the godammed things weren't even in the vaults when I looked?"

There was an unexpected plea in Mulholland's voice.

"No, I guess not. But there was no way of being sure at the time. We couldn't just take this shit-head's word that he'd produce them."

Picking up his coffee mug from the floor, Schroeder took a deep gulp. He wiped away the wet ring round his mouth with the back of

247

his other hand. He gestured towards the documents held by the major. "That list of those names?" he asked. "Is it there?"

Mulholland's eyes gleamed triumphantly. "I've only had a quick look so far, but the records seem to be complete."

Schroeder grasped the bar above his head and pulled himself to his feet. "You'll let them know in Okinawa?"

Mulholland's voice was quiet. "I'll radio as soon as I can."

The lieutenant gave a snort as he lumbered towards the exit.

"OK then. I'll tell the others. Mebbe, now, we can all go home."

His protesting body stiffened when he heard Tatiana's voice.

"You must not leave," she was telling him. She was standing by the open door of the compartment near the tail, where Yukovlev's body had been placed.

"Aw shit!" he groaned and sank back in his seat. The pistol in her hand looked too business-like for argument. Mulholland glared at her. "Just what the hell do you think you are doing?"

"I was saying good-bye to a comrade," she replied. "The one whom you betrayed."

Now Schroeder remembered having seen her enter the storeroom soon after the plane had landed.

"Just how do you figure that out?" Mulholland snarled. "We got the godammed papers didn't we?"

Tears ridged her filth covered cheeks. There was a tremor in her voice. "Those other men," she said. "The evil ones who made Pingfan, they should be made to pay. I did not know you protected them."

Mulholland's voice turned smooth as he looked at the exhausted woman. "Well! That's just what we are aiming to do. Make 'em pay!" He sidled a little closer as he spoke, his eye fixed on the gun, as it wavered in her tired grip. "We're taking them back home to be tried. What the hell's wrong with that?"

"Look out sir!" Schroeder's voice cracked out a warning as an armed Russian guard appeared at the boarding hatch behind them. The man levelled his rifle menacingly at the startled group, whilst moving away from the open door to allow someone else to enter.

Schroeder's tired body shook with relief. "Thank God it's you," he gasped.

Petrokov was unsmiling as he returned Schroeder's gaze. He then looked thoughtfully at Mulholland, before turning his attention to Naguchi and the other two men. Schroeder slumped back in his seat. His lips took on a cynical twist as he looked at the stern-faced Russian.

"What the hell's going on?" Mulholland shouted. "Tell that godammed guard of yours to get off this American plane."

Petrokov shook his head. "You are all under arrest," he told them. "It is you who must leave the plane."

Mulholland hunched his shoulders threateningly. "Just who the hell do you think you are?"

"My name, I think you already know. I have the rank of major in the Intelligence Service of the Soviet Army." Petrokov still wore his own grimy uniform. Dark shadows circled his pale blue eyes, but his voice was cold and firm.

Schroeder's lips trembled. He gulped hard to hold back a hysterical laugh when he saw the fury on Mulholland's face, "You double-crossing bastard," the major grated. "You were on to us from the start?"

The Russian officer replied with a grim smile. "Our friend Schroeder's arrival at the hotel was too good an opportunity to miss. Yes major, there was a purpose in our journey from Dairen."

Mulholland picked him up. "You said 'our', then Yukovlev was in it with you?"

The Russian's face became grim again at the mention of the doctor's name. "The whole idea was his. He knew that scientists were escaping from Pingfan. He suspected that they were coming to you."

"Then I was right," Mulholland breathed.

Schroeder was slowly recovering from the shock of Petrokov's revelations.

"Right about what, for Chrisake?"

The major's eyes took on a inward look. "I had the feelin' somehow, that he was the one in control, even when he listened to my orders. It was almost as though he wanted me to know," he smiled wryly and shook his head. "I just refused to believe, I guess, that a dying man would take on this kind of mission."

"He'd made himself a promise," Schroeder broke in quietly. "He wanted to see those Pingfan monsters rounded up."

"He knew about this one." Petrokov gazed with contempt at their watchful captive, whose mild, brown eyes were ranging nervously round the confined cabin. "He didn't know his whereabouts, or how you'd get him out, so he felt we had to go along with your plan."

Mulholland, whose thoughts had seemed far away, jerked his gaze back to Petrokov. "So, I guess you've found the others?"

The Russian inclined his head, with a return of his familiar grin. "But of course," he replied. "It was not too difficult. They were already aboard your other aeroplane. My men only had to surround it. Your guards who were with them objected at first. But I'm happy to say that no blood was shed."

Tatiana had been watching with incredulous eyes. In the threatening silence, her hand which held the pistol dropped limply to her side. The small sound made Mulholland look behind him. "Was she part of your godammed plan?" he rasped.

Petrokov shook his head. "No. I'm afraid she is a woman as well as a soldier. She wanted to help the Mukden prisoners." There was an ill-concealed sneer in his voice. He darted a quick glance towards Schroeder, who was getting to his feet. "Perhaps there were some personal loyalties too. Don't move any further," he warned the American.

"I'm too godammed tired for all this crap," Schroeder muttered. He looked at the glowering Mulholland. "Tell him to keep the godammed lot, and let's be on our way."

The stubborn Mulholland refused to give in. "What say if we do a deal?" he suggested in a cautious voice. "If this shit-head is so important, you can have him and we'll take the rest. What do you say?" He was reaching into his pocket for a cigar, but the guard's pointing rifle made him pause.

Petrokov's features hardened. "There will be no deal," he replied softly. "These people will remain here, to be tried in Russia."

"What about us?" Mulholland demanded. There was an ugly ring in his voice.

"We will keep you for a little while, until you have answered some questions."

Schroeder looked wonderingly at the determined Russian.

250

"What the hell are you saying," he asked him. "You know damn well that the names of the infected prisoners must be sent on to Okinawa. Time is important, for Chrisake."

"Come on godammit!" Mulholland burst out. "Some of them could be carrying diseases which will wipe out whole populations."

The Russian was smiling again as he shook his head, but his eyes held a cruel glint. "That would be very sad," he replied.

His features froze in a stupid stare as the guard by his side staggered backwards with a howl of pain. His weapon clattered on the metal floor as he clutched at his shattered shoulder.

Mulholland had ducked as the deafening gunshot had exploded close to his ear. Behind him, Tatiana's face was deathly pale as she pointed the pistol at Petrokov.

"You will not betray those men who are on the ship," she panted. She licked her lips, glancing towards the dumbfounded Schroeder. "Take his pistol," she urged.

The young American officer leapt to do her bidding. One of the Russian guards was half-way up the ladder. He fell back with a startled yell as Schroeder, using Petrokov's pistol, loosed off a single shot. He held the pistol to Petrokov's head. "Now tell your men to back-off," he snarled.

Naguchi snatched up the rifle of the wounded guard. He jabbed it against Petrokov's ribs. "Do as he godammed says," he hissed.

The Russian's face was twisted with rage as he turned towards the exit. He shouted something to the cluster of guards outside. Reluctantly, they moved away from the foot of the ladder as he started to descend.

"One wrong godammed move and you're dead." Mulholland watched him carefully from the door of the plane. "Stay close and keep him covered," he warned Naguchi as the interpreter swiftly followed the seething Russian. He was joined on the runway a moment later by Schroeder.

Petrokov looked at the pistol in Schroeder's hand, as though daring him to use it. But by now a cold-eyed Dum-Dum had returned and deliberately pointed his heavy rifle.

Mulholland was still in the plane. He moved towards the exit. He paused to toss his pistol to Naguchi's friend.

"Keep that bastard covered," he rasped, with a jerk of his head towards the watchful scientist. The American agent expertly caught

251

the gun. He took his place alongside Tatiana, as she leaned against the store-room door. Her eyes were fixed on the blood-soaked guard who was moaning as he writhed on the floor.

"Tell your guards to drop their rifles," Mulholland told the scowling Petrokov. The Russian wavered until Dum-Dum's gun made a threatening move.

Schroeder breathed a sigh of relief, as the officer growled an order. With Mulholland closely watching, the guards slowly placed their weapons on the ground. The shadows from the huge bulk of the DC.3 made their shapes uncertain.

Schroeder could hear the major's harsh breathing as he spoke to Naguchi and Dum-Dum. "Collect their weapons, and keep the bastards here for now," he told them. "Lieutenant Schroeder and me are goin' over with Petrokov to the other plane." He picked up one of the rifles himself, and waved it under the Russian's nose. "We're going to get those other egg-heads back aren't we my friend?" he jeered.

Petrokov's lips were tightly drawn. He hesitated, before turning under the thrust of the major's rifle.

Schroeder looked at Mulholland. "Can we do it?" he muttered.

"We're sure as hell going to try." Mulholland replied, as they walked slowly behind Petrokov to where the other Dakota was standing further along the runway.

"There aren't too many Russkis here at present," Mulholland went on in a low voice. "They're not due to take over 'til after midnight. I think this deal is mostly Petrokov's idea. There were only a half dozen men round our own plane. My guess is that it'll be the same for the other."

As they drew closer to the parked aircraft, Mulholland gave Petrokov another jab with his rifle. "Tell your men you're comin'," he growled. "But if you try to warn them, I'll blow your godammed brains out."

The Russian stumbled in the semi-darkness. He half-turned with a curse, but moved forward again as the major's rifle threatened him once more. They were close enough now to the other plane for the cabin lights to show up Mulholland's watchful eyes.

Petrokov called out in Russian to a guard who had spotted their approach.

Schroeder was giving an approving grunt, when he saw a

stealthy movement from the corner of his eye. He caught his breath in sudden fear. The moving shadow he had glimpsed was now behind them, close to the tail of the plane. An involuntary spasm ran down his spine as he waited for the impact of a bullet.

"Stop here!" Mulholland's low-voiced order to Petrokov wrenched Schroeder's attention back to the two men. They had halted opposite the open cabin door. A patch of light showed from inside the aircraft. It outlined the shape of a Russian guard standing at the entrance to the plane.

Schroeder swung swiftly round, his skin still prickling, the pistol held firmly in his hand. There was no one to be seen apart from the half dozen Russians who were lined up near the foot of the ladder.

Mulholland had halted his small group just beyond the range of the illuminated patches cast by the plane's lighted windows.

"Tell your guys who you are."

Petrokov stifled a curse as the major's rifle ground once more into his spine.

Schroeder listened carefully as the Russian major identified himself in an angry voice, telling the men to stay in line. Behind Petrokov, the two Americans were standing in deep shadow. The Russian guards peered suspiciously and fidgeted with their weapons, as they strained their eyes to see who else was there.

"Tell 'em we're coming closer and they have to follow your orders." Mulholland spoke very carefully, his lips close to Petrokov's ear.

Schroeder cocked his pistol as the Russian seemed to hesitate. Petrokov barked out a command, then moved forward quickly, taking the Americans by surprise.

"Don't try any tricks godammit."

Schroeder could make out Mulholland's narrowed eyes as he warned the tense Russian officer.

A guard stepped forward to salute as the trio moved towards them. He stopped with an uncertain look on his face when he saw the dim shapes behind Petrokov.

It was Schroeder who gave the next order in Russian.

"Tell your men to lay down their weapons."

In a louder voice he shouted to the others, "Major Petrokov is a prisoner. He will be killed unless you carry out your orders."

Watching the man's every movement, Schroeder saw the surprise change to anger. The Russian N.C.O's fingers tightened involuntarily around the stock of his rifle. Mulholland's harsh voice froze the man. "Drop it!" he said.

They were close enough now, for Schroeder to glimpse the alarmed faces of the Japanese scientists behind the windows of the plane. Even as the Russian sergeant barked an order and Schroeder heard the rifles clattering to the ground, he cursed himself for being a fool. They had forgotten the guard who was inside the aircraft! A bullet from the man's rifle struck sparks from the runway. The next one sang past his ear. He heard a startled grunt behind him. As he flung himself flat against the concrete, he turned his head to stare into Mulholland's sightless eyes. Blood still spurted from the hole in the major's skull, forming a dark pool on the runway.

Schroeder heard his own voice sobbing with rage as he rolled over behind the twitching body. He emptied his pistol in the direction of the shouting Russians, who were scuffling for their scattered weapons.

"They're not worth it godammit," he screamed, "Those Jap shitheads should all be in hell."

He grabbed Mulholland's rifle and squeezed the trigger time after time.

He became aware of confused yells coming from the scattered guards. They were rolling around or running for shelter, as the stutter of a sub-machine gun broke through their cries. The sound of shouting American voices added to the turmoil of Schroeder's baffled senses.

"Come on, lootenant. Let's start runnin'!"

It was Dead-Eye bending down to shake his shoulder. As the officer scrambled to his feet, he remembered the half-seen figure he had passed a few minutes earlier.

The pair of them lunged across the runway to where some grappling men still battled on the ground. Others, mostly Americans, attempted to separate them. A small group of sullen Russians cursed and spat at a group of G.Is. The Americans were covering them with the Russians own weapons, which had been snatched up from the ground. Dead-Eye loosed off several rounds into the air. He kicked the nearest squirming bodies. "Cut it out godammit!"

The struggling gradually stopped as panting Yanks and Russians slowly separated. Dead-Eye covered the ex-combatants with his own gun. "All you godammed Russkis git over there!" He jerked his weapon towards the others already under guard. A few of them were nursing minor wounds.

Two men in American uniform remained sprawled on the ground. Schroeder darted across to the first one. The head lolled loosely as he turned the body onto its back. The other man was groaning, with blood gouting fiercely from his thigh.

"Somebody get a dressing on there," he barked at the panting men.

"I found where our guys were being kept, lootenant, and turned 'em loose." Dead-Eye's glass orb glinted in a ray from a cabin window as Schroeder turned towards him. "The trouble was, they had no weapons. When the major made the Russkis drop their rifles, we went for 'em." They both looked towards Mulholland's body when Dead-Eye mentioned his name.

"Get him aboard," Schroeder said tersely. "The other two as well," he added. He still held the empty rifle loosely in his hand when he called to the other Americans. "Four of you take those Russkis and find some godammed place to lock 'em up in 'til we can get the hell out of here."

Schroeder's eyes searched quickly around, trying to pierce the darkness. "Any sign of Petrokov?" he asked the panting Dead-Eye, who had been hurrying the men loading the casualties.

The soldier shook his head. "Nope! He must've run when the shootin' started."

"Sonofabitch," Schroeder swore. "Keep a lookout. He won't quit now."

Some sounds from the direction of the control tower made the pair of them turn their heads. Doors were being slammed in the buildings grouped tightly around its base.

"He'll be back any moment with extra help." Schroeder flung the words over his shoulder as he ran back down the runway. "Tell the pilot to run her up," he shouted. "I'm goin' to pick up Naguchi and the others."

Dum-Dum whipped round as he heard Schroeder's stumbling feet. Naguchi sprang up from beside the guard, whose belt he had been using to truss him. The man's comrades were already bound, squirming face-down on the concrete.

Schroeder's lungs were pumping as he reached the group. The patches of light and darkness around the standing plane were blended by the grey mist at the back of his eyes.

"Good work!" he gasped. "Where's Tatiana?"

"She's inside the ship with Ikari, watching that Pingfan V.I.P." There was a vicious note in Dum-Dum's voice. "Why don't we just shoot the bastard?"

His words were drowned by the roar from the other plane as the pilot switched on the port engine.

"Get 'em out"!" Schroeder shouted. Tatiana appeared at the open hatch. He saw the pale shadow of her face before she flung up an arm to protect it from the dust and noise as the pilot gunned both engines of the waiting plane further along the runway.

He sprang to the ladder to hurry her down. Behind him Dum-Dum's gun began to chatter. Brown uniformed figures running towards them flung themselves flat on the ground.

The scared-looking scientist behind Tatiana leapt back into the plane as bullets whipped about their heads. Naguchi yelled a warning as his friend Ikari struggled to force the prisoner out. One of the attacking Russians was using a sub-machine gun. Heavy slugs thudded into the fuselage as Schroeder reached for Tatiana.

The dishevelled figure of Petrokov was leading a rush towards the plane. Schroeder saw the pointing pistol. He tried in vain to swing the woman away, but she resisted fiercely. Her body jack-knifed as it took the bullet intended for him.

The shooting redoubled in fury as he and Naguchi dragged Tatiana to the shelter of the wheels. A ripple of flame appeared on the trailing edge of the wing above their heads.

"She's goin' up!" Dum-Dum yelled. "Get movin'! I'll cover you.!"

He fired a few short bursts before the weapon clicked uselessly in his hands. With a shout of rage, the American ran clear of the blazing aircraft. Holding the gun across his chest, he threw himself at Petrokov. Schroeder shot a helpless glance towards the thrashing limbs, as he and Naguchi supported Tatiana's body. The interpreter's voice was high-pitched with fear as he shrieked for Schroeder to move.

256

"Come on! The godammed tank's goin' to blow."

A figure dropped from the flame-filled hatch above their heads. He rolled on the ground, his clothing ablaze. Naguchi released the woman. He fell on top of the rolling shape, smothering the flames. He gasped as he recognised Ikari.

"Where's Kikuchi? Has the bastard got away?"

The agent shook his head. He managed to move his blistered lips. "He's still in there. Took a bullet in the chest"

Schroeder had hoisted Tatiana across his shoulders. He staggered towards the other plane, the blood from her wound oozing over his hand.

Dim shapes were scurrying in his direction from where the Dakota's thundering engines strained against its brakes. Dead-Eye appeared from the darkness, his face contorted with apprehension, when he recognised Schroeder's burden.

With great tenderness, heedless of the noise and the bullets and the danger from the blazing hulk behind them, he took her limp body in his arms.

"Come on with me, baby," he said. "It's time to take you home."

A great blast of air shook the overloaded plane as it rose clumsily from the ground. Schroeder looked back through a window which glowed with orange light as flames leapt skywards from the blazing wreck below.

He pressed his face closer to the small glass panel, as though striving to see the bodies of Yukovlev and the Japanese scientist through the pillar of smoke and flame.

"Goodbye Nicolai Yukovlev," he muttered, "I hope you see that bastard in hell!"

Chapter 14

His head flopped sideways to his shoulder as he sank back in the canvas seat.

A few moments later the navigator was shaking him awake.

"Here you are old buddy," he was grinning. "Try a slug of this. You sure look like you need it." He was holding out a battered army water bottle.

Schroeder gasped as the pungent liquid hit his empty stomach. He forced his eyes to stay open whilst he looked along the crowded fuselage.

Tatiana was lying on her back in the space near the boarding hatch. Dead-Eye knelt anxiously near her head. He had found an old buoyancy jacket to use as a pillow. "Is she goin' to be OK ?" he asked.

The Japanese doctor who was dressing the wound in the fleshy part of her side, nervously smiled his encouragement.

"If she gets to hospital soon, she will be OK"

Dead-Eye covered her with part of a parachute, which he had ripped from its pack, despite the protests of the pilot, its owner. "The godammed captain stays with the ship," the fierce looking Dead-Eye had growled.

As he watched Tatiana's smile, whilst the rugged soldier gently patted her hand, Schroeder's jaw dropped in surprise.

"Well I'll be dammed!" he said under his breath.

Something crackled in the pocket of his boiler-suit, as he raised a hand to rub his blood-shot eyes. He withdrew the papers he had taken from Mulholland's body. They were crumpled and barely legible, stained with sweat and the major's blood. He held them close to his face, squinting to make out the Japanese characters. Some of them were printed in red. He rose painfully from his seat to lurch unsteadily along the aisle, past the apprehensive scientists and the exhausted soldiers, and stood behind the pilot.

"Is the radio OK?" he enquired hoarsely.

"Sure it's OK" The roar of the engines almost drowned the pilot's voice.

Schroeder clutched the back of the pilot's seat. "How soon can you raise Tokyo?" he asked.

The young man looked closely at his watch. "Mebbe in about thirty minutes."

Schroeder asked him for a writing pad, then beckoned for Naguchi. They squatted together in the cramped space behind the two man crew. Naguchi scanned the closely printed characters on the discoloured papers which Schroeder had thrust into his hands.

"Copy the names which are printed in red."

The interpreter's eyes became gradually narrower as he wrote on the borrowed pad. When he finally dropped his arm, Schroeder took the pad from him.

"Are you sure this is the lot?"

"Yes that's it. There are thirty names."

Naguchi's expression was bleak with loathing as his gaze took in the two rows of miserable looking scientists facing each other across the aisle.

Schroeder handed the crudely scrawled list to the man by the pilot's side.

"Get this off to G.H.Q. in Tokyo as soon as you can. Make sure it's given top priority."

He sank down on his haunches, with his back against the cold fuselage. "What's goin' to happen to those poor bastards?" he wondered. He pulled the peak of his cap firmly over his eyes to shield them from the intruding lights. A few moments later he was fast asleep.

* * *

The four high-ranking officers who sat around a table in a quiet room in Tokyo were listening intently to a fifth man. His voice was grave and he spoke in carefully chosen sentences.

"That, then, gentlemen," he was saying, "Is the unanimous conclusion of myself and every medical colleague with whom I could consult."

One of his listeners, a wiry American wearing Admiral's rank, looked serious. He held up the sheet of paper in his hand.

"Am I to understand," he asked, "that the men whose names

we have here, must never be allowed to mix with other people?"

The senior medical officer, who had been speaking, nodded soberly. "There is no other way," he said, "to prevent the possibility of uncontrolled epidemics."

"But why, godammit?" a walnut-skinned general broke in. "Those men will want to go back to their families. Surely you medics can control a few diseases?"

The doctor shook his head. "I am afraid these will not be simple diseases," he said. "I wish to God they were."

A grizzled looking Air-Force colonel spoke in a thoughtful voice.

"I seem to remember the Japs used something in China, before we came into the war. They were spraying stuff from the air."

The doctor looked grim. "That was bubonic plague," he confirmed. "They also used anthrax and typhoid. No one knows how many civilians died. Hundreds of thousands were reported."

As his listeners remained silent, the worried looking officer continued. "But new epidemics could be much worse. At Pingfan, the Japanese scientists were working on more virulent mutations of these diseases, among God knows how many others." The speaker paused to look earnestly round at the seated men. "I must stress, gentlemen," he continued, "that the human immune system has no response, nor has medical science any answer, to the disasters which these men could be taking with them."

"Well – how come that the poor devils are still alive?" The general was looking puzzled.

"Because, so far, they are only carriers." The doctor's voice was low, and precise "The scientists discovered methods of inhibiting these pathogens for indefinite periods of time."

The air force officer whistled softly. "That means the diseases could break out at any time in the future?"

The doctor leaned forward, his fingers splayed on the polished table. "Exactly," he said. "One month, six months, mebbe even ten years. And if an outbreak occurred, there wouldn't be a single dammed thing we could do about it."

The admiral referred to his papers. "These men," he said, "they're American, British and Australian?"

The medical officer's face was strained. "Yes," he said, "Three different parts of the globe - three separate continents."

The admiral turned to the fourth man, who had so far remained silent. He wore a colonel's insignia on his shoulders. His uniform was immaculate.

"You were in touch with Major Mulholland, I believe?" The admiral's voice was formal.

"Yes sir," the colonel replied. "We were in day-to-day contact throughout the time of his mission in Manchuria."

The admiral consulted his documents. "I see he made certain recommendations to be followed in the event of his death?"

"That is so, sir." The colonel's reply was clipped.

"I want you to carry them out."

The admiral's expression was sombre as the officer saluted and left the room. Those remaining shuffled their papers uneasily. The admiral gazed round at the watching eyes. He spoke to them briefly. "That, gentlemen," he said, "concludes this meeting."

* * *

The noise from the B24's four engines drummed out all other sounds as the silver machine made its stately progress towards Manila. "Clapped out old cow," the flight engineer grumbled. "Why did we have to change from 'Able Mabel'?"

The hapless passengers being transported sat shoulder to shoulder on narrow wooden planks in the giant aircraft's bomb-bays. They had taken off three hours earlier from the airfield at Okinawa. Their plane was the last one of the forty that had left the island that morning.

"When will it be our bloody turn?" the impatient Taffy had voiced his indignation.

Standing idly in the inevitable line, they had waited for their names to be called. "Seems to me we're goin' to be the bleeding last," Lockie had added morosely. "I don't trust these bleedin' aeroplanes, anyway."

"You didn't like the godammed ship much, either." Tiny hitched the belt of his slacks as he spoke. The newly-issued khaki-drill uniform hung shapelessly on his bony figure.

"What the hell does it matter, for Christ's sake? Stop bloody moaning." Jim glared irritably around, as he spoke.

"Well it looks like Lockie was right," said Johno, some time
261

later. He looked at the others still waiting, about thirty men he guessed. "We'll just about fit into one plane."

Now at 8000 feet, with an icy gale blowing through the gap between the bomb-bay doors, he tried to keep his teeth from chattering. He avoided leaning his back against the control rods which shifted from time to time behind him.

"Can't be much longer now," he thought, as he looked along the two rows of pinched faces.

The bored pilot checked the instruments in front of him, then switched on his intercom. "Better take a fix," he said to the navigator. "I guess we're running right on schedule." He leaned back and stretched his arms.

Almost beneath them, a lean American Navy frigate rolled and pitched in the long Pacific swells. Two men on the bridge held binoculars to their eyes, as they watched a slim silver shape in the sky.

A bright white spark appeared near the tail of the plane. The ship's captain, a navy lieutenant, tightened his shoulders. He gave an involuntary gasp which covered the sound of the small explosion.

The huge machine rolled into a side-slip as the tail assembly fell away. Slowly, at first, then with gathering speed, the fuselage began to spin. First one wing broke off, then the other. The horrified lieutenant spoke quickly into the speaking- tube. "Steer 030 degrees," he ordered. "Take her to maximum revs."

The man by his side continued to watch until the tumbling object was concealed by the horizon. He lowered his binoculars before speaking to the younger officer.

"Please cancel that last order, lieutenant," he said. "There'll be no hope of rescue."

The young man's eyes were hot with anger. "How the hell do you know that?" he exploded.

The army officer unbuttoned a pocket and produced a printed card. "I want you to radio Tokyo," he said, ignoring the younger man's outburst. "Make it 'Top Secret'," he continued, "to the man whose name you see here."

The lieutenant's wrath had subsided when he handed back the card. "I'm sorry I questioned your order," he said. "I didn't realise..."

"Forget it," the Colonel interrupted. He stopped speaking,

whilst he stared moodily over the rail of the tiny bridge.

"Just report that you saw a godammed aeroplane and it fell into the sea."

MARUTA (Log of Wood)

This novel is drawn partly on the real-life experiences of the author, who was a prisoner of the Japanese in a notorious camp in Manchuria. The use of POW's, by the Japanese, as guinea-pigs (Maruta) for germ-warfare experiments, is entirely factual, though the events in this story are fictitious.

A detachment of American paratroopers, led by the aggressive Major Mulholland, is dropped into Manchuria to make contact with allied POW's following the Japanese surrender. Russian forces are also on their way!

Meanwhile, the prisoners are on their way to the coast, under escort from a detachment of Russians under a woman NCO and supervised by Mulholland's number two, Lieutenant Shroeder. Conflict arises between the prisoners and their escort on their two day journey. But this is nothing compared to the information that Mulholland has gleaned from the Japanese scientists – that many of the prisoners have been infected with a delayed action plague bacilli!

An action packed thriller that will keep you

ISBN 1 86185 122 7